INCREDIBLE
PIRATE TALES

INCREDIBLE PIRATE TALES

Nineteen Classic Stories of the
Outlaws of the High Seas

New and Expanded Edition

Edited and with an introduction by
Tom McCarthy

Guilford, Connecticut

An imprint of Rowman & Littlefield

Distributed by NATIONAL BOOK NETWORK

Copyright © 2016 by Rowman & Littlefield

Designed by Steven Plaziak

British Library Cataloguing in Publication Information Available

Library of Congress Cataloging-in-Publication Data Available

ISBN 978-1-4930-1878-9 (pbk.)
ISBN 978-1-4930-2418-6 (e-book)

♾™ The paper used in this publication meets the minimum requirements of American National Standard for Information Sciences—Permanence of Paper for Printed Library Materials, ANSI/NISO Z39.48-1992.

To Narci, for giving
my imagination flight

CONTENTS

~ Contents ~

INTRODUCTION TO THE
NEW AND EXPANDED EDITION

Putting together the first edition of *Incredible Pirate Tales* was a labor of love, and I was at a loss after I sent in the manuscript. The job, if one can even call it that, was such a joy I lost track of the time I spent daydreaming, immersed in the intriguingly gnarly world of pirates and their misdeeds.

I could not stop collecting and disappearing into books and stories and firsthand accounts of plunder and attack and righteous comeuppance for the, shall I say, boringly conforming merchants who thought they could sail quietly and unnoticed on their way to profit and good commerce. But as always in these tales, the enmity of the rebellious buccaneers holds sway. Ships are plundered, loot is hauled away and hidden. It's a classic confrontation, the stiff and formal and accepted versus the scurvy underdog. Who doesn't root for the underdog? Hasn't that been at the crux of this enduring romance of readers for pirate stories?

After compiling the first edition I was drawn into the world of pirates in a way I could not escape. I couldn't stop reading pirate stories, and the more I read the more I became a true aficionado. There is something magnetic about these scurrilous dogs. And viewed from a distance, on paper and not through the lens of real life, they can seem downright admirable.

After the first edition went to press I began collecting other stories like a kleptomaniac in a large department store. I hoarded them, reread them, rated them. Putting together the first edition was not exactly a difficult job because I loved the task of reading volume upon volume of stories and choosing the best. The most difficult thing about the job was making the difficult choice of what to leave out. So of course I was delighted when I was told there would be an expanded edition. I felt like Captain Kidd in pursuit of a crippled merchantman. I would have another chance.

But why this phenomenon of pirates?

I'm certainly not the only one who has been hypnotized by this phenomenon. Why do so many readers admire pirates? Maybe it's just vicarious rebellion against the workaday world of dreary jobs and bills and lawns to mow and neighbors to appease and rules to abide by.

For this new edition, I once again faced the difficult task of making choices, mostly because of the enormous number of stories I had collected over the intervening years. Please excuse me while I pat myself on the back, but I believe this time I have outdone myself with these new stories.

You'll find here, in addition to the existing tales that have already entertained so many, a story that describes a gruesome beheading off the coast of Cuba, some fatal brainings and losses of limbs, and even one lipless and scarred pirate who came up on the wrong side of a cutlass. All in good pirate fun, of course.

These new stories will take you from the South Atlantic to the Caribbean, and from the Bay of Fundy to the Mediterranean.

Because pirates got around, of course.

And the new stories will take you from the sixteenth-century Barbary pirates of the one-armed Barbarossa to three hundred years later when Confederate Civil War commerce raider Mogul Mackenzie went rogue after the war ended.

Because pirates have always been around, of course.

Again, why?

In the words of one author herein, written more than a hundred years ago, pirates went after "the holders of fat positions and the gilded idlers who swaggered and ruffled it on their riches." In other words, those lazy idlers had it coming to them. Much could be said today for admiring someone who was tormenting holders of fat positions and gilded idlers. I might give it a shot myself.

In the romance of the pirate, which we celebrate with this collection, those who pursued that dark craft embodied the romance of the sea at its highest expression. And the fact remains that in the lore of the sea the pirate is a picturesque figure—and the more real and crass and bloody his career, the more interest he inspires.

Find a chair, rediscover your imagination, and, if you dare, grab a flagon of Captain Morgan and enjoy the read.

I was mesmerized by these stories and I hope they will have the same effect on you, rum or not.

L'OLONNOIS THE CRUEL

Frank R. Stockton

CHAPTER ONE

We have seen that the buccaneers had at last become so numerous and so formidable that it was dangerous for a Spanish ship laden with treasure from the new world to attempt to get out of the Caribbean Sea into the Atlantic, and that thus failing to find enough richly laden vessels to satisfy their ardent cravings for plunder, the buccaneers were forced to make some change in their methods of criminal warfare; and from capturing Spanish galleons, they formed themselves into well-organized bodies and attacked towns.

Among the buccaneer leaders who distinguished themselves as land pirates was a thoroughbred scoundrel by the name of Francis L'Olonnois, who was born in France. In those days it was the custom to enforce servitude upon people who were not able to take care of themselves. Unfortunate debtors and paupers of all classes were sold to people who had need of their services. The only difference sometimes between master and servant depended entirely upon the fact that one had money, and the other had none. Boys and girls were sold for a term of years, somewhat as if they had been apprentices, and it so happened that the boy L'Olonnois was sold to a master who took him to the West Indies. There he led the life of a slave until he was of age, and then, being no longer subject to ownership, he became one of the freest and most independent persons who ever walked this earth.

He began his career on the island of Hispaniola, where he took up the business of hunting and butchering cattle; but he very soon gave up this life for that of a pirate, and enlisted as a common sailor on one of their ships. Here he gave signs of such great ability as a brave and unscrupulous scoundrel that one of the leading pirates on the island of Tortuga gave him a ship and a crew, and set him up in business on his own account. The piratical career of L'Olonnois was very much like that of other buccaneers of the day, except that he was so abominably cruel to the Spanish prisoners whom he captured that he gained a reputation for vile humanity, surpassing that of any other rascal on the western continent. When he captured a prisoner, it seemed to delight his soul as much to torture and mutilate him before killing him as to take away whatever valuables he possessed. His reputation for ingenious wickedness spread all over the West Indies, so that the crews of Spanish ships, attacked by this demon, would rather die on their decks or sink to the bottom in their ships than be captured by L'Olonnois.

All the barbarities, the brutalities, and the fiendish ferocity which have ever been attributed to the pirates of the world were united in the character of this inhuman wretch, who does not appear to be so good an example of the true pirate as Roc, the Brazilian. He was not so brave, he was not so able, and he was so utterly base that it would be impossible for any one to look upon him as a hero. After having attained in a very short time the reputation of being the most bloody and wicked pirate of his day, L'Olonnois was unfortunate enough to be wrecked upon the coast, not far from the town of Campeachy. He and his crew got safely to shore, but it was not long before their presence was discovered by the people of the town, and the Spanish soldiers thereupon sallied out and attacked them. There was a fierce fight, but the Spaniards were the stronger, and the buccaneers were utterly defeated. Many of them were killed, and most of the rest wounded or taken prisoners.

Among the wounded was L'Olonnois, and as he knew that if he should be discovered he would meet with no mercy, he got behind some bushes, scooped up several handfuls of sand, mixed it with his blood, and with it rubbed his face so that it presented the pallor of a corpse. Then he lay down among the bodies of his dead companions, and when the Spaniards afterwards walked over the battlefield, he was looked upon as one of the common pirates whom they had killed.

When the soldiers had retired into the town with their prisoners, the make-believe corpse stealthily arose and made his way into the woods, where he stayed until his wounds were well enough for him to walk about. He divested himself of his great boots, his pistol belt, and the rest of his piratical costume, and, adding to his scanty raiment a cloak and hat which he had stolen from a poor cottage, he boldly approached the town and entered it. He looked like a very ordinary person, and no notice was taken of him by the authorities. Here he found shelter and something to eat, and he soon began to make himself very much at home in the streets of Campeachy.

It was a very gay time in the town, and, as everybody seemed to be happy, L'Olonnois was very glad to join in the general rejoicing, and these hilarities gave him particular pleasure as he found out that he was the cause of them. The buccaneers who had been captured, and who were imprisoned in the fortress, had been interrogated over and over again by the Spanish officials in regard to L'Olonnois, their commander, and, as they had invariably answered that he had been killed, the Spanish were forced to believe the glad tidings, and they celebrated the death of the monster as the greatest piece of public good fortune which could come to their community. They built bonfires, they sang songs about the death of the black-hearted buccaneer, and services of thanksgiving were held in their churches.

All this was a great delight to L'Olonnois, who joined hands with the young men and women, as they danced around the bonfires; he assisted in a fine bass voice in the choruses which told of his death and his dreadful doom, and he went to church and listened to the priests and the people as they gave thanks for their deliverance from his enormities.

But L'Olonnois did not waste all his time chuckling over the baseless rejoicings of the people of the town. He made himself acquainted with some of the white slaves, men who had been brought from England, and finding some of them very much discontented with their lot, he ventured to tell them that he was one of the pirates who had escaped, and offered them riches and liberty if they would join him in a scheme he had concocted. It would have been easy enough for him to get away from the town by himself, but this would have been of no use to him unless he obtained some sort of a vessel, and some men to help him navigate it. So he proposed to the slaves that they should steal a small boat belonging to the master of one of them, and in this, under cover of the night, the little party safely left Campeachy and set sail for Tortuga, which, as we have told, was then the headquarters of the buccaneers, and "the common place of refuge of all sorts or wickedness, and the seminary, as it were, of all manner of pirates."

When L'Olonnois arrived at Tortuga he caused great astonishment among his old associates; that he had come back a comparative pauper surprised no one, for this was a common thing to happen to a pirate, but the wonder was that he got back at all.

He had no money, but, by the exercise of his crafty abilities, he managed to get possession of a ship, which he manned with a crew of about a score of impecunious dare-devils who were very anxious to do something to mend their fortunes.

Having now become very fond of land-fighting, he did not go out in search of ships, but directed his vessel to a little village called de los Cayos, on the coast of Cuba, for here, he thought, was a chance for a good and easy stroke of business. This village was the abode of industrious people, who were traders in tobacco, hides, and sugar, and who were obliged to carry on their traffic in a rather peculiar manner. The sea near their town was shallow, so that large ships could not approach very near, and thus the villagers were kept busy carrying goods and supplies in small boats, backwards and forwards from the town to the vessels at anchor. Here was a nice little prize that could not get away from him, and L'Olonnois had plenty of time to make his preparations to seize it. As he could not sail a ship directly up to the town, he cruised about the coast at some distance from de los Cayos, endeavoring to procure two small boats in which to approach the town, but although his preparations were made as quietly as possible, the presence of his vessel was discovered by some fishermen. They knew that it was a pirate ship, and some of them who had seen L'Olonnois recognized that dreaded pirate upon the deck. Word of the impending danger was taken to the town, and the people there immediately sent a message by land to Havana, informing the Governor of the island that the cruel pirate L'Olonnois was in a ship a short distance from their village, which he undoubtedly intended to attack.

When the Governor heard this astonishing tale, it was almost impossible for him to believe it. The good news of the death of L'Olonnois had come from Campeachy to Havana, and the people of the latter town also rejoiced greatly. To be now told that this scourge of the West Indies was alive, and was about to fall upon a peaceful little village on the island over which he ruled, filled the Governor with rage as well as amazement, and he ordered a well-armed ship, with a large crew of fighting men, to sail immediately for de los Cayos, giving the captain express orders that he was not to come back until he had obliterated from the face of the earth the whole of the wretched gang with the exception of the leader. This extraordinary villain was to be brought to Havana to be treated as the Governor should see fit. In order that his commands should be executed promptly and effectually, the Governor sent a big negro slave in the ship, who was charged with the duty of hanging every one of the pirates except L'Olonnois.

By the time the war-vessel had arrived at de los Cayos, L'Olonnois had made his preparation to attack the place. He had procured two large canoes, and in these he had intended to row up to the town and land with his men. But now there was a change in the state of affairs, and he was obliged to alter his plans. The ordinary person in command of two small boats, who should suddenly discover that a village which he supposed almost defenceless, was protected by a large man-of-war, with cannon and a well-armed crew, would have altered his plans so completely that he would have left that part of the coast of Cuba with all possible expedition. But the pirates of that day seemed to pay very little attention to the element of odds; if they met an enemy who was weak, they would fall upon him, and if they met with one who was a good deal stronger than themselves, they would fall upon him all the same. When the time came to fight they fought.

Of course L'Olonnois could not now row leisurely up to the town and begin to pillage it as he had intended, but no intention of giving up his project entered his mind. As the Spanish vessel was in his way, he would attack her and get her out of his way if the thing could be done.

In this new state of affairs he was obliged to use stratagem, and he also needed a larger force than he had with him, and he therefore captured some men who were fishing along the coast and put them into his canoes to help work the oars. Then by night he proceeded slowly in the direction of the Spanish vessel. The man-of-war was anchored not very far from the town, and when about two o'clock in the morning the watch on deck saw some canoes approaching they supposed them to be boats from shore, for, as has been said, such vessels were continually plying about those shallow waters. The canoes were hailed, and after having given an account of themselves they were asked if they knew anything about the pirate ship upon the coast. L'Olonnois understood very well that it would not do for him or his men to make answer to these inquiries, for their speech would have shown they did not belong to those parts.

Therefore he made one of his prisoner fishermen answer that they had not seen a pirate vessel, and if there had been one there, it must have sailed away when its captain heard the Spanish ship was coming. Then the canoes were allowed to go their way, but their way was a very different one from any which could have been expected by the captain of the ship.

They rowed off into the darkness instead of going toward the town, and waited until nearly daybreak, then they boldly made for the man-of-war, one canoe attacking her on one side and the other on the other. Before the Spanish could comprehend what had happened there were more than twenty pirates upon their decks, the dreaded L'Olonnois at their head.

In such a case as this cannon were of no use, and when the crew tried to rush upon deck, they found that cutlasses and pistols did not avail very much better. The pirates had the advantage; they had over-powered the watch, and were defending the deck against all comers from below. It requires a very brave sailor to stick his head out of a hatchway when he sees three or four cutlasses ready to split it open. But there was some stout fighting on board; the officers came out of their cabins, and some of the men were able to force their way out into the struggle. The pirates knew, however, that they were but few and that were their enemies allowed to get on deck they would prove entirely too strong, and they fought, each scoundrel of them, like three men, and the savage fight ended by every Spanish sailor or officer who was not killed or wounded being forced to stay below decks, where the hatches were securely fastened down upon them.

L'Olonnois now stood a proud victor on the deck of his prize, and, being a man of principle, he determined to live up to the distinguished reputation which he had acquired in that part of the world. Baring his muscular and hairy right arm, he clutched the handle of his sharp and heavy cutlass and ordered the prisoners to be brought up from below, one at a time, and conducted to the place where he stood. He wished to give Spain a lesson which would make her understand that he was not to be interfered with in the execution of his enterprises, and he determined to allow himself the pleasure of personally teaching this lesson.

As soon as a prisoner was brought to L'Olonnois he struck off his head, and this performance he continued, beginning with number one, and going on until he had counted ninety. The last one brought to him was the negro slave. This man, who was not a soldier, was desperately frightened and begged piteously for his life. L'Olonnois, finding that the man was willing to tell everything he knew, questioned him about the sending of this vessel from Havana, and when the poor fellow had finished by telling that he had come there, not of his own accord, but simply for the purpose of obeying his master, to hang all the pirates except their leader, that great buccaneer laughed, and, finding he could get nothing more from the negro, cut off his head likewise, and his body was tumbled into the sea after those of his companions.

Now there was not a Spaniard left on board the great ship except one man, who had been preserved from the fate of the others because L'Olonnois had some correspondence to attend to, and he needed a messenger to carry a letter. The pirate captain went into the cabin, where he found writing-materials ready to his hand, and there he composed a letter to the Governor of Havana, a part of which read as follows: "I shall never henceforward give quarter unto any Spaniard whatsoever. And I have great hopes that I shall execute on your own person the very same punishment I have done to them you sent against me. Thus I have retaliated the kindness you designed unto me and my companions."

When this message was received by the dignified official who filled the post of Governor of Cuba, he stormed and fairly foamed at the mouth. To be utterly foiled and discomfited by this resurrected pirate, and to be afterwards addressed in terms of such unheard-of insolence and abuse, was more than he could bear, and, in the presence of many of his officials and attendants, he swore a terrible oath that after that hour he would never again give quarter to any buccaneer, no matter when or where he was captured, or what he might be doing at the time. Every man of the wretched band should die as soon as he could lay hands upon him.

But when the inhabitants of Havana and the surrounding villages heard of this terrible resolution of their Governor they were very much disturbed. They lived in constant danger of attack, especially those who were engaged in fishing or maritime pursuits, and they feared that when it became known that no buccaneer was to receive quarter, the Spanish colonists would be treated in the same way, no matter where they might be found and taken. Consequently, it was represented to the Governor that his plan of vengeance would work most disastrously for the Spanish settlers, for the buccaneers could do far more damage to them than he could possibly do to these dreadful Brethren of the Coast, and that, unless he wished to bring upon them troubles greater than those of famine or pestilence, they begged that he would retract his oath.

When the high dignitary had cooled down a little, he saw that there was a good deal of sense in what the representative of the people had said to him, and he consequently felt obliged, in consideration of the public safety, to take back what he had said, and to give up the purpose, which would have rendered unsafe the lives of so many peaceable people.

L'Olonnois was now the possessor of a fine vessel which had not been in the least injured during the battle in which it had been won. But his little crew, some of whom had been killed and wounded, was insufficient to work such a ship upon an important cruise on the high seas, and he also discovered, much to his surprise, that there were very few provisions on board, for when the vessel was sent from Havana it was supposed she would make but a very short cruise. This savage swinger of the cutlass thereupon concluded that he would not try to do any great thing for the present, but, having obtained some booty and men from the woe-begone town of de los Cayos, he sailed away, touching at several other small ports for the purpose of pillage, and finally anchoring at Tortuga.

When L'Olonnois landed on the disreputable shores of Tortuga, he was received by all circles of the vicious society of the island with loud acclamation. He had not only taken a fine Spanish ship, he had not only bearded the Governor of Havana in his fortified den, but he had struck off ninety heads with his own hand. Even people who did not care for him before reverenced him now. In all the annals of piracy no hero had ever done such a deed as this, and the best records of human butchering had been broken.

Now grand and ambitious ideas began to swell the head of this champion slaughterer, and he conceived the plan of getting up a grand expedition to go forth and capture the important town of Maracaibo, in New Venezuela. This was an enterprise far above the ordinary aims of a buccaneer, and it would require more than ordinary force to accomplish it. He therefore set himself to work to enlist a large number of men and to equip a fleet of vessels, of which he was to be chief commander or admiral. There were a great many unemployed pirates in Tortuga at that time, and many a brawny rascal volunteered to sail under the flag of the daring butcher of the seas.

But in order to equip a fleet, money was necessary as well as men, and therefore L'Olonnois thought himself very lucky when he succeeded in interesting the principal piratical capitalist of Tortuga in his undertaking. This was an old and seasoned buccaneer by the name of Michael de Basco, who had made money enough by his piratical exploits to retire from business and live on his income. He held the position of Mayor of the island and was an important man among his fellow miscreants. When de Basco heard of the great expedition which L'Olonnois was about to undertake, his whole soul was fired and he could not rest tamely in his comfortable quarters when such great things were to be done, and he offered to assist L'Olonnois with funds and join in the expedition if he were made commander of the land forces. This offer was accepted gladly, for de Basco had a great reputation as a fighter in Europe as well as in America.

When everything had been made ready, L'Olonnois set sail for Maracaibo with a fleet of eight ships. On the way they captured two Spanish vessels, both of which were rich prizes, and at last they arrived before the town which they intended to capture.

Maracaibo was a prosperous place of three or four thousand inhabitants; they were rich people living in fine houses, and many of them had plantations which extended out into the country. In every way the town possessed great attractions to piratical marauders, but there were difficulties in the way; being such an important place, of course it had important defences. On an island in the harbor there was a strong fort, or castle, and on another island a little further from the town there was a tall tower, on the top of which a sentinel was posted night and day to give notice of any approaching enemy. Between these two islands was the only channel by which the town could be approached from the sea. But in preparing these defences the authorities had thought only of defending themselves against ordinary naval forces and had not anticipated the extraordinary naval methods of the buccaneers who used to be merely sea-robbers, who fell upon ships after they had left their ports, but who now set out to capture not only ships at sea but towns on land.

L'Olonnois had too much sense to run his ships close under the guns of the fortress, against which he could expect to do nothing, for the buccaneers relied but little upon their cannon, and so they paid no more attention to the ordinary harbor than if it had not been there, but sailed into a fresh-water lake at some distance from the town, and out of sight of the tower. There L'Olonnois landed his men, and, advancing upon the fort from the rear, easily crossed over to the little island and marched upon the fort. It was very early in the morning. The garrison was utterly amazed by this attack from land, and although they fought bravely for three hours, they were obliged to give up the defence of the walls, and as many of them as could do so got out of the fort and escaped to the mainland and the town.

L'Olonnois now took possession of the fort, and then, with the greater part of his men, he returned to his ships, brought them around to the entrance of the bay, and then boldly sailed with his whole fleet under the very noses of the cannon and anchored in the harbor in front of the town.

When the citizens of Maracaibo heard from the escaping garrison that the fort had been taken, they were filled with horror and dismay, for they had no further means of defence. They knew that the pirates had come there for no other object than to rob, pillage, and cruelly treat them, and consequently as many as possible hurried away into the woods and the surrounding country with as many of their valuables as they could carry. They resembled the citizens of a town attacked by the cholera or the plague, and in fact, they would have preferred a most terrible pestilence to this terrible scourge of piracy from which they were about to suffer.

As soon as L'Olonnois and his wild pirates had landed in the city they devoted themselves entirely to eating and drinking and making themselves merry. They had been on short commons during the latter part of their voyage, and they had a royal time with the abundance of food and wine which they found in the houses of the town. The next day, however, they set about attending to the business which had brought them there, and parties of pirates were sent out into the surrounding country to find the people who had run away and to take from them the treasures they had carried off. But although a great many of the poor, miserable, unfortunate citizens were captured and brought back to the town, there was found upon them very little money, and but few jewels or ornaments of value. And now L'Olonnois began to prove how much worse his presence was than any other misfortune which could have happened to the town. He tortured the poor prisoners, men, women, and children, to make them tell where they had hidden their treasures, sometimes hacking one of them with his sword, declaring at the same time that if he did not tell where his money was hidden he would immediately set to work to cut up his family and his friends.

The cruelties inflicted upon the inhabitants by this vile and beastly pirate and his men were so horrible that they could not be put into print. Even John Esquemeling, who wrote the account of it, had not the heart to tell everything that had happened. But after two weeks of horror and torture, the pirates were able to get but comparatively little out of the town, and they therefore determined to go somewhere else, where they might do better.

At the southern end of Lake Maracaibo, about forty leagues from the town which the pirates had just desolated and ruined, lay Gibraltar, a good-sized and prosperous town, and for this place L'Olonnois and his fleet now set sail; but they were not able to approach unsuspected and unseen, for news of their terrible doings had gone before them, and their coming was expected. When they drew near the town they saw the flag flying from the fort, and they knew that every preparation had been made for defence. To attack such a place as this was a rash undertaking; the Spaniards had perhaps a thousand soldiers, and the pirates numbered but three hundred and eighty, but L'Olonnois did not hesitate. As usual, he had no thought of bombardment, or any ordinary method of naval warfare; but at the first convenient spot he landed all his men, and having drawn them up in a body, he made them an address. He made them understand clearly the difficult piece of work which was before them; but he assured them that pirates were so much in the habit of conquering Spaniards that if they would all promise to follow him and do their best, he was certain he could take the town. He assured them that it would be an ignoble thing to give up such a grand enterprise as this simply because they found the enemy strong and so well prepared to meet them, and ended by stating that if he saw a man flinch or hold back for a second, he would pistol him with his own hand. Whereupon the pirates all shook hands and promised they would follow L'Olonnois wherever he might lead them.

This they truly did, and L'Olonnois, having a very imperfect knowledge of the proper way to the town, led them into a wild bog, where this precious pack of rascals soon found themselves up to their knees in mud and water, and in spite of all the cursing and swearing which they did, they were not able to press through the bog or get out of it. In this plight they were discovered by a body of horsemen from the town, who began firing upon them. The Spaniards must now have thought that their game was almost bagged and that all they had to do was to stand on the edge of the bog and shoot down the floundering fellows who could not get away from them. But these fellows were bloody buccaneers, each one of them a great deal harder to kill than a cat, and they did not propose to stay in the bog to be shot down. With their cutlasses they hewed off branches of trees and threw these down in the bog, making a sort of rude roadway by means of which they were able to get out on solid ground. But here they found themselves confronted by a large body of Spaniards, entrenched behind earthworks. Cannon and musket were opened upon the buccaneers, and the noise and smoke were so terrible they could scarcely hear the commands of their leaders.

Never before, perhaps, had pirates been engaged in such a land battle as this. Very soon the Spaniards charged from behind their earthworks, and then L'Olonnois and his men were actually obliged to fly back. If he could have found any way of retreating to his ships, L'Olonnois would doubtless have done so, in spite of his doughty words, when he addressed his men, but this was now impossible, for the Spaniards had felled trees and had made a barricade between the pirates and their ships. The buccaneers were now in a very tight place; their enemy was behind defences and firing at them steadily, without showing any intention of coming out to give the pirates a chance for what they considered a fair fight. Every now and then a buccaneer would fall, and L'Olonnois saw that as it would be utterly useless to endeavor to charge the barricade he must resort to some sort of trickery or else give up the battle.

Suddenly he passed the word for every man to turn his back and run away as fast as he could from the earthworks. Away scampered the pirates, and from the valiant Spaniards there came a shout of victory. The soldiers could not be restrained from following the fugitives and putting to death every one of the cowardly rascals. Away went the buccaneers, and after them, hot and furious, came the soldiers. But as soon as the Spaniards were so far away from their entrenchments that they could not get back to them, the crafty L'Olonnois, who ran with one eye turned behind him, called a halt, his men turned, formed into battle array, and began an onslaught upon their pursuing enemy, such as these military persons had never dreamed of in their wildest imagination. We are told that over two hundred Spaniards perished in a very short time. Before a furious pirate with a cutlass a soldier with his musket seemed to have no chance at all, and very soon the Spaniards who were left alive broke and ran into the woods.

The buccaneers formed into a body and marched toward the town, which surrendered without firing a gun, and L'Olonnois and his men,

who, but an hour before, had been in danger of being shot down by
their enemy as if they had been rabbits in a pen, now marched boldly
into the centre of the town, pulled down the Spanish flag, and hoisted
their own in its place. They were the masters of Gibraltar. Never had
ambitious villany been more successful.

When L'Olonnois and his buccaneers entered the town of Gibraltar they found that the greater part of the inhabitants had fled, but
there were many people left, and these were made prisoners as fast
as they were discovered. They were all forced to go into the great
church, and then the pirates, fearing that the Spaniards outside of
the town might be reënforced and come back again to attack them,
carried a number of cannon into the church and fortified the building. When this had been done, they felt safe and began to act as if
they had been a menagerie of wild beasts let loose upon a body of defenceless men, women, and children. Not only did these wretched
men rush into the houses, stealing everything valuable they could
find and were able to carry away, but when they had gathered together all they could discover they tortured their poor prisoners by
every cruel method they could think of, in order to make them tell
where more treasures were concealed. Many of these unfortunates
had had nothing to hide, and therefore could give no information to
their brutal inquisitors, and others died without telling what they had
done with their valuables. When the town had been thoroughly
searched and sifted, the pirates sent men out into the little villages
and plantations in the country, and even hunters and small farmers
were captured and made to give up everything they possessed which
was worth taking.

For nearly three weeks these outrageous proceedings continued,
and to prove that they were lower than the brute beasts they allowed
the greater number of the prisoners collected in the church to perish
of hunger. There were not provisions enough in the town for the pirates' own uses and for these miserable creatures also, and so, with the
exception of a small quantity of mule flesh, which many of the prisoners could not eat, they got nothing whatever, and slowly starved.

When L'Olonnois and his friends had been in possession of Gibraltar for about a month, they thought it was time to leave, but their

greedy souls were not satisfied with the booty they had already obtained, and they therefore sent messages to the Spaniards who were still concealed in the forests, that unless in the course of two days a ransom of ten thousand pieces of eight were paid to them, they would burn the town to the ground. No matter what they thought of this heartless demand, it was not easy for the scattered citizens to collect such a sum as this, and the two days passed without the payment of the ransom, and the relentless pirates promptly carried out their threat and set the town on fire in various places. When the poor Spaniards saw this and perceived that they were about to lose even their homes, they sent to the town and promised that if the pirates would put out the fires they would pay the money. In the hope of more money, and not in the least moved by any feeling of kindness, L'Olonnois ordered his men to help put out the fires, but they were not extinguished until a quarter of the town was entirely burned and a fine church reduced to ashes.

When the buccaneers found they could squeeze nothing more out of the town, they went on board their ships, carrying with them all the plunder and booty they had collected, and among their spoils were about five hundred slaves, of all ages and both sexes, who had been offered an opportunity to ransom themselves, but who, of course, had no money with which to buy their freedom, and who were now condemned to a captivity worse than anything they had ever known before.

Now the eight ships with their demon crews sailed away over the lake toward Maracaibo. It was quite possible for them to get out to sea without revisiting this unfortunate town, but as this would have been a very good thing for them to do, it was impossible for them to do it; no chance to do anything wicked was ever missed by these pirates. Consequently L'Olonnois gave orders to drop anchor near the city, and then he sent some messengers ashore to inform the already half-ruined citizens that unless they sent him thirty thousand pieces of eight he would enter their town again, carry away everything they had left, and burn the place to the ground. The poor citizens sent a committee to confer with the pirates, and while the negotiations were going on some of the conscienceless buccaneers went on shore and carried off from one of the great churches its images, pictures, and even its bells. It was at last arranged that the citizens should pay twenty thousand pieces of eight, which was the utmost sum they could possibly raise, and, in addition to this, five hundred head of beef-cattle, and the pirates promised that if this were done they would depart and molest the town no more. The money was paid, the cattle were put on board the ships, and to the unspeakable relief of the citizens, the pirate fleet sailed away from the harbor.

But it would be difficult to express the horror and dismay of those same citizens when, three days afterward, those pirate ships all came back again. Black despair now fell upon the town; there was nothing more to be stolen, and these wretches must have repented that they had left the town standing, and had returned to burn it down. But when one man came ashore in a boat bringing the intelligence that L'Olonnois could not get his largest ship across a bar at the entrance to the lake, and that he wanted a pilot to show him the channel, then the spirits of the people went up like one great united rocket, bursting into the most beautiful coruscations of sparks and colors. There was nothing on earth that they would be so glad to furnish him as a pilot to show him how to sail away from their shores. The pilot was instantly sent to the fleet, and L'Olonnois and his devastating band departed.

They did not go directly to Tortuga, but stopped at a little island near Hispaniola, which was inhabited by French buccaneers, and this delay was made entirely for the purpose of dividing the booty. It seems strange that any principle of right and justice should have been regarded by these dishonest knaves, even in their relations to each other, but they had rigid rules in regard to the division of their spoils, and according to these curious regulations the whole amount of plunder was apportioned among the officers and crews of the different ships.

Before the regular allotment of shares was made, the claims of the wounded were fully satisfied according to their established code. For the loss of a right arm a man was paid about six hundred dollars or six slaves; for the loss of a left arm, five hundred dollars, or five slaves; for a missing right leg, five hundred dollars, or five slaves; for a missing left leg, four hundred dollars, or four slaves; for an eye or a finger, one hundred dollars, or one slave. Then the rest of the money and spoils were divided among all the buccaneers without reference to what had been paid to the wounded. The shares of those who had been killed were given to friends or acquaintances, who undertook to deliver them to their families.

The spoils in this case consisted of two hundred and sixty thousand dollars in money and a great quantity of valuable goods, besides many slaves and precious stones and jewels. These latter were apportioned among the men in the most ridiculous manner, the pirates having no idea of the relative value of the jewels, some of them preferring large and worthless colored stones to smaller diamonds and rubies. When all their wickedly gained property had been divided, the pirates sailed to Tortuga, where they proceeded, without loss of time, to get rid of the wealth they had amassed. They ate, they drank, they gambled; they crowded the taverns as taverns have never been crowded before; they sold their valuable merchandise for a twentieth part of its value to some of the more level-headed people of the place; and having rioted, gambled, and committed every sort of extravagance for about three weeks, the majority of L'Olonnois' rascally crew found themselves as poor as when they had started off on their expedition. It took them almost as long to divide their spoils as it did to get rid of them.

As these precious rascals had now nothing to live upon, it was necessary to start out again and commit some more acts of robbery and ruin; and L'Olonnois, whose rapacious mind seems to have been filled with a desire for town-destroying, projected an expedition to Nicaragua, where he proposed to pillage and devastate as many towns and villages as possible. His reputation as a successful commander was now so high that he had no trouble in getting men, for more offered themselves than he could possibly take.

He departed with seven hundred men and six ships, stopping on the way near the coast of Cuba, and robbing some poor fishermen of their boats, which he would need in shallow water. Their voyage was a very long one, and they were beset by calms, and instead of reaching Nicaragua, they drifted into the Gulf of Honduras. Here they found themselves nearly out of provisions, and were obliged to land and scour the country to find something to eat. Leaving their ships, they began a land march through the unfortunate region where they now found themselves. They robbed Indians, they robbed villages; they devastated little towns, taking everything that they cared for, and burning what they did not want, and treating the people they captured with viler cruelties than any in which the buccaneers had yet indulged. Their great object was to take everything they could find, and then try to make the people confess where other things were hidden. Men and women were hacked to pieces with swords; it was L'Olonnois' pleasure, when a poor victim had nothing to tell, to tear out his tongue with his own hands, and it is said that on some occasions his fury was so great that he would cut out the heart of a man and bite at it with his great teeth. No more dreadful miseries could be conceived than those inflicted upon the peaceful inhabitants of the country through which these wretches passed. They frequently met ambuscades of Spaniards, who endeavored to stop their progress; but this was impossible. The pirates were too strong in number and too savage in disposition to be resisted by ordinary Christians, and they kept on their wicked way.

At last they reached a town called San Pedro, which was fairly well defended, having around it a great hedge of prickly thorns; but thorns cannot keep out pirates, and after a severe fight the citizens surrendered, on condition that they should have two hours' truce. This was given, and the time was occupied by the people in running away into the woods and carrying off their valuables. But when the two hours had expired, L'Olonnois and his men entered the town, and instead of rummaging around to see what they could find, they followed the unfortunate people into the woods, for they well understood what they wanted when they asked for a truce, and robbed them of nearly everything they had taken away.

But the capture of this town was not of much service to L'Olonnois, who did not find provisions enough to feed his men. Their supplies ran very low, and it was not long before they were in danger of starvation. Consequently they made their way by the most direct course to the coast, where they hoped to be able to get something to eat. If they could find nothing else, they might at least catch fish. On their way every rascal of them prepared himself a net, made out of the fibres of a certain plant, which grew in abundance in those regions, in order that he might catch himself a supper when he reached the sea.

After a time the buccaneers got back to their fleet and remained on the coast about three months, waiting for some expected Spanish ships, which they hoped to capture. They eventually met with one, and after a great deal of ordinary fighting and stratagem they boarded and took her, but found her not a very valuable prize.

Now L'Olonnois proposed to his men that they should sail for Guatemala, but he met with an unexpected obstacle; the buccaneers who had enlisted under him had expected to make great fortunes in this expedition, but their high hopes had not been realized. They had had very little booty and very little food, they were hungry and disappointed and wanted to go home, and the great majority of them declined to follow L'Olonnois any farther. But there were some who declared that they would rather die than go home to Tortuga as poor as when they left it, and so remained with L'Olonnois on the biggest ship of the fleet, which he commanded. The smaller vessels now departed for Tortuga, and after some trouble L'Olonnois succeeded in getting his vessel out of the harbor where it had been anchored, and sailed for the islands of de las Pertas. Here he had the misfortune to run his big vessel hopelessly aground.

When they found it absolutely impossible to get their great vessel off the sand banks, the pirates set to work to break her up and build a boat out of her planks. This was a serious undertaking, but it was all they could do. They could not swim away, and their ship was of no use to them as she was. But when they began to work they had no idea it would take so long to build a boat. It was several months before the unwieldy craft was finished, and they occupied part of the time in gardening, planting French beans, which came to maturity in six weeks, and gave them some fresh vegetables. They also had some stores and portable stoves on board their dismantled ship, and made bread from some wheat which was among their provisions, thus managing to live very well.

L'Olonnois was never intended by nature to be a boat-builder, or anything else that was useful and honest, and when the boat was finished it was discovered that it had been planned so badly that it would not hold them all, so all they could do was to draw lots to see who should embark in her, for one-half of them would have to stay until the others came back to release them. Of course L'Olonnois went away in the boat, and reached the mouth of the Nicaragua River. There his party was attacked by some Spaniards and Indians, who killed more than half of them and prevented the others from landing. L'Olonnois and the rest of his men got safely away, and they might now have sailed back to the island where they had left their comrades, for there was room enough for them all in the boat. But they did nothing of the sort, but went to the coast of Cartagena.

The pirates left on the island were eventually taken off by a buccaneering vessel, but L'Olonnois had now reached the end of the string by which the devil had allowed him to gambol on this earth for so long a time. On the shores where he had now landed he did not find prosperous villages, treasure houses, and peaceful inhabitants, who could be robbed and tortured, but instead of these he came upon a community of Indians, who were called by the Spaniards Bravos, or wild men. These people would never have anything to do with the whites. It was impossible to conquer them or to pacify them by kind treatment. They hated the white man and would have nothing to do with him. They had heard of L'Olonnois and his buccaneers, and when they found this notorious pirate upon their shores they were filled with a fury such as they had never felt for any others of his race.

These bloody pirates had always conquered in their desperate fights because they were so reckless and so savage, but now they had fallen among thoroughbred savages, more cruel and more brutal and pitiless than themselves. Nearly all the buccaneers were killed, and L'Olonnois was taken prisoner. His furious captors tore his living body apart, piece by piece, and threw each fragment into the fire, and when the whole of this most inhuman of inhuman men had been entirely consumed, they scattered his ashes to the winds so that not a trace should remain on earth of this monster. If, in his infancy, he had died of croup, the history of the human race would have lost some of its blackest pages.

BLACK BARTLEMY'S TREASURE

Jeffrey Farnol

CHAPTER TWO

The Frenchman beside me had been dead since dawn. His scarred and shackled body swayed limply back and forth with every sweep of the great oar as we, his less fortunate bench-fellows, tugged and strained to keep time to the stroke.

Two men had I seen die beside me, yet Death ever passed me by, nay, it seemed rather that despite the pain of stripes, despite the travail and hardship, my strength waxed the mightier; upon arm and thigh, burnt nigh black by fierce suns, the muscles showed hard and knotted; within my body, scarred by the lash, the life leapt and glowed yet was the soul of me sick unto death. But it seemed I could not die—finding thereby blessed rest and a surcease from this agony of life as had this Frenchman, who of all the naked wretches about me, was the only one with whom I had any sort of fellowship. He had died (as I say) with the dawn, so quietly that at first I thought he but fainted and pitied him, but, when I knew, pity changed to bitterness.

Therefore, as I strove at the heavy oar I prayed 'twixt gnashing teeth a prayer I had often prayed, and the matter of my praying was thus:

"O God of Justice, for the agony I needs must now endure, for the bloody stripes and bitter anguish give to me vengeance—vengeance, O God, on mine enemy!"

So prayed I, hoarse-panting and with the sweat trickling down whiles I stared at the naked back of him that rowed before me—a great, fat fellow he had been once, but now the skin hung in numberless creases whereon were many weals, some raw and bloody, that crossed and re-crossed each other after the manner of lace-work.

"Justice, O God, upon mine enemy! Since Death is not for me let me live until I be avenged; for the pain I suffer so may I see him suffer, for the anguish that is mine so may I watch his agony. Thou art a just God, so, God of Justice, give to me vengeance!"

The sun rose high and higher over our quarter, beating down upon our naked backs and adding greatly to our torments thereby, waking the pain of old stripes and lending an added sting to new.

Ever and anon would come the sharp crack of the drivers' whips followed by the squealing cry of quivering flesh (a cry wherein was none of the human) the which, dying to a whine, was lost in the stir and bustle of the great galleass. But ever and always, beneath the hoarse voices of the mariners, beneath the clash of armour and tramp of feet, beneath the creak and rumble of the long oars, came yet another sound, rising and falling yet never ceasing, a dull, low sound the like of which you shall sometimes hear among trees when the wind is high—the deep, sobbing moan that was the voice of our anguish as we poor wretches urged the great *Esmeralda* galleass upon her course.

The oar whereto I was chained along with my three bench-mates had at some time been badly sprung, so that the armourers had made shift to strengthen it with a stout iron fillet some six inches wide. Now it so happened that my grasp came upon this fillet, and, with every stroke of the oar, day after day, week in and week out, it had become my wont to rub the links of my chain to and fro across this iron band, whereby they had become very smooth and shining.

The words of my prayer were yet upon my lips, when, chancing to look upon one of these links, I beheld that which set my heart a-leaping and my riotous blood a-tingle to my fingers' ends; yet 'twas a very small thing, no more than a mark that showed upon the polished surface of the link, a line not so thick as a hair and not to be noticed without close looking; but when I bore upon the link this hair-line grew and widened, it needed but a sudden wrench and I should be free. This threw me into such a rapturous transport that I had much ado to contain myself, howbeit after some while I lifted my eyes to the heaven all flushed and rosy with the young day, for it seemed that God had indeed heard my prayer.

Presently, along the gangway amidships, comes none other than that accursed Portugal, Pedro the whip-master, who, espying the drooping form of the Frenchman beside me, forthwith falls a-cursing in his vile tongue and gives a prodigious flourish with his whip. Now by reason of much practice they do become very expert with these same whips, insomuch that they shall (with a certain cunning flick of the lash) gash you a man as it were with a knife, the like of which none may bear and not cry out for the exceeding pain of it. "Ha, thou lazy dog!" cries he, "Think ye to snore and take your ease whiles Pedro is aboard?" And with the word the long lash hissed and cracked upon the Frenchman's naked back like a pistol-shot.

And lo! He (that meseemed was dead) stirred. I felt the scarred body leap and quiver, the swooning eyes opened, rolling dim and sightless and the pallid face was twisted in sharp anguish; but, even as I watched, the lines of agony were smoothed away, into the wild eyes came a wondrous light, and uttering a great, glad cry he sank forward across the oar-shaft and hung there. Hereupon this accursed Pedro betook him to his whip, smiting right heartily, but, seeing the Frenchman stirred not and perceiving, moreover, the blood to come but slow and in no great quantity, he presently desisted and bade us cease rowing one and all.

This sudden respite from labour served but to teach me how stiff and painful were my limbs, more especially my left wrist and ankle where the fetters had worn great sores.

The wind was fallen light and there rose that hot, sickening reek, that suffocating stench that is like unto nothing on earth save one of these floating hells, and the which, if a man hath but smelled it once, he shall nevermore forget.

After some while, back cometh Pedro with certain of the armourers, and (having by diverse methods learned the Frenchman was in sooth dead) they struck off his fetters, hand and leg, in the doing of which they must needs free me also (since we were chained together, he and I) and, binding a great shot to his feet, made ready to heave him overboard.

And now, seeing no man heeded me, I snapped asunder the cracked link and was free, save for the heavy chain that cumbered my leg. Stooping, I lifted this chain and crouched to spring for the bulwark; but now (even in this moment), remembering all that I had suffered at the hands of this most accursed Pedro, I turned, and wrapping the broken oar-chain about my fist, crept towards where he stood to oversee the armourers. His back was towards me and I was within a yard of him when he turned, and, seeing me, uttered a shout and raised his whip, but ere the blow could fall I leapt and smote him. My iron-bound fist took him full betwixt the eyes, and looking down upon his crushed and spattered face as he lay I knew that Pedro the whip-master would whip men no more these many days.

Then (not minded to die by the whip or upon a pike-head) turned I and sprang for the ship's side, but the chain about my leg hampered me sorely, and ere I could mount the high bulwark I was beset from behind. So would I have faced them and died fighting but fierce strokes battered me to my knees, fierce hands wrenched and tore at me, and grown faint with blows I was overborne, my hands lashed behind me, and thus helpless I was dragged along the gangway and so up the ladder to the poop where, plain to all men's sight, a whipping-post had been set up. Yet even so I struggled still, panting out curses on them, French and Spanish and English, drawing upon all the vile abuse of the rowing-bench and lazarette since fain would I have them slay me out of hand the rather than endure the miseries and anguish of my lot. Yet this might not be (since slaves were hard to come by and I was mighty and strong) wherefore I struggled no more, but suffered them to strike off my broken fetters and bind me to the whipping-post as they listed. Yet scarce had they made an end when there comes a loud hail from the masthead, whereupon was sudden mighty to-do of men running hither and yon, laughing and shouting one to another, some buckling on armour as they ran, some casting loose the great ordnance, while eyes turned and hands pointed in the one direction; but turn and twist me how I might I could see nought of any strange sail by reason of the high bulkhead beside me.

Of a sudden all voices were hushed as up the poop-ladder comes the [pirate] commander Don Miguel in his black armour, who, looking long and steadily to windward, gives a sign with his gauntleted hand, whereon divers of the officers go off hot-foot, some to muster the long files of arquebusiers, others to overlook the setting of more sail and the like. And now was a prodigious cracking of whips followed by groans and cries and screaming curses, and straightway the long oars began to swing with a swifter beat. From where I stood in my bonds I could look down upon the poor, naked wretches as they rose and fell, each and all at the same moment, in time to the stroke.

For maybe half an hour the chase was kept up and then all at once the decks quivered 'neath the discharge of one of the forward culverins; and presently, as the great galleass altered her course, obedient to the motion of Don Miguel's hand, I beheld, some half-league to windward, the towering stern of the ship we were pursuing, whose length gradually grew upon me as we overhauled her until she was fairly in view. She was a small ship, and by her build I did not doubt but that she was English; even as I watched, up to her mizzen-peak fluttered the English flag. And hereupon a great yearning came upon me, insomuch that of a sudden her high, weatherbeaten sides, her towering masts and patched canvas grew all blurred and indistinct.

Thrice already our guns had roared, yet (though she was now so close that I made out her very rope and spar) she made no sign. In a little our guns fell silent also, wherefore, looking about, I beheld Don Miguel standing beside the tiller yet with his impassive gaze ever bent upon the foe; and, as I watched, I read his deadly purpose, and a great fear for the English ship came upon me, and I fell a-praying beneath my breath, for we carried a weapon more terrible than any culverin that was ever cast, the long, sharp ram below the water.

The English ship was now so near that I could see the yawning muzzles of her guns, while her high, curving sides seemed to tower over us. As I gazed, with my heart full of a pitiful fear for her, I saw a head appear above her quarter-railing, a very round head whereon was a mariner's red cap. Came a puff of smoke, the sharp crack of a caliver, and one of the officers beside Don Miguel threw up his hands and, twisting on his heels, fell clashing in his armour. When I looked again for the red cap, it was gone. But Don Miguel waited, silent and impassive as ever. Suddenly he gestured with his hand, I saw the heave of the steersmen's shoulders as they obeyed, while the air rang with shouts of command as, the starboard oars holding water, the larboard thrashed and churned amain and the great *Esmeralda* galleass (turning thus well-nigh in her own length) drove straight for the side of her foe.

Never had I seen it better done, and I set my teeth, waiting for the grinding crash that was to send the English ship to the bottom, but lo! her creaking yards were braced round, and, paying off before the wind (which now blew strongly) she stood away upon a course at right angles to her old, whereby both vessels were running parallel as before. Yet it had been close, so very close indeed that as we drove past her I heard the sickening crack of our oars as they snapped off one after the other against her side, tossing those that manned them in bloody, struggling heaps.

And now from every English gun leaped roaring flame; the air was full of shrieks and groans and the crash of splintering wood, and through the eddying smoke I could see many of our soldiery that lay in strange, contorted attitudes while others crawled, sobbing on hands and knees; but on the scarlet-dropping rowing-benches I dared not look.

Hotter waxed the fight, louder swelled the din and tumult with the never-ceasing thunder of the guns; and amid it all Don Miguel paced to and fro, impassive as always, the blade of his long rapier gleaming here and there as he directed the fire.

Up rolled the smoke thicker and denser, but, ever and anon, through some rift I might catch a glimpse of the scarred, blackened side of the English ship, or the litter and confusion of our decks. Twice shots ploughed up the planking hard by me, and once my post itself was struck, so that for a moment I had some hope of winning free of my bonds, yet struggle how I would I could not move; the which filled me with a keen despair, for I made no doubt (what with the smoke and tumult) I might have plunged overboard unnoticed and belike have gained the English ship.

Slowly and by degrees our fire slackened, one by one the guns fell silent and in their place rose the more hateful sounds of anguish. Now as I stood thus, my eyes smarting with burnt powder, my ears yet ringing with the din, I grew aware how the deck sloped in strange fashion; at first I paid small heed, yet with every minute this slope became steeper, and with this certainty came the knowledge that we were sinking and, moreover (judging by the angle of the deck) sinking by the stern.

Hereupon, impelled by that lust of life the which is implanted in each one of us, I fell to a wild struggling against my bonds, until, seeing in a little the hopelessness of this, I grew resigned to despair, and, ceasing my passionate efforts, looked about me, for the smoke was thinned away. And truly an evil sight was this great galleass, with its shot-torn decks and huddled heaps of dead, its litter of broken spars and dismantled guns, and with everywhere great gouts and pools of blood, while below and beyond were the shattered rowing-benches cumbered now with awful red heaps, silent for the most part, yet some there were who screamed high and shrill.

Save for myself and divers of the dead the poop lay deserted, but forward such of the soldiers and mariners who yet lived were fighting for the boats, and all was riot and confusion.

As I stared about me thus I espied Don Miguel lying among the wreckage of a dismantled gun; his face was towards me and looked as I had seen it an hundred times, save for a smear of blood upon his cheek. Even as I gazed his eyes met mine full and square. For a moment he lay without motion, then (his face a-twitch with the effort) he came slowly to his elbow, gazed about him and so back to me again. Then I saw his hand creep down to the dagger at his hip, to fumble weakly there—howbeit, at the third essay he drew the blade and began to creep towards me. Very slowly and painfully he dragged himself along, and once I heard him groan, but he stayed not till he was come within striking distance, yet was he sore wounded and so weak withal that he was fain to rest him awhile. And ever his impassive eyes looked up into mine the while I nerved myself to meet the blow unflinching (and it might be so). Once more he raised himself, his arm lifted slowly, the dagger gleamed and fell, its keen edge severing the cords that bound me, and with a sudden effort I broke free and stood staring down into those impassive eyes as one in a dream. Then, lifting a feeble hand, he pointed to the tattered sails of the English ship hard by, and so, resting his head upon his arm as one that is very weary, he sighed; and with the sigh I think the life passed out of him.

Turning, I was upon the quarter-railing in a single leap, and, without a glance at the red havoc behind me, I plunged over and down.

The sharp sting of the brine struck me like a myriad needle-points, but the sweet cool of the waters was wondrous grateful to my sun-scorched body as, coming to the surface, I struck out for the English ship though sore hampered by my chain.

Presently coming beneath her lofty stern I found hanging therefrom a tangle of ropes and cordage whereby I contrived to clamber aboard, and so beheld a man in a red seaman's bonnet who sat upon the wreckage of one of the quarter guns tying up a splinter-gash in his arm with hand and teeth; perceiving me he rolled a pair of blue eyes up at me and nodded:

"Welcome aboard, lad!" says he, having knotted the bandage to his liking. "Be ye one as can understand good English?"

"Aye!," says I, nodding.

"Why then bear witness as I be a patient soul and marciful. Be witness as I held my fire so long as any marciful soul might by token that I knew what a broadside can do among crowded rowing-benches—having rowed aboard one o' they Spanish hells afore now—so I held my fire till yon devil's craft came nigh cutting me asunder—and marcy hath its limits. Timothy Spence o' the *Tiger*, master, is me, homeward bound for the Port of London, and by this fight am short five good men. But you're a proper big 'un. Go for'ard to the bo'sun, you shall know him by reason that he lacketh his starboard yere. Ask him for clothes to cover thy nakedness, lad, and—Oho, there goeth yon devil's craft—!" Turning as he spoke I saw the sharp bows of the *Esmeralda* lift and lift, high and higher, and, with a long-drawn gurgling roar, the great galleass plunged down stern foremost, burying her shame and misery from the eyes of man for evermore.

Thus then I sailed with Master Timothy Spence aboard the *Tiger*, a free man after five years of anguish.

THE GHOST OF CAPTAIN BRAND

Howard Pyle

CHAPTER THREE

It is not so easy to tell why discredit should be cast upon a man because of something that his grandfather may have done amiss, but the world, which is never overnice in its discrimination as to where to lay the blame, is often pleased to make the innocent suffer in the place of the guilty.

Barnaby True was a good, honest, biddable lad, as boys go, but yet he was not ever allowed altogether to forget that his grandfather had been that very famous pirate, Capt. William Brand, who, after so many marvelous adventures (if one may believe the catchpenny stories and ballads that were written about him), was murdered in Jamaica by Capt. John Malyoe, the commander of his own consort, the *Adventure* galley.

It has never been denied, that ever I heard, that up to the time of Captain Brand's being commissioned against the South Sea pirates he had always been esteemed as honest, reputable a sea captain as could be.

When he started out upon that adventure it was with a ship, the *Royal Sovereign*, fitted out by some of the most decent merchants of New York. The governor himself had subscribed to the adventure, and had himself signed Captain Brand's commission. So, if the unfortunate man went astray, he must have had great temptation to do so, many others behaving no better when the opportunity offered in those faraway seas where so many rich purchases might very easily be taken and no one the wiser.

To be sure, those stories and ballads made our captain to be a most wicked, profane wretch; and if he were, why, God knows he suffered and paid for it, for he laid his bones in Jamaica, and never saw his home or his wife and daughter again after he had sailed away on the *Royal Sovereign* on that long misfortunate voyage, leaving them in New York to the care of strangers.

At the time when he met his fate in Port Royal Harbor he had obtained two vessels under his command—the *Royal Sovereign*, which was the boat fitted out for him in New York, and the *Adventure* galley, which he was said to have taken somewhere in the South Seas. With these he lay in those waters of Jamaica for over a month after his return from the coasts of Africa, waiting for news from home, which, when it came, was of the very blackest; for the colonial authorities were at that time stirred up very hot against him to take him and hang him for a pirate, so as to clear their own skirts for having to do with such a fellow. So maybe it seemed better to our captain to hide his ill-gotten treasure there in those far-away parts, and afterward to try and bargain with it for his life when he should reach New York, rather than to sail straight for the Americas with what he had earned by his piracies, and so risk losing life and money both.

However that might be, the story was that Captain Brand and his gunner, and Captain Malyoe of the *Adventure* and the sailing master of the *Adventure* all went ashore together with a chest of money (no one of them choosing to trust the other three in so nice an affair), and buried the treasure somewhere on the beach of Port Royal Harbor. The story then has it that they fell a-quarreling about a future division or the money, and that, as a wind-up to the affair, Captain Malyoe shot Captain Brand through the head, while the sailing master of the *Adventure* served the gunner of the *Royal Sovereign* after the same fashion through the body, and that the murderers then went away, leaving the two stretched out in their own blood on the sand in the staring sun, with no one to know where the money was hid but they two who had served their comrades so.

It is a mighty great pity that anyone should have a grandfather who ended his days in such a sort as this, but it was no fault of Barnaby True's, nor could he have done anything to prevent it, seeing that he was not even born into the world at the time that his grandfather turned pirate, and was only one year old when he so met his tragical end. Nevertheless, the boys with whom he went to school never tired of calling him "Pirate," and would sometimes sing for his benefit that famous catchpenny song beginning thus:

> *Oh, my name was Captain Brand,*
> *A-sailing,*
> *And a-sailing;*
> *Oh, my name was Captain Brand,*
> *A-sailing free.*
> *Oh, my name was Captain Brand,*
> *And I sinned by sea and land,*
> *For I broke God's just command,*
> *A-sailing free.*

'Twas a vile thing to sing at the grandson of so misfortunate a man, and oftentimes little Barnaby True would double up his fists and would fight his tormentors at great odds, and would sometimes go back home with a bloody nose to have his poor mother cry over him and grieve for him.

Not that his days were all of teasing and torment, neither; for if his comrades did treat him so, why, then, there were other times when he and they were as great friends as could be, and would go in swimming together where there was a bit of sandy strand along the East River above Fort George, and that in the most amicable fashion. Or, maybe the very next day after he had fought so with his fellows, he would go a-rambling with them up the Bowerie Road, perhaps to help them steal cherries from some old Dutch farmer, forgetting in such adventure what a thief his own grandfather had been.

Well, when Barnaby True was between sixteen and seventeen years old he was taken into employment in the countinghouse of Mr. Roger Hartright, the well-known West India merchant, and Barnaby's own stepfather.

It was the kindness of this good man that not only found a place for Barnaby in the countinghouse, but advanced him so fast that before our hero was twenty-one years old he had made four voyages as super-cargo to the West Indies in Mr. Hartright's ship, the *Belle Helen*, and soon after he was twenty-one undertook a fifth. Nor was it in any such subordinate position as mere supercargo that he acted, but rather as the confidential agent of Mr. Hartright, who, having no children of his own, was very jealous to advance our hero into a position of trust and responsibility in the countinghouse, as though he were indeed a son, so that even the captain of the ship had scarcely more consideration aboard than he, young as he was in years.

As for the agents and correspondents of Mr. Hartright throughout these parts, they also, knowing how the good man had adopted his interests, were very polite and obliging to Master Barnaby—especially, be it mentioned, Mr. Ambrose Greenfield, of Kingston, Jamaica, who, upon the occasions of his visits to those parts, did all that he could to make Barnaby's stay in that town agreeable and pleasant to him.

So much for the history of our hero to the time of the beginning of this story, without which you shall hardly be able to understand the purport of those most extraordinary adventures that befell him shortly after he came of age, nor the logic of their consequence after they had occurred.

For it was during his fifth voyage to the West Indies that the first of those extraordinary adventures happened of which I shall have presently to tell.

At that time he had been in Kingston for the best part of four weeks, lodging at the house of a very decent, respectable widow, by name Mrs. Anne Bolles, who, with three pleasant and agreeable daughters, kept a very clean and well-served lodging house in the outskirts of the town.

One morning, as our hero sat sipping his coffee, clad only in loose cotton drawers, a shirt, and a jacket, and with slippers upon his feet, as is the custom in that country, where everyone endeavors to keep as cool as may be while he sat thus sipping his coffee, Miss Eliza, the youngest of the three daughters, came and gave him a note, which, she said, a stranger had just handed in at the door, going away again without waiting for a reply. You may judge of Barnaby's surprise when he opened the note and read as follows:

MR. BARNABY TRUE.

SIR,—Though you don't know me, I know you, and I tell you this: if you will be at Pratt's Ordinary on Harbor Street on Friday next at eight o'clock of the evening, and will accompany the man who shall say to you, "The Royal Sovereign *is come in," you shall learn something the most to your advantage that ever befell you. Sir, keep this note, and show it to him who shall address these words to you, so to certify that you are the man he seeks.*

Such was the wording of the note, which was without address, and without any superscription whatever.

The first emotion that stirred Barnaby was one of extreme and profound amazement. Then the thought came into his mind that some witty fellow, of whom he knew a good many in that town—and wild, waggish pranks they were was attempting to play off some smart jest upon him. But all that Miss Eliza could tell him when he questioned her concerning the messenger was that the bearer of the note was a tall, stout man, with a red neckerchief around his neck and copper buckles to his shoes, and that he had the appearance of a sailorman, having a great big queue hanging down his back. But, Lord! What was such a description as that in a busy seaport town, full of scores of men to fit such a likeness? Accordingly, our hero put away the note into his wallet, determining to show it to his good friend Mr. Greenfield that evening, and to ask his advice upon it. So he did show it, and that gentleman's opinion was the same as his—that some wag was minded to play off a hoax upon him, and that the matter of the letter was all nothing but smoke.

Nevertheless, though Barnaby was thus confirmed in his opinion as to the nature of the communication he had received, he yet determined in his own mind that he would see the business through to the end, and would be at Pratt's Ordinary, as the note demanded, upon the day and at the time specified therein.

Pratt's Ordinary was at that time a very fine and well-known place of its sort, with good tobacco and the best rum that ever I tasted, and had a garden behind it that, sloping down to the harbor front, was planted pretty thick with palms and ferns grouped into clusters with flowers and plants. Here were a number of little tables, some in little grottoes, like our Vauxhall in New York, and with red and blue and white paper lanterns hung among the foliage, whither gentlemen and ladies used sometimes to go of an evening to sit and drink lime juice and sugar and water (and sometimes a taste of something stronger), and to look out across the water at the shipping in the cool of the night.

Thither, accordingly, our hero went, a little before the time appointed in the note, and passing directly through the Ordinary and the garden beyond, chose a table at the lower end of the garden and close to the water's edge, where he would not be easily seen by anyone coming into the place. Then, ordering some rum and water and a pipe of tobacco, he composed himself to watch for the appearance of those witty fellows whom he suspected would presently come thither to see the end of their prank and to enjoy his confusion.

The spot was pleasant enough; for the land breeze, blowing strong and full, set the leaves of the palm tree above his head to rattling and clattering continually against the sky, where, the moon then being about full, they shone every now and then like blades of steel. The waves also were splashing up against the little landing place at the foot of the garden, sounding very cool in the night, and sparkling all over the harbor where the moon caught the edges of the water. A great many vessels were lying at anchor in their ridings, with the dark, prodigious form of a man-of-war looming up above them in the moonlight.

There our hero sat for the best part of an hour, smoking his pipe of tobacco and sipping his grog, and seeing not so much as a single thing that might concern the note he had received.

It was not far from half an hour after the time appointed in the note, when a rowboat came suddenly out of the night and pulled up to the landing place at the foot of the garden above mentioned, and three or four men came ashore in the darkness. Without saying a word among themselves they chose a near-by table and, sitting down, ordered rum and water, and began drinking their grog in silence. They might have sat there about five minutes, when, by and by, Barnaby

True became aware that they were observing him very curiously; and then almost immediately one, who was plainly the leader of the party, called out to him:

"How now, messmate! Won't you come and drink a dram of rum with us?"

"Why, no," says Barnaby, answering very civilly; "I have drunk enough already, and more would only heat my blood."

"All the same," quoth the stranger, "I think you will come and drink with us; for, unless I am mistook, you are Mr. Barnaby True, and I am come here to tell you that the *Royal Sovereign* is come in."

Now I may honestly say that Barnaby True was never more struck aback in all his life than he was at hearing these words uttered in so unexpected a manner. He had been looking to hear them under such different circumstances that, now that his ears heard them addressed to him, and that so seriously, by a perfect stranger, who, with others, had thus mysteriously come ashore out of the darkness, he could scarce believe that his ears heard aright. His heart suddenly began beating at a tremendous rate, and had he been an older and wiser man, I do believe he would have declined the adventure, instead of leaping blindly, as he did, into that of which he could see neither the beginning nor the ending. But being barely one-and-twenty years of age, and having an adventurous disposition that would have carried him into almost anything that possessed a smack of uncertainty or danger about it, he contrived to say, in a pretty easy tone (though God knows how it was put on for the occasion):

"Well, then, if that be so, and if the *Royal Sovereign* is indeed come in, why, I'll join you, since you are so kind as to ask me." And therewith he went across to the other table, carrying his pipe with him, and sat down and began smoking, with all the appearance of ease he could assume upon the occasion.

"Well, Mr. Barnaby True," said the man who had before addressed him, so soon as Barnaby had settled himself, speaking in a low tone of voice, so there would be no danger of any others hearing the words—"Well, Mr. Barnaby True—for I shall call you by your name, to show you that though I know you, you don't know me—I am glad to see that you are man enough to enter thus into an affair, though you can't see to the bottom of it. For it shows me that you are a man of mettle, and are deserving of the fortune that is to befall you to-night. Nevertheless, first of all, I am bid to say that you must show me a piece of paper that you have about you before we go a step farther."

"Very well," said Barnaby; "I have it here safe and sound, and see it you shall." And thereupon and without more ado he fetched out his wallet, opened it, and handed his interlocutor the mysterious note he had received the day or two before. Whereupon the other, drawing to him the candle, burning there for the convenience of those who would smoke tobacco, began immediately reading it.

This gave Barnaby True a moment or two to look at him. He was a tall, stout man, with a red handkerchief tied around his neck, and with copper buckles on his shoes, so that Barnaby True could not but wonder whether he was not the very same man who had given the note to Miss Eliza Bolles at the door of his lodging house.

"'Tis all right and straight as it should be," the other said, after he had so glanced his eyes over the note. "And now that the paper is read" (suiting his action to his words), "I'll just burn it, for safety's sake."

And so he did, twisting it up and setting it to the flame of the candle.

"And now," he said, continuing his address, "I'll tell you what I am here for. I was sent to ask you if you're man enough to take your life in your own hands and to go with me in that boat down there? Say 'Yes,' and we'll start away without wasting more time, for the devil is ashore here at Jamaica—though you don't know what that means— and if he gets ahead of us, why, then we may whistle for what we are after. Say 'No,' and I go away again, and I promise you you shall never be troubled again in this sort. So now speak up plain, young gentleman, and tell us what is your mind in this business, and whether you will adventure any farther or not."

If our hero hesitated it was not for long. I cannot say that his courage did not waver for a moment; but if it did, it was, I say, not for long, and when he spoke up it was with a voice as steady as could be.

"To be sure I'm man enough to go with you," he said, "and if you mean me any harm I can look out for myself; and if I can't, why, here is something can look out for me," and therewith he lifted up the flap of his coat pocket and showed the butt of a pistol he had fetched with him when he had set out from his lodging house that evening.

At this the other burst out a-laughing. "Come," says he, "you are indeed of right mettle, and I like your spirit. All the same, no one in all the world means you less ill than I, and so, if you have to use that barker, 'twill not be upon us who are your friends, but only upon one who is more wicked than the devil himself. So come, and let us get away."

Thereupon he and the others, who had not spoken a single word for all this time, rose from the table, and he having paid the scores of all, they all went down together to the boat that still lay at the landing place at the bottom of the garden.

Thus coming to it, our hero could see that it was a large yawl boat manned with half a score of black men for rowers, and there were two lanterns in the stern sheets, and three or four iron shovels.

The man who had conducted the conversation with Barnaby True for all this time, and who was, as has been said, plainly the captain of the party, stepped immediately down into the boat; our hero followed, and the others followed after him; and instantly they were seated the boat was shoved off and the black men began pulling straight out into the harbor, and so, at some distance away, around under the stern of the man-of-war.

Not a word was spoken after they had thus left the shore, and presently they might all have been ghosts, for the silence of the party. Barnaby True was too full of his own thoughts to talk—and serious enough thoughts they were by this time, with crimps to trepan a man at every turn, and press gangs to carry a man off so that he might never be heard of again. As for the others, they did not seem to choose to say anything now that they had him fairly embarked upon their enterprise.

And so the crew pulled on in perfect silence for the best part of an hour, the leader of the expedition directing the course of the boat straight across the harbor, as though toward the mouth of the Rio Cobra River. Indeed, this was their destination, as Barnaby could after a while see, by the low point of land with a great long row of coconut palms upon it (the appearance of which he knew very well), which by and by began to loom up out of the milky dimness of the moonlight.

As they approached the river they found the tide was running strong out of it, so that some distance away from the stream it gurgled and rippled alongside the boat as the crew of black men pulled strongly against it. Thus they came up under what was either a point of land or an islet covered with a thick growth of mangrove trees. But still no one spoke a single word as to their destination, or what was the business they had in hand.

The night, now that they were close to the shore, was loud with the noise of running tide-water, and the air was heavy with the smell of mud and marsh, and over all the whiteness of the moonlight, with a few stars pricking out here and there in the sky; and all so strange and silent and mysterious that Barnaby could not divest himself of the feeling that it was all a dream.

So, the rowers bending to the oars, the boat came slowly around from under the clump of mangrove bushes and out into the open water again.

Instantly it did so the leader of the expedition called out in a sharp voice, and the black men instantly lay on their oars.

Almost at the same instant Barnaby True became aware that there was another boat coming down the river toward where they lay, now drifting with the strong tide out into the harbor again, and he knew that it was because of the approach of that boat that the other had called upon his men to cease rowing.

The other boat, as well as he could see in the distance, was full of men, some of whom appeared to be armed, for even in the dusk of the darkness the shine of the moonlight glimmered sharply now and then on the barrels of muskets or pistols, and in the silence that followed after their own rowing had ceased Barnaby True could hear the chug! chug! of the oars sounding louder and louder through the watery stillness of the night as the boat drew nearer and nearer. But he knew nothing of what it all meant, nor whether these others were friends or enemies, or what was to happen next.

The oarsmen of the approaching boat did not for a moment cease their rowing, not till they had come pretty close to Barnaby and his companions. Then a man who sat in the stern ordered them to cease rowing, and as they lay on their oars he stood up. As they passed by, Barnaby True could see him very plain, the moonlight shining full upon him—a large, stout gentleman with a round red face, and clad in a fine laced coat of red cloth. Amidship of the boat was a box or chest about the bigness of a middle-sized traveling trunk, but covered all over with cakes of sand and dirt. In the act of passing, the gentleman, still standing, pointed at it with an elegant gold-headed cane which he held in his hand. "Are you come after this, Abraham Dawling?" says he, and thereat his countenance broke into as evil, malignant a grin as ever Barnaby True saw in all of his life.

The other did not immediately reply so much as a single word, but sat as still as any stone. Then, at last, the other boat having gone by, he suddenly appeared to regain his wits, for he bawled out after it, "Very well, Jack Malyoe! Very well, Jack Malyoe! You've got ahead of us this time again, but next time is the third, and then it shall be our turn, even if William Brand must come back from hell to settle with you."

This he shouted out as the other boat passed farther and farther away, but to it my fine gentleman made no reply except to burst out into a great roaring fit of laughter.

There was another man among the armed men in the stern of the passing boat—a villainous, lean man with lantern jaws, and the top of his head as bald as the palm of my hand. As the boat went away into the night with the tide and the headway the oars had given it, he grinned so that the moonlight shone white on his big teeth. Then, flourishing a great big pistol, he said, and Barnaby could hear every word he spoke, "Do but give me the word, Your Honor, and I'll put another bullet through the son of a sea cook."

But the gentleman said some words to forbid him, and therewith the boat was gone away into the night, and presently Barnaby could hear that the men at the oars had begun rowing again, leaving them lying there, without a single word being said for a long time.

By and by one of those in Barnaby's boat spoke up. "Where shall you go now?" he said.

At this the leader of the expedition appeared suddenly to come back to himself, and to find his voice again. "Go?" he roared out. "Go to the devil! Go? Go where you choose! Go? Go back again—that's where we'll go!" and therewith he fell a-cursing and swearing until he foamed at the lips, as though he had gone clean crazy, while the black men began rowing back again across the harbor as fast as ever they could lay oars into the water.

They put Barnaby True ashore below the old custom house; but so bewildered and shaken was he by all that had happened, and by what he had seen, and by the names that he heard spoken, that he was scarcely conscious of any of the familiar things among which he found himself thus standing. And so he walked up the moonlit street toward his lodging like one drunk or bewildered; for "John Malyoe" was the name of the captain of the *Adventure* galley—he who had shot Barnaby's own grandfather—and "Abraham Dawling" was the name of the gunner of the *Royal Sovereign* who had been shot at the same time with the pirate captain, and who, with him, had been left stretched out in the staring sun by the murderers.

The whole business had occupied hardly two hours, but it was as though that time was no part of Barnaby's life, but all a part of some other life, so dark and strange and mysterious that it in no wise belonged to him.

As for that box covered all over with mud, he could only guess at that time what it contained and what the finding of it signified.

But of this our hero said nothing to anyone, nor did he tell a single living soul what he had seen that night, but nursed it in his own mind, where it lay so big for a while that he could think of little or nothing else for days after.

Mr. Greenfield, Mr. Hartright's correspondent and agent in these parts, lived in a fine brick house just out of the town, on the Mona Road, his family consisting of a wife and two daughters—brisk, lively young ladies with black hair and eyes, and very fine bright teeth that shone whenever they laughed, and with a plenty to say for themselves. Thither Barnaby True was often asked to a family dinner; and, indeed, it was a pleasant home to visit, and to sit upon the veranda and smoke a cigarro with the good old gentleman and look out toward the mountains, while the young ladies laughed and talked, or played upon the guitar and sang. And oftentimes so it was strongly upon Barnaby's mind to speak to the good gentleman and tell him what he had beheld that night out in the harbor; but always he would think better of it and hold his peace, falling to thinking, and smoking away upon his cigarro at a great rate.

A day or two before the *Belle Helen* sailed from Kingston Mr. Greenfield stopped Barnaby True as he was going through the office to bid him to come to dinner that night (for there within the tropics they breakfast at eleven o'clock and take dinner in the cool of the evening, because of the heat, and not at midday, as we do in more temperate latitudes). "I would have you meet," says Mr. Greenfield, "your chief passenger for New York, and his granddaughter, for whom the state cabin and the two staterooms are to be fitted as here ordered [showing a letter]—Sir John Malyoe and Miss Marjorie Malyoe. Did you ever hear tell of Capt. Jack Malyoe, Master Barnaby?"

Now I do believe that Mr. Greenfield had no notion at all that old Captain Brand was Barnaby True's own grandfather and Capt. John Malyoe his murderer, but when he so thrust at him the name of that man, what with that in itself and the late adventure through which he himself had just passed, and with his brooding upon it until it was so prodigiously big in his mind, it was like hitting him a blow to so fling the questions at him. Nevertheless, he was able to reply, with a pretty straight face, that he had heard of Captain Malyoe and who he was.

"Well," says Mr. Greenfield, "if Jack Malyoe was a desperate pirate and a wild, reckless blade twenty years ago, why, he is Sir John Malyoe now and the owner of a fine estate in Devonshire. Well, Master Barnaby, when one is a baronet and come into the inheritance of a fine estate (though I do hear it is vastly cumbered with debts), the world will wink its eye to much that he may have done twenty years ago. I do hear say, though, that his own kin still turn the cold shoulder to him."

To this address Barnaby answered nothing, but sat smoking away at his cigarro at a great rate.

And so that night Barnaby True came face to face for the first time with the man who murdered his own grandfather—the greatest beast of a man that ever he met in all of his life.

That time in the harbor he had seen Sir John Malyoe at a distance and in the darkness; now that he beheld him near by it seemed to him that he had never looked at a more evil face in all his life. Not that the man was altogether ugly, for he had a good nose and a fine double chin; but his eyes stood out like balls and were red and watery, and he winked them continually, as though they were always smarting; and

41

his lips were thick and purple-red, and his fat, red cheeks were mottled here and there with little clots of purple veins; and when he spoke his voice rattled so in his throat that it made one wish to clear one's own throat to listen to him. So, what with a pair of fat, white hands, and that hoarse voice, and his swollen face, and his thick lips sticking out, it seemed to Barnaby True he had never seen a countenance so distasteful to him as that one into which he then looked.

But if Sir John Malyoe was so displeasing to our hero's taste, why, the granddaughter, even this first time he beheld her, seemed to him to be the most beautiful, lovely young lady that ever he saw. She had a thin, fair skin, red lips, and yellow hair—though it was then powdered pretty white for the occasion—and the bluest eyes that Barnaby beheld in all of his life. A sweet, timid creature, who seemed not to dare so much as to speak a word for herself without looking to Sir John for leave to do so, and would shrink and shudder whenever he would speak of a sudden to her or direct a sudden glance upon her. When she did speak, it was in so low a voice that one had to bend his head to hear her, and even if she smiled would catch herself and look up as though to see if she had leave to be cheerful.

As for Sir John, he sat at dinner like a pig, and gobbled and ate and drank, smacking his lips all the while, but with hardly a word to either her or Mrs. Greenfield or to Barnaby True; but with a sour, sullen air, as though he would say, "Your damned victuals and drink are no better than they should be, but I must eat 'em or nothing." A great bloated beast of a man!

Only after dinner was over and the young lady and the two misses sat off in a corner together did Barnaby hear her talk with any ease. Then, to be sure, her tongue became loose, and she prattled away at a great rate, though hardly above her breath, until of a sudden her grandfather called out, in his hoarse, rattling voice, that it was time to go. Whereupon she stopped short in what she was saying and jumped up from her chair, looking as frightened as though she had been caught in something amiss, and was to be punished for it.

Barnaby True and Mr. Greenfield both went out to see the two into their coach, where Sir John's man stood holding the lantern. And who should he be, to be sure, but that same lean villain with bald head who had offered to shoot the leader of our hero's expedition out on the harbor that night! For, one of the circles of light from the lantern shining up into his face, Barnaby True knew him the moment he clapped eyes upon him. Though he could not have recognized our hero, he grinned at him in the most impudent, familiar fashion, and never so much as touched his hat either to him or to Mr. Greenfield; but as soon as his master and his young mistress had entered the coach, banged to the door and scrambled up on the seat alongside the driver, and so away without a word, but with another impudent grin, this time favoring both Barnaby and the old gentleman.

Such were these two, master and man, and what Barnaby saw of them then was only confirmed by further observation—the most hateful couple he ever knew; though, God knows, what they afterward suffered should wipe out all complaint against them.

The next day Sir John Malyoe's belongings began to come aboard the *Belle Helen*, and in the afternoon that same lean, villainous manservant comes skipping across the gangplank as nimble as a goat, with two black men behind him lugging a great sea chest. "What!" he cried out, "and so you is the supercargo, is you? Why, I thought you was more account when I saw you last night a-sitting talking with His Honor like his equal. Well, no matter; 'tis something to have a brisk, genteel young fellow for a supercargo. So come, my hearty, lend a hand, will you, and help me set His Honor's cabin to rights."

What a speech was this to endure from such a fellow, to be sure! and Barnaby so high in his own esteem, and holding himself a gentleman! Well, what with his distaste for the villain, and what with such odious familiarity, you can guess into what temper so impudent an address must have cast him. "You'll find the steward in yonder," he said, "and he'll show you the cabin," and therewith turned and walked away with prodigious dignity, leaving the other standing where he was.

As he entered his own cabin he could not but see, out of the tail of his eye, that the fellow was still standing where he had left him, regarding him with a most evil, malevolent countenance, so that he had the satisfaction of knowing that he had made one enemy during that voyage who was not very likely to forgive or forget what he must regard as a slight put upon him.

The next day Sir John Malyoe himself came aboard, accompanied by his granddaughter, and followed by this man, and he followed again by four black men, who carried among them two trunks, not large in size, but prodigious heavy in weight, and toward which Sir John and his follower devoted the utmost solicitude and care to see that they were properly carried into the state cabin he was to occupy. Barnaby True was standing in the great cabin as they passed close by him; but though Sir John Malyoe looked hard at him and straight in the face, he never so much as spoke a single word, or showed by a look or a sign that he knew who our hero was. At this the serving man, who saw it all with eyes as quick as a cat's, fell to grinning and chuckling to see Barnaby in his turn so slighted.

The young lady, who also saw it all, flushed up red, then in the instant of passing looked straight at our hero, and bowed and smiled at him with a most sweet and gracious affability, then the next moment recovering herself, as though mightily frightened at what she had done.

The same day the *Belle Helen* sailed, with as beautiful, sweet weather as ever a body could wish for.

There were only two other passengers aboard, the Rev. Simon Styles, the master of a flourishing academy in Spanish Town, and his wife, a good, worthy old couple, but very quiet, and would sit in the great cabin by the hour together reading, so that, what with Sir John Malyoe staying all the time in his own cabin with those two trunks he held so precious, it fell upon Barnaby True in great part to show attention to the young lady; and glad enough he was of the opportunity, as anyone may guess. For when you consider a brisk, lively young man of one-and-twenty and a sweet, beautiful miss of seventeen so thrown together day after day for two weeks, the weather being very fair, as I have said, and the ship tossing and bowling along before a fine humming breeze that sent white caps all over the sea, and with nothing to do but sit and look at that blue sea and the bright sky overhead, it is not hard to suppose what was to befall, and what pleasure it was to Barnaby True to show attention to her.

But, oh! those days when a man is young, and, whether wisely or no, fallen in love! How often during that voyage did our hero lie awake in his berth at night, tossing this way and that without sleep—not that he wanted to sleep if he could, but would rather lie so awake thinking about her and staring into the darkness!

Poor fool! He might have known that the end must come to such a fool's paradise before very long. For who was he to look up to Sir John Malyoe's granddaughter, he, the supercargo of a merchant ship, and she the granddaughter of a baronet.

Nevertheless, things went along very smooth and pleasant, until one evening, when all came of a sudden to an end. At that time he and the young lady had been standing for a long while together, leaning over the rail and looking out across the water through the dusk toward the westward, where the sky was still of a lingering brightness. She had been mightily quiet and dull all that evening, but now of a sudden she began, without any preface whatever, to tell Barnaby about herself and her affairs. She said that she and her grandfather were going to New York that they might take passage thence to Boston town, there to meet her cousin Captain Malyoe, who was stationed in garrison at that place. Then she went on to say that Captain Malyoe was the next heir to the Devonshire estate, and that she and he were to be married in the fall.

But, poor Barnaby! what a fool was he, to be sure! Methinks when she first began to speak about Captain Malyoe he knew what was coming. But now that she had told him, he could say nothing, but stood there staring across the ocean, his breath coming hot and dry as ashes in his throat. She, poor thing, went on to say, in a very low voice, that she had liked him from the very first moment she had seen him, and had been very happy for these days, and would always think of him as a dear friend who had been very kind to her, who had so little pleasure in life, and so would always remember him.

Then they were both silent, until at last Barnaby made shift to say, though in a hoarse and croaking voice, that Captain Malyoe must be a very happy man, and that if he were in Captain Malyoe's place he would be the happiest man in the world. Thus, having spoken, and so found his tongue, he went on to tell her, with his head all in a whirl, that he, too, loved her, and that what she had told him struck him to the heart, and made him the most miserable, unhappy wretch in the whole world.

She was not angry at what he said, nor did she turn to look at him, but only said, in a low voice, he should not talk so, for that it could only be a pain to them both to speak of such things, and that whether she would or no, she must do everything as her grandfather bade her, for that he was indeed a terrible man.

To this poor Barnaby could only repeat that he loved her with all his heart, that he had hoped for nothing in his love, but that he was now the most miserable man in the world.

It was at this moment, so tragic for him, that some one who had been hiding nigh them all the while suddenly moved away, and Barnaby True could see in the gathering darkness that it was that villain manservant of Sir John Malyoe's and knew that he must have overheard all that had been said.

The man went straight to the great cabin, and poor Barnaby, his brain all atingle, stood looking after him, feeling that now indeed the last drop of bitterness had been added to his trouble to have such a wretch overhear what he had said.

The young lady could not have seen the fellow, for she continued leaning over the rail, and Barnaby True, standing at her side, not moving, but in such a tumult of many passions that he was like one bewildered, and his heart beating as though to smother him.

So they stood for I know not how long when, of a sudden, Sir John Malyoe comes running out of the cabin, without his hat, but carrying his gold-headed cane, and so straight across the deck to where Barnaby and the young lady stood, that spying wretch close at his heels, grinning like an imp.

"You hussy!" bawled out Sir John, so soon as he had come pretty near them, and in so loud a voice that all on deck might have heard the words; and as he spoke he waved his cane back and forth as though he would have struck the young lady, who, shrinking back almost upon the deck, crouched as though to escape such a blow. "You hussy!" he bawled out with vile oaths, too horrible here to be set down. "What do you do here with this Yankee supercargo, not fit for a gentlewoman to wipe her feet upon? Get to your cabin, you hussy" (only it was something worse he called her this time), "before I lay this cane across your shoulders!"

What with the whirling of Barnaby's brains and the passion into which he was already melted, what with his despair and his love, and his anger at this address, a man gone mad could scarcely be less accountable for his actions than was he at that moment. Hardly knowing what he did, he put his hand against Sir John Malyoe's breast and thrust him violently back, crying out upon him in a great, loud, hoarse voice for threatening a young lady, and saying that for a farthing he would wrench the stick out of his hand and throw it overboard.

Sir John went staggering back with the push Barnaby gave him, and then caught himself up again. Then, with a great bellow, ran roaring at our hero, whirling his cane about, and I do believe would have struck him (and God knows then what might have happened) had not his manservant caught him and held him back.

"Keep back!" cried out our hero, still mighty hoarse. "Keep back! If you strike me with that stick I'll fling you overboard!"

By this time, what with the sound of loud voices and the stamping of feet, some of the crew and others aboard were hurrying up, and the next moment Captain Manly and the first mate, Mr. Freesden, came running out of the cabin. But Barnaby, who was by this fairly set agoing, could not now stop himself.

"And who are you, anyhow," he cried out, "to threaten to strike me and to insult me, who am as good as you? You dare not strike me! You may shoot a man from behind, as you shot poor Captain Brand on the Rio Cobra River, but you won't dare strike me face to face. I know who you are and what you are!"

By this time Sir John Malyoe had ceased to endeavor to strike him, but stood stock-still, his great bulging eyes staring as though they would pop out of his head.

"What's all this?" cries Captain Manly, bustling up to them with Mr. Freesden. "What does all this mean?"

But, as I have said, our hero was too far gone now to contain himself until all that he had to say was out.

"The damned villain insulted me and insulted the young lady," he cried out, panting in the extremity of his passion, "and then he threatened to strike me with his cane. But I know who he is and what he is. I know what he's got in his cabin in those two trunks, and where he found it, and whom it belongs to. He found it on the shores of the Rio Cobra River, and I have only to open my mouth and tell what I know about it."

At this Captain Manly clapped his hand upon our hero's shoulder and fell to shaking him so that he could scarcely stand, calling out to him the while to be silent. "What do you mean?" he cried. "An officer of this ship to quarrel with a passenger of mine! Go straight to your cabin, and stay there till I give you leave to come out again."

At this Master Barnaby came somewhat back to himself and into his wits again with a jump. "But he threatened to strike me with his cane, Captain," he cried out, "and that I won't stand from any man!"

"No matter what he did," said Captain Manly, very sternly. "Go to your cabin, as I bid you, and stay there till I tell you to come out again, and when we get to New York I'll take pains to tell your step-father of how you have behaved. I'll have no such rioting as this aboard my ship."

Barnaby True looked around him, but the young lady was gone. Nor, in the blindness of his frenzy, had he seen when she had gone nor whither she went. As for Sir John Malyoe, he stood in the light of a lantern, his face gone as white as ashes, and I do believe if a look could kill, the dreadful malevolent stare he fixed upon Barnaby True would have slain him where he stood.

After Captain Manly had so shaken some wits into poor Barnaby he, unhappy wretch, went to his cabin, as he was bidden to do, and there, shutting the door upon himself, and flinging himself down, all dressed as he was, upon his berth, yielded himself over to the pro-foundest passion of humiliation and despair.

There he lay for I know not how long, staring into the darkness, until by and by, in spite of his suffering and his despair, he dozed off into a loose sleep, that was more like waking than sleep, being pos-sessed continually by the most vivid and distasteful dreams, from which he would awaken only to doze off and to dream again.

It was from the midst of one of these extravagant dreams that he was suddenly aroused by the noise of a pistol shot, and then the noise of another and another, and then a great bump and a grinding jar, and then the sound of many footsteps running across the deck and down into the great cabin. Then came a tremendous uproar of voices in the great cabin, the struggling as of men's bodies being tossed about, strik-ing violently against the partitions and bulkheads. At the same instant arose a screaming of women's voices, and one voice, and that Sir John Malyoe's, crying out as in the greatest extremity: "You villains! You damned villains!" and with the sudden detonation of a pistol fired into the close space of the great cabin.

Barnaby was out in the middle of his cabin in a moment, and taking only time enough to snatch down one of the pistols that hung at the head of his berth, flung out into the great cabin, to find it as black as night, the lantern slung there having been either blown out or dashed out into darkness. The prodigiously dark space was full of uproar, the hubbub and confusion pierced through and through by that keen sound of women's voices screaming, one in the cabin and the other in the stateroom beyond. Almost immediately Barnaby pitched headlong over two or three struggling men scuffling together upon the deck, falling with a great clatter and the loss of his pistol, which, however, he regained almost immediately.

What all the uproar meant he could not tell, but he presently heard Captain Manly's voice from somewhere suddenly calling out, "You bloody pirate, would you choke me to death?" wherewith some notion of what had happened came to him like a dash, and that they had been attacked in the night by pirates.

Looking toward the companionway, he saw, outlined against the darkness of the night without, the blacker form of a man's figure, standing still and motionless as a statue in the midst of all this hubbub, and so by some instinct he knew in a moment that that must be the master maker of all this devil's brew. Therewith, still kneeling upon the deck, he covered the bosom of that shadowy figure point blank, as he thought, with his pistol, and instantly pulled the trigger.

In the flash of red light, and in the instant stunning report of the pistol shot, Barnaby saw, as stamped upon the blackness, a broad, flat face with fishy eyes, a lean, bony forehead with what appeared to be a great blotch of blood upon the side, a cocked hat trimmed with gold lace, a red scarf across the breast, and the gleam of brass buttons. Then the darkness, very thick and black, swallowed everything again.

But in the instant Sir John Malyoe called out, in a great loud voice: "My God! 'Tis William Brand!" Therewith came the sound of someone falling heavily down.

The next moment, Barnaby's sight coming back to him again in the darkness, he beheld that dark and motionless figure still standing exactly where it had stood before, and so knew either that he had missed it or else that it was of so supernatural a sort that a leaden bullet might do it no harm. Though if it was indeed an apparition that Barnaby beheld in that moment, there is this to say, that he saw it as plain as ever he saw a living man in all of his life.

This was the last our hero knew, for the next moment somebody—whether by accident or design he never knew—struck him such a terrible violent blow upon the side of the head that he saw forty thousand stars flash before his eyeballs, and then, with a great humming in his head, swooned dead away.

When Barnaby True came back to his senses again it was to find himself being cared for with great skill and nicety, his head bathed with cold water, and a bandage being bound about it as carefully as though a chirurgeon was attending to him.

He could not immediately recall what had happened to him, nor until he had opened his eyes to find himself in a strange cabin, extremely well fitted and painted with white and gold, the light of a lantern shining in his eyes, together with the gray of the early daylight through the dead-eye. Two men were bending over him—one, a negro in a striped shirt, with a yellow handkerchief around his head and silver earrings in his ears; the other, a white man, clad in a strange outlandish dress of a foreign make, and with great mustachios hanging down, and with gold earrings in his ears.

It was the latter who was attending to Barnaby's hurt with such extreme care and gentleness.

All this Barnaby saw with his first clear consciousness after his swoon. Then remembering what had befallen him, and his head beating as though it would split asunder, he shut his eyes again, contriving with great effort to keep himself from groaning aloud, and wondering as to what sort of pirates these could be who would first knock a man in the head so terrible a blow as that which he had suffered, and then take such care to fetch him back to life again, and to make him easy and comfortable.

Nor did he open his eyes again, but lay there gathering his wits together and wondering thus until the bandage was properly tied about his head and sewed together. Then once more he opened his eyes, and looked up to ask where he was.

Either they who were attending to him did not choose to reply, or else they could not speak English, for they made no answer, excepting by signs; for the white man, seeing that he was now able to speak, and so was come back into his senses again, nodded his head three or four times, and smiled with a grin of his white teeth, and then pointed, as though toward a saloon beyond. At the same time the negro held up our hero's coat and beckoned for him to put it on, so that Barnaby, seeing that it was required of him to meet some one without, arose, though with a good deal of effort, and permitted the negro to help him on with his coat, still feeling mightily dizzy and uncertain upon his legs, his head beating fit to split, and the vessel rolling and pitching at a great rate, as though upon a heavy ground swell.

So, still sick and dizzy, he went out into what was indeed a fine saloon beyond, painted in white and gilt like the cabin he had just quitted, and fitted in the nicest fashion, a mahogany table, polished very bright, extending the length of the room, and a quantity of bottles, together with glasses of clear crystal, arranged in a hanging rack above.

Here at the table a man was sitting with his back to our hero, clad in a rough pea-jacket, and with a red handkerchief tied around his throat, his feet stretched out before him, and he smoking a pipe of tobacco with all the ease and comfort in the world.

As Barnaby came in he turned round, and, to the profound astonishment of our hero, presented toward him in the light of the lantern, the dawn shining pretty strong through the skylight, the face of that very man who had conducted the mysterious expedition that night across Kingston Harbor to the Rio Cobra River.

This man looked steadily at Barnaby True for a moment or two, and then burst out laughing; and, indeed, Barnaby, standing there with the bandage about his head, must have looked a very droll picture of that astonishment he felt so profoundly at finding who was this pirate into whose hands he had fallen.

"Well," says the other, "and so you be up at last, and no great harm done, I'll be bound. And how does your head feel by now, my young master?"

To this Barnaby made no reply, but, what with wonder and the dizziness of his head, seated himself at the table over against the speaker, who pushed a bottle of rum toward him, together with a glass from the swinging shelf above.

He watched Barnaby fill his glass, and so soon as he had done so began immediately by saying: "I do suppose you think you were treated mightily ill to be so handled last night. Well, so you were treated ill enough—though who hit you that crack upon the head I know no more than a child unborn. Well, I am sorry for the way you were handled, but there is this much to say, and of that you may believe me, that nothing was meant to you but kindness, and before you are through with us all you will believe that well enough."

Here he helped himself to a taste of grog, and sucking in his lips, went on again with what he had to say. "Do you remember," said he, "that expedition of ours in Kingston Harbor, and how we were all of us balked that night?"

"Why, yes," said Barnaby True, "nor am I likely to forget it."

"And do you remember what I said to that villain, Jack Malyoe, that night as his boat went by us?"

"As to that," said Barnaby True, "I do not know that I can say yes or no, but if you will tell me, I will maybe answer you in kind."

"Why, I mean this," said the other. "I said that the villain had got the better of us once again, but that next time it would be our turn, even if William Brand himself had to come back from hell to put the business through."

"I remember something of the sort," said Barnaby, "now that you speak of it, but still I am all in the dark as to what you are driving at."

The other looked at him very cunningly for a little while, his head on one side, and his eyes half shut. Then, as if satisfied, he suddenly burst out laughing. "Look hither," said he, "and I'll show you something," and therewith, moving to one side, disclosed a couple of traveling cases or small trunks with brass studs, so exactly like those that

Sir John Malyoe had fetched aboard at Jamaica that Barnaby, putting this and that together, knew that they must be the same.

Our hero had a strong enough suspicion as to what those two cases contained, and his suspicions had become a certainty when he saw Sir John Malyoe struck all white at being threatened about them, and his face lowering so malevolently as to look murder had he dared do it. But, Lord! What were suspicions or even certainty to what Barnaby True's two eyes beheld when that man lifted the lids of the two cases—the locks thereof having already been forced—and, flinging back first one lid and then the other, displayed to Barnaby's astonished sight a great treasure of gold and silver! Most of it tied up in leathern bags, to be sure, but many of the coins, big and little, yellow and white, lying loose and scattered about like so many beans, brimming the cases to the very top.

Barnaby sat dumb-struck at what he beheld; as to whether he breathed or no, I cannot tell; but this I know, that he sat staring at that marvelous treasure like a man in a trance, until, after a few seconds of this golden display, the other banged down the lids again and burst out laughing, whereupon he came back to himself with a jump.

"Well, and what do you think of that?" said the other. "Is it not enough for a man to turn pirate for? But," he continued, "it is not for the sake of showing you this that I have been waiting for you here so long a while, but to tell you that you are not the only passenger aboard, but that there is another, whom I am to confide to your care and attention, according to orders I have received; so, if you are ready, Master Barnaby, I'll fetch her in directly." He waited for a moment, as though for Barnaby to speak, but our hero not replying, he arose and, putting away the bottle of rum and the glasses, crossed the saloon to a door like that from which Barnaby had come a little while before. This he opened, and after a moment's delay and a few words spoken to some one within, ushered thence a young lady, who came out very slowly into the saloon where Barnaby still sat at the table.

It was Miss Marjorie Malyoe, very white, and looking as though stunned or bewildered by all that had befallen her.

Barnaby True could never tell whether the amazing strange voyage that followed was of long or of short duration; whether it occupied three days or ten days. For conceive, if you choose, two people of flesh and blood moving and living continually in all the circumstances and surroundings as of a nightmare dream, yet they two so happy together that all the universe beside was of no moment to them! How was anyone to tell whether in such circumstances any time appeared to be long or short? Does a dream appear to be long or to be short?

The vessel in which they sailed was a brigantine of good size and build, but manned by a considerable crew, the most strange and outlandish in their appearance that Barnaby had ever beheld—some white, some yellow, some black, and all tricked out with gay colors, and gold earrings in their ears, and some with great long mustachios, and others with handkerchiefs tied around their heads, and all talking a language together of which Barnaby True could understand not a single word, but which might have been Portuguese from one or two phrases he caught. Nor did this strange, mysterious crew, of God knows what sort of men, seem to pay any attention whatever to Barnaby or to the young lady. They might now and then have looked at him and her out of the corners of their yellow eyes, but that was all; otherwise they were indeed like the creatures of a nightmare dream. Only he who was the captain of this outlandish crew would maybe speak to Barnaby a few words as to the weather or what not when he would come down into the saloon to mix a glass of grog or to light a pipe of tobacco, and then to go on deck again about his business. Otherwise our hero and the young lady were left to themselves, to do as they pleased, with no one to interfere with them.

As for her, she at no time showed any great sign of terror or of fear, only for a little while was singularly numb and quiet, as though dazed with what had happened to her. Indeed, methinks that wild beast, her grandfather, had so crushed her spirit by his tyranny and his violence that nothing that happened to her might seem sharp and keen, as it does to others of an ordinary sort.

But this was only at first, for afterward her face began to grow singularly clear, as with a white light, and she would sit quite still, permitting Barnaby to gaze, I know not how long, into her eyes, her face so transfigured and her lips smiling, and they, as it were, neither of them breathing, but hearing, as in another far-distant place, the outlandish jargon of the crew talking together in the warm, bright sunlight, or the sound of creaking block and tackle as they hauled upon the sheets.

Is it, then, any wonder that Barnaby True could never remember whether such a voyage as this was long or short?

It was as though they might have sailed so upon that wonderful voyage forever. You may guess how amazed was Barnaby True when, coming upon deck one morning, he found the brigantine riding upon an even keel, at anchor off Staten Island, a small village on the shore, and the well-known roofs and chimneys of New York town in plain sight across the water.

'Twas the last place in the world he had expected to see.

And, indeed, it did seem strange to lie there alongside Staten Island all that day, with New York town so nigh at hand and yet so impossible to reach. For whether he desired to escape or no, Barnaby True could not but observe that both he and the young lady were so closely watched that they might as well have been prisoners, tied hand and foot and laid in the hold, so far as any hope of getting away was concerned.

All that day there was a deal of mysterious coming and going aboard the brigantine, and in the afternoon a sailboat went up to the town, carrying the captain, and a great load covered over with a tarpaulin in the stern. What was so taken up to the town Barnaby did not then guess, but the boat did not return again till about sundown.

For the sun was just dropping below the water when the captain came aboard once more and, finding Barnaby on deck, bade him come down into the saloon, where they found the young lady sitting, the broad light of the evening shining in through the skylight, and making it all pretty bright within.

The captain commanded Barnaby to be seated, for he had something of moment to say to him; whereupon, as soon as Barnaby had taken his place alongside the young lady, he began very seriously, with a preface somewhat thus: "Though you may think me the captain of this brigantine, young gentleman, I am not really so, but am under orders, and so have only carried out those orders of a superior in all these things that I have done." Having so begun, he went on to say that there was one thing yet remaining for him to do, and that the greatest thing of all. He said that Barnaby and the young lady had not been fetched away from the *Belle Helen* as they were by any mere chance of accident, but that 'twas all a plan laid by a head wiser than his, and carried out by one whom he must obey in all things. He said that he hoped that both Barnaby and the young lady would perform willingly what they would be now called upon to do, but that whether they did it willingly or no, they must, for that those were the orders of one who was not to be disobeyed.

You may guess how our hero held his breath at all this; but whatever might have been his expectations, the very wildest of them all did not reach to that which was demanded of him. "My orders are these," said the other, continuing: "I am to take you and the young lady ashore, and to see that you are married before I quit you; and to that end a very good, decent, honest minister who lives ashore yonder in the village was chosen and hath been spoken to and is now, no doubt, waiting for you to come. Such are my orders, and this is the last thing I am set to do; so now I will leave you alone together for five minutes to talk it over, but be quick about it, for whether willing or not, this thing must be done."

Thereupon he went away, as he had promised, leaving those two alone together, Barnaby like one turned into stone, and the young lady, her face turned away, flaming as red as fire in the fading light.

Nor can I tell what Barnaby said to her, nor what words he used, but only, all in a tumult, with neither beginning nor end he told her that God knew he loved her, and that with all his heart and soul, and that there was nothing in all the world for him but her; but, neverthe-less, if she would not have it as had been ordered, and if she were not willing to marry him as she was bidden to do, he would rather die than lend himself to forcing her to do such a thing against her will. Never-theless, he told her she must speak up and tell him yes or no, and that God knew he would give all the world if she would say "yes."

All this and more he said in such a tumult of words that there was no order in their speaking, and she sitting there, her bosom rising and falling as though her breath stifled her. Nor may I tell what she replied to him, only this, that she said she would marry him. At this he took her into his arms and set his lips to hers, his heart all melting away in his bosom.

So presently came the captain back into the saloon again, to find Barnaby sitting there holding her hand, she with her face turned away, and his heart beating like a trip hammer, and so saw that all was settled as he would have it. Wherewith he wished them both joy, and gave Barnaby his hand.

The yawlboat belonging to the brigantine was ready and waiting alongside when they came upon deck, and immediately they descended to it and took their seats. So they landed, and in a little while were walking up the village street in the darkness, she clinging to his arm as though she would swoon, and the captain of the brigantine and two other men from aboard following after them. And so to the minister's house, finding him waiting for them, smoking his pipe in the warm evening, and walking up and down in front of his own door. He immediately conducted them into the house, where, his wife having fetched a candle, and two others of the village folk being present, the good man having asked several questions as to their names and their age and where they were from, the ceremony was performed, and the certificate duly signed by those present—excepting the men who had come ashore from the brigantine, and who refused to set their hands to any paper.

The same sailboat that had taken the captain up to the town in the afternoon was waiting for them at the landing place, whence, the captain, having wished them Godspeed, and having shaken Barnaby very heartily by the hand, they pushed off, and, coming about, ran away with the slant of the wind, dropping the shore and those strange beings alike behind them into the night.

As they sped away through the darkness they could hear the creaking of the sails being hoisted aboard of the brigantine, and so knew that she was about to put to sea once more. Nor did Barnaby True ever set eyes upon those beings again, nor did anyone else that I ever heard tell of.

It was nigh midnight when they made Mr. Hartright's wharf at the foot of Wall Street, and so the streets were all dark and silent and deserted as they walked up to Barnaby's home.

You may conceive of the wonder and amazement of Barnaby's dear stepfather when, clad in a dressing gown and carrying a lighted candle in his hand, he unlocked and unbarred the door, and so saw who it was had aroused him at such an hour of the night, and the young and beautiful lady whom Barnaby had fetched with him.

The first thought of the good man was that the *Belle Helen* had come into port; nor did Barnaby undeceive him as he led the way into the house, but waited until they were all safe and sound in privily together before he should unfold his strange and wonderful story.

"This was left for you by two foreign sailors this afternoon, Barnaby," the good old man said, as he led the way through the hall, holding up the candle at the same time, so that Barnaby might see an object that stood against the wainscoting by the door of the dining room.

Nor could Barnaby refrain from crying out with amazement when he saw that it was one of the two chests of treasure that Sir John Malyoe had fetched from Jamaica, and which the pirates had taken from the *Belle Helen*. As for Mr. Hartright, he guessed no more what was in it than the man in the moon.

The next day but one brought the *Belle Helen* herself into port, with the terrible news not only of having been attacked at night by pirates, but also that Sir John Malyoe was dead. For whether it was the sudden shock of the sight of his old captain's face—whom he himself had murdered and thought dead and buried—flashing so out against the darkness, or whether it was the strain of passion that overset his brains, certain it is that when the pirates left the *Belle Helen*, carrying with them the young lady and Barnaby and the traveling trunks, those left aboard the *Belle Helen* found Sir John Malyoe lying in a fit upon the floor, frothing at the mouth and black in the face, as though he had been choked, and so took him away to his berth, where, the next morning about ten o'clock, he died, without once having opened his eyes or spoken a single word.

As for the villain manservant, no one ever saw him afterward; though whether he jumped overboard, or whether the pirates who so attacked the ship had carried him away bodily, who shall say?

Mr. Hartright, after he had heard Barnaby's story, had been very uncertain as to the ownership of the chest of treasure that had been left by those men for Barnaby, but the news of the death of Sir John Malyoe made the matter very easy for him to decide. For surely if that treasure did not belong to Barnaby, there could be no doubt that it must belong to his wife, she being Sir John Malyoe's legal heir. And so it was that that great fortune (in actual computation amounting to upward of sixty-three thousand pounds) came to Barnaby True, the grandson of that famous pirate, William Brand; the English estate in Devonshire, in default of male issue of Sir John Malyoe, descended to Captain Malyoe, whom the young lady was to have married.

As for the other case of treasure, it was never heard of again, nor could Barnaby ever guess whether it was divided as booty among the pirates, or whether they had carried it away with them to some strange and foreign land, there to share it among themselves.

And so the ending of the story, with only this to observe, that whether that strange appearance of Captain Brand's face by the light of the pistol was a ghostly and spiritual appearance, or whether he was present in flesh and blood, there is only to say that he was never heard of again; nor had he ever been heard of till that time since the day he was so shot from behind by Capt. John Malyoe on the banks of the Rio Cobra River in the year 1733.

ATTACKED BY PIRATES

Charles Reade

CHAPTER FOUR

Wind down at noon next day, and a dead calm.

At two P.M. the weather cleared; the sun came out high in heaven's center; and a balmy breeze from the west.

At six twenty-five, the grand orb set calm and red, and the sea was gorgeous with miles and miles of great ruby dimples: it was the first glowing smile of southern latitude. The night stole on so soft, so clear, so balmy, all were loth to close their eyes on it: the passengers lingered long on deck, watching the Great Bear dip, and the Southern Cross rise, and overhead a whole heaven of glorious stars most of us have never seen, and never shall see in this world. No belching smoke obscured, no plunging paddles deafened; all was musical; the soft air sighing among the sails; the phosphorescent water bubbling from the ship's bows; the murmurs from little knots of men on deck subdued by the great calm; home seemed near, all danger far; Peace ruled the sea, the sky, the heart: the ship, making a track of white fire on the deep, glided gently yet swiftly homeward, urged by snowy sails piled up like alabaster towers against a violent sky, out of which looked a thousand eyes of holy tranquil fire. So melted the sweet night away.

Now carmine streaks tinged the eastern sky at the water's edge; and that water blushed; now the streaks turned orange, and the waves below them sparkled. Thence splashes of living gold flew and settled on the ship's white sails, the deck, and the faces; and with no more prologue, being so near the line, up came majestically a huge, fiery, golden sun, and set the sea flaming liquid topaz.

Instantly the look-out at the foretop-gallant-mast-head hailed the deck below.

"Strange sail! Right ahead!"

The strange sail was reported to Captain Dodd, then dressing in his cabin. He came soon after on deck and hailed the look-out: "Which way is she standing?"

"Can't say, sir. Can't see her move any."

Dodd ordered the boatswain to pipe to breakfast; and taking is deck glass went lightly up to the fore-top-gallant-mast crosstrees. Thence, through the light haze of a glorious morning, he espied a long low schooner, lateen-rigged, lying close under Point Leat, a small island about nine miles distant on the weather bow, and nearly in the Agra's course, then approaching the Straits of Gaspar, 4 latitude S.

"She is hove-to," said Dodd very gravely.

At eight o'clock, the stranger lay about two miles to windward, and still hove-to.

By this time all eyes were turned upon her, and half a dozen glasses. Everybody, except the captain, delivered an opinion. She was a Greek lying-to for water: she was a Malay coming north with canes, and short of hands: she was a pirate watching the Straits.

The captain leaned silent and somber with his arms on the bulwarks, and watched the suspected craft.

Mr. Fullalove joined the group, and leveled a powerful glass, of his own construction. He inspection was long and minute, and while the glass was at his eye, Sharpe asked him half in a whisper, could he make out anything?

"Wal," said he, "the varmint looks considerable snaky." Then, without removing his glass, he let drop a word at a time, as if the facts were trickling into his telescope at the lens, and out at the sight. "One—two—four—seven, false ports."

There was a momentary murmur among the officers all round. But British sailors are undemonstrative: Colonel Kenealy, strolling the deck with his cigar, saw they were watching another ship with maritime curiosity, and making comments; but he discerned no particular emotion nor anxiety in what they said, nor in the grave low tones they said it in. Perhaps a brother seaman would though.

The next observation that trickled out of Fullalove's tube was this: "I judge there are too few hands on deck, and too many—white—eyeballs—glittering at the portholes."

"Confound it," muttered Bayliss, uneasily; "how can you see that?"

Fullalove replied only by quietly handing his glass to Dodd. The captain thus appealed to, glued his eye to the tube.

"Well, sir; see the false ports, and the white eyebrows?" asked Sharpe ironically.

"I see this is the best glass I ever looked through," said Dodd doggedly, without interrupting his inspection.

"I think he is a Malay pirate," said Mr. Grey.

Sharpe took him up very quickly, and indeed angrily: "Nonsense. And if he is, he won't venture on a craft of this size."

"Says the whale to the swordfish," suggested Fullalove, with a little guttural laugh.

The captain, with the American glass at his eye, turned half round to the man at the wheel: "Starboard!"

"Starboard it is."

"Steer south-south-east."

"Ay, ay, sir." And the ship's course was thus altered two points.

This order lowered Dodd fifty per cent in Mr. Sharpe's estimation. He hold his tongue as long as he could: but at last his surprise and dissatisfaction burst out of him, "Won't that bring him out on us!"

"Very likely, sir," replied Dodd.

"Begging your pardon, captain, would it not be wiser to keep our course, and show the blackguard we don't fear him?"

"When we do! Sharpe, he has made up his mind an hour ago whether to lie still or bite; my changing my course two points won't change his mind, but it may make him declare it; and I must know what he does intend before I run the ship into the narrows ahead."

"Oh, I see," said Sharpe, half convinced.

The alteration in the *Agra*'s course produced no movement on the part of the mysterious schooner. She lay-to under the land still, and with only a few hands on deck, while the *Agra* edged away from her and entered the Straits between Long Island and Point Leat, leaving the schooner about two miles and a half distant to the N.W.

Ah! The stranger's deck swarms black with men.

His sham ports fell as if by magic, his guns grinned through the gaps like black teeth; his huge fossil rose and filled, and out he came in chase.

The breeze was a kiss from Heaven, the sky a vaulted sapphire, the sea a million dimples of liquid, lucid gold.

The way the pirate dropped the mask, showed his black teeth, and bore up in chase, was terrible: so dilates and bounds the sudden tiger on his unwary prey. There were stout hearts among the officers of the peaceable *Agra*; but danger in a new form shakes the brave, and this was their first pirate: their dismay broke out in ejaculations not loud but deep. "Hush," said Dodd doggedly, "the lady!"

Mrs. Beresford had just come on deck to enjoy the balmy morning.

"Sharpe," said Dodd, in a tone that conveyed no suspicion to the newcomer, "set the royals and flying jib.—Port!"

"Port it is," cried the man at the helm.

"Steer due south!" And, with these words in his mouth, Dodd dived to the gun-deck.

By this time elastic Sharpe had recovered the first shock, and the order to crows sail on the ship galled his pride and his manhood. He muttered indignantly, "The white feather!" This eased his mind, and he obeyed orders briskly as ever. While he and his hands were setting every rag the ship could carry on that tack, the other officers having unluckily no orders to execute, stood gloomy and helpless, with their eyes glued, by a sort of somber fascination, on that coming fate; and they literally jumped and jarred when Mrs. Beresford, her heart opened by the lovely day, broke in on their nerves with her light treble.

"What a sweet morning, gentlemen! After all, a voyage is a delight-ful thing. Oh, what a splendid sea! and the very breeze is warm. Ah! and there's a little ship sailing along: here, Freddy, Freddy darling, leave off beating the sailor's legs, and come here and see this pretty ship. What a pity it is so far off. Ah! Ah! what is that dreadful noise?"

For her horrible small talk, that grated on those anxious souls like the mockery of some infantine fiend, was cut short by ponderous blows and tremendous smashing below. It was the captain staving in water-casks: the water poured out at the scuppers.

"Clearing the lee guns," said a middy, off his guard.

Colonel Kenealy pricked up his ears, drew his cigar from his mouth, and smelt powder. "What, for action?" said he briskly. "Where's the enemy?"

Fullalove made him a signal, and they went below.

Mrs. Beresford had not heard or not appreciated the remark: she prattled on till she made the mates and midshipmen shudder.

Realize the situation, and the strange incongruity between the senses and the mind in these poor fellows! The day had ripened its beauty; beneath a purple heaven shone, sparkled, and laughed a blue sea, in whose waves the tropical sun seemed to have fused his beams; and beneath that fair, sinless, peaceful sky, wafted by a balmy breeze over those smiling, transparent, golden waves, a bloodthirsty pirate bore down on them with a crew of human tigers; and a lady babble babble babble babble babble babble babbled in their quivering ears.

But now the captain came bustling on deck, eyed the loftier sails, saw they were drawing well, appointed four midshipmen a staff to convey his orders: gave Bayliss charge of the carronades, Grey of the cutlasses, and directed Mr. Tickell to break the bad news gently to Mrs. Beresford, and to take her below to the orlop deck; ordered the purser to serve out beef, biscuit, and grog to all hands, saying, "Men can't work on an empty stomach: and fighting is hard work;" then beckoned the officers to come round him. "Gentlemen," said he, confidentially, "in crowding sail on this ship I had no hope of escaping that fellow on this tack, but I was, and am, most anxious to gain the open sea, where I can square my yards and run for it, if I see a chance. At present I shall carry on till he comes within range: and then, to keep the Company's canvas from being shot to rags, I shall shorten sail; and to save ship and cargo and all our lives, I shall fight while a plank of her swims. Better be killed in hot blood than walk the plank in cold."

The officers cheered faintly; the captain's dogged resolution stirred up theirs.

The pirate had gained another quarter of a mile and more. The ship's crew were hard at their beef and grog, and agreed among themselves it was a comfortable ship. They guessed what was coming, and woe to the ship in that hour if the captain had not won their respect. Strange to say, there were two gentlemen in the *Agra* to whom the pirate's approach was not altogether unwelcome. Colonel Kenealy and Mr. Fullalove were rival sportsmen and rival theorists. Kenealy stood out for a smooth bore and a four-ounce ball; Fullalove for a rifle of his own construction. Many a doughty argument they had, and many a bragging march; neither could convert the other. At last Fullalove hinted that by going ashore at the Cape, and getting each behind a tree at one hundred yards, and popping at one another, one or other would be convinced.

"Well, but," said Kenealy, "if he is dead, he will be no wiser. Besides, to a fellow like me, who has had the luxury of popping at his enemies, popping at a friend is poor insipid work."

"That is true," said the other regretfully. "But I reckon we shall never settle it by argument."

Theorists are amazing; and it was plain, by the alacrity with which these good creatures loaded the rival instruments, that to them the pirate came not so much as a pirate as a solution. Indeed, Kenealy, in the act of charging his piece, was heard to mutter, "Now, this is lucky." However, these theorists were no sooner loaded than something occurred to make them more serious. They were sent for in haste to Dodd's cabin; they found him giving Sharpe a new order.

"Shorten sail to the taupsles and jib, get the colors ready on the halyards, and then send the men aft."

Sharpe ran out full of zeal, and tumbled over Ramgolam, who was stooping remarkably near the keyhole. Dodd hastily bolted the cabin-door, and looked with trembling lip and piteous earnestness in Kenealy's face and Fullalove's. They were mute with surprise at a gaze so eloquent and yet mysterious.

He manned himself, and opened his mind to them with deep emotion, yet not without a certain simple dignity.

"Colonel," said he, "you are an old friend; you sir, are a new one; but I esteem you highly, and what my young gentlemen chaff you about, you calling all men brothers, and making that poor negro love you instead of fear you, that shows me you have a great heart. My dear friends, I have been unlucky enough to bring my children's fortune on board this ship: here it is under my shirt. Fourteen thousand pounds! This weighs me down. Oh, if they should lose it after all! Do pray give me a hand apiece and pledge your sacred words to take it home safe to my wife at Barkington, if you, or either of you, should see this bright sun set today, and I should not."

"Why, Dodd, old fellow," said Kenealy cheerfully, "this is not the way to go into action."

"Colonel," replied Dodd, "to save this ship and cargo, I must be wherever the bullets are, and I will too,"

Fullalove, more sagacious than the worthy colonel, said earnestly—

"Captain Dodd, may I never see Broadway again, and never see Heaven at the end of my time, if I fail you. There's my hand."

"And mine," said Kenealy warmly.

They all three joined hands, and Dodd seemed to cling to them.

"God bless you both! God bless you! Oh, what a weight your true hands have pulled off my heart. Good-by, for a few minutes. The time is short. I'll just offer a prayer to the Almighty for wisdom, and then I'll come up and say a word to the men and fight the ship, according to my lights."

Sail was no sooner shortened and the crew ranged, than the captain came briskly on deck, saluted, jumped on a carronade, and stood erect. He was not the man to show the crew his forebodings.

(Pipe.) "Silence fore and aft."

"My men, the schooner coming up on our weather quarter is a Portuguese pirate. His character is known; he scuttles all the ships he boards, dishonors the women, and murders the crew. We cracked on to get out of the narrows, and now we have shortened sail to fight this blackguard, and teach him to molest a British ship. I promise, in the Company's name, twenty pounds prize-money to every man before the mast if we beat him off or out-maneuver him; thirty if we sink him; and forty if we tow him astern into a friendly port. Eight guns are clear below, three on the weather side, five on the lee; for, if he knows his business, he will come up on the lee quarter: if he doesn't, that is no fault of yours nor mine. The muskets are all loaded, the cutlasses ground like razors—"

"Hurrah!"

"We have got women to defend—"

"Hurrah!"

"A good ship under our feet, the God of justice overhead, British hearts in our bosoms, and British colors flying—run 'em up!—over our heads." (The ship's colors flew up to the fore, and the Union Jack to the mizzen peak.) "Now, lads, I mean to fight this ship while a plank of her (stamping on the deck) swims beneath my foot, and—what do you say?"

The reply was a fierce "hurrah!" from a hundred throats, so loud, so deep, so full of volume, it made the ship vibrate, and rang in the creeping-on pirate's ears. Fierce, but cunning, he saw mischief in those shortened sails, and that Union Jack, the terror of his tribe, rising to a British cheer; he lowered his mainsail, and crawled up on the weather quarter. Arrived within a cable's length, he double-reefed his foresail to reduce his rate of sailing nearly to that of the ship; and the next moment a tongue of flame, and then a gush of smoke, issued from his lee bow, and the ball flew screaming like a seagull over the *Agra's* mizzen top. He then put his helm up, and fired his other bow-chaser, and sent the shot hissing and skipping on the water past the ship. This prologue made the novices wince. Bayliss wanted to reply with a carronade; but Dodd forbade him sternly, saying, "If we keep him aloof we are done for."

The pirate drew nearer, and fired both guns in succession, hulled the *Agra* amidships, and sent an eighteen-pound ball through her foresail. Most of the faces were pale on the quarter-deck; it was very trying to be shot at, and hit, and make no return. The next double discharge sent one shot smash through the stern cabin window, and splintered the bulwark with another, wounding a seaman slightly.

"LIE DOWN FORWARD!" shouted Dodd. "Bayliss, give him a shot."

The carronade was fired with a tremendous report, but no visible effect. The pirate crept nearer, steering in and out like a snake to avoid the carronades, and firing those two heavy guns alternately into the devoted ship. He hulled the *Agra* now nearly every shot.

The two available carronades replied noisily, and jumped as usual; they sent one thirty-two pound shot clean through the schooner's deck and side; but that was literally all they did worth speaking of.

"Curse them!" cried Dodd; "Load them with grape! They are not to be trusted with ball. And all my eighteen-pounders dumb! The coward won't come alongside and give them a chance."

At the next discharge the pirate chipped the mizzen mast, and knocked a sailor into dead pieces on the forecastle. Dodd put his helm down ere the smoke cleared, and got three carronades to bear, heavily laden with grape. Several pirates fell, dead or wounded, on the crowded deck, and some holes appeared in the foresail; this one interchange was quite in favor of the ship.

But the lesson made the enemy more cautious; he crept nearer, but steered so adroitly, now right astern, now on the quarter, that the ship could seldom bring more than one carronade to bear, while he raked her fore and aft with grape and ball.

In this alarming situation, Dodd kept as many of the men below as possible; but, for all he could do, four were killed and seven wounded.

Fullalove's word came too true: it was the swordfish and the whale: it was a fight of hammer and anvil; one hit, the other made a noise. Cautious and cruel, the pirate hung on the poor hulking creature's quarters and raked her a point-blank distance. He made her pass a bitter time. And her captain! To see the splintering hull, the parting shrouds, the shivered gear, and hear the shrieks and groans of his wounded; and he unable to reply in kind! The sweat of agony poured down his face. Oh, if he could but reach the open sea, and square his yards, and make a long chase of it; perhaps fall in with aid. Wincing under each heavy blow, he crept doggedly, patiently on towards that one visible hope.

At last, when the ship was cloved with shot, and peppered with grape, the channel opened; in five minutes more he could put her dead before the wind.

No! The pirate, on whose side luck had been from the first, got half a broadside to bear at long musket-shot, killed a midshipman by Dodd's side, cut away two of the *Agra*'s mizzen shrouds, wounded the gaff, and cut the jibstay. Down fell that powerful sail into the water, and dragged across the ship's forefoot, stopping her way to the open sea she panted for. The mates groaned; the crew cheered stoutly, as British tars do in any great disaster: the pirates yelled with ferocious triumph, like the devils they looked.

But most human events, even calamities, have two sides. The *Agra* being brought almost to a standstill, the pirate forged ahead against his will, and the combat took a new and terrible form. The elephant gun popped and the rifle cracked in the *Agra*'s mizzen top, and the man at the pirate's helm jumped into the air and fell dead: both theorists claimed him. Then the three carronades peppered him hotly; and he hurled an iron shower back with fatal effect. Then at last the long eighteen-pounders on the gun-deck got a word in. The old Niler was not the man to miss a vessel alongside in a quiet sea: he sent two round shot clean through him; the third splintered his bulwark and swept across his deck.

"His masts—fire at his masts!" roared Dodd to Monk, through his trumpet. He then got the jib clear, and made what sail he could without taking all the hands from the guns.

This kept the vessels nearly alongside a few minutes, and the fight was hot as fire. The pirate now for the first time hoisted his flag. It was black as ink. His crew yelled as it rose: the Britons, instead of quailing, cheered with fierce derision; the pirate's wild crew of yellow Malays, black chinless Papuans, and bronzed Portuguese served their side guns, twelve-pounders, well, and with ferocious cries. The white Britons, drunk with battle now, naked to the waist, grimed with powder, and spotted like leopards with blood, their own and their mates', replied with loud undaunted cheers and a deadly hail of grape from the quarter-deck; while the master-gunner and his mates, loading with a rapidity the mixed races opposed could not rival, hulled the schooner well between wind and water, and then fired chain-shot at her masts, as ordered, and began to play the mischief with her shrouds and rigging. Meantime, Fullalove and Kenealy, aided by Vespasian, who loaded, were quietly butchering the pirate crew two a minute, and hoped to settle the question they were fighting for: smooth bore v. rifle; but unluck-ily neither fired once without killing; so "there was nothing proven."

The pirate, bold as he was, got sick of fair fighting first. He hoisted his mainsail and drew rapidly ahead, with a slight bearing to windward, and dismounted a carronade and stove in the ship's quarter-boat, by way of a parting kick.

The men hurled a contemptuous cheer after him; they thought they had beaten him off. But Dodd knew better. He was but retiring a little way to make a more deadly attack than ever: he would soon wear, and cross the *Agra*'s defenseless bows, to rake her fore and aft at pistol-shot distance; or grapple, and board the enfeebled ship, two hundred strong.

Dodd flew to the helm and with his own hands put it hard a-weather, to give the deck-guns one more chance, the last, of sinking or disabling the *Destroyer*. As the ship obeyed, and a deck-gun bellowed below him, he saw a vessel running out from Long Island, and coming swiftly up on his lee quarter.

It was a schooner. Was she coming to his aid?

Horror! A black flag floated from her foremast head.

While Dodd's eyes were staring almost out of his head at this deathblow to hope, Monk fired again; and just then a pale face came close to Dodd's, and a solemn voice whispered in his ear: "Our ammunition is nearly done!"

Dodd seized Sharpe's hand convulsively, and pointed to the pirate's consort coming up to finish them; and said, with the calm of a brave man's despair, "Cutlasses! And die hard!"

At that moment the master-gunner fired his last gun. It sent a chain-shot on board the retiring pirate, took off a Portuguese head and spun it clean into the sea ever so far to windward, and cut the schooner's foremast so nearly through that it trembled and nodded, and presently snapped with a loud crack, and came down like a bro-ken trees, with the yard and sail; the latter overlapping the deck and burying itself, black flag and all, in the sea; and there, in one moment, lay the *Destroyer* buffeting and wriggling—like a heron on the water with his long wings broken—an utter cripple.

The victorious crew raised a stunning cheer.

"Silence!" roared Dodd, with his trumpet. "All hands make sail!"

He set his courses, bent a new jib, and stood out to windward close hauled, in hopes to make a good offing, and then put his ship dead before the wind, which was now rising to a stiff breeze. In doing this he crossed the crippled pirate's bows, within eighty yards, and sore was the temptation to rake him; but his ammunition being short, and his danger being imminent from the other pirate, he had the self-command to resist the great temptation.

He hailed the mizzen top: "Can you two hinder them from firing that gun?"

"I rather think we can," said Fullalove, "eh, Colonel?" and he tapped his long rifle.

The ship no sooner crossed the schooner's bows than a Malay ran forward with a linstock. Pop went the colonel's ready carbine, and the Malay fell over dead, and the linstock flew out of his hand. A tall Portuguese, with a movement of rage, snatched it up and darted to the gun: the Yankee rifle cracked, but a moment too late. Bang! went the pirate's bowchaser, and crashed into the *Agra*'s side, and passed nearly through her.

"Ye missed him! Ye missed him!" cried the rival theorist, joyfully. He was mistaken; the smoke cleared, and there was the pirate captain leaning wounded against he mainmast with a Yankee bullet in his shoulder, and his crew uttering yellows of dismay and vengeance. They jumped, and raged, and brandished their knives, and made horrid gesticulations of revenge; and the white eyeballs of the Malays and Papuans glittered fiendishly; and the wounded captain raised his sound arm and had a signal hoisted to his consort, and she bore up in chase, and jamming her fore lateen flat as a board, lay far nearer the wind than the *Agra* could, and sailed three feet to her two besides. On this superiority being made clear, the situation of the merchant vessel, though not so utterly desperate as before Monk fired his lucky shot, became pitiable enough. If she ran before the wind, the fresh pirate would cut her off: if she lay to windward, she might postpone the inevitable and fatal collision with a foe as strong as that she had only escaped by a rare piece of luck; but this would give the crippled pirate time to refit and unite to destroy her. Add to this the failing ammunition and the thinned crew!

Dodd cast his eyes all round the horizon for help.

The sea was blank.

The bright sun was hidden now; drops of rain fell, and the wind was beginning to sing, and the sea to rise a little.

"Gentlemen," said he, "let us kneel down and pray for wisdom, in this sore strait."

He and his officers kneeled on the quarter-deck. When they rose, Dodd stood rapt about a minute; his great thoughtful eye saw no more the enemy, the sea, nor anything external; it was turned inward. His officers looked at him in silence.

"Sharpe," said he at last, "there must be a way out of them both with such a breeze as this is now; if we could but see it."

"Ay, *if*," groaned Sharpe.

Dodd mused again.

"About ship!" said he softly, like an absent man.

"Ay, ay, sir!"

"Steer due north!" said he, still like one whose mind was elsewhere.

While the ship was coming about, he gave minute orders to the mates and the gunner, to ensure co-operation in the delicate and dangerous maneuvers that were sure to be at hand.

The wind was W.N.W.: he was standing north; one pirate lay on his lee beam stopping a leak between wind and water, and hacking the deck clear of his broken mast and yards. The other, fresh, and thirsting for the easy prey, came up to weather on him and hang on his quarter, pirate fashion.

When they were distant about a cable's length, the fresh pirate, to meet the ship's change of tactics, changed his own, luffed up, and gave the ship a broadside, well aimed but not destructive, the guns being loaded with ball.

Dodd, instead of replying immediately, put his helm hard up and ran under the pirate's stern, while he was jammed up in the wind, and with his five eighteen pounders raked him fore and aft, then paying off, gave him three carronades crammed with grape and canister. The rapid discharge of eight guns made the ship tremble, and enveloped her in thick smoke; loud shrieks and groans were heard from the schooner: the smoke cleared; the pirate's mainsail hung on deck, his jib-boom was cut off like a carrot and the sail struggling; his foresail looked lace, lanes of dead and wounded lay still or writhing on his deck, and his lee scuppers ran blood into the sea. Dodd squared his yards and bore away.

The ship rushed down the wind, leaving the schooner staggered and all abroad. But not for long; the pirate wore and fired his bow chasers at the now flying *Agra*, split one of the carronades in two, and killed a Lascar, and made a hole in the foresail. This done, he hoisted his mainsail again in a trice, sent his wounded below, flung his dead overboard, to the horror of their foes, and came after the flying ship, yawing and firing his bow chasers. The ship was silent. She had no shot to throw away. Not only did she take these blows like a coward, but all signs of life disappeared on her, except two men at the wheel and the captain on the main gangway.

Dodd had ordered the crew out of the rigging, armed them with cutlasses, and laid them flat on the forecastle. He also compelled Kenealy and Fullalove to come down out of harm's way, no wiser on the smooth bore question than they went up.

The great patient ship ran environed by her foes; one destroyer right in her course, another in her wake, following her with yells of vengeance, and pounding away at her—but no reply.

Suddenly the yells of the pirates on both sides ceased, and there was a moment of dead silence on the sea.

Yet nothing fresh had happened.

Yes, this had happened: the pirates to windward and the pirates to leeward of the *Agra* had found out, at one and the same moment, that the merchant captain they had lashed, and bullied, and tortured was a patient but tremendous man. It was not only to rake the fresh schooner he had put his ship before the wind, but also by a double, daring, masterstroke to hurl his monster ship bodily on the other. Without a foresail she could never get out of her way. The pirate crew had stopped the leak, and cut away and unshipped the broken foremast, and were stepping a new one, when they saw the huge ship bearing down in full sail. Nothing easier than to slip out of her way could they get the foresail to draw; but the time was short, the deadly intention manifest, the coming destruction swift.

After that solemn silence came a storm of cries and curses, as their seamen went to work to fit the yard and raise the sail; while their fighting men seized their matchlocks and trained the guns. They were well commanded by an heroic able villain. Astern the consort thundered; but the *Agra*'s response was a dead silence more awful than broadsides.

For then was seen with what majesty the enduring Anglo-Saxon fights.

One of that indomitable race on the gangway, one at the foremast, two at the wheel, conned and steered the great ship down on a hundred matchlocks and a grinning broadside, just as they would have conned and steered her into a British harbor.

"Starboard!" said Dodd, in a deep calm voice, with a motion of his hand.

"Starboard it is."

The pirate wriggled ahead a little. The man forward made a silent signal to Dodd.

"Port!" said Dodd quietly.

"Port it is."

But at this critical moment the pirate astern sent a mischievous shot and knocked one of the men to atoms at the helm.

Dodd waved his hand without a word, and another man rose from the deck, and took his place in silence, and laid his unshaking hand on the wheel stained with that man's warm blood whose place he took.

The high ship was now scarce sixty yards distant; she seemed to know: she reared her lofty figure-head with great awful shoots into the air.

But now the panting pirates got their new foresail hoisted with a joyful shout: it drew, the schooner gathered way, and their furious consort close on the *Agra*'s heels just then scourged her deck with grape.

"Port!" said Dodd calmly.

"Port it is."

The giant prow darted at the escaped pirate. That acre of coming canvas took the wind out of the swift schooner's foresail; it flapped: oh, then she was doomed! That awful moment parted the races on board her: the Papuans and Sooloos, their black faces livid and blue with horror, leaped yelling into the sea, or crouched and whimpered; the yellow Malays and brown Portuguese, though blanched to one color now, turned on death like dying panthers, fired two cannon slap into the ship's bows, and snapped their muskets and matchlocks at their solitary executioner on the ship's gangway, and out flew their knives like crushed wasp's stings. CRASH! The Indiaman's cutwater in thick smoke beat in the schooner's broadside: down went her masts to leeward like fishing-rods whipping the water; there was a horrible shrieking yell; wild forms leaped off on the *Agra,* and were hacked to pieces almost ere they reached the deck—a surge, a chasm in the sea, filled with an instant rush of engulphing waves, a long, awful, grating, grinding noise, never to be forgotten in this world, all along under the ship's keel—and the fearful majestic monster passed on over the blank she had made, with a pale crew standing silent and awestruck on her deck; a cluster of wild heads and staring eyeballs bobbing like corks in her foaming wake, sole relic of the blotted-out *Destroyer*; and a wounded man staggering on the gangway, with hands uplifted and staring eyes.

Shot in two places, the head and the breast!

With a loud cry of pity and dismay, Sharpe, Fullalove, Kenealy, and others rushed to catch him, but, ere they got near, the captain of the triumphant ship fell down on his hands and knees, his head sunk over the gangway, and his blood ran fast and pattered in the midst of them on the deck he had defended so bravely.

THE GHOST PIRATES

William Hope Hodgson

C H A P T E R   F I V E

At four o'clock, when again we went on deck, the Second Mate told me to go on with a paunch mat I was making; while Tammy, he sent to get out his sinnet. I had the mat slug on the fore side of the mainmast, between it and the after end of the house; and, in a few minutes, Tammy brought his sinnet and yarns to the mast, and made fast to one of the pins.

"What do you think it was, Jessop?" he asked, abruptly, after a short silence.

I looked at him.

"What do you think?" I replied.

"I don't know what to think," he said. "But I've a feeling that it's something to do with all the rest," and he indicated aloft, with his head.

"I've been thinking, too," I remarked.

"That it is?" he inquired.

"Yes," I answered, and told him how the idea had come to me at my dinner, that the strange men-shadows which came aboard might come from that indistinct vessel we had seen down in the sea.

"Good Lord!" he exclaimed, as he got my meaning. And then for a little, he stood and thought.

"That's where they live, you mean?" he said, at last, and paused again.

"Well," I replied. "It can't be the sort of existence *we* should call life."

He nodded, doubtfully.

77

"No," he said, and was silent again.

Presently, he put out an idea that had come to him.

"You *think*, then, that that—vessel has been with us for some time, if we'd only known?" he asked.

"All along," I replied. "I mean ever since these things started."

"Supposing there are others," he said, suddenly.

I looked at him.

"If there are," I said "you can pray to God that they won't stumble across us. It strikes me that whether they're ghosts, or not ghosts, they're blood-gutted pirates."

"It seems horrible," he said solemnly, "to be talking seriously like this, about—you know, about such things."

"I've tried to stop thinking that way," I told him. "I've felt I should go cracked, if I didn't. There's damned queer things happen at sea, I know; but this isn't one of them."

"It seems so strange and unreal, one moment, doesn't it?" he said. "And the next, you *know* it's really true, and you can't understand why you didn't always know. And yet they'd never believe, if you told them ashore about it."

"They'd believe, if they'd been in this packet in the middle watch this morning," I said.

"Besides," I went on. "They don't understand. We didn't . . . I shall always feel different now, when I read that some packet hasn't been heard of."

Tammy stared at me.

"I've heard some of the old shellbacks talking about things," he said. "But I never took them really seriously."

"Well," I said. "I guess we'll have to take this seriously. I wish to God we were home!"

"My God! So do I," he said.

For a good while after that, we both worked on in silence; but, presently, he went off on another tack.

"Do you think we'll really shorten her down every night before it gets dark?" he asked.

"Certainly," I replied. "They'll never get the men to go aloft at night, after what's happened."

"But, but—supposing they ordered us aloft—" he began.

"Would you go?" I interrupted.

"No!" he said, emphatically. "I'd jolly well be put in irons first!"

"That settles it, then," I replied. "You wouldn't go, nor would any one else."

At this moment the Second Mate came along.

"Shove that mat and that sinnet away, you two," he said. "Then get your brooms and clear up."

"I, i, Sir," we said, and he went on forrard.

"Jump on the house, Tammy," I said. "And let go the other end of this rope, will you?"

"Right" he said, and did as I had asked him. When he came back, I got him to give me a hand to roll up the mat, which was a very large one.

"I'll finish stopping it," I said. "You go and put your sinnet away."

"Wait a minute," he replied, and gathered up a double handful of shakins from the deck, under where I had been working. Then he ran to the side.

"Here!" I said. "Don't go dumping those. They'll only float, and the Second Mate or the Skipper will be sure to spot them."

"Come here, Jessop!" he interrupted, in a low voice, and taking no notice of what I had been saying.

I got up off the hatch, where I was kneeling. He was staring over the side.

"What's up?" I asked.

"For God's sake, hurry!" he said, and I ran, and jumped on to the spar, alongside of him.

"Look!" he said, and pointed with a handful of shakins, right down, directly beneath us.

Some of the shakins dropped from his hand, and blurred the water, momentarily, so that I could not see. Then, as the ripples cleared away, I saw what he meant.

"Two of them!" he said, in a voice that was scarcely above a whisper. "And there's another out there," and he pointed again with the handful of shakins.

"There's another a little further aft," I muttered.

"Where?—where?" he asked.

"There," I said, and pointed.

"That's four," he whispered. "Four of them!"

I said nothing; but continued to stare. They appeared to me to be a great way down in the sea, and quite motionless. Yet, though their outlines were somewhat blurred and indistinct, there was no mistaking that they were very like exact, though shadowy, representations of vessels. For some minutes we watched them, without speaking. At last Tammy spoke.

"They're real, right enough," he said, in a low voice.

"I don't know," I answered.

"I mean we weren't mistaken this morning," he said.

"No," I replied. "I never thought we were."

"Away forrard," I heard the Second Mate, returning aft. He came nearer, and saw us.

"What's up now, you two?" he called, sharply. "This isn't clearing up!"

I put out my hand to warn him not to shout, and draw the attention of the rest of the men.

He took several steps towards me.

"What is it? what is it?" he said, with a certain irritability; but in a lower voice.

"You'd better take a look over the side, Sir," I replied.

My tone must have given him an inkling that we had discovered something fresh; for, at my words, he made one spring, and stood on the spar, alongside of me.

"Look, Sir," said Tammy. "There's four of them."

The Second Mate glanced down, saw something and bent sharply forward.

"My God!" I heard him mutter, under his breath.

After that, for some half-minute, he stared, without a word.

"There are two more out there, Sir," I told him, and indicated the place with my finger.

It was a little time before he managed to locate these and when he did, he gave them only a short glance. Then he got down off the spar, and spoke to us.

"Come down off there," he said, quickly. "Get your brooms and clear up. Don't say a word!—It may be nothing."

He appeared to add that last bit, as an afterthought, and we both knew it meant nothing. Then he turned and went swiftly aft.

"I expect he's gone to tell the Old Man," Tammy remarked, as we went forrard, carrying the mat and his sinnet.

"H'm," I said, scarcely noticing what he was saying; for I was full of the thought of those four shadowy craft, waiting quietly down there.

We got our brooms, and went aft. On the way, the Second Mate and the Skipper passed us. They went forrard too by the fore brace, and got up on the spar. I saw the Second point up at the brace and he appeared to be saying something about the gear. I guessed that this was done purposely, to act as a blind, should any of the other men be looking. Then the Old Man glanced down over the side, in a casual sort of manner; so did the Second Mate. A minute or two later, they came aft, and went back, up on to the poop. I caught a glimpse of the Skipper's face as he passed me, on his return. He struck me as looking worried—bewildered, perhaps, would be a better word.

Both Tammy and I were tremendously keen to have another look; but when at last we got a chance, the sky reflected so much on the water, we could see nothing below.

We had just finished sweeping up when four bells went, and we cleared below for tea. Some of the men got chatting while they were grubbing.

"I 'ave 'eard," remarked Quoin, "as we're goin' ter shorten 'er down afore dark."

"Eh?" said old Jaskett, over his pannikin of tea.

Quoin repeated his remark.

"'Oo says so?" inquired Plummer.

"I 'eard it from ther Doc," answered Quoin, "'E got it from ther Stooard."

"'Ow would 'ee know?" asked Plummer.

"I dunno," said Quoin. "I 'spect 'e's 'eard 'em talkin' 'bout it arft."

Plummer turned to me.

"'Ave you 'eard anythin', Jessop?" he inquired.

"What, about shortening down?" I replied.

"Yes," he said. "Weren't ther Old Man talkin' ter yer, up on ther poop this mornin'?"

"Yes," I answered. "He said something to the Second Mate about shortening down; but it wasn't to me."

"They are!" said Quoin, "'Aven't I just said so?"

At that instant, one of the chaps in the other watch poked his head in through the starboard doorway.

"All hands shorten sail!" he sung out; at the same moment the Mate's whistle came sharp along the decks.

Plummer stood up, and reached for his cap.

"Well," he said. "It's evydent they ain't goin' ter lose no more of us!"

Then we went out on deck.

It was a dead calm; but all the same, we furled the three royals, and then the three t'gallants. After that, we hauled up the main and foresail, and stowed them. The crossjack, of course, had been furled some time, with the wind being plumb aft.

It was while we were up at the foresail, that the sun went over the edge of the horizon. We had finished stowing the sail, out upon the yard, and I was waiting for the others to clear in, and let me get off the foot-rope. Thus it happened that having nothing to do for nearly a minute, I stood watching the sun set, and so saw something that otherwise I should, most probably, have missed. The sun had dipped nearly half-way below the horizon, and was showing like a great, red dome of dull fire. Abruptly, far away on the starboard bow, a faint mist drove up out of the sea. It spread across the face of the sun, so that its light shone now as though it came through a dim haze of smoke.

Quickly, this mist or haze grew thicker; but, at the same time, separating and taking strange shapes, so that the red of the sun struck through ruddily between them. Then, as I watched, the weird mistiness collected and shaped and rose into three towers. These became more definite, and there was something elongated beneath them. The shaping and forming continued, and almost suddenly I saw that the thing had taken on the shape of a great ship. Directly afterwards, I saw that it was moving. It had been broadside on to the sun. Now it was swinging. The bows came round with a stately movement, until the three masts bore in a line. It was heading directly towards us. It grew larger; but yet less distinct. Astern of it, I saw now that the sun had sunk to a mere line of light. Then, in the gathering dusk it seemed to me that the ship was sinking back into the ocean. The sun went beneath the sea, and the thing I had seen became merged, as it were, into the monotonous greyness of the coming night.

A voice came to me from the rigging. It was the Second Mate's. He had been up to give us a hand.

"Now then, Jessop," he was saying. "Come along! Come along!"

I turned quickly, and realised that the fellows were nearly all off the yard.

"I, i, Sir," I muttered, and slid in along the foot-rope, and went down on deck. I felt fresh dazed and frightened.

A little later, eight bells went, and, after roll call, I cleared up, on to the poop, to relieve the wheel. For a while as I stood at the wheel my mind seemed blank, and incapable of receiving impressions. This sensation went, after a time, and I realised that there was a great stillness over the sea. There was absolutely no wind, and even the everlasting creak, creak of the gear seemed to ease off at times.

At the wheel there was nothing whatever to do. I might just as well have been forrard, smoking in the fo'cas'le. Down on the main-deck, I could see the loom of the lanterns that had been lashed up to the sherpoles in the fore and main rigging. Yet they showed less than they might, owing to the fact that they had been shaded on their after sides, so as not to blind the officer of the watch more than need be.

The night had come down strangely dark, and yet of the dark and the stillness and the lanterns, I was only conscious in occasional flashes of comprehension. For, now that my mind was working, I was thinking chiefly of that queer, vast phantom of mist, I had seen rise from the sea, and take shape.

I kept staring into the night, towards the West, and then all round me; for, naturally, the memory predominated that she had been coming towards us when the darkness came, and it was a pretty disquieting sort of thing to think about. I had such a horrible feeling that something beastly was going to happen any minute.

Yet, two bells came and went, and still all was quiet—strangely quiet, it seemed to me. And, of course, besides the queer, misty vessel I had seen in the West I was all the time remembering the four shadowy craft lying down in the sea, under our port side. Every time I remembered them, I felt thankful for the lanterns round the main deck, and I wondered why none had been put in the mizzen rigging. I wished to goodness that they had, and made up my mind I would speak to the Second Mate about it, next time he came aft. At the time, he was leaning over the rail across the break of the poop. He was not smoking, as I could tell; for had he been, I should have seen the glow of his pipe, now and then. It was plain to me that he was uneasy. Three times already he had been down on to the main deck, prowling about. I guessed that he had been to look down into the sea, for any signs of those four grim craft. I wondered whether they would be visible at night.

Suddenly, the time-keeper struck three bells, and the deeper notes of the bell forrard, answered them. I gave a start. It seemed to me that they had been struck close to my elbow. There was something unaccountably strange in the air that night. Then, even as the Second Mate answered the look-out's "All's well," there came the sharp whir and rattle of running gear, on the port side of the mainmast.

Simultaneously, there was the shrieking of a parrel, up the main; and I knew that someone, or something, had let go the main-topsail haul-yards. From aloft there came the sound of something parting; then the crash of the yard as it ceased falling.

The Second Mate shouted out something unintelligible, and jumped for the ladder. From the maindeck there came the sound of running feet, and the voices of the watch, shouting. Then I caught the Skipper's voice; he must have run out on deck, through the saloon doorway.

"Get some more lamps! Get some more lamps!" he was singing out. Then he swore.

He sung out something further. I caught the last two words.

" . . . carried away," they sounded like.

"No, Sir," shouted the Second Mate. "I don't think so."

A minute of some confusion followed; and then came the click of pawls. I could tell that they had taken the haulyards to the after capstan. Odd words floated up to me.

" . . . all this water?" I heard in the Old Man's voice. He appeared to be asking a question.

"Can't say, Sir," came the Second Mate's.

There was a period of time, filled only by the clicking of the pawls and the sounds of the creaking parrel and the running gear. Then the Second Mate's voice came again.

"Seems all right, Sir," I heard him say.

I never heard the Old Man's reply; for in the same moment, there came to me a chill of cold breath at my back. I turned sharply, and saw something peering over the taff rail. It had eyes that reflected the binnacle light, weirdly, with a frightful, tigerish gleam; but beyond that, I could see nothing with any distinctness. For the moment, I just stared. I seemed frozen. It was so close. Then movement came to me, and I jumped to the binnacle and snatched out the lamp. I twitched round, and shone the light towards it. The thing, whatever it was, had come more forward over the rail; but now, before the light, it recoiled with a queer, horrible litheness. It slid back, and down, and so out of sight. I have only a confused notion of a wet glistening Something, and two vile eyes. Then I was running, crazy, towards the break of the poop. I sprang down the ladder, and missed my footing, and landed on my stern, at the bottom. In my left hand I held the still burning binnacle lamp. The men were putting away the capstan-bars; but at my abrupt appearance, and the yell I gave out at falling, one or two of them fairly ran backwards a short distance, in sheer funk, before they realised what it was.

From somewhere further forrard, the Old Man and the Second Mate came running aft.

"What the devil's up now?" sung out the Second, stopping and bending to stare at me. "What's to do, that you're away from the wheel?"

I stood up and tried to answer him; but I was so shaken that I could only stammer.

"I—I—there—" I stuttered.

"Damnation!" shouted the Second Mate, angrily. "Get back to the wheel!"

I hesitated, and tried to explain.

"Do you damned well hear me?" he sung out.

"Yes, Sir; but—" I began.

"Get up on to the poop, Jessop!" he said.

I went. I meant to explain, when he came up. At the top of the ladder, I stopped. I was not going back alone to that wheel. Down below, I heard the Old Man speaking.

"What on earth is it now, Mr. Tulipson?" he was saying.

The Second Mate made no immediate reply; but turned to the men, who were evidently crowding near.

"That will do, men!" he said, somewhat sharply.

I heard the watch start to go forrard. There came a mutter of talk from them. Then the Second Mate answered the Old Man. He could not have known that I was near enough to overhear him.

"It's Jessop, Sir. He must have seen something; but we mustn't frighten the crowd more than need be."

"No," said the Skipper's voice.

They turned and came up the ladder, and I ran back a few steps, as far as the skylight. I heard the Old Man speak as they came up.

"How is it there are no lamps, Mr. Tulipson?" he said, in a surprised tone.

"I thought there would be no need up here, Sir," the Second Mate replied. Then he added something about saving oil.

"Better have them, I think," I heard the Skipper say.

"Very good, Sir," answered the Second, and sung out to the timekeeper to bring up a couple of lamps.

Then the two of them walked aft, to where I stood by the skylight.

"What are you doing, away from the wheel?" asked the Old Man, in a stern voice.

I had collected my wits somewhat by now.

"I won't go, Sir, till there's a light," I said.

The Skipper stamped his foot, angrily; but the Second Mate stepped forward.

"Come! Come, Jessop!" he exclaimed. "This won't do, you know! You'd better get back to the wheel without further bother."

"Wait a minute," said the Skipper, at this juncture. "What objection have you to going back to the wheel?" he asked.

"I saw something," I said. "It was climbing over the taffrail, Sir—"

"Ah!" he said, interrupting me with a quick gesture. Then, abruptly: "Sit down! sit down; you're all in a shake, man."

I flopped down on to the skylight seat. I was, as he had said, all in a shake, and the binnacle lamp was wobbling in my hand, so that the light from it went dancing here and there across the deck.

"Now," he went on. "Just tell us what you saw."

I told them, at length, and while I was doing so, the time-keeper brought up the lights and lashed one up on the sheerpole in each rigging.

"Shove one under the spanker boom," the Old Man sung out, as the boy finished lashing up the other two. "Be smart now."

"I, i, Sir," said the 'prentice, and hurried off.

"Now then," remarked the Skipper when this had been done "You needn't be afraid to go back to the wheel. There's a light over the stern, and the Second Mate or myself will be up here all the time."

I stood up.

"Thank you, Sir," I said, and went aft. I replaced my lamp in the binnacle, and took hold of the wheel; yet, time and again, I glanced behind and I was very thankful when, a few minutes later, four bells went, and I was relieved.

Though the rest of the chaps were forrard in the fo'cas'le, I did not go there. I shirked being questioned about my sudden appearance at the foot of the poop ladder; and so I lit my pipe and wandered about the maindeck. I did not feel particularly nervous, as there were now two lanterns in each rigging, and a couple standing upon each of the spare top-masts under the bulwarks.

Yet, a little after five bells, it seemed to me that I saw a shadowy face peer over the rail, a little abaft the fore lanyards. I snatched up one of the lanterns from off the spar, and flashed the light towards it, whereupon there was nothing. Only, on my mind, more than my sight, I fancy, a queer knowledge remained of wet, peery eyes. Afterwards, when I thought about them, I felt extra beastly. I knew then how brutal they had been . . . Inscrutable, you know. Once more in that same watch I had a somewhat similar experience, only in this instance it had vanished even before I had time to reach a light. And then came eight bells, and our watch below.

When we were called again, at a quarter to four, the man who roused us out, had some queer information.

"Toppin's gone—clean vanished!" he told us, as we began to turn out. "I never was in such a damned, hair-raisin' hooker as this here. It ain't safe to go about the bloomin' decks."

"'Oo's gone?" asked Plummer, sitting up suddenly and throwing his legs over his bunk-board.

"Toppin, one of the 'prentices," replied the man. "We've been huntin' all over the bloomin' show. We're still at it—but we'll never find him," he ended, with a sort of gloomy assurance.

"Oh, I dunno," said Quoin. "P'raps 'e's snoozin' somewheres 'bout."

"Not him," replied the man. "I tell you we've turned everythin' upside down. He's not aboard the bloomin' ship.

"Where was he when they last saw him?" I asked.

"Someone must know something, you know!"

"Keepin' time up on the poop," he replied. "The Old Man's nearly shook the life out of the Mate and the chap at the wheel. And they say they don't know nothin'."

"How do you mean?" I inquired. "How do you mean, nothing?"

"Well," he answered. "The youngster was there one minute, and then the next thing they knew, he'd gone. They've both sworn black an' blue that there wasn't a whisper. He's just disappeared off of the face of the bloomin' earth."

I got down on to my chest, and reached for my boots.

Before I could speak again, the man was saying something fresh.

"See here, mates," he went on. "If things is goin' on like this, I'd like to know where you an' me'll be befor' long!"

"We'll be in 'ell," said Plummer.

"I dunno as I like to think 'bout it," said Quoin.

"We'll have to think about it!" replied the man. "We've got to think a bloomin' lot about it. I've talked to our side, an' they're game."

"Game for what?" I asked.

"To go an' talk straight to the bloomin' Capting," he said, wagging his finger at me. "It's make tracks for the nearest bloomin' port, an' don't you make no bloomin' mistake."

I opened my mouth to tell him that the probability was we should not be able to make it, even if he could get the Old Man to see the matter from his point of view. Then I remembered that the chap had no idea of the things I had seen, and thought out; so, instead, I said:

"Supposing he won't?"

"Then we'll have to bloomin' well make him," he replied.

"And when you got there," I said. "What then? You'd be jolly well locked up for mutiny."

"I'd sooner be locked up," he said. "It don't kill you!"

There was a murmur of agreement from the others, and then a moment of silence, in which, I know, the men were thinking.

Jaskett's voice broke into it.

"I never thought at first as she was 'aunted—" he commenced; but Plummer cut in across his speech.

"We mustn't 'urt any one, yer know," he said. "That'd mean 'angin', an' they ain't been er bad crowd.

"No," assented everyone, including the chap who had come to call us.

"All the same," he added. "It's got to be up hellum, an' shove her into the nearest bloomin' port."

"Yes," said everyone, and then eight bells went, and we cleared out on deck.

Presently, after roll-call—in which there had come a queer, awkward little pause at Toppin's name—Tammy came over to me. The rest of the men had gone forrard, and I guessed they were talking over mad plans for forcing the Skipper's hand, and making him put into port—poor beggars!

I was leaning over the port rail, by the fore brace-lock, staring down into the sea, when Tammy came to me. For perhaps a minute he said nothing. When at last he spoke, it was to say that the shadow vessels had not been there since daylight.

"What?" I said, in some surprise. "How do you know?"

"I woke up when they were searching for Toppin," he replied. "I've not been asleep since. I came here, right away." He began to say something further; but stopped short.

"Yes," I said encouragingly.

"I didn't know—" he began, and broke off. He caught my arm. "Oh, Jessop!" he exclaimed. "What's going to be the end of it all? Surely something can be done?"

I said nothing. I had a desperate feeling that there was very little we could do to help ourselves.

"Can't we do something?" he asked, and shook my arm. "Anything's better than this! We're being murdered!"

Still, I said nothing; but stared moodily down into the water. I could plan nothing; though I would get mad, feverish fits of thinking.

"Do you hear?" he said. He was almost crying.

"Yes, Tammy," I replied. "But I don't know! I don't know!"

"You don't know!" he exclaimed. "You don't know! Do you mean we're just to give in, and be murdered, one after another?"

"We've done all we can," I replied. "I don't know what else we can do, unless we go below and lock ourselves in, every night."

"That would be better than this," he said. "There'll be no one to go below, or anything else, soon!"

"But what if it came on to blow?" I asked. "We'd be having the sticks blown out of her."

"What if it came on to blow *now*?" he returned. "No one would go aloft, if it were dark, you said, yourself! Besides, we could shorten her *right* down, first. I tell you, in a few days there won't be a chap alive aboard this packet unless they jolly well do something!"

"Don't shout," I warned him. "You'll have the Old Man hearing you." But the young beggar was wound up, and would take no notice.

"I will shout," he replied. "I want the Old Man to hear. I've a good mind to go up and tell him."

He started on a fresh tack.

"Why don't the men do something?" he began. "They ought to damn well make the Old Man put us into port! They ought—"

"For goodness sake, shut up, you little fool!" I said. "What's the good of talking a lot of damned rot like that? You'll be getting yourself into trouble."

"I don't care," he replied. "I'm not going to be murdered!"

"Look here," I said. "I told you before, that we shouldn't be able to see the land, even if we made it."

"You've no proof," he answered. "It's only your idea."

"Well," I replied. "Proof, or no proof, the Skipper would only pile her up, if he tried to make the land, with things as they are now."

"Let him pile her up," he answered. "Let him jolly well pile her up! That would be better than staying out here to be pulled overboard, or chucked down from aloft!"

"Look here, Tammy—" I began; but just then the Second Mate sung out for him, and he had to go. When he came back, I had started to walk to and from, across the fore side of the mainmast. He joined me, and after a minute, he started his wild talk again.

"Look here, Tammy," I said, once more. "It's no use your talking like you've been doing. Things are as they are, and it's no one's fault, and nobody can help it. If you want to talk sensibly, I'll listen; if not, then go and gas to someone else."

With that, I returned to the port side, and got up on the spar, again, intending to sit on the pinrail and have a bit of a talk with him. Before sitting down I glanced over, into the sea. The action had been almost mechanical; yet, after a few instants, I was in a state of the most intense excitement, and without withdrawing my gaze, I reached out and caught Tammy's arm to attract his attention.

"My God!" I muttered. "Look!"

"What is it?" he asked, and bent over the rail, beside me. And this is what we saw: a little distance below the surface there lay a pale-coloured, slightly-domed disc. It seemed only a few feet down. Below it, we saw quite clearly, after a few moment's staring, the shadow of a royal-yard, and, deeper, the gear and standing-rigging of a great mast. Far down among the shadows I thought, presently, that I could make out the immense, indefinite stretch of vast decks.

"My God!" whispered Tammy, and shut up. But presently, he gave out a short exclamation, as though an idea had come to him; and got down off the spar, and ran forrard on to the fo'cas'le head. He came running back, after a short look into the sea, to tell me that there was the truck of another great mast coming up there, a bit off the bow, to within a few feet of the surface of the sea.

In the meantime, you know, I had been staring like mad down through the water at the huge, shadowy mast just below me. I had traced out bit by bit, until now I could clearly see the jackstay, running along the top of the royal mast; and, you know, the royal itself was *set*.

But, you know, what was getting at me more than anything, was a feeling that there was movement down in the water there, among the rigging. I *thought* I could actually see, at times, things moving and glinting faintly and rapidly to and fro in the gear. And once, I was practically certain that something was on the royal-yard, moving in to the mast; as though, you know, it might have come up the leech of the sail. And this way, I got a beastly feeling that there were things swarming down there.

Unconsciously, I must have leant further and further out over the side, staring; and suddenly—good Lord! how I yelled—I overbalanced. I made a sweeping grab, and caught the fore brace, and with that, I was back in a moment upon the spar. In the same second, almost, it seemed to me that the surface of the water above the submerged truck was broken, and I am sure *now*, I saw something a moment in the air against the ship's side—a sort of shadow in the air; though I did not realise it at the time.

Anyway, the next instant, Tammy gave out an awful scream, and was head downwards over the rail, in a second. I had an idea *then* that he was jumping overboard. I collared him by the waist of his britchers, and one knee, and then I had him down on the deck, and sat plump on him; for he was struggling and shouting all the time, and I was so breathless and shaken and gone to mush, I could not have trusted my hands to hold him.

You see, I never thought then it was anything but some influence at work on him; and that he was trying to get loose to go over the side. But I know now that I saw the shadow-man that had him. Only, at the time, I was so mixed up, and with the one idea in my head, I was not really able to notice anything, properly. But, afterwards, I comprehended a bit (you can understand, can't you?) what I had seen at the time without taking in.

And even now looking back, I know that the shadow was only like a faint-seen greyness in the daylight, against the whiteness of the decks, clinging against Tammy.

And there was I, all breathless and sweating, and quivery with my own tumble, sitting on the little screeching beggar, and he fighting like a mad thing; so that I thought I should never hold him.

And then I heard the Second Mate shouting and there came running feet along the deck. Then many hands were pulling and hauling, to get me off him.

"Bloody cowyard!" sung out someone.

"Hold him! Hold him!" I shouted. "He'll be overboard!"

At that, they seemed to understand that I was not ill-treating the youngster; for they stopped manhandling me, and allowed me to rise; while two of them took hold of Tammy, and kept him safe.

"What's the matter with him?" the Second Mate was singing out. "What's happened?"

"He's gone off his head, I think," I said.

"What?" asked the Second Mate. But before I could answer him, Tammy ceased suddenly to struggle, and flopped down upon the deck.

"'E's fainted," said Plummer, with some sympathy. He looked at me, with a puzzled, suspicious air. "What's 'appened? What's 'e been doin'?"

"Take him aft into the berth!" ordered the Second Mate, a bit abruptly. It struck me that he wished to prevent questions. He must have tumbled to the fact that we had seen something, about which it would be better not to tell the crowd.

Plummer stooped to lift the boy.

"No," said the Second Mate. "Not you, Plummer. Jessop, you take him." He turned to the rest of the men. "That will do," he told them and they went forrard, muttering a little.

I lifted the boy, and carried him aft.

"No need to take him into the berth," said the Second Mate. "Put him down on the after hatch. I've sent the other lad for some brandy."

Then the brandy came, we dosed Tammy and soon brought him round. He sat up, with a somewhat dazed air. Otherwise, he seemed quiet and sane enough.

"What's up?" he asked. He caught sight of the Second Mate. "Have I been ill, Sir?" he exclaimed.

"You're right enough now, youngster," said the Second Mate. "You've been a bit off. You'd better go and lie down for a bit."

"I'm all right now, Sir," replied Tammy. "I don't think—"

"You do as you're told!" interrupted the Second. "Don't always have to be told twice! If I want you, I'll send for you."

Tammy stood up, and made his way, in rather an unsteady fashion, into the berth. I fancy he was glad enough to lie down.

"Now then, Jessop," exclaimed the Second Mate, turning to me. "What's been the cause of all this? Out with it now, smart!"

I commenced to tell him; but, almost directly, he put up his hand.

"Hold on a minute," he said. "There's the breeze!"

He jumped up the port ladder, and sung out to the chap at the wheel. Then down again.

"Starboard fore brace," he sung out. He turned to me. "You'll have to finish telling me afterwards," he said.

"I, i, Sir," I replied, and went to join the other chaps at the braces.

As soon as we were braced sharp up on the port tack, he sent some of the watch up to loose the sails. Then he sung out for me.

"Go on with your yarn now, Jessop," he said.

I told him about the great shadow vessel, and I said something about Tammy—I mean about my not being sure now whether he had tried to jump overboard. Because, you see, I began to realise that I had seen the shadow; and I remembered the stirring of the water above the submerged truck. But the Second did not wait, of course, for any theories, but was away, like a shot, to see for himself. He ran to the side, and looked down. I followed, and stood beside him; yet, now that the surface of the water was blurred by the wind, we could see nothing.

"It's no good," he remarked, after a minute. "You'd better get away from the rail before any of the others see you. Just be taking those halyards aft to the capstan."

From then, until eight bells, we were hard at work getting the sail upon her, and when at last eight bells went, I made haste to swallow my breakfast, and get a sleep.

At midday, when we went on deck for the afternoon watch, I ran to the side; but there was no sign of the great shadow ship. All that watch, the Second Mate kept me working at my paunch mat, and Tammy he put on to his sinnet, telling me to keep an eye on the youngster. But the boy was right enough; as I scarcely doubted now, you know; though—a most unusual thing—he hardly opened his lips the whole afternoon. Then at four o'clock, we went below for tea.

At four bells, when we came on deck again, I found that the light breeze, which had kept us going during the day, had dropped, and we were only just moving. The sun was low down, and the sky clear. Once or twice, as I glanced across to the horizon, it seemed to me that I caught again that odd quiver in the air that had preceded the coming of the mist; and, indeed on two separate occasions, I saw a thin whisp of haze drive up, apparently out of the sea. This was at some little distance on our port beam; otherwise, all was quiet and peaceful; and though I stared into the water, I could make out no vestige of that great shadow ship, down in the sea.

It was some little time after six bells that the order came for all hands to shorten sail for the night. We took in the royals and t'gallants, and then the three courses. It was shortly after this, that a rumour went round the ship that there was to be no look-out that night after eight o'clock. This naturally created a good deal of talk among the men; especially as the yarn went that the fo'cas'le doors were to be shut and fastened as soon as it was dark, and that no one was to be allowed on deck.

"'Oo's goin' ter take ther wheel?" I heard Plummer ask.

"I s'pose they'll 'ave us take 'em as usual," replied one of the men. "One of ther officers is bound ter be on ther poop; so we'll 'ave company."

Apart from these remarks, there was a general opinion that—if it were true—it was a sensible act on the part of the Skipper. As one of the men said:

"It ain't likely that there'll be any of us missin' in ther mornin', if we stays in our bunks all ther blessed night."

And soon after this, eight bells went.

At the moment when eight bells actually went, I was in the fo'cas'le, talking to four of the other watch. Suddenly, away aft, I heard shouting, and then on the deck overhead came the loud thudding of someone pomping with a capstan-bar. Straightway, I turned and made a run for the port doorway, along with the four other men. We rushed out through the doorway on to the deck. It was getting dusk; but that did not hide from me a terrible and extraordinary sight. All along the port rail there was a queer, undulating greyness, that moved downwards inboard, and spread over the decks. As I looked, I found that I saw more clearly, in a most extraordinary way. And, suddenly, all the moving greyness resolved into hundreds of strange men. In the half-light, they looked unreal and impossible, as though there had come upon us the inhabitants of some fantastic dream-world. My God! I thought I was mad. They swarmed in upon us in a great wave of murderous, living shadows. From some of the men who must have been going aft for roll-call, there rose into the evening air a loud, awful shouting.

"Aloft!" yelled someone; but, as I looked aloft, I saw that the horrible things were swarming there in scores and scores.

"Jesus Christ—!" shrieked a man's voice, cut short, and my glance dropped from aloft, to find two of the men who had come out from the fo'cas'le with me, rolling upon the deck. They were two indistinguishable masses that writhed here and there across the planks. The brutes fairly covered them. From them, came muffled little shrieks and gasps; and there I stood, and with me were the other two men. A man darted past us into the fo'cas'le, with two grey men on his back, and I heard them kill him. The two men by me, ran suddenly across the fore hatch, and up the starboard ladder on to the fo'cas'le head. Yet, almost in the same instant, I saw several of the grey men disappear up the other ladder. From the fo'cas'le head above, I heard the two men commence to shout, and this died away into a loud scuffling. At that, I turned to see whether I could get away. I stared round, hopelessly; and then with two jumps, I was on the pigsty, and from there upon the top of the deckhouse. I threw myself flat, and waited, breathlessly.

All at once, it seemed to me that it was darker than it had been the previous moment, and I raised my head, very cautiously. I saw that the ship was enveloped in great billows of mist, and then, not six feet from me, I made out someone lying, face downwards. It was Tammy. I felt safer now that we were hidden by the mist, and I crawled to him. He gave a quick gasp of terror when I touched him; but when he saw who it was, he started to sob like a little kid.

"Hush!" I said. "For God's sake be quiet!" But I need not have troubled; for the shrieks of the men being killed, down on the decks all around us, drowned every other sound.

I knelt up, and glanced round and then aloft. Overhead, I could make out dimly the spars and sails, and now as I looked, I saw that the t'gallants and royals had been unloosed and were hanging in the bunt-lines. Almost in the same moment, the terrible crying of the poor beggars about the decks, ceased; and there succeeded an awful silence, in which I could distinctly hear Tammy sobbing. I reached out, and shook him.

"Be quiet! Be quiet!" I whispered, intensely. "THEY'LL hear us!"

At my touch and whisper, he struggled to become silent; and then, overhead, I saw the six yards being swiftly mast-headed. Scarcely were the sails set, when I heard the swish and flick of gaskets being cast adrift on the lower yards, and realised that ghostly things were at work there.

For a moment or so there was silence, and I made my way cautiously to the after end of the house, and peered over. Yet, because of the mist, I could see nothing. Then, abruptly, from behind me, came a single wail of sudden pain and terror from Tammy. It ended instantly in a sort of choke. I stood up in the mist and ran back to where I had left the kid; but he had gone. I stood dazed. I felt like shrieking out loud. Above me I heard the flaps of the course being tumbled off the yards. Down upon the decks, there were the noises of a multitude working in a weird, inhuman silence. Then came the squeal and rattle of blocks and braces aloft. They were squaring the yards.

I remained standing. I watched the yards squared, and then I saw the sails fill suddenly. An instant later, the deck of the house upon which I stood became canted forrard. The slope increased, so that I could scarcely stand, and I grabbed at one of the wire-winches. I wondered, in a stunned sort of way, what was happening. Almost directly afterwards, from the deck on the port side of the house, there came a sudden, loud, human scream; and immediately, from different parts of the decks, there rose, afresh, some most horrible shouts of agony from odd men. This grew into an intense screaming that shook my heart up; and there came again a noise of desperate, brief fighting. Then a breath of cold wind seemed to play in the mist, and I could see down the slope of the deck. I looked below me, towards the bows. The jib-boom was plunged right into the water, and, as I stared, the bows disappeared into the sea. The deck of the house became a wall to me, and I was swinging from the winch, which was now above my head. I watched the ocean lap over the edge of the fo'cas'le head, and rush down on to the maindeck, roaring into the empty fo'cas'le. And still all around me came crying of the lost sailor-men. I heard something strike the corner of the house above me, with a dull thud, and then I saw Plummer plunge down into the flood beneath. I remembered that he had been at the wheel. The next instant, the water had leapt to my feet; there came a drear chorus of bubbling screams, a roar of waters, and I was going swiftly down into the darkness. I let go of the winch, and struck out madly, trying to hold my breath. There was a loud singing in my ears. It grew louder. I opened my mouth. I felt I was dying. And then, thank God! I was at the surface, breathing. For the moment, I was blinded with the water, and my agony of breathlessness. Then, growing easier, I brushed the water from my eyes and so, not three hundred yards away, I made out a large ship, floating almost motionless. At first, I could scarcely believe I saw aright. Then, as I realized that indeed there was yet a chance of living, I started to swim towards you.

You know the rest—

THE JOASSAMEE PIRATES

Charles Ellms

The line of coast from Cape Mussenndom to Bahrain, on the Arabian side of the Persian Gulf, had been from time immemorial occupied by a tribe of Arabs called Joassamees. These, from local position, were all engaged in maritime pursuits. Some traded in their own small vessels to Bussorah, Bushire, Muscat, and even India; others annually fished in their own boats on the pearl banks of Bahrain; and a still greater number hired themselves out as sailors to navigate the coasting small craft of the Persian Gulf.

The Joassamees at length perceiving that their local position enabled them to reap a rich harvest by plundering vessels in passing this great highway of nations, commenced their piratical career. The small coasting vessels of the gulf, from their defenceless state, were the first object of their pursuit, and these soon fell an easy prey; until, emboldened by success, they directed their views to more arduous enterprises, and having tasted the sweets of plunder in the increase of their wealth, had determined to attempt more promising victories.

About the year 1797, one of the East India Company's vessels of war, the *Viper*, of ten guns, was lying at anchor in the inner roads of Bushire. Some dows of the Joassamees were at the same moment anchored in the harbor; but as their warfare had hitherto been waged only against what are called native vessels, and they had either feared or respected the British flag, no hostile measures were ever pursued against them by the British ships. The commanders of these dows had applied to the Persian agent of the East India Company there, for a supply of gunpowder and cannon shot for their cruise: and as this man had no suspicions of their intentions, he furnished them with an order to the commanding officer on board for the quantity required. The captain of the *Viper* was on shore at the time, in the agent's house, but the order being produced to the officer on board, the powder and shot were delivered, and the dows weighed and made sail. The crew of the *Viper* were at this moment taking their breakfast on deck, and the officers below; when on a sudden, a cannonading was opened on them by two of the dows, who attempted also to board.

The officers, leaping on deck, called the crew to quarters, and cutting their cable, got sail upon the ship, so as to have the advantage of manoeuvring. A regular engagement now took place between this small cruiser and four dows, all armed with great guns, and full of men. In the contest Lieut. Carruthers, the commanding officer, was once wounded by a ball in the loins; but after girding a handkerchief round his waist, he still kept the deck, till a ball entering his forehead, he fell. Mr. Salter, the midshipman on whom the command devolved, continued the fight with determined bravery, and after a stout resistance, beat them off, chased them some distance out to sea, and subsequently regained the anchorage in safety.

Several years elapsed before the wounds of the first defeat were sufficiently healed to induce a second attempt on vessels under the British flag, though a constant state of warfare was still kept up against the small craft of the gulf. In 1804, the East India Company's cruiser, *Fly*, was taken by a French privateer, off the Island of Kenn, in the Persian Gulf; but before the enemy boarded her, she ran into shoal water, near that island, and sunk the government dispatches, and some treasure with which they were charged, in about two and a half fathoms of water, taking marks for the recovery of them, if possible, at some future period. The passengers and crew were taken to Bushire where they were set at liberty, and having purchased a country dow by subscription, they fitted her out and commenced their voyage down the gulf, bound for Bombay. On their passage down, as they thought it would be practicable to recover the government packet and treasure sunk off Kenn, they repaired to that island, and were successful, after much exertion, in recovering the former, which being in their estimation of the first importance, as the dispatches were from England to Bombay, they sailed with them on their way thither, without loss of time.

Near the mouth of the gulf, they were captured by a fleet of Joassamee boats, after some resistance, in which several were wounded and taken into their chief port at Ras-el-Khyma. Here they were detained in hope of ransom, and during their stay were shown to the people of the town as curiosities, no similar beings having been before seen there within the memory of man. The Joassamee ladies were so minute in their enquiries, indeed, that they were not satisfied without determining in what respect an uncircumcised infidel differed from a true believer.

When these unfortunate Englishmen had remained for several months in the possession of the Arabs, and no hope of their ransom appeared, it was determined to put them to death, and thus rid themselves of unprofitable enemies. An anxiety to preserve life, however, induced the suggestion, on their parts, of a plan for the temporary prolongation of it, at least. With this view they communicated to the chief of the pirates the fact of their having sunk a quantity of treasure near the island of Kenn, and of their knowing the marks of the spot, by the bearings of objects on shore, with sufficient accuracy to recover it, if furnished with good divers. They offered, therefore, to purchase their own liberty, by a recovery of this money for their captors; and on the fulfillment of their engagement it was solemnly promised to be granted to them.

They soon sailed for the spot, accompanied by divers accustomed to that occupation on the pearl banks of Bahrain; and, on their anchoring at the precise points of bearing taken, they commenced their labors. The first divers who went down were so successful, that all the crew followed in their turns, so that the vessel was at one time almost entirely abandoned at anchor. As the men, too, were all so busily occupied in their golden harvest, the moment appeared favorable for escape; and the still captive Englishmen were already at their stations to overpower the few on board, cut the cable, and make sail. Their motions were either seen or suspected, as the divers repaired on board in haste, and the scheme was thus frustrated. They were now given their liberty as promised, by being landed on the island of Kenn, where, however, no means offered for their immediate escape. The pirates, having at the same time landed themselves on the island, commenced a general massacre of the inhabitants, in which their released prisoners, fearing they might be included, fled for shelter to clefts and hiding places in the rocks. During their refuge here, they lived on such food as chance threw in their way; going out under cover of the night to steal a goat and drag it to their haunts. When the pirates had at length completed their work of blood, and either murdered or driven off every former inhabitant of the island, they quitted it themselves, with the treasure which they had thus collected from the sea and shore. The Englishmen now ventured to come out from their hiding places, and to think of devising some means of escape. Their good fortune in a moment of despair, threw them on the wreck of a boat, near the beach, which was still capable of repair. In searching about the now deserted town, other materials were found, which were of use to them, and sufficient plank and logs of wood for the construction of a raft. These were both completed in a few days, and the party embarked on them in two divisions, to effect a passage to the Persian shore. One of these rafts was lost in the attempt, and all on board her perished; while the raft, with the remainder of the party reached land.

Having gained the main land they now set out on foot towards Bushire, following the line of the coast for the sake of the villages and water. In this they are said to have suffered incredible hardships and privations of every kind. No one knew the language of the country perfectly, and the roads and places of refreshment still less; they were in general destitute of clothes and money, and constantly subject to plunder and imposition, poor as they were. Their food was therefore often scanty, and always of the worst kind; and they had neither shelter from the burning sun of the day, nor from the chilling dews of night.

The Indian sailors, sipakees, and servants, of whom a few were still remaining when they set out, had all dropped off by turns; and even Europeans had been abandoned on the road, in the most affecting way, taking a last adieu of their comrades, who had little else to expect but soon to follow their fate. One instance is mentioned of their having left one who could march no further, at the distance of only a mile from a village; and on returning to the spot on the morrow, to bring him in, nothing was found but his mangled bones, as he had been devoured in the night by jackals. The packet being light was still, however, carried by turns, and preserved through all obstacles and difficulties; and with it they reached at length the island of Busheap, to which they crossed over in a boat from the main. Here they were detained by the Sheikh, but at length he provided them with a boat for the conveyance of themselves and dispatches to Bushire. From this place they proceeded to Bombay, but of all the company only two survived. A Mr. Jowl, an officer of a merchant ship, and an English sailor named Penmel together with the bag of letters and dispatches.

In the following year, two English brigs, the *Shannon*, Capt. Babcock, and the *Trimmer*, Capt. Cummings, were on their voyage from Bombay to Bussorah. These were both attacked, near the Islands of Polior and Kenn, by several boats, and after a slight resistance on the part of the *Shannon* only, were taken possession of, and a part of the crew of each, cruelly put to the sword. Capt. Babcock, having been seen by one of the Arabs to discharge a musket during the contest, was taken by them on shore; and after a consultation on his fate, it was determined that he should forfeit the arm by which this act of resistance was committed. It was accordingly severed from his body by one stroke of a sabre, and no steps were taken either to bind up the wound, or to prevent his bleeding to death. The captain, himself, had yet sufficient presence of mind left, however, to think of his own safety, and there being near him some clarified butter, he procured this to be heated, and while yet warm, thrust the bleeding stump of his arm into it. It had the effect of lessening the effusion of blood, and ultimately of saving a life that would otherwise most probably have been lost. The crew were then all made prisoners, and taken to a port of Arabia, from whence they gradually dispersed and escaped. The vessels themselves were additionally armed, one of them mounting twenty guns, manned with Arab crews, and sent from Ras-el-Khyma to cruise in the gulf, where they committed many piracies.

In the year 1808, the force of the Joassamees having gradually increased, and becoming flushed with the pride of victory, their insulting attacks on the British flag were more numerous and more desperate than ever. The first of these was on the ship *Minerva*, of

Bombay, on her voyage to Bussorah. The attack was commenced by several boats (for they never cruize singly) and a spirited resistance in a running fight was kept up at intervals for several days in succession. A favorable moment offered, however, for boarding; the ship was overpowered by numbers, and carried amidst a general massacre. The captain was said to have been cut up into separate pieces, and thrown overboard by fragments; the second mate and carpenter alone were spared, probably to make use of their services; and an Armenian lady, the wife of Lieut. Taylor, then at Bushire, was reserved perhaps for still greater sufferings, but was subsequently ransomed for a large sum.

A few weeks after this, the *Sylph*, one of the East India Company's cruisers, of sixty tons and mounting eight guns, was accompanying the mission under Sir Hartford Jones, from Bombay, to Persia; when being separated from the rest of the squadron, she was attacked in the gulf by a fleet of dows. These bore down with all the menacing attitude of hostility; but as the commander, Lieut. Graham had received orders from the Bombay government, not to open his fire on any of these vessels until he had been first fired on himself, the ship was hardly prepared for battle, and the colors were not even hoisted to apprise them to what nation she belonged. The dows approached, threw their long overhanging prows across the *Sylph*'s beam, and pouring in a shower of stones on her deck, beat down and wounded almost every one who stood on it. They then boarded, and made the ship an easy prize, before more than a single shot had been fired, and in their usual way, put every one whom they found alive to the sword. Lieut. Graham fell, covered with wounds, down the fore hatchway of his own vessel, where he was dragged by some of the crew into a store room, in which they had secreted themselves, and barricaded the door with a crowbar from within. The cruiser was thus completely in the possession of the enemy, who made sail on her, and were bearing her off in triumph to their own port, in company with their boats. Soon after, however, the commodore of the squadron in the *Neried* frigate hove in sight, and perceiving this vessel in company with the dows, judged her to be a prize to the pirates. She accordingly gave them all chase, and coming up with the brig, the Arabs took to their boats and abandoned her. The chase was continued after the dows, but without success.

These repeated aggressions at length opened the eyes of the East India Government, and an expedition was accordingly assembled at Bombay. The naval force consisted of *La Chiffone*, frigate, Capt. Wainwright, as commodore. The *Caroline* of thirty-eight guns; and eight of the East India Company's cruisers, namely, the *Mornington*, *Ternate*, *Aurora*, *Prince of Wales*, *Ariel*, *Nautilus*, *Vestal* and *Fury*, with four large transports, and the *Stromboli* bomb-ketch. The fleet sailed from Bombay in September, and after a long passage they reached Muscat, where it remained for many days to refresh and arrange their future plans; they sailed and soon reached Ras-el-Khyma, the chief port of the pirates within the gulf. Here the squadron anchored abreast of the town, and the troops were landed under cover of the ships and boats. The inhabitants of the town assembled in crowds to repel the invaders; but the firm line, the regular volleys, and the steady charge of the troops at the point of the bayonet, overcame every obstacle, and multiplied the heaps of the slain. A general conflagration was then ordered, and a general plunder to the troops was permitted. The town was set on fire in all parts, and about sixty sail of boats and dows, with the *Minerva*, a ship which they had taken, then lying in the roads were all burnt and destroyed.

The complete conquest of the place was thus effected with very trifling loss on the part of the besiegers, and some plunder collected; though it was thought that most of the treasure and valuables had been removed into the interior. This career of victory was suddenly damped by the report of the approach of a large body of troops from the interior, and although none of these were seen, this ideal reinforcement induced the besiegers to withdraw. The embarkation took place at daylight in the morning; and while the fleet remained at anchor during the whole of the day, parties were still seen assembling on the shore, displaying their colors, brandishing their spears, and firing muskets from all points; so that the conquest was scarcely as complete as could be wished, since no formal act of submission had yet been shown. The expedition now sailed to Linga, a small port of the Joassamees, and burnt it to the ground. The force had now become separated, the greater portion of the troops being sent to Muscat for supplies, or being deemed unnecessary, and some of the vessels sent on separate services of blockading passages, &c. The remaining portion of the blockading squadron consisting of *La Chiffone*, frigate, and four of the cruisers, the *Mornington, Ternate, Nautilus,* and *Fury,* and two transports, with five hundred troops from Linga, then proceeded to Luft, another port of the Joassamees. As the channel here was narrow and difficult of approach, the ships were warped into their stations of anchorage, and a summons sent on shore, as the people had not here abandoned their town, but were found at their posts of defence, in a large and strong castle with many batteries, redoubts, &c. The summons being treated with disdain, the troops were landed with Col. Smith at their head; and while forming on the beach a slight skirmish took place with such of the inhabitants of the town, as fled for shelter to the castle. The troops then advanced towards the fortress, which is described to have had walls fourteen feet thick, pierced with loop holes, and only one entrance through a small gate, well cased with iron bars and bolts, in the strongest manner. With a howitzer taken for the occasion, it was intended to have blown this gate open, and to have taken the place by storm; but on reaching it while the ranks opened, and the men sought to surround the castle to seek for some other entrance at the same time, they were picked off so rapidly and unexpectedly from the loop holes above, that a general flight took place, the howitzer was abandoned, even before it had been fired, and both the officers and the troops sought shelter by lying down behind the ridges of sand and little hillocks immediately underneath the castle walls. An Irish officer, jumping up from his hiding place, and calling on some of his comrades to follow him in an attempt to rescue the howitzer, was killed in the enterprise. Such others as even raised their heads to look around them, were picked off by the musketry from above; and the whole of the troops lay therefore hidden in this way, until the darkness of the night favored their escape to the beach, where they embarked after sunset, the enemy having made no sally on them from the fort. A second summons was sent to the chief in the castle, threatening to bombard the town from a nearer anchorage if he did not submit, and no quarter afterwards shown. With the dawn of morning, all eyes were directed to the fortress, when, to the surprise of the whole squadron, a man was seen waving the British Union flag on the summit of its walls. It was Lieutenant Hall, who commanded the *Fury* which was one of the vessels nearest the shore. During the night he had gone on shore alone, taking an Union-Jack in his hand, and advanced singly to the castle gate. The fortress had already been abandoned by the greater number of the inhabitants, but some few still remained there. These fled at the approach of an individual supposing him to be the herald of those who were to follow. Be this as it may, the castle was entirely abandoned, and the British flag waved on its walls by this daring officer, to the surprise and admiration of all the fleet. The town and fortifications were then taken possession of. After sweeping round the bottom of the gulf, the expedition returned to Muscat.

On the sailing of the fleet from hence, the forces were augmented by a body of troops belonging to the Imaun of Muscat, destined to assist in the recovery of a place called Shenaz, on the coast, taken by the Joassamees. On their arrival at this place, a summons was sent, commanding the fort to surrender, which being refused, a bombardment was opened from the ships and boats, but without producing much effect. On the following morning, the whole of the troops were landed, and a regular encampment formed on the shore, with sand batteries, and other necessary works for a siege. After several days bombardment, in which about four thousand shot and shells were discharged against the fortress, to which the people had fled for refuge after burning down the town, a breach was reported to be practicable, and the castle was accordingly stormed. The resistance still made was desperate; the Arabs fighting as long as they could wield the sword, and even thrusting their spears up through the fragments of towers, in whose ruins they remained irrevocably buried. The loss in killed and wounded was upwards of a thousand men. Notwithstanding that the object of this expedition might be said to be incomplete, inasmuch as nothing less than a total extirpation of their race could secure the tranquility of these seas, yet the effect produced by this expedition was such, as to make them reverence or dread the British flag for several years afterwards.

At length in 1815, their boats began to infest the entrance to the Red Sea; and in 1816, their numbers had so increased on that coast, that a squadron of them commanded by a chief called Ameer Ibrahim, captured within sight of Mocha, four vessels bound from Surat to that port, richly laden and navigating under the British flag, and the crews were massacred.

A squadron consisting of His Majesty's ship *Challenger*, Captain Brydges, and the East India Company's cruisers, *Mercury*, *Ariel*, and *Vestal*, were despatched to the chief port of the Joassamees, Ras-el-Khyma. Mr. Buckingham, the Great Oriental traveller, accompanied the expedition from Bushire. Upon their arrival at Ras-el-Khyma, a demand was made for the restoration of the four Surat vessels and their cargoes; or in lieu thereof twelve lacks of rupees. Also that the commander of the piratical squadron, Ameer Ibrahim, should be delivered up for punishment. The demand was made by letter, and answer being received, Captain Brydges determined to go on shore and have an interview with the Pirate Chieftain. Mr. Buckingham says, "He requested me to accompany him on shore as an interpreter. I readily assented. We quitted the ship together about 9 o'clock, and pulled straight to the shore, sounding all the way as we went, and gradually shoaling our water from six to two fathoms, within a quarter of a mile of the beach, where four large dows lay at anchor, ranged in a line, with their heads seaward, each of them mounting several pieces of cannon, and being full of men. On landing on the beach, we found its whole length guarded by a line of armed men, some bearing muskets, but the greater part armed with swords, shields, and spears; most of them were negroes, whom the Joassamees spare in their wars, looking on them rather as property and merchandise, than in the light of enemies. We were permitted to pass this line, and upon our communicating our wish to see the chief, we were conducted to the gate of the principal building, nearly in the centre of the town, and were met by the Pirate Chieftain attended by fifty armed men. I offered him the Mahometan salutation of peace, which he returned without hesitation.

"The chief, Hassan ben Rahma, whom we had seen, was a small man, apparently about forty years of age, with an expression of cunning in his looks, and something particularly sarcastic in his smile. He was dressed in the usual Arab garments, with a cashmeer shawl, turban, and a scarlet benish, of the Persian form, to distinguish him from his followers. There were habited in the plainest garments. One of his eyes had been wounded, but his other features were good, his teeth beautifully white and regular, and his complexion very dark.

"The town of Ras-el-Khyma stands on a narrow tongue of sandy land, pointing to the northeastward, presenting its northwest edge to the open sea, and its southeast one to a creek, which runs up within it to the southwestward, and affords a safe harbor for boats. There appeared to be no continued wall of defence around it, though round towers and portions of walls were seen in several parts, probably once connected in line, but not yet repaired since their destruction. The strongest points of defence appear to be in a fortress at the northeast angle, and a double round tower, near the centre of the town; in each of which, guns are mounted; but all the other towers appear to afford only shelter for musketeers. The rest of the town is composed of ordinary buildings of unhewn stone, and huts of rushes and long grass, with narrow avenues winding between them. The present number of inhabitants may be computed at ten thousand at least. They are thought to have at present (1816), sixty large boats out from their own port, manned with crews of from eighty, to three hundred men each, and forty other boats that belong to other ports. Their force concentrated, would probably amount to at least one hundred boats and eight thousand fighting men. After several fruitless negociations, the signal was now made to weigh, and stand closer in towards the town. It was then followed by the signal to engage the enemy. The squadron bore down nearly in line, under easy sail, and with the wind right aft, or on shore; the *Mercury* being on the starboard bow, the *Challenger* next in order, in the centre, the *Vestal* following in the same line, and the *Ariel* completing the division.

"A large fleet of small boats were seen standing in from Cape Mussundum, at the same time; but these escaped by keeping closer along shore, and at length passing over the bar and getting into the back water behind the town. The squadron continued to stand on in a direct line towards the four anchored dows, gradually shoaling from the depth of our anchorage to two and a half fathoms, where stream anchors were dropped under foot, with springs on the cables, so that each vessel lay with her broadside to the shore. A fire was now opened by the whole squadron, directed to the four dows. These boats were full of men, brandishing their weapons in the air, their whole number exceeding, probably, six hundred. Some of the shot from the few long guns of the squadron reached the shore, and were buried in the sand; others fell across the bows and near the hulls of the dows to which they were directed; but the cannonades all fell short, as we were then fully a mile from the beach.

"The Arab colors were displayed on all the forts; crowds of armed men were assembled on the beach, bearing large banners on poles, and dancing around them with their arms, as if rallying around a sacred standard, so that no sign of submission or conquest was witnessed throughout. The *Ariel* continued to discharge about fifty shot after all the others had desisted, but with as little avail as before, and thus ended this wordy negociation, and the bloodless battle to which it eventually led."

In 1818, these pirates grew so daring that they made an irruption into the Indian Ocean, and plundered vessels and towns on the islands and coasts. A fleet was sent against them, and intercepted them off Ashlola Island, proceeding to the westward in three divisions; and drove them back into the gulf. The *Eden* and *Psyche* fell in with two trankies, and these were so closely pursued that they were obliged to drop a small captured boat they had in tow. The *Thetes* one day kept in close chase of seventeen vessels, but they were enabled to get away owing to their superior sailing. The cruisers met with the Joassamees seventeen times and were constantly employed in hunting them from place to place.

At length, in 1819, they became such a scourge to commerce that a formidable expedition under the command of Major General Sir W. Grant Keir, sailed against them. It arrived before the chief town in December, and commenced operations. In his despatches Gen. Keir says—

"I have the satisfaction to report the town of Ras-el Khyma, after a resistance of six days, was taken possession of this morning by the force under my command.

"On the 18th, after completing my arrangements at Muscat, the Liverpool sailed for the rendezvous at Kishme; on the 21st, we fell in with the fleet of the Persian Gulf and anchored off the island of Larrack on the 24th November.

"As it appeared probable that a considerable period would elapse before the junction of the ships which were detained at Bombay, I conceived it would prove highly advantageous to avail myself of all the information that could be procured respecting the strength and resources of the pirates we had to deal with.

"No time was lost in making the necessary preparations for landing, which was effected the following morning without opposition, at a spot which had been previously selected for that purpose, about two miles to the westward of the town. The troops were formed across the isthmus connecting the peninsula on which the town is situated with the neighboring country, and the whole of the day was occupied in getting the tents on shore, to shelter the men from rain, landing engineers, tools, sand bags, &c., and making arrangements preparatory to commencing our approaches the next day. On the morning of the 4th, our light troops were ordered in advance, supported by the pickets, to dislodge the enemy from a bank within nine hundred yards of the outer fort, which was expected to afford good cover for the men. The whole of the light companies of the force under Capt. Backhouse, moved forward, and drove the Arabs with great gallantry from a date grove, and over the bank close under the walls of the fort, followed by the pickets under Major Molesworth, who took post at the sand banks, whilst the European light troops were skirmishing in front. The enemy kept up a sharp fire of musketry and cannon; during these movements, Major Molesworth, a gallant officer, was here killed. The troops kept their position during the day, and in the night effected a lodgment within three hundred yards of the southernmost tower, and erected a battery of four guns, together with a mortar battery.

"The weather having become rather unfavorable for the disembarkation of the stores required for the siege, but this important object being effected on the morning of the 6th, we were enabled to open three eighteen pounders on the fort, a couple of howitzers, and six pounders were also placed in the battery on the right, which played on the defences of the towers and nearly silenced the enemy's fire, who, during the whole of our progress exhibited a considerable degree of resolution in withstanding, and ingenuity in counteracting our attacks, sallied out at 8 o'clock this evening along the whole front of our entrenchments, crept close up to the mortar battery without being perceived, and entered it over the parapet, after spearing the advance sentries. The party which occupied it were obliged to retire, but being immediately reinforced charged the assailants, who were driven out of the battery with great loss. The enemy repeated his attacks towards morning but was vigorously repulsed. During the seventh every exertion was made to land and bring up the remaining guns and mortars, which was accomplished during the night. They were immediately placed in the battery, together with two twenty-four pounders which were landed from the Liverpool, and in the morning the whole of the ordnance opened on the fort and fired with scarcely any intermission till sunset, when the breach on the curtain was reported nearly practicable and the towers almost untenable. Immediate arrangements were made for the assault, and the troops ordered to move down to the entrenchments by daylight the next morning. The party moved forward about 8 o'clock, and entered the fort through the breaches without firing a shot, and it soon appeared the enemy had evacuated the place. The town was taken possession of and found almost entirely deserted, only eighteen or twenty men, and a few women remaining in their houses.

"The expedition next proceeded against Rumps, a piratical town, eight miles north of Ras-el-Khyma, but the inhabitants abandoned the town and took refuge in the hill fort of Zyah, which is situated at the head of a navigable creek nearly two miles from the sea coast. This place was the residence of Hussein Bin Alley, a sheikh of considerable importance among the Joassamee tribes, and a person who from his talents and lawless habits, as well as from the strength and advantageous situation of the fort, was likely to attempt the revival of the piratical system upon the first occasion. It became a desirable object to reduce the power of this chieftain.

"On the 18th December, the troops embarked at Ras-el-Khyma, at day break in the boats of the fleet under command of Major Warren, with the 65th regiment and the flank companies of the first and second regiment, and at noon arrived within four miles of their destination. This operation was attended with considerable difficulty and risk, owing to the heavy surf that beat on the shore; and which was the occasion of some loss of ammunition, and of a few boats being upset and stove in."

"At half past three P.M., having refreshed the men," says Major Warren, "we commenced our march, and fording the creek or back water, took up our position at sunset, to the northeastward of the fort, the enemy firing at us as we passed, notwithstanding that our messenger, whom we had previously sent in to summon the Sheikh, was still in the place; and I lost no time in pushing our riflemen and pickets as far forward as I could without exposing them too much to the firing of the enemy, whom I found strongly posted under secure cover in the date tree groves in front of the town. Captain Cocke, with the light company of his battalion, was at the same time sent to the westward, to cut off the retreat of the enemy on that side.

"At day break the next morning, finding it necessary to drive the enemy still further in, to get a nearer view of his defences, I moved forward the rifle company of the 65th regiment, and after a considerable opposition from the enemy, I succeeded in forcing him to retire some distance; but not without disputing every inch of ground, which was well calculated for resistance, being intersected at every few yards, by banks and water courses raised for the purpose of irrigation, and covered with date trees. The next morning the riflemen, supported by the pickets, were again called into play, and soon established their position within three and four hundred yards of the town, which with the base of the hill, was so completely surrounded, as to render the escape of any of the garrison now almost impossible. This advantage was gained by a severe loss. Two twenty-four pounders and the two twelves, the landing of which had been retarded by the difficulty of communication with the fleet from which we derived all our supplies, having been now brought on shore, we broke ground in the evening, and notwithstanding the rocky soil, had them to play next morning at daylight.

"Aware, however, that the families of the enemy were still in the town, and humanity dictating that some effort should be made to save the innocent from the fate that awaited the guilty; an opportunity was afforded for that purpose by an offer to the garrison of security to their women and children, should they be sent out within the hour; but the infatuated chief, either from an idea that his fort on the hill was not to be reached by our shot, or with the vain hope to gain time by procrastination, returning no answer to our communication, while he detained our messenger; we opened our fire at half past eight in the morning, and such was the precision of the practice, that in two hours we perceived the breach would soon be practicable. I was in the act of ordering the assault, when a white flag was displayed; and the enemy, after some little delay in assembling from the different quarters of the place, marched out without their arms, with Hussein Bin Alley at their head, to the number of three hundred and ninety-eight; and at half past one P.M., the British flags were hoisted on the hill fort and at the Sheikh's house. The women and children to the number of four hundred, were at the same time collected together in a place of security, and sent on board the fleet, together with the men. The service has been short but arduous; the enemy defended themselves with great obstinacy and ability worthy of a better cause."

From two prisoners retaken from the Joassamees, they learnt that the plunder is made a general stock, and distributed by the chief, but in what proportions the deponents cannot say; water is generally very scarce. There is a quantity of fish caught on the bank, upon which and dates they live. There were a few horses, camels, cows, sheep, and goats; the greatest part of which they took with them; they were in general lean, as the sandy plain produces little or no vegetation, except a few dates and cocoa-nut trees. The pirates who abandoned Ras-el-Khyma, encamped about three miles in the interior, ready to retreat into the desert at a moment's warning. The Sheikh of Rumps is an old man, but looks intelligent, and is said to be the man who advises upon all occasions the movements of the different tribes of pirates on the coast, and when he was told that it was the wish of the Company to put a stop to their piracy, and make an honest people of them by encouraging them to trade, seemed to regret much that those intentions were not made known, as they would have been most readily embraced. Rumps is the key to Ras-el-Khyma, and by its strength is defended from a strong banditti infesting the mountains, as also the Bedouin Arabs who are their enemies. A British garrison of twelve hundred men was stationed at Ras-el-Khyma, and a guard-ship. The other places sent in tokens of submission, as driven out of their fortresses on the margin of the sea, they had to contend within with the interior hostile tribes.

DEVIL WITH DEVIL

Daniel Defoe

CHAPTER SEVEN

Thieving, lying, swearing, forswearing, joined to the most abominable lewdness, was the stated practice of the ship's crew; adding to it, that, with the most insufferable boasts of their own courage, they were, generally speaking, the most complete cowards that I ever met with; and the consequence of their cowardice was evident upon many occasions. However, there was here and there one among them that was not so bad as the rest; and, as my lot fell among them, it made me have the most contemptible thoughts of the rest, as indeed they deserved.

I was exactly fitted for their society indeed; for I had no sense of virtue or religion upon me. I had never heard much of either, except what a good old parson had said to me when I was a child of about eight or nine years old; nay, I was preparing and growing up apace to be as wicked as anybody could be, or perhaps ever was. Fate certainly thus directed my beginning, knowing that I had work which I had to do in the world, which nothing but one hardened against all sense of honesty or religion could go through; and yet, even in this state of original wickedness, I entertained such a settled abhorrence of the abandoned vileness of the Portuguese, that I could not but hate them most heartily from the beginning, and all my life afterwards. They were so brutishly wicked, so base and perfidious, not only to strangers but to one another, so meanly submissive when subjected, so insolent, or barbarous and tyrannical, when superior, that I thought there was something in them that shocked my very nature. Add to this that it is natural to an Englishman to hate a coward, it all joined together to make the devil and a Portuguese equally my aversion.

However, according to the English proverb, he that is shipped with the devil must sail with the devil; I was among them, and I managed myself as well as I could. My master had consented that I should assist the captain in the office, as above; but, as I understood afterwards that the captain allowed my master half a moidore a month for my service, and that he had my name upon the ship's books also, I expected that when the ship came to be paid four months' wages at the Indies, as they, it seems, always do, my master would let me have something for myself.

But I was wrong in my man, for he was none of that kind; he had taken me up as in distress, and his business was to keep me so, and make his market of me as well as he could, which I began to think of after a different manner than I did at first, for at first I thought he had entertained me in mere charity, upon seeing my distressed circumstances, but did not doubt but when he put me on board the ship, I should have some wages for my service.

But he thought, it seems, quite otherwise; and when I procured one to speak to him about it, when the ship was paid at Goa, he flew into the greatest rage imaginable, and called me English dog, young heretic, and threatened to put me into the Inquisition. Indeed, of all the names the four-and-twenty letters could make up, he should not have called me heretic; for as I knew nothing about religion, neither Protestant from Papist, or either of them from a Mahometan, I could never be a heretic. However, it passed but a little, but, as young as I was, I had been carried into the Inquisition, and there, if they had asked me if I was a Protestant or a Catholic, I should have said yes to that which came first. If it had been the Protestant they had asked first, it had certainly made a martyr of me for I did not know what.

But the very priest they carried with them, or chaplain of the ship, as we called him, saved me; for seeing me a boy entirely ignorant of religion, and ready to do or say anything they bid me, he asked me some questions about it, which he found I answered so very simply, that he took it upon him to tell them he would answer for my being a good

Catholic, and he hoped he should be the means of saving my soul, and he pleased himself that it was to be a work of merit to him; so he made me as good a Papist as any of them in about a week's time.

I then told him my case about my master; how, it is true, he had taken me up in a miserable case on board a man-of-war at Lisbon; and I was indebted to him for bringing me on board this ship; that if I had been left at Lisbon, I might have starved, and the like; and therefore I was willing to serve him, but that I hoped he would give me some little consideration for my service, or let me know how long he expected I should serve him for nothing.

It was all one; neither the priest nor any one else could prevail with him, but that I was not his servant but his slave, that he took me in the Algerine, and that I was a Turk, only pretended to be an English boy to get my liberty, and he would carry me to the Inquisition as a Turk.

This frighted me out of my wits, for I had nobody to vouch for me what I was, or from whence I came; but the good Padre Antonio, for that was his name, cleared me of that part by a way I did not understand; for he came to me one morning with two sailors, and told me they must search me, to bear witness that I was not a Turk. I was amazed at them, and frighted, and did not understand them, nor could I imagine what they intended to do to me.

However, stripping me, they were soon satisfied, and Father Antony bade me be easy, for they could all witness that I was no Turk. So I escaped that part of my master's cruelty.

And now I resolved from that time to run away from him if I could, but there was no doing of it there, for there were not ships of any nation in the world in that port, except two or three Persian vessels from Ormus, so that if I had offered to go away from him, he would have had me seized on shore, and brought on board by force; so that I had no remedy but patience.

And this he brought to an end too as soon as he could, for after this he began to use me ill, and not only to straiten my provisions, but to beat and torture me in a barbarous manner for every trifle, so that, in a word, my life began to be very miserable.

The violence of this usage of me, and the impossibility of my escape from his hands, set my head a-working upon all sorts of mischief, and in particular I resolved, after studying all other ways to deliver myself, and finding all ineffectual, I say, I resolved to murder him. With this hellish resolution in my head, I spent whole nights and days contriving how to put it in execution, the devil prompting me very warmly to the fact. I was indeed entirely at a loss for the means, for I had neither gun or sword, nor any weapon to assault him with; poison I had my thoughts much upon, but knew not where to get any; or, if I might have got it, I did not know the country word for it, or by what name to ask for it.

In this manner I quitted the fact, intentionally, a hundred and a hundred times; but Providence, either for his sake or for mine, always frustrated my designs, and I could never bring it to pass; so I was obliged to continue in his chains till the ship, having taken in her loading, set sail for Portugal.

I can say nothing here to the manner of our voyage, for, as I said, I kept no journal; but this I can give an account of, that having been once as high as the Cape of Good Hope, as we call it, or Cabo de Bona Speranza, as they call it, we were driven back again by a violent storm from the W.S.W., which held us six days and nights a great way to the eastward, and after that, standing afore the wind for several days more, we at last came to an anchor on the coast of Madagascar.

The storm had been so violent that the ship had received a great deal of damage, and it required some time to repair her; so, standing in nearer the shore, the pilot, my master, brought the ship into a very good harbour, where we rid in twenty-six fathoms water, about half a mile from the shore.

While the ship rode here there happened a most desperate mutiny among the men, upon account of some deficiency in their allowance, which came to that height that they threatened the captain to set him on shore, and go back with the ship to Goa. I wished they would with all my heart, for I was full of mischief in my head, and ready enough to do any. So, though I was but a boy, as they called me, yet I prompted the mischief all I could, and embarked in it so openly, that I escaped very little being hanged in the first and most early part of my life; for the captain had some notice that there was a design laid by some of the company to murder him; and having, partly by money and promises, and partly by threatening and torture, brought two fellows to confess the particulars, and the names of the persons concerned, they were presently apprehended, till, one accusing another, no less than sixteen men were seized and put into irons, whereof I was one.

The captain, who was made desperate by his danger, resolving to clear the ship of his enemies, tried us all, and we were all condemned to die. The manner of his process I was too young to take notice of; but the purser and one of the gunners were hanged immediately, and I expected it with the rest. I do not remember any great concern I was under about it, only that I cried very much, for I knew little then of this world, and nothing at all of the next.

However, the captain contented himself with executing these two, and some of the rest, upon their humble submission and promise of future good behaviour, were pardoned; but five were ordered to be set on shore on the island and left there, of which I was one. My master used all his interest with the captain to have me excused, but could not obtain it; for somebody having told him that I was one of them who was singled out to have killed him, when my master desired I might not be set on shore, the captain told him I should stay on board if he desired it, but then I should be hanged, so he might choose for me which he thought best. The captain, it seems, was particularly provoked at my being concerned in the treachery, because of his having been so kind to me, and of his having singled me out to serve him, as I have said above; and this, perhaps, obliged him to give my master such a rough choice, either to set me on shore or to have me hanged on board. And had my master, indeed, known what good-will I had for him, he would not have been long in choosing for me; for I had certainly determined to do him a mischief the first opportunity I had for it. This was, therefore, a good providence for me to keep me from dipping my hands in blood, and it made me more tender afterwards in matters of blood than I believe I should otherwise have been. But as to my being one of them that was to kill the captain, that I was wronged in, for I was not the person, but it was really one of them that were pardoned, he having the good luck not to have that part discovered.

I was now to enter upon a part of independent life, a thing I was indeed very ill prepared to manage, for I was perfectly loose and dissolute in my behaviour, bold and wicked while I was under government, and now perfectly unfit to be trusted with liberty, for I was as ripe for any villainy as a young fellow that had no solid thought ever placed in his mind could be supposed to be. Education, as you have heard, I had none; and all the little scenes of life I had passed through had been full of dangers and desperate circumstances; but I was either so young or so stupid, that I escaped the grief and anxiety of them, for want of having a sense of their tendency and consequences.

This thoughtless, unconcerned temper had one felicity indeed in it, that it made me daring and ready for doing any mischief, and kept off the sorrow which otherwise ought to have attended me when I fell into any mischief; that this stupidity was instead of a happiness to me, for it left my thoughts free to act upon means of escape and deliverance in my distress, however great it might be; whereas my companions in the misery were so sunk by their fear and grief, that they abandoned themselves to the misery of their condition, and gave over all thought but of their perishing and starving, being devoured by wild beasts, murdered, and perhaps eaten by cannibals, and the like.

I was but a young fellow, about seventeen or eighteen; but hearing what was to be my fate, I received it with no appearance of discouragement; but I asked what my master said to it, and being told that he had used his utmost interest to save me, but the captain had answered I should either go on shore or be hanged on board, which he pleased, I then gave over all hope of being received again. I was not very thankful in my thoughts to my master for his soliciting the captain for me, because I knew that what he did was not in kindness to me so much as in kindness to himself; I mean, to preserve the wages which he got for me, which amounted to above six dollars a month, including what the captain allowed him for my particular service to him.

When I understood that my master was so apparently kind, I asked if I might not be admitted to speak with him, and they told me I might, if my master would come down to me, but I could not be allowed to come up to him; so then I desired my master might be spoke to come to me, and he accordingly came to me. I fell on my knees to him, and begged he would forgive me what I had done to displease him; and indeed the resolution I had taken to murder him lay with some horror upon my mind just at that time, so that I was once just a-going to confess it, and beg him to forgive me, but I kept it in. He told me he had done all he could to obtain my pardon of the captain, but could not and he knew no way for me but to have patience, and submit to my fate; and if they came to speak with any ship of their nation at the Cape, he would endeavour to have them stand in, and fetch us off again, if we might be found.

Then I begged I might have my clothes on shore with me. He told me he was afraid I should have little need of clothes, for he did not see how we could long subsist on the island, and that he had been told that the inhabitants were cannibals or men-eaters (though he had no reason for that suggestion), and we should not be able to live among them. I told him I was not so afraid of that as I was of starving for want of victuals; and as for the inhabitants being cannibals, I believed we should be more likely to eat them than they us, if we could but get at them. But I was mightily concerned, I said, we should have no weapons with us to defend ourselves, and I begged nothing now, but that he would give me a gun and a sword, with a little powder and shot.

He smiled, and said they would signify nothing to us, for it was impossible for us to pretend to preserve our lives among such a populous and desperate nation as the people of this island were. I told him that, however, it would do us this good, for we should not be devoured or destroyed immediately; so I begged hard for the gun. At last he told me he did not know whether the captain would give him leave to give me a gun, and if not, he durst not do it; but he promised to use his interest to obtain it for me, which he did, and the next day he sent me a gun, with some ammunition, but told me the captain would not suffer the ammunition to be given us til we were set all on shore, and till he was just going to set sail. He also sent me the few clothes I had in the ship, which indeed were not many.

Two days after this, we were all carried on shore together; the rest of my fellow-criminals hearing I had a gun, and some powder and shot, solicited for liberty to carry the like with them, which was also granted them; and thus we were set on shore to shift for ourselves.

At our first coming into the island we were terrified exceedingly with the sight of the barbarous people, whose figure was made more terrible to us than it really was by the report we had of them from the seamen; but when we came to converse with them awhile, we found they were not cannibals, as was reported, or such as would fall immediately upon us and eat us up; but they came and sat down by us, and wondered much at our clothes and arms, and made signs to give us some victuals, such as they had, which was only roots and plants dug out of the ground for the present, but they brought us fowls and flesh afterwards in good plenty.

This encouraged the other four men that were with me very much, for they were quite dejected before; but now they began to be very familiar with them, and made signs, that if they would use us kindly, we would stay and live with them; which they seemed glad of, though they knew little of the necessity we were under to do so, or how much we were afraid of them.

However, upon second thoughts we resolved that we would only stay in that part so long as the ship rid in the bay, and then making them believe we were gone with the ship, we would go and place ourselves, if possible, where there were no inhabitants to be seen, and so live as we could, or perhaps watch for a ship that might be driven upon the coast as we were.

The ship continued a fortnight in the roads, repairing some damage which had been done her in the late storm, and taking in wood and water; and during this time, the boat coming often on shore, the men brought us several refreshments, and the natives believing we only belonged to the ship, were civil enough. We lived in a kind of a tent on the shore, or rather a hut, which we made with the boughs of trees, and sometimes in the night retired to a wood a little out of their way, to let them think we were gone on board the ship. However, we found them barbarous, treacherous, and villainous enough in their nature, only civil from fear, and therefore concluded we should soon fall into their hands when the ship was gone.

The sense of this wrought upon my fellow-sufferers even to distraction; and one of them, being a carpenter, in his mad fit, swam off to the ship in the night, though she lay then a league to sea, and made such pitiful moan to be taken in, that the captain was prevailed with at last to take him in, though they let him lie swimming three hours in the water before he consented to it.

Upon this, and his humble submission, the captain received him, and, in a word, the importunity of this man (who for some time petitioned to be taken in, though they hanged him as soon as they had him) was such as could not be resisted; for, after he had swam so long about the ship, he was not able to reach the shore again; and the captain saw evidently that the man must be taken on board or suffered to drown, and the whole ship's company offering to be bound for him for his good behaviour, the captain at last yielded, and he was taken up, but almost dead with his being so long in the water.

When this man was got in, he never left importuning the captain, and all the rest of the officers, in behalf of us that were behind, but to the very last day the captain was inexorable; when, at the time their preparations were making to sail, and orders given to hoist the boats into the ship, all the seamen in a body came up to the rail of the quarter-deck, where the captain was walking with some of his officers, and appointing the boatswain to speak for them, he went up, and falling on his knees to the captain, begged of him, in the humblest manner possible, to receive the four men on board again, offering to answer for their fidelity, or to have them kept in chains till they came to Lisbon, and there to be delivered up to justice, rather than, as they said, to have them left to be murdered by savages, or devoured by wild beasts. It was a great while ere the captain took any notice of them, but when he did, he ordered the boatswain to be seized, and threatened to bring him to the capstan for speaking for them.

Upon this severity, one of the seamen, bolder than the rest, but still with all possible respect to the captain, besought his honour, as he called him, that he would give leave to some more of them to go on shore, and die with their companions, or, if possible, to assist them to resist the barbarians. The captain, rather provoked than cowed with this, came to the barricade of the quarter-deck, and speaking very prudently to the men (for had he spoken roughly, two-thirds of them would have left the ship, if not all of them), he told them, it was for their safety as well as his own that he had been obliged to that severity; that mutiny on board a ship was the same thing as treason in a king's palace, and he could not answer it to his owners and employers to trust the ship and goods committed to his charge with men who had entertained thoughts of the worst and blackest nature; that he wished heartily that it had been anywhere else that they had been set on shore, where they might have been in less hazard from the savages; that, if he had designed they should be destroyed, he could as well have executed them on board as the other two; that he wished it had been in some other part of the world, where he might have delivered them up to the civil justice, or might have left them among Christians; but it was better their lives were put in hazard than his life, and the safety of the ship; and that though he did not know that he had deserved so ill of any of them as that they should leave the ship rather than do their duty, yet if any of them were resolved to do so unless he would consent to take a gang of traitors on board, who, as he had proved before them all, had conspired to murder him, he would not hinder them, nor for the present would he resent their importunity; but, if there was nobody left in the ship but himself, he would never consent to take them on board.

This discourse was delivered so well, was in itself so reasonable, was managed with so much temper, yet so boldly concluded with a negative, that the greatest part of the men were satisfied for the present. However, as it put the men into juntos and cabals, they were not composed for some hours; the wind also slackening towards night, the captain ordered not to weigh till next morning.

The same night twenty-three of the men, among whom was the gunner's mate, the surgeon's assistant, and two carpenters, applying to the chief mate told him, that as the captain had given them leave to go on shore to their comrades, they begged that he would speak to the captain not to take it ill that they were desirous to go and die with their companions; and that they thought they could do no less in such an extremity than go to them; because, if there was any way to save their lives, it was by adding to their numbers, and making them strong enough to assist one another in defending themselves against the savages, till perhaps they might one time or other find means to make their escape, and get to their own country again.

The mate told them, in so many words, that he durst not speak to the captain upon any such design, and was very sorry they had no more respect for him than to desire him to go upon such an errand;

but, if they were resolved upon such an enterprise, he would advise them to take the long-boat in the morning betimes, and go off, seeing the captain had given them leave, and leave a civil letter behind them to the captain, and to desire him to send his men on shore for the boat, which should be delivered very honestly, and he promised to keep their counsel so long.

Accordingly, an hour before day, those twenty-three men, with every man a firelock and a cutlass, with some pistols, three halberds or half-pikes, and good store of powder and ball, without any provision but about half a hundred of bread, but with all their chests and clothes, tools, instruments, books, &c., embarked themselves so silently, that the captain got no notice of it till they were gotten half the way on shore.

As soon as the captain heard of it he called for the gunner's mate, the chief gunner being at the time sick in his cabin, and ordered to fire at them; but, to his great mortification, the gunner's mate was one of the number, and was gone with them; and indeed it was by this means they got so many arms and so much ammunition. When the captain found how it was, and that there was no help for it, he began to be a little appeased, and made light of it, and called up the men, and spoke kindly to them, and told them he was very well satisfied in the fidelity and ability of those that were now left, and that he would give to them, for their encouragement, to be divided among them, the wages which were due to the men that were gone, and that it was a great satisfaction to him that the ship was free from such a mutinous rabble, who had not the least reason for their discontent.

The men seemed very well satisfied, and particularly the promise of the wages of those who were gone went a great way with them. After this, the letter which was left by the men was given to the captain by his boy, with whom, it seems, the men had left it. The letter was much to the same purpose of what they had said to the mate, and which he declined to say for them, only that at the end of their letter they told the captain that, as they had no dishonest design, so they had taken nothing away with them which was not their own, except some arms and ammunition, such as were absolutely necessary to them, as well for their defence against the savages as to kill fowls or beasts for their food, that they might not perish; and as there were considerable sums due to them for wages, they hoped he would allow the arms and ammunition upon their accounts. They told him that, as to the ship's longboat, which they had taken to bring them on shore, they knew it was necessary to him, and they were very willing to restore it to him, and if he pleased to send for it, it should be very honestly delivered to his men, and not the least injury offered to any of those who came for it, nor the least persuasion or invitation made use of to any of them to stay with them; and, at the bottom of the letter, they very humbly besought him that, for their defence, and for the safety of their lives, he would be pleased to send them a barrel of powder and some ammunition, and give them leave to keep the mast and sail of the boat, that if it was possible for them to make themselves a boat of any kind, they might shift off to sea, to save themselves in such part of the world as their fate should direct them to.

Upon this the captain, who had won much upon the rest of his men by what he had said to them, and was very easy as to the general peace (for it was very true that the most mutinous of the men were gone), came out to the quarter-deck, and, calling the men together, let them know the substance of the letter, and told the men that, however they had not deserved such civility from him, yet he was not willing to expose them more than they were willing to expose themselves; he was inclined to send them some ammunition, and as they had desired but one barrel of powder, he would send them two barrels, and shot, or lead and moulds to make shot, in proportion; and, to let them see that he was civiller to them than they deserved, he ordered a cask of arrack and a great bag of bread to be sent them for subsistence till they should be able to furnish themselves.

The rest of the men applauded the captain's generosity, and every one of them sent us something or other, and about three in the afternoon the pinnace came on shore, and brought us all these things, which we were very glad of, and returned the long-boat accordingly; and as to the men that came with the pinnace, as the captain had singled out such men as he knew would not come over to us, so they had positive orders not to bring any one of us on board again, upon pain of death; and indeed both were so true to our points, that we neither asked them to stay, nor they us to go.

We were now a good troop, being in all twenty-seven men, very well armed, and provided with everything but victuals; we had two carpenters among us, a gunner, and, which was worth all the rest, a surgeon or doctor; that is to say, he was an assistant to a surgeon at Goa, and was entertained as a supernumerary with us. The carpenters had brought all their tools, the doctor all his instruments and medicines, and indeed we had a great deal of baggage, that is to say, on the whole, for some of us had little more than the clothes on our backs, of whom I was one; but I had one thing which none of them had, viz., I had the twenty-two moidores of gold which I had stole at the Brazils, and two pieces of eight. The two pieces of eight I showed, and one moidore, and none of them ever suspected that I had any more money in the world, having been known to be only a poor boy taken up in charity, as you have heard, and used like a slave, and in the worst manner of a slave, by my cruel master the pilot.

It will be easy to imagine we four that were left at first were joyful, nay, even surprised with joy at the coming of the rest, though at first we were frighted, and thought they came to fetch us back to hang us; but they took ways quickly to satisfy us that they were in the same condition with us, only with this additional circumstance, theirs was voluntary, and ours by force.

The first piece of news they told us after the short history of their coming away was, that our companion was on board, but how he got thither we could not imagine, for he had given us the slip, and we never imagined he could swim so well as to venture off to the ship, which lay at so great a distance; nay, we did not so much as know that he could swim at all, and not thinking anything of what really happened, we thought he must have wandered into the woods and was devoured, or was fallen into the hands of the natives, and was murdered; and these thoughts filled us with fears enough, and of several kinds, about its being some time or other our lot to fall into their hands also. But hearing how he had with much difficulty been received on board the ship again and pardoned, we were much better satisfied than before.

Being now, as I have said, a considerable number of us, and in condition to defend ourselves, the first thing we did was to give every one his hand that we would not separate from one another upon any occasion whatsoever, but that we would live and die together; that we would kill no food, but that we would distribute it in public; and that we would be in all things guided by the majority, and not insist upon our own resolutions in anything if the majority were against it; that we would appoint a captain among us to be our governor or leader during pleasure; that while he was in office we would obey him without reserve, on pain of death; and that every one should take turn, but the captain was not to act in any particular thing without advice of the rest, and by the majority.

Having established these rules, we resolved to enter into some measures for our food, and for conversing with the inhabitants or natives of the island for our supply. As for food, they were at first very useful to us, but we soon grew weary of them, being an ignorant, ravenous, brutish sort of people, even worse than the natives of any other country that we had seen; and we soon found that the principal part of our subsistence was to be had by our guns, shooting of deer and other creatures, and fowls of all other sorts, of which there is abundance.

We found the natives did not disturb or concern themselves much about us; nor did they inquire, or perhaps know, whether we stayed among them or not, much less that our ship was gone quite away, and had cast us off, as was our case; for the next morning, after we had sent back the long-boat, the ship stood away to the south-east, and in four hours' time was out of our sight.

The next day two of us went out into the country one way, and two another, to see what kind of a land we were in; and we soon found the country was very pleasant and fruitful, and a convenient place enough to live in; but, as before, inhabited by a parcel of creatures scarce human, or capable of being made social on any account whatsoever.

We found the place full of cattle and provisions; but whether we might venture to take them where we could find them or not, we did not know; and though we were under a necessity to get provisions, yet we were loth to bring down a whole nation of devils upon us at once, and therefore some of our company agreed to try to speak with some of the country, if we could, that we might see what course was to be taken with them. Eleven of our men went on this errand, well armed and furnished for defence. They brought word that they had seen some of the natives, who appeared very civil to them, but very shy and afraid, seeing their guns, for it was easy to perceive that the natives knew what their guns were, and what use they were of.

They made signs to the natives for some food, and they went and fetched several herbs and roots, and some milk; but it was evident they did not design to give it away, but to sell it, making signs to know what our men would give them.

Our men were perplexed at this, for they had nothing to barter; however, one of the men pulled out a knife and showed them, and they were so fond of it that they were ready to go together by the ears for the knife. The seaman seeing that, was willing to make a good market of his knife, and keeping them chaffering about it a good while, some offered him roots, and others milk; at last one offered him a goat for it, which he took. Then another of our men showed them another knife, but they had nothing good enough for that, whereupon one of them made signs that he would go and fetch something; so our men stayed three hours for their return, when they came back and brought him a small-sized, thick, short cow, very fat and good meat, and gave him for his knife.

This was a good market, but our misfortune was we had no merchandise; for our knives were as needful to us as to them, and but that we were in distress for food, and must of necessity have some, these men would not have parted with their knives.

However, in a little time more we found that the woods were full of living creatures, which we might kill for our food, and that without giving offence to them; so that our men went daily out a-hunting, and never failed in killing something or other; for, as to the natives, we had no goods to barter; and for money, all the stock among us would not have subsisted us long. However, we called a general council to see what money we had, and to bring it all together, that it might go as far as possible; and when it came to my turn, I pulled out a moidore and the two dollars I spoke of before.

This moidore I ventured to show, that they might not despise me too much for adding too little to the store, and that they might not pretend to search me; and they were very civil to me, upon the presumption that I had been so faithful to them as not to conceal anything from them.

But our money did us little service, for the people neither knew the value or the use of it, nor could they justly rate the gold in proportion with the silver; so that all our money, which was not much when it was all put together, would go but a little way with us, that is to say, to buy us provisions.

Our next consideration was to get away from this cursed place, and whither to go. When my opinion came to be asked, I told them I would leave that all to them, and I told them I had rather they would let me go into the woods to get them some provisions, than consult with me, for I would agree to whatever they did; but they would not agree to that, for they would not consent that any of us should go into the woods alone; for though we had yet seen no lions or tigers in the woods, we were assured there were many in the island, besides other creatures as dangerous, and perhaps worse, as we afterwards found by our own experience.

We had many adventures in the woods, for our provisions, and often met with wild and terrible beasts, which we could not call by their names; but as they were, like us, seeking their prey, but were themselves good for nothing, so we disturbed them as little as possible.

Our consultations concerning our escape from this place, which, as I have said, we were now upon, ended in this only, that as we had two carpenters among us, and that they had tools almost of all sorts with them, we should try to build us a boat to go off to sea with, and that then, perhaps, we might find our way back to Goa, or land on some more proper place to make our escape. The counsels of this assembly were not of great moment, yet as they seem to be introductory of many more remarkable adventures which happened under my conduct hereabouts many years after, I think this miniature of my future enterprises may not be unpleasant to relate.

To the building of a boat I made no objection, and away they went to work immediately; but as they went on, great difficulties occurred, such as the want of saws to cut our plank; nails, bolts, and spikes, to fasten the timbers; hemp, pitch, and tar, to caulk and pay her seams, and the like. At length, one of the company proposed that, instead of building a bark or sloop, or shallop, or whatever they would call it, which they found was so difficult, they would rather make a large peri-agua, or canoe, which might be done with great ease.

It was presently objected, that we could never make a canoe large enough to pass the great ocean, which we were to go over to get to the coast of Malabar; that it not only would not bear the sea, but it would never bear the burden, for we were not only twenty-seven men of us, but had a great deal of luggage with us, and must, for our provision, take in a great deal more.

I never proposed to speak in their general consultations before, but finding they were at some loss about what kind of vessel they should make, and how to make it, and what would be fit for our use, and what not, I told them I found they were at a full stop in their counsels of every kind; that it was true we could never pretend to go over to Goa on the coast of Malabar in a canoe, which though we could all get into it, and that it would bear the sea well enough, yet would not hold our provisions, and especially we could not put fresh water enough into it for the voyage; and to make such an adventure would be nothing but mere running into certain destruction, and yet that nevertheless I was for making a canoe.

They answered, that they understood all I had said before well enough, but what I meant by telling them first how dangerous and impossible it was to make our escape in a canoe, and yet then to advise making a canoe, that they could not understand.

To this I answered, that I conceived our business was not to attempt our escape in a canoe, but that, as there were other vessels at sea besides our ship, and that there were few nations that lived on the sea-shore that were so barbarous, but that they went to sea in some boats or other, our business was to cruise along the coast of the island, which was very long, and to seize upon the first we could get that was better than our own, and so from that to another, till perhaps we might at last get a good ship to carry us wherever we pleased to go.

"Excellent advice," says one of them. "Admirable advice," says another. "Yes, yes," says the third (which was the gunner), "the English dog has given excellent advice; but it is just the way to bring us all to the gallows. The rogue has given us devilish advice, indeed, to go a-thieving, till from a little vessel we came to a great ship, and so we shall turn downright pirates, the end of which is to be hanged."

"You may call us pirates," says another, "if you will, and if we fall into bad hands, we may be used like pirates; but I care not for that, I'll be a pirate, or anything, nay, I'll be hanged for a pirate rather than starve here, therefore I think the advice is very good." And so they cried all, "Let us have a canoe." The gunner, over-ruled by the rest, submitted; but as we broke up the council, he came to me, takes me by the hand, and, looking into the palm of my hand, and into my face too, very gravely, "My lad," says he, "thou art born to do a world of mischief; thou hast commenced pirate very young; but have a care of the gallows, young man; have a care, I say, for thou wilt be an eminent thief."

WOLVES OF THE SEA

Randall Parrish

CHAPTER EIGHT

It was a fair, calm night, but moonless, with but little wind stirring, and a slight haze in the air, obscuring the vision. The windows of the great house above, which earlier in the evening had blazed with lights, were now darkened, and the distant sounds of voices and laughter had entirely ceased. The only noise discernible as I lay quiet was the soft lapping of waves against the side of the sloop or about the piling supporting the wharf to which we were moored. The others must have fallen asleep immediately, but my own mind remained far too active to enable me to lose consciousness. At last, despairing of slumber, and perchance urged by some indistinct premonition of danger, I sat up once more and gazed about. The three men were lying not far apart, close in to the galley wall, merely dark, shapeless shadows, barely to be distinguished in the gloom. With no longer any fear of disturbing them, I arose to my feet, and stepping carefully past their recumbent forms, moved silently aft toward the more open space near the wheel. I had been standing there hardly a minute, staring blankly out into the misty dimness of the Bay, when my startled eyes caught glimpse of a speck of white emerging from the black shadows—the spectral glimmer of a small sail. I was scarcely convinced I had seen it, yet as swiftly crouched lower, hiding myself behind the protection of the rail, instantly alert to learn the meaning of this strange apparition. An instant told me this was no deceit. The strange craft swept past, so far out that those on board no doubt believed themselves beyond sight from the shore, heading apparently for a point of land, which I vaguely remembered as jutting out to the northward. Even my eyes, accustomed to the darkness, and strained to the utmost, could detect scarcely more than the faintest shadow gliding silently by, yet sufficient to recognize the outlines of a small keel boat, propelled by a single lug sail, and even imagined I could discern the stooped figure of a man at the helm.

I had in truth hardly more than grasped the reality of the boat's presence—it seemed so spectral a thing amid the mists of the night—when it had vanished utterly once more behind the curtain of darkness. There was no sound to convince me my eyes had not deceived; that I had actually perceived a boat, flying before the wind, under complete control, and headed to the northward. No echo of a voice came across the water, no slight flap of sail, no distant creak of pulley, or groaning of rope—merely that fleeting vision, seemingly a phantom of imagination, a vision born from sea and cloud. Yet I knew I was not deceived. Where the craft could be bound; for what secret purpose it was afloat; who were aboard, were but so many unanswerable questions arising in my mind. I stared vainly into the darkness, puzzled and uncertain, impressed alone by the one controlling thought, that some mysterious object, some hidden purpose alone could account for that swift, silent passage. Where could they have come from, unless from that strange Dutch bark riding at anchor off the point below? The passing craft had impressed me as a ship's boat, and no craft of fishermen; and if it really came from the Namur of Rotterdam, had it been sent in answer to·some signal by Sanchez? I could think of nothing else. They must have chosen this late hour purposely; they had doubtless endeavored to slip past us unobserved, seeking some more desolate spot on the coast where they might land unseen. Possibly, deceived by the night, the helmsman had approached closer to the wharf than he had intended; yet, nevertheless, if he held to his present course, he must surely touch shore not more than five hundred yards distant. In all probability that was his purpose.

I stood up, tempted at first to arouse Sam, but deciding almost as quickly that at present this was unnecessary. I had no wish to be the occasion for laughter; it would be better first to ascertain who these parties were, rather than create an unwarranted alarm. The reason-

able probability was they composed merely a party of innocent fishermen, returning home after a day of sport—plantation servants possibly, who having stolen away unobserved, were now endeavoring to
beach their stolen boat, and reach quarters without being seen. This
theory appeared far more reasonable than the other, and, if it proved
true, to arouse the sleepers on deck, would only result in making me
a butt for ridicule. It appeared safe enough for me to adventure alone,
and I was at least determined to assure myself as to the identity of
these strangers. If they had actually landed it would require only a few
moments to ascertain the truth, and I could accomplish this fully as
well by myself, as though accompanied by others—indeed with less
danger of discovery. I quietly lowered my body over the rail, and found
footing on the wharf.

My knowledge of the path to be pursued was extremely vague, for
our arrival had been in the dusk of the evening, so that any observation of the shore lines had been quite casual. I merely remembered
that the bluff rose rather steeply from the water's edge, the path leading upward toward the house crowning the summit, turning and twisting in order to render the climb easier, and finally vanishing entirely
as it approached the crest. Beside this, leading downward straight to
the shore end of the wharf, was the broad slide, along which the bales
and hogsheads of tobacco were sent hurtling on their way to market.
My impression remained that the strip of beach was decidedly narrow,
and generally bordered by a rather thick growth of dwarfed shrub. The
point of land beyond clung dimly in my memory as sparsely wooded,
tapering at its outer extremity into a sand bar against which the restless waves of the Bay broke in lines of foam. The only feasible method
of approach to the spot I now sought would be by following this narrow strip of beach, yet this might be attempted safely, as my movements would be concealed by the darker background of the high bluff
at the left.

In spite of the unfamiliarity of this passage, I succeeded in making
excellent progress, advancing silently along the soft sand, assured I
was safe from observation by reason of the intense darkness. The
waves lapping the beach helped muffle my footsteps, but no other
sound reached my ears, nor could my eyes perceive the slightest

movement along the water surface within reach of vision. The distance proved somewhat greater than anticipated, because of the deep curve in the shore, and I had nearly reached the conclusion that the boat must have rounded the point and gone on, when suddenly I was brought to a halt by a voice speaking in Spanish—one of those harsh, croaking voices never to be reduced to a whisper. Imperfect as was my knowledge of the tongue, I yet managed a fair understanding of what was being said.

"Not the spot, Manuel? Of course it is; do you not suppose I know? The cursed fog made me run in close ashore to where I could see the sloop, so as not to mistake. This is the place, and now there is nothing to do but wait. The Senor—he will be here presently."

"Ay, unless you misread the signal," a somewhat more discreet, but piping voice replied doubtfully. "I saw nothing of all you tell about."

"Because you knew no meaning, nor read the instructions," a touch of anger in the tone. "I tell you it was all written out in that letter brought to me from England on the *Wasp*. They were his last orders, and it was because of them that we anchored off the point yonder, and explored this coast. You saw the Senor touch the handkerchief to his cheek?"

"As he went forward alone—yes, surely."

"It was that motion which bade us come here, Manuel. Once for each cursed plantation along this west coast from the point. He touched the cloth to his cheek but the once, and this is the first. I watched for the sign with care for he is not one with whom to make a mistake."

"Dios de Dios! Do I not know, Estada? Have I not a scar here which tells?"

"True, enough; and have I not received also my lesson—eight hours staked face upward in the sun. So 'tis my very life wagered on this being the place named. Besides 'tis proven by the sloop lying thereby the wharf."

"Where then is the Captain?" perversely unsatisfied.

"At the house yonder on the hill—where else? He knew how it would be, for this is not his first visit to the Bay. 'Twas because of his knowledge he could plan in England. 'Tis the custom of these planters to stop by night along the way, and go ashore; not to camp, but as guests of some friend. Only beforehand it was not possible for him to know which plantation would be the one chosen. That was what he must signal. You see it now?"

"Clearly, Estada; he is the same wary fox as of old."

"Never do they catch him napping," proudly. "Santa Maria! Have I not seen it tried often in ten years?"

"About his plan here? He wrote you his purpose?"

"Not so much as a word; merely the order what to do. Dios! He tells nothing, for he trusts no man. A good thing that. Yet I have my own thought, Manuel."

"And what is that?"

The other hesitated, as though endeavoring to rearrange the idea in his own mind, and possibly doubtful of how much to confide to his companion. When he finally replied his words came forth so swiftly I could scarcely grasp their meaning with my slight knowledge of the tongue.

"'Tis no more than that I make a guess, friend, yet I have been with the Captain for ten years now, and know his way. This planter Fairfax is rich. The letter says nothing of that—no, not a word; but I made inquiries ashore. There is no one more wealthy in these Colonies, and he returns now from London, after the sale of his tobacco crop. No doubt he sold for his neighbors also. 'Tis the way they do, form a combine, and send an agent to England to get the best price. He will surely bear back with him a great sum. This the Senor knows; nor is it the first time he has done the trick, Manuel. Santa Maria! 'Tis the easiest one of all. Then there is the girl."

"The one who was aboard the sloop?"

"Of course. I knew nothing of her, but I have keen eyes, and I have been long with the Senor. Marked you not how he approached her? No sea rover ever had greater desire for women, or won them easier. 'Tis a bright eye and red lip that wins him from all else. Even to me this one looked a rare beauty; yet am I sorry he found her, for it may delay the task here."

"Why must you fear that?"

"Bah! But you are stupid. Who will take by force what may be won by a few soft words?" He paused suddenly, evidently struck by a new thought. "Yet I think, Manuel, the Captain may have failed in this case. I watched their greeting, and her's was not that of love. If this be true, we strike at once, while it is safe."

"Here, you mean—tonight?"

"And why not here, and tonight? Is there a better spot or time? With another night the sloop will be far up the Bay, while now from where we are anchored, we could be beyond the Capes by daybreak, with the broad ocean before us. We are five—six with the Senor—and our ship lies but a short league away, ready for sea. There are only four men on the sloop, with some servants above—spiritless fellows. Why else should he have signaled our coming, unless there was work to do? That will be the plan, to my notion—the money and the girl in one swoop; then a quick sail to the southward. Pist! 'Tis boys' play."

The other seemed to lick his lips, as though the picture thus drawn greatly pleased him.

"Gracioso Dios! I hope 'tis so. It has been dull enough here this month past. I am for blue water, and an English ship to sack."

"Or, better yet, a week at Porto Grande—hey, Manuel? The girls are not so bad, with clink of gold in the pocket after a cruise. Wait, though—there is someone coming down."

I crouched backward into the bushes, and, a moment later, the newcomer moved past me scarcely a yard distant, along the narrow strip of sand. He appeared no more than a black shadow, wrapped in a loose cloak, thus rendered so shapeless as to be scarcely recognizable. Directly opposite my covert he paused peering forward in uncertainty.

"Estada." He spoke the name cautiously, and in doubt.

"Ay, Captain," and another figure, also shapeless, and ill-defined, emerged noiselessly from the gloom. "We await you."

"Good," the tone one of relief. "I rather questioned if you caught my signal. I was watched, and obliged to exercise care. How many have you here?"

"Four, Senor, with Manuel Estevan."

"Quite sufficient; and how about the others?"

"All safely aboard, Senor; asleep in their bunks by now, but ready. Francois LeVere has charge of the deck watch."

"Ah! how happens it the quadroon is with you? A good choice, yet that must mean the *Vengeance* is still at Porto Grande. For what reason?"

"Because of greater injuries than we supposed, Captain. There were two shots in her below the water line, and to get at them we were obliged to beach her. LeVere came with us, expecting this job would be done before now, for by this time the schooner should be in water again, her sides scraped clean of barnacles, fit for any cruise. We have been waiting for you along this coast for several weeks."

"Yes, I know. The boat we intended to take met with an accident, while the one we did take proved the slowest tub that ever sailed. How is it here? Are there suspicions?"

"None, Senor. We have cruised outside most of the time. Only once were we hailed; while Manuel, with a boat crew, was ashore for nearly a week, picking up such news as he might. There is no warship in these waters."

"So I discovered on landing; indeed I was told as much in England. However your disguise is perfect."

Estada laughed.

"There is no mistaking where the *Namur* came from, Senor; she's Holland from keel to topmast, but the best sailing Dutchman I ever saw. You said you were being watched on the sloop. Are you known?" The other uttered an oath snarling through his teeth.

"'Tis nothing," he explained contemptuously. "No more than the bite of a harmless snake in the grass. A dog of a servant who came over with us—one of Monmouth's brood. He has no knowledge of who I am, nor suspicion of my purpose. It is not that, yet the fellow watches me like a hawk. We had some words aboard and there is hate between us"

"If he was indentured, how came he on the sloop?"

"Fairfax bought him. The fellow won the interest of the girl coming over, and she interceded in his behalf. It was my plan to get him into my own hands. I'd have taught him a lesson, but the papers were signed before we landed. Yet the lad is not through with me; I do not let go in a hurry."

"May I ask you your plans, Senor?"

"Yes, I am here to explain. Are we out of ear-shot?"

"None can hear us. Manuel has gone back to the boat."

"Then listen. This planter, Fairfax, has returned from England with a large sum. It is in gold and notes. I have been unable to learn the exact amount, but it represents the proceeds in cash of the tobacco crop of himself, and a number of his neighbors. They pooled, and made him their agent. Without doubt, from all I could ascertain, it will be upward of fifty thousand pounds—not a bad bit of pocket money. This still remains in his possession, but a part will be dispersed tomorrow; so if we hope to gain the whole, we must do so now."

"Fifty thousand pounds, you say? Gracioso Dios! a sum worth fighting for."

"Ay; we've done some hard fighting for less. It is here under our very hands, and there could be no better place than this in which to take it. Everything is ready, and there is not the slightest suspicion of danger—not even a guard set over the treasure. I assured myself of this before coming down."

"Then it is at the house?"

"In an iron-bound chest, carried up from the sloop, and placed in the room assigned to Fairfax for the night. He considers it perfectly safe under his bed. But before we attempt reaching this, we must attend to those men left below on the boat. They are the only dangerous ones, for there are none of the fighting sort up above. Only two servants sleep in the main house, the cook, and a maid, both women. The others are in the slave quarters, a half mile away. Fairfax is vigorous, and will put up a fight, if he has any chance. He must be taken care of, before he does have any. Travers is an old man, to be knocked out with a blow. All we have to fear are those fellows on the sloop, and they will have to be attended to quietly, without any alarm reaching the house. I am going to leave that job to you—it's not your first."

"The old sea orders, Captain?"

"Ay, that will be quicker, and surer," The voice hardened in gust of sudden ferocity. "But, mark you, with one exception—the Englishman is not to be killed, if he can be taken alive. I would deal with him."

"How are we to recognize him from the others?"

"Pish! A blind man would know—he is the only one of that blood on board, taller, and heavier of build, with blond hair. A mistake, and you pay for it. Besides him there are two negroes, and an Irish fool. It matters not what happens to them; a knife to the heart is the more silent; but I would have this Geoffry Carlyle left alive to face me. You will do well to remember."

"I will pass the word to the men."

"See that you do. Then after that," Sanchez went on deliberately, as though murder was of small account, "you will follow me up the bluff. Who are the others with you?"

"Carl Anderson, Pedro Mendez, and Cochose."

"Well chosen; Mendez is the least valuable, and we will leave him with the prisoner at the boat. The big negro, Cochose, together with Manuel, can attend to Travers, and the two negresses—they sleep below. That will leave you and the Swede to get the chest. No firearms, if they can be avoided."

"You are certain of the way, Senor—in the dark?"

"I have been over the house, and drawn a rude diagram. You can look it over in the cabin of the sloop, after affairs have been attended to there. The stairs lead up from the front hall. I will go with you to the door of Fairfax's room."

Estada hesitated, as though afraid to further question his chief, yet finally, in spite of this fear, the query broke from his lips.

"And you, Senor—the girl?"

"What know you of any girl?"

"That there was one on the deck of the sloop—an English beauty. It was when you turned to greet her that you gave me the signal. I merely thought that perhaps—"

"Then stop thinking," burst forth Sanchez, enraged. "Thinking has nothing to do with your work. If there is a girl, I attend to her. Let that suffice. Dios! Am I chief here, or are you? You have my orders, now obey them, and hold your tongue. Bring the men up here."

Without a word, evidently glad to escape thus easily, Estada vanished into the gloom, leaving behind only the vague figure of Sanchez pacing the sands, his lips muttering curses. I dared not move, scarcely indeed to breathe, so closely did he skirt my covert. To venture forth would mean certain discovery; nor could I hope to steal away through the bushes, where any twig might snap beneath my foot. What could I do? How could I bring warning to those sleeping victims? This heartless discussion of robbery and murder left me cold with horror, yet helpless to lift a hand. I had no thought of myself, of my possible fate when once delivered into the hands of this monster, this arch villain, but all my agony of mind centered on the imminent danger confronting Dorothy Fairfax, and those unsuspecting men. All my preconceived impressions of Sanchez had vanished; he was no longer in my imagination a weakling, a boastful, cowardly bravado, a love-sick fool; but a leader of desperate men, a villain of the deepest dye—the dreaded pirate, Black Sanchez, whose deeds of crime were without number, and whose name was infamous. Confronted by Fairfax's ill-guarded gold, maddened by the girl's contemptuous indifference, no deed of violence and blood was too revolting for him to commit. What he could not win by words, he would seize by force and make his own. As coolly as another might sell a bolt of cloth, he would plan murder and rape, and then smilingly watch the execution. And I—what could I do?

The little band of men emerged from the concealment of the fog noiselessly, and gathered into a group about the figure of Sanchez, where he stood motionless awaiting them. I could distinguish no faces, scarcely indeed the outlines of their separate forms in the gloom, but one was an unusually big fellow, far taller and heavier than his companions. When he spoke he possessed a negro's voice, and I recognized him at once for Cochose. The Captain swept his impatient eyes about the circle.

"Lads," he said, incisively, a sharper note of leadership in the tone "it has been a bit quiet for you lately; but now I am back again, and we'll try our luck at sea once more. There must be many a laden ship waiting for us. Does that sound good?"

There was a savage growl of response, a sudden leaning forward of dark figures.

"I thought it would. We'll begin on a job tonight. There are fifty thousand pounds for us in that house yonder, and I waive my share. Estada will explain to you the work I want done; see that you do it quietly and well. By daylight we shall be on blue water, with our course set for Porto Grande. How is it, bullies, do you sniff the salt sea?"

"Ay, ay, Captain."

"And see the pretty girls waiting—and hear the chink of gold?"

"Ay, Senor."

"Then do not fail me tonight—and remember, it is to be the knife. Estada."

"Here, Senor."

"I have forgotten one thing—scuttle the sloop before joining me. 'Tis better to make all safe; and now, strong arms, and good luck. Go to your task, and if one fails me, it will mean the lash at the mast-butt."

They moved off one by one, Estada leading, along the narrow strip of sand, five of them, on their mission of murder. The leader remained alone, his back toward where I crouched, his eyes following their vanishing figures, until the night had swallowed them. I arose silently to my feet, conscious of possessing no weapon, yet fully aware that all hope of thwarting this villainy lay in immediate action. But I must await the right moment. Even with the advantage of surprise, there would inevitably be the noise of struggle. I had in the past despised Sanchez, but I had never yet tested him as a fighting man, and, indeed, no longer considered the fellow to be a mean antagonist. Remembering who he was, I now realized fully the desperate nature of my attempt, the need of quick, remorseless action. Nevertheless I dared not attack until assured that those men he had just dispatched were safely beyond ear-shot. I could hear or see nothing of them; they had vanished utterly, and the soft sand returned no echo of their footsteps. Time alone gave me judgment as to the distance they would travel. If I yielded too much of this, they might attain the sloop before I could sound an alarm; while if I moved too quickly the noise would bring them back to the rescue. The moments were agony, as I bent tensely forward, poised for a leap. God! I could wait no longer!

Sanchez had turned slightly, apparently immersed in thought, and stood with his face toward the Bay. Even in that darkness his position was that of a man intently listening for the slightest sound to reach him out of the black night. I ventured a cautious step forward, and stood on the open sand, scarcely a yard to his rear, every nerve throbbing, my lips still silently counting the seconds. I could not, I dared not wait longer. Some vague sense of my presence must have influenced the man, for he swung suddenly about, uttering a stifled cry of startled

143

surprise, as we met face to face. For an instant we were locked so closely within each other's desperate grip, his head bent beneath my arm, with my fingers clutching at his throat to block any call for help, that he possessed no knowledge of his assailant's identity. But the man was like a tiger, possessed of immense strength encased in a wiry frame. The surprise of attack was to my advantage, yet almost before I realized what was being done, he had rallied, broken my first hold, and his eyes were glaring straight into mine. Then he knew me, signaling his discovery with an oath, his free hand instantly grasping at the knife concealed beneath his loose cloak. Even as he jerked it forth, I crushed his wrist within my fingers, forcing his fore-arm back. Breast to breast we wrestled for mastery, every muscle strained, our feet firm planted on the sand. There was no outcry, no noise, except that of our heavy breathing, and trampling feet. Personal hatred had ascendancy in both our hearts—I doubt if he ever thought of aught else but the desire to kill me there with his own hands. Only once did he even utter a word, hissing out the sentence as though it were a poison:

"To hell with you, you sneaking English cur!"

"Then I travel that road not alone," I muttered back. "There will be one less of the devil's brood afloat."

What followed has to me no clearness, no consistency. I remember, yet it is as though memory played me a thousand tricks. Never have I fought more wickedly, nor with deeper realization that I needed every ounce of strength, and every trick of wit and skill. I had not before dreamed he was such a man; but now I knew the fellow possessed greater knowledge of the game than I, and a quicker movement; I alone excelled in weight of body, and coolness of brain. His efforts were those of an infuriated animal, his uncontrolled outburst of hatred rendering him utterly reckless of results in his struggle to overcome me at any cost. It was this blind blood-lust which gave me victory. I know not clearly how it was done; my only memory being his frantic efforts to drive home the knife point, and mine to defeat the thrust. Twice he pricked me deep enough to draw blood, before I succeeded in twisting backward the arm with which he held the blade. It was a sailor's trick of last resort, heartlessly cruel in its agony, but I felt then no call to mercy. He met the game too late, falling half back upon one knee, hoping thus to foil my purpose, yet my greater weight saved me. There was the sharp crack of a bone, as his useless fingers let the knife drop, a snarled curse of pain, and then, with the rage of a mad dog, Sanchez struck his teeth deep into my cheek. The sharp pang of pain drove me to frenzy, and for the first time I lost all control, my one free hand seeking to reach the lost knife. With a thrill of exultation I gripped it, driving instantly the keen blade to its hilt into the man's side. He made no cry, no struggle—the set teeth unlocked, and he fell limply back on the sand, his head lapped by the waves.

I remained poised above him, spent and breathless from struggle, scarcely conscious even as to what had occurred so swiftly, the dripping knife in my hand, blood streaming down my cheek, and still infuriated by blind passion. The fellow lay motionless, his face upturned to the sky, but invisible except in dim outline. It did not seem possible he could actually be dead; I had struck blindly, with no knowledge as to where the keen blade had penetrated—a mere desperate lunge. I rested my ear over his heart, detecting no murmur of response; touched the veins of his wrist, but found there no answering throb of life. Still dazed and uncertain, I arose staggering to my feet, conscious at last that the man must actually be dead, yet, for the moment, so surprised by the discovery as to scarcely realize its significance. Not that I regretted the act, not that I experienced the slightest remorse, yet, for an instant, the shock seemed to leave me nerveless and unstrung. Only a moment since I was engaged in desperate struggle, and now I could only stare down at the dark lines of that motionless body outstretched upon the sand.

Then I remembered those others—the unconscious sleepers on the deck of the sloop; those blood-stained villains creeping toward them through the black shadows of the night. The memory was like a dash of water in the face. With the death-dealing knife still gripped in my hand, I raced forward along the narrow strip of sand, reckless of what I might encounter, eager only to arrive in time to give utterance to a shout of warning. I could not have covered more than half the distance when the first sound of attack reached me—far-off, gurgling cry of agony, which pierced the darkness like the scream of a dying soul. The heart leaped into my throat, yet I ran on, unhalted, unseen, until the planks of the wharf were beneath my feet, the low side of the sloop looming black before me. There was confusion aboard, the sounds of struggle, mingled with curses and blows. With one upward swing of my body I was safely aboard, knife still in hand, peering eagerly forward. Through the gloom concealing the deck, I could perceive only dim figures, a riot of men, battling furiously hand to hand, yet out of the ruck loomed through the darkness in larger outline than the others—Cochose, the negro. I leaped at the fellow, and struck with the keen knife, missing the heart, but plunging the blade deep into the flesh of the shoulder. The next instant I was in a bear's grip, the very breath crushed out of me, yet, by some chance, my one arm remained free, and I drove the sharp steel into him twice before he forced the weapon from my fingers. Through a wrestler's trick, although my wrist was as numb as if dead from his fierce grip, I thrust an elbow beneath the brute's chin, and thus forced his head back, until the neck cracked.

This respite served merely for the moment, yet sufficiently long to win me a firm foot-hold on deck, and a breath of night air. He was too strong, too immense of stature. Apparently unweakened by his wounds, the giant negro, thoroughly aroused, exerted his mighty muscles, and, despite my utmost effort at resistance, thrust me back against the stern rail, where the weight of his body pinned me helplessly. With a roar of rage he drove his huge fist into my face, but happily was too close to give much force to the blow. My own hands, gripping the neck-band of his coarse shirt, twisted it tight about the great throat, until, in desperation, panting for breath, the huge brute actually lifted me in his arms, and hurled me backward, headlong over the rail. I struck something as I fell, yet rebounding from this, splashed into the deep water, and went down so nearly unconscious as to make not even the slightest struggle. I had no strength left in me, no desire to save myself, and I sank like a stone. And yet I came up once more to the surface, arising by sheer chance, directly beneath the small dory—which my body must have struck as I fell—towing by a painter astern of the sloop, and fortunately retained sense enough to cling desperately to this first thing my hands touched, and thus remained concealed.

This occurred through complete exhaustion, rather than the exercising of any judgment, for, had it not been for this providential support, I would surely have drowned without a struggle. Every breath I drew was in pain; I felt as though my ribs had been crushed in, while I had lost sufficient blood to leave me as weak as a babe. I simply clung there desperately, hopelessly, yet the salt water soon served to revive me physically, and even my brain began to arouse from its daze to a faint realization of the conditions. The small dory to which I clung, caught in some mysterious current, floated at the very extremity of its slender towline, and in consequence the sloop appeared little more than a mere smudge, when my eyes endeavored to discover its outlines. Evidently the bloody work had been completed, for now all was silent on board. I could not even detect the sound of a footstep on the deck. Then, clear enough to be distinctly heard across the narrow strip of water, came the voice of Estada, in a gruff inquiry:

"So you are hiding here, Cochose? What are you looking for in the sea?"

"What? Why that damned Englishman." The response was a savage growl, intensified by husky dialect. "Mon Dieu! He fought me like a mad rat."

"The Englishman, you say? He was here then? It was he you battled with? What became of the fellow?"

"He went down there, Senor. The dog stabbed me three times. It was either he or I to go."

"You mean you threw him overboard?"

"Ay, with his ribs crushed in, and not a breath left in his damned body. He's never come up even—I've watched, and there has not been so much as a ripple where he sank."

The two must have hung in silence over the rail staring down. I dared not advance my head to look, nor even move a muscle of my body in the water, but both were still standing there when Estada finally gave utterance to an oath.

"How know you it was the man?"

"Who else could it have been? You have the others."

"Ay, true enough; yet it will go hard with you, Cochose, when the Captain learns of this—he would have the fellow alive."

"As well attempt to take a tiger with bare hands—see, the blood yet runs; a single inch to the left, and it would be I fed to the fishes. Pah! What is the difference, Senor, so the man dies?"

"Right enough, no doubt; anyway it is not I who must face Sanchez, and it is too late now to change fate. Let's to the rest of our task. You can still do your part?"

The giant negro growled.

"Ay; I have been worse hurt, yet a bit of cloth would help me."

"Let Carl see to that, while I gain glimpse at this map of the house up yonder. Come forward with me to the cabin, till I light a candle. How came you aft here?"

"Because that fellow leaped the rail from the wharf. I saw him, and we met at the wheel."

"From the wharf, you say? He was not aboard then? Santa Maria! I know not what that may mean. Yet what difference, so he be dead. Anderson, Mendez, throw that carrion overboard—no, bullies, never mind; let them lie where they are, and sink an auger in the sloop's bottom. That will settle the whole matter. What is that out yonder, Cochose?"

"A small boat, Senor—a dory, I make it."

"Cut the rope, and send it adrift. Now come along with me."

The darker loom of the sloop vanished slowly, as the slight current sweeping about the end of the wharf drifted the released boat to which I clung outward into the Bay. The faint echo of a voice floated to my ears across the widening expanse of water, and then all was silent as the night closed in darkly between. There was scarcely a ripple to the sea, and yet I felt that the boat was steadily drifting out into deeper water. I was still strangely weak, barely able to retain my grasp, with a peculiar dullness in my head, which made me fearful that at any moment I might let go. I was not even conscious of thinking, or capable of conceiving clearly my situation, yet I must have realized vaguely the immediate necessity of action, for finally I mustered every ounce of remaining energy in one supreme effort, and succeeded in dragging my body up out of water over the boat's stern, sinking helplessly forward into the bottom. The moment this was accomplished every sense deserted me, and I lay there motionless, totally unconscious.

I shall never know how long I remained thus, the little dory in which I lay rocked aimlessly about by the waves, and constantly drifting in the grasp of unseen currents farther and farther out into the Bay. The blackness of the night swallowed us, as tossed by wind and sea, we were borne on through the waste unguided. Yet this time could not have been great. As though awakening from sleep a faint consciousness returned, causing me to lift my head, and stare hopelessly about into the curtain of mist overhanging the water. At first, with nothing surrounding to awaken memory into action, only that dull vista of sea and sky, my mind refused to respond to any impression; then the sharp pain of my wounds, accented by the sting of salt water, brought me swift realization of where I was, and the circumstances bringing methere. My wet clothing had partially dried on my body as I lay there motionless in the bottom of the boat, and now, with every movement, chafed the raw spots, rendering the slightest motion a physical agony. I had evidently lost considerable blood, yet this had already ceased to flow, and a very slight examination served to convince me that the knife slashes were none of them serious. Beyond these punctures of the flesh, while I ached from head to foot, my other injuries were merely bruises to add to my discomfort—the result of blows dealt me by Sanchez and Cochose, aggravated by the bearlike hug of the giant negro. Indeed, I awoke to the discovery that I was far from being a dead man; and, inspired by this knowledge, the various incidents of the night flashed swiftly back into my mind. How long had I been lying there unconscious, adrift in the open boat? How far had we floated from land? Where were we now, and in the meantime what had occurred ashore? These were questions impossible to answer. I could not even attempt their solution. No gleam of light appeared in any direction; no sound echoed across the dark waste of water. Far above, barely visible through a floating veil of haze, I was able to detect the faint gleam of stars, and was sailor enough to determine through their guidance some certainty as to the points of compass; yet possessed no means by which to ascertain the time of night, or the position of the boat. With this handicap it was clearly impossible for me to attempt any return to the wharf through the impenetrable black curtain which shut me in. What then could I do? What might I still hope to accomplish? At first thought the case appeared hopeless. Those fellows had swept the sloop clean, and had doubtless long ago scuttled it. This ruthless deed once accomplished, their orders were to raid the house on the bluff. But would they go on with their bloody work? They would suddenly find themselves leaderless, unguided. Would that suffice to stop them? The vivid memory came to me anew of that arch villain, Sanchez, lying where I had left him, his head resting in the surf—dead. Would the discovery of his body halt his followers, and send them rushing back to their boat, eager only to get safely away? This did not seem likely. Estada knew of my boarding the sloop from the wharf, and would at once connect the fact of my being ashore with the killing of Sanchez. This would satisfy him there was no further danger. Besides, these were not men to be easily frightened at sight of a dead body, even that of their own captain. They might hesitate, discuss, but they would never flee in panic. Surely not with that ruffian Estada yet alive to lead them, and the knowledge that fifty thousand pounds was yonder in that unguarded house, with no one to protect the treasure but two old men asleep, and the women. The women!—Dorothy! What would become of her? Into whose hands would she fall in that foul division of spoils? Estada's? Good God—yes! And I, afloat and helpless in this boat, what could I do?

THE SUCCESSFUL PIRATE

Charles Ellms

CHAPTER NINE

All other pirates were destined to be eclipsed in fame by Henry Every, alias Bridgman, who now made his appearance in the Indian seas. His exploits, the great wealth he amassed by piracy, and his reputed marriage with a Mogul princess, continued to excite the public mind long after he had disappeared from the scene. Several biographies of him were written, one of them attributed to Defoe, all of them containing great exaggerations; and a play, *The Successful Pirate*, was written in his honour. His biographers generally give his name as John Avery, but it was as is here given. According to the account of Van Broeck, a Dutchman, who was detained on board his ship for a time, and was on good terms with him, he was born at Plymouth, the son of a trading captain who had served in the navy under Blake. Every himself served in the navy, in the *Resolution* and *Edgar*, before he got the command of a merchant ship, in which he made several voyages to the West Indies. In May, 1694, he was first mate of the *Charles the Second*, one of the small squadron of English ships hired from Sir James Houblon, by the Spanish Government, to act against French smugglers who were troubling their Peruvian trade.

The Spaniards were bad paymasters, and Houblon's squadron was detained at Corunna three or four months, while the crews became more and more discontented as their wages remained unpaid. As their sense of grievance increased, a plot was formed among the most turbulent spirits to seize a ship and turn rovers, under Every's command.

On the night of the 30th May, the captain of the *Charles the Second* was made prisoner while in bed. A boat-load of men sent from the James to prevent the capture, joined the mutineers; the cables were cut, and the ship ran out of harbour. The captain and all who were unwilling to join were put into a boat, and the *Charles*, renamed the *Fancy*, was headed south for the coast of Africa. The only man detained against his will was the doctor, as he was a useful man.

Some months were spent on the Guinea coast, where some negroes were captured, and five ships—three English and two Danish—were plundered and burnt. Before the end of the year Every was east of the Cape, intent on the Red Sea traders. The first intelligence of him that reached Bombay was in May, 1695, when three outward-bound merchantmen reported that they had seen him at Johanna.

> *Your Honor's ships going into that island gave him chase, but he was too nimble for them by much, having taken down a great deale of his upper works and made her exceeding snugg, which advantage being added to her well sailing before, causes her to sail so hard now, that she fears not who follows her. This ship will undoubtedly (go) into the Red Sea, which will procure infinite clamours at Surat.*

Accompanying this report came the following characteristic letter from Every:

> *February y'e 28th, 1695/4.*

> *To all English. Commanders lett this Satisfye that I was Riding here att this Instant in y'e Ship fancy man of Warr formerly the Charles of y'e Spanish Expedition who departed from Croniae y'e 7th of May, 94: Being and am now in A Ship of 46 guns 150 Men & bound to Seek our fortunes I have Never as Yett Wronged any English or Dutch nor never Intend whilst I am Commander. Wherefore as I Commonly Speake w'th all Ships I Desire who ever Comes to y'e perusal of this to take this Signall that if you or aney whome you may informe*

*are desirous to know w't wee are att a Distance then make
your Antient Vp in a Ball or Bundle and hoyst him att y'e
Mizon Peek y'e Mizon Being furled I shall answere w'th y'e
same & Never Molest you: for my men are hungry Stout and
Resolute: & should they Exceed my Desire I cannott help my
selfe as Yett.*

An Englishman's friend
HENRY EVERY.

*Here is 160 od French armed men now att Mohilla who waits
for Opportunity of getting aney ship, take Care of your Selves.*

According to Van Broeck, he was a man of good natural disposition, who had been soured by the bad treatment he received at the hands of his relations. The letter shows him to have been a man of some education, and during his short but active career in the Indian seas he appears to have attacked native ships only. The Company's records do not mention the loss of a single English ship at Every's hands, a circumstance that no doubt told heavily against the English in native opinion at Surat.

The same ships that brought Every's letter to Sir John Gayer brought intelligence of a well-known French pirate having got aground at Mohilla. The three Company's ships watering at Johanna heard of the occurrence, and proceeded to the spot, burnt the French ship after taking out what treasure was on board, and captured six of the Frenchmen, who were brought to Bombay. Every's friendly warning about the "160 od French armed men" evidently referred to the wrecked crew.

The value of Perim, or Bab's Key, as it was then called by mariners, to command the trade of the Red Sea, was at once perceived by Every, who attempted to make a settlement there. After some unprofitable digging for water, he abandoned the project, and established himself in Madagascar, which had before this become known as a pirate resort. During the next thirty years the only traders who dared show themselves on the Madagascar coast were those who did business with the pirates, owing to the number of pirate settlements that sprang up at different points; the best known being at St. Mary's Island, St. Augustine's, Port Dauphin, and Charnock's Point. They built themselves forts and established a reign of terror over the surrounding country, sometimes taking a part in native quarrels, and sometimes fighting among themselves; dubbing themselves kings, and living in squalid dignity with large seraglios of native women. Captain Woodes Rogers, who touched at Madagascar for slaves, sixteen years after Every's time, described those he met as having been on the islands above twenty-five years, with a motley crowd of children and grandchildren.

> *Having been so many years upon this Island, it may be imagined their Cloaths had long been worn out, so that their Majesties were extremely out at the Elbows: I cannot say they were ragged, since they had no Cloaths, they had nothing to cover them but the Skins of Beasts without any tanning, but with all the Hair on, nor a Shoe nor Stocking, so they looked like the Pictures of Hercules in the Lion's Skin; and being overgrown with Beard, and Hair upon their Bodies, they appeared the most savage Figures that a Man's Imagination can frame.*

One remarkable settlement was founded in the north, near Diego Suarez, by Misson, a Frenchman, and the most humane of pirates, with whom was allied Tew, the English pirate. Misson's aim was to build a fortified town "that they might have some place to call their own; and a receptacle, when age and wounds had rendered them incapable of hardship, where they might enjoy the fruits of their labour and go to their graves in peace." The settlement was named Libertatia. Slavery was not permitted, and freed slaves were encouraged to settle there. The harbour was strongly fortified, as a Portuguese squadron that attacked them found to its cost. A dock was made; crops were sown; a Lord Conservator was appointed for three years, with a Parliament to make laws. The colony was still in its infancy when it was surprised and destroyed by the natives, while Misson was away on a cruise; and so Libertatia came to an end. Tew succeeded in escaping to his sloop with a quantity of diamonds and gold in bars. On Misson rejoining him, they determined to go to America. Misson's ship foundered in a storm, while Tew made his way to Rhode Island, and lived there for a time unquestioned. But the fascinations of a rover's life were too much for him. He fitted out a sloop and made again for the Red Sea, and was killed in action there with a Mogul ship.

From their Madagascar settlements the pirates scoured the east coast of Africa, the Indian Ocean as far as Sumatra, the mouth of the Red Sea, where the Mocha ships offered many rich prizes, the Malabar coast, and the Gulf of Oman. From time to time, ships from New England and the West Indies brought supplies and recruits, taking back those who were tired of the life, and who wished to enjoy their booty. European prisoners were seldom treated barbarously when there was no resistance, and the pirate crews found many recruits among captured merchantmen. Their worst cruelties were reserved for the native merchants of India who fell into their hands. They believed all native traders to be possessed of jewels, as was indeed often the case, and the cruellest tortures were inflicted on them to make them surrender their valuables. One unhappy Englishman we hear of, Captain Sawbridge, who was taken by pirates, while on a voyage to Surat with a ship-load of Arab horses from Bombay. His complaints and expostulations were so annoying to his captors that, after repeatedly telling him to hold his tongue, they took a sail needle and twine and sewed his lips together. They kept him thus several hours, with his hands tied behind him, while they plundered his ship, which they afterwards set on fire, burning her and the horses in her. Sawbridge and his people were carried to Aden and set on shore, where he died soon after.

Before long, Every made some notable captures. Off Aden he found five pirate ships of English nationality, three of them from America, commanded by May, Farrell, and Wake. In the Gulf of Aden he burned the town of Mahet on the Somali coast because the people refused to trade with him. In September, while cruising off Socotra with the *Fancy*, two sloops, and a galley, he took the *Futteh Mahmood* with a valuable cargo, belonging to Abdool Quffoor, the wealthiest and most influential merchant in Surat. A few days later he took off Sanjan, north of Bombay, a ship belonging to the Emperor, called the *Gunj Suwaie* (*Exceeding Treasure*).

This was the great capture that made Every famous. According to the legend, there was a granddaughter of Aurungzeeb on board, whom Every wedded by the help of a moollah, and carried off to Madagascar. But the story is only the most sensational of the many romantic inventions that have accumulated round Every's name. The native historian who relates the capture of the *Gunj Suwaie*, and who had friends on board, would certainly not have refrained from mentioning such an event if it had occurred; nor would the Mogul Emperor have failed to wreak vengeance on the English for such an insult to his family.

The *Gunj Suwaie* was the largest ship belonging to the port of Surat. It carried eighty guns and four hundred matchlocks, besides other warlike implements, and was deemed so strong that it disdained the help of a convoy. On this occasion it was returning from the Red Sea with the result of the season's trading, amounting to fifty-two lakhs of rupees in silver and gold, and having on board a number of Mahommedan ladies returning from pilgrimage to Mecca. In spite of the disparity of force, Every bore down and engaged. The first gun was fired by the *Gunj Suwaie* burst, killing three or four men and wounding others. The main mast was badly damaged by Every's broadsides, and the *Fancy* ran alongside and boarded. This was the moment when a decent defence should have been made.

The sailor's cutlass was a poor match for the curved sword and shield, so much so that the English were notorious in the East for their want of boldness in sword-play. But Ibrahim Khan, the captain, was a coward, and ran below at the sight of the white faces. His crew followed his example, and the vessel was taken almost without resistance.

So rich a prize was not to be relinquished without a very complete search. For a whole week the *Gunj Suwaie* was rummaged from stem to stern, while the crew of the *Fancy* indulged in a horrible orgy, excited beyond measure by the immense booty that had fallen into their hands. Several of the women threw themselves into the sea or slew themselves with daggers; the last piece of silver was sought out and carried on board the *Fancy*, the last jewel torn from the passengers and crew, and then the *Gunj Suwaie* was left to find its way to Surat as it best could.

The vials of long-accumulated wrath were poured out on the English. Instigated by Abdul Guffoor, the populace of Surat flew to arms to wreak vengeance on the factory. The Governor, Itimad Khan, was well disposed to the English, but popular excitement ran so high that he found it difficult to protect them. Guards were placed on the factory to save it from plunder. A mufti urged that the English should be put to death in revenge for the death of so many true believers, and quoted an appropriate text from the Koran. Soon came an order from Aurungzeeb directing the Seedee to march on Bombay, and for all the English in Surat and Broach to be made prisoners. President Annesley and the rest, sixty-three in all, were placed in irons, and so remained eleven months. To make matters worse, news arrived of Every having captured the *Rampura*, a Cambay ship with a cargo valued at Rs.1,70,000.

"It is strange," wrote Sir John Gayer, "to see how almost all the merchants are incensed against our nation, reproaching the Governor extremely for taking our part, and as strange to see that notwithstanding all, he stems the stream against them more than well could be imagined, considering his extreme timorous nature."

The strangeness of the merchants' hostility is hardly apparent, but it is not too much to say that Itimad Khan's friendly behaviour alone saved English trade from extinction. The Dutch, always hostile in the East, whatever might be the relations between Holland and England in Europe, strove to improve the occasion by fomenting popular excitement, and tried to get the English permanently excluded from the Indian trade. In the words of Sir John Grayer, "they retained their Edomitish principles, and rejoice to see Jacob laid low." But Itimad Khan knew that the pirates were of all nationalities, and refused to hold the English alone responsible. To propitiate the Governor, Sir John Gayer made over to him the six French pirates taken at Mohilla, not without qualms at handing over Christians to Mahommedan mercies. He fully expected that the treasure taken out of the wreck would also be demanded of him; but Itimad Khan was not an avaricious man, and no such demand was made. "His contempt of money is not to be paralleled by any of the King's Umbraws or Governors," Sir John wrote, a year later, when Itimad Khan was dead. To forestall the Dutch with the Emperor, Gayer sent an agent offering to convoy the Red Sea fleet for the future, in return for a yearly payment of four lakhs a year. The offer was refused, but it served to place the English in a more favourable light, and to procure the cancelling of orders that had been given for attacking Bombay and Madras. Had it been accepted, the Seedee would have been added to the number of the Company's enemies. The Dutch, not to be outdone, offered to perform the same service in return for a monopoly of trade in the Emperor's dominions.

This brought all other Europeans into line against the Dutch proposal, and the intrigue was defeated. The embargo on all European trade at Surat was maintained, while the Dutch, French, and English were directed to scour the seas and destroy the pirates. It was further ordered that Europeans on shore were not to carry arms or use palanquins, and their ships were forbidden to hoist their national flags. The Dutch and French hung back. They would not send a ship to sea without payment, except for their own affairs. Sir John Gayer, more wisely, sent armed ships to convoy the Mocha fleet, at the Company's charge, and so the storm passed off.

Meanwhile, Every, glutted with booty, made up his mind to retire with his enormous gains. According to Johnson, he gave the slip, at night, to his consorts, sailed for Providence in the Bahamas, where his crew dispersed, and thence made his way to England, just at the time a royal proclamation offering £500 for his apprehension was published. The reward was doubled by an offer of four thousand rupees from the Company; eight rupees being the equivalent of a pound at that time. Several of his crew also straggled home and were captured; but before he left the Indian coast, twenty-five Frenchmen, fourteen Danes, and some English were put ashore, fearing to show themselves in Europe or America. This fact would seem to throw some doubt on the account of his having left his consorts by stealth.

On the 19th October, 1696, six of his crew were tried and sentenced at the Old Bailey, and a true bill was found and an indictment framed against Every himself, though he had not been apprehended. According to Johnson, Every changed his name and lived unostentatiously, while trying to sell the jewels he had amassed. The merchant in whose hands he had placed them, suspecting how they had been come by, threatened him.

Every fled to Ireland, leaving his jewels in the merchant's hands, and finally died in Devonshire in extreme poverty. But the authority for this, as for most of the popular accounts of Every, is extremely doubtful. That he was cheated out of some of his ill-gotten gains is probable enough, but it is in the highest degree improbable that he was known to be living in poverty, and yet that the large reward offered for his apprehension was not earned. What is alone certain is that he was never apprehended, and that in a few months he carried off an amount of plunder such as never before was taken out of the Indian seas by a single rover. For long he was the hero of every seaport town in England and North America; innumerable legends gathered round his name, and an immense impulse was given to piracy.

THE LIFE OF LAFITTE

Charles Ellms

CHAPTER TEN

Jean Lafitte was born at St. Maloes in France, in 1781, and went to sea at the age of thirteen; after several voyages in Europe, and to the coast of Africa, he was appointed mate of a French East Indiaman, bound to Madras. On the outward passage they encountered a heavy gale off the Cape of Good Hope, which sprung the mainmast and otherwise injured the ship, which determined the captain to bear up for the Mauritius, where he arrived in safety; a quarrel having taken place on the passage out between Lafitte and the captain, he abandoned the ship and refused to continue the voyage. Several privateers were at this time fitting out at this island, and Lafitte was appointed captain of one of these vessels; after a cruise during which he robbed the vessels of other nations, besides those of England, and thus committing piracy, he stopped at the Seychelles, and took in a load of slaves for the Mauritius; but being chased by an English frigate as far north as the equator, he found himself in a very awkward condition; not having provisions enough on board his ship to carry him back to the French Colony. He therefore conceived the bold project of proceeding to the Bay of Bengal, in order to get provisions from on board some English ships. In his ship of two hundred tons, with only two guns and twenty-six men, he attacked and took an English armed schooner with a numerous crew. After putting nineteen of his own crew on board the schooner, he took the command of her and proceeded to cruise upon the coast of Bengal. He there fell in with the *Pagoda*, a vessel belonging to the English East India Company, armed with twenty-six twelve pounders and manned with one hundred and fifty men. Expecting that the enemy would take him for a pilot of the Ganges, he manoeuvred accordingly. The *Pagoda* manifested no suspicions, whereupon he suddenly darted with his brave followers upon her decks, overturned all who opposed them, and speedily took the ship. After a very successful cruise he arrived safe at the Mauritius, and took the command of *La Confiance* of twenty-six guns and two hundred and fifty men, and sailed for the coast of British India. Off the Sand Heads in October, 1807, Lafitte fell in with the *Queen East Indiaman*, with a crew of near four hundred men, and carrying forty guns; he conceived the bold project of getting possession of her. Never was there beheld a more unequal conflict; even the height of the vessel compared to the feeble privateer augmented the chances against Lafitte; but the difficulty and danger far from discouraging this intrepid sailor, acted as an additional spur to his brilliant valor. After electrifying his crew with a few words of hope and ardor, he manoeuvred and ran on board of the enemy. In this position he received a broadside when close too; but he expected this, and made his men lay flat upon the deck. After the first fire they all rose, and from the yards and tops, threw bombs and grenades into the forecastle of the *Indiaman*. This sudden and unforeseen attack caused a great havoc. In an instant, death and terror made them abandon a part of the vessel near the mizen-mast. Lafitte, who observed every thing, seized the decisive moment, beat to arms, and forty of his crew prepared to board, with pistols in their hands and daggers held between their teeth. As soon as they got on deck, they rushed upon the affrighted crowd, who retreated to the steerage, and endeavored to defend themselves there. Lafitte thereupon ordered a second division to board, which he headed himself; the captain of the Indiaman was killed, and all were swept away in a moment. Lafitte caused a gun to be loaded with grape, which he pointed towards the place where the crowd was assembled, threatening to exterminate them. The English deeming resistance fruitless, surrendered, and Lafitte hastened to put a stop to the slaughter. This exploit, hitherto unparalleled, resounded through India, and the name of Lafitte became the terror of English commerce in these latitudes.

As British vessels now traversed the Indian Ocean under strong convoys, game became scarce, and Lafitte determined to visit France;

and after doubling the Cape of Good Hope, he coasted up to the Gulf of Guinea, and in the Bight of Benin, took two valuable prizes loaded with gold dust, ivory, and palm oil; with this booty he reached St. Maloes in safety. After a short stay at his native place he fitted out a brigantine, mounting twenty guns and one hundred and fifty men, and sailed for Gaudaloupe; amongst the West India Islands, he made several valuable prizes; but during his absence on a cruise the island having been taken by the British, he proceeded to Carthagena, and from thence to Barrataria. After this period, the conduct of Lafitte at Barrataria does not appear to be characterized by the audacity and boldness of his former career; but he had amassed immense sums of booty, and as he was obliged to have dealings with the merchants of the United States, and the West Indies, who frequently owed him large sums, and the cautious dealings necessary to found and conduct a colony of Pirates and Smugglers in the very teeth of a civilized nation, obliged Lafitte to cloak as much as possible his real character.

As we have said before, at the period of the taking of Gaudaloupe by the British, most of the privateers commissioned by the government of that island, and which were then on a cruise, not being able to return to any of the West India Islands, made for Barrataria, there to take in a supply of water and provisions, recruit the health of their crews, and dispose of their prizes, which could not be admitted into any of the ports of the United States, we being at that time in peace with Great Britain. Most of the commissions granted to privateers by the French government at Gaudaloupe, having expired sometime after the declaration of the independence of Carthagena, many of the privateers repaired to that port, for the purpose of obtaining from the new government commissions for cruising against Spanish vessels. Having duly obtained their commissions, they in a manner blockaded for a long time all the ports belonging to the royalists, and made numerous captives, which they carried into Barrataria. Under this denomination is comprised part of the coast of Louisiana to the west of the mouths of the Mississippi, comprehended between Bastien bay on the east, and the mouths of the river or bayou la Fourche on the west. Not far from the sea are lakes called the great and little lakes of Barrataria, communicating with one another by several large bayous with a great number of branches. There is also the island of

Barrataria, at the extremity of which is a place called the Temple, which denomination it owes to several mounds of shells thrown up there by the Indians. The name of Barrataria is also given to a large basin which extends the whole length of the cypress swamps, from the Gulf of Mexico to three miles above New Orleans. These waters disembogue into the gulf by two entrances of the bayou Barrataria, between which lies an island called Grand Terre, six miles in length, and from two to three miles in breadth, running parallel with the coast. In the western entrance is the great pass of Barrataria, which has from nine to ten feet of water. Within this pass about two leagues from the open sea, lies the only secure harbor on the coast, and accordingly this was the harbor frequented by the Pirates, so well known by the name of Barratarians.

At Grand Jerre, the privateers publicly made sale by auction, of the cargoes of their prizes. From all parts of Lower Louisiana, people resorted to Barrataria, without being at all solicitous to conceal the object of their journey. The most respectable inhabitants of the state, especially those living in the country, were in the habit of purchasing smuggled goods coming from Barrataria.

The government of the United States sent an expedition under Commodore Patterson, to disperse the settlement of marauders at Barrataria; the following is an extract of his letter to the secretary of war.

"Sir—I have the honor to inform you that I departed from this city on the 11th June, accompanied by Col. Ross, with a detachment of seventy of the 44th regiment of infantry. On the 12th, reached the schooner *Carolina*, of Plaquemine, and formed a junction with the gun vessels at the Balize on the 13th, sailed from the southwest pass on the evening of the 15th, and at half past 8 o'clock, A.M. on the 16th, made the Island of Barrataria, and discovered a number of vessels in the harbor, some of which shewed Carthagenian colors. At 2 o'clock, perceived the pirates forming their vessels, ten in number, including prizes, into a line of battle near the entrance of the harbor, and making every preparation to offer me battle. At 10 o'clock, wind light and variable, formed the order of battle with six gun boats and the *Sea Horse* tender, mounting one six pounder and fifteen men, and a launch mounting one twelve pound carronade; the schooner *Carolina*, drawing too much water to cross the bar. At half past 10 o'clock, perceived several smokes along the coasts as signals, and at the same time a white flag hoisted on board a schooner at the fort, an American flag at the mainmast head and a Carthagenian flag (under which the pirates cruise) at her topping lift; replied with a white flag at my main; at 11 o'-clock, discovered that the pirates had fired two of their best schooners; hauled down my white flag and made the signal for battle; hoisting with a large white flag bearing the words 'Pardon for Deserters'; having heard there was a number on shore from the army and navy. At a quarter past 11 o'clock, two gun boats grounded and were passed agreeably to my previous orders, by the other four which entered the harbor, manned by my barge and the boats belonging to the grounded vessels, and proceeded in to my great disappointment. I perceived that the pirates abandoned their vessels, and were flying in all directions. I immediately sent the launch and two barges with small boats in pursuit of them. At meridian, took possession of all their vessels in the harbor consisting of six schooners and one felucca, cruisers, and prizes of the pirates, one brig, a prize, and two armed schooners under the Carthagenian flag, both in the line of battle, with the armed vessels of the pirates, and apparently with an intention to aid them in any resistance they might make against me, as their crews were at quarters, tompions out of their guns, and matches lighted. Col. Ross at the same time landed, and with his command took possession of their establishment on shore, consisting of about forty houses of different sizes, badly constructed, and thatched with palmetto leaves.

"When I perceived the enemy forming their vessels into a line of battle I felt confident from their number and very advantageous position, and their number of men, that they would have fought me; their not doing so I regret; for had they, I should have been enabled more effectually to destroy or make prisoners of them and their leaders; but it is a subject of great satisfaction to me, to have effected the object of my enterprise, without the loss of a man.

"The enemy had mounted on their vessels twenty pieces of cannon of different calibre; and as I have since learnt, from eight hundred, to one thousand men of all nations and colors.

"Early in the morning of the 20th, the *Carolina* at anchor, about five miles distant, made the signal of a 'strange sail in sight to eastward';

immediately after she weighed anchor, and gave chase the strange sail, standing for Grand Terre, with all sail; at half past 8 o'clock, the chase hauled her wind off shore to escape; sent acting Lieut. Spedding with four boats manned and armed to prevent her passing the harbor; at 9 o'clock A.M., the chase fired upon the *Carolina*, which was returned; each vessel continued firing during the chase, when their long guns could reach. At 10 o'clock, the chase grounded outside of the bar, at which time the *Carolina* was from the shoalness of the water obliged to haul her wind off shore and give up the chase; opened a fire upon the chase across the island from the gun vessels. At half past 10 o'clock, she hauled down her colors and was taken possession of. She proved to be the armed schooner Gen. Boliver; by grounding she broke both her rudder pintles and made water; took from her her armament, consisting of one long brass eighteen pounder, one long brass six pounder, two twelve pounders, small arms, &c., and twenty-one packages of dry goods. On the afternoon of the 23d, got underway with the whole squadron, in all seventeen vessels, but during the night one escaped, and the next day arrived at New Orleans with my whole squadron."

At different times the English had sought to attack the pirates at Barrataria, in hopes of taking their prizes, and even their armed vessels. Of these attempts of the British, suffice it to instance that of June 23d, 1813, when two privateers being at anchor off Cat Island, a British sloop of war anchored at the entrance of the pass, and sent her boats to endeavor to take the privateers; but they were repulsed with considerable loss.

Such was the state of affairs, when on the 2d Sept., 1814, there appeared an armed brig on the coast opposite the pass. She fired a gun at a vessel about to enter, and forced her to run aground; she then tacked and shortly after came to an anchor at the entrance of the pass. It was not easy to understand the intentions of this vessel, who, having commenced with hostilities on her first appearance now seemed to announce an amicable disposition. Mr. Lafitte then went off in a boat to examine her, venturing so far that he could not escape from the pinnace sent from the brig, and making towards the shore, bearing British colors and a flag of truce. In this pinnace were two naval officers. One was Capt. Lockyer, commander of the brig. The first question they asked was, where was Mr. Lafitte? He not choosing to make himself known to them, replied that the person they inquired for was on shore. They then delivered to him a packet directed to Mr. Lafitte, Barrataria, requesting him to take particular care of it, and to deliver it into Mr. Lafitte's hands. He prevailed on them to make for the shore, and as soon as they got near enough to be in his power, he made himself known, recommending to them at the same time to conceal the business on which they had come. Upwards of two hundred persons lined the shore, and it was a general cry amongst the crews of the privateers at Grand Terre, that those British officers should be made prisoners and sent to New Orleans as spies. It was with much difficulty that Lafitte dissuaded the multitude from this intent, and led the officers in safety to his dwelling. He thought very prudently that the papers contained in the packet might be of importance towards the safety of the country and that the officers if well watched could obtain no intelligence that might turn to the detriment of Louisiana. He now examined the contents of the packet, in which he found a proclamation addressed by Col. Edward Nichalls, in the service of his Brittanic Majesty, and commander of the land forces on the coast of Florida, to the inhabitants of Louisiana. A letter from the same to Mr. Lafitte, the commander of Barrataria; an official letter from the honorable W.H. Percy, captain of the sloop of war *Hermes*, directed to Lafitte. When he had perused these letters, Capt. Lockyer enlarged on the subject of them and proposed to him to enter into the service of his Brittanic Majesty with the rank of post captain and to receive the command of a 44-gun frigate. Also all those under his command, or over whom he had sufficient influence. He was also offered thirty thousand dollars, payable at Pensacola, and urged him not to let slip this opportunity of acquiring fortune and consideration. On Lafitte's requiring a few days to reflect upon these proposals, Capt. Lockyer observed to him that no reflection could be necessary, respecting proposals that obviously precluded hesitation, as he was a Frenchman and proscribed by the American government. But to all his splendid promises and daring insinuations, Lafitte replied that in a few days he would give a final answer; his object in this procrastination being to gain time to inform the officers of the state government of this nefarious project. Having occasion to go to some distance for a short time, the persons who had proposed to send the British officers prisoners to New Orleans, went and seized them in his absence, and confined both them and the crew of the pinnace, in a secure place, leaving a guard at the door. The British officers sent for Lafitte; but he, fearing an insurrection of the crews of the privateers, thought it advisable not to see them until he had first persuaded their captains and officers to desist from the measures on which they seemed bent. With this view he represented to the latter that, besides the infamy that would attach to them if they treated as prisoners people who had come with a flag of truce, they would lose the opportunity of discovering the projects of the British against Louisiana.

Early the next morning Lafitte caused them to be released from their confinement and saw them safe on board their pinnace, apologizing the detention. He now wrote to Capt. Lockyer the following letter.

To CAPTAIN LOCKYER.

Barrataria, 4th Sept. 1814.
Sir—The confusion which prevailed in our camp yesterday and
this morning, and of which you have a complete knowledge,
has prevented me from answering in a precise manner to the
object of your mission; nor even at this moment can I give you
all the satisfaction that you desire; however, if you could grant
me a fortnight, I would be entirely at your disposal at the end of
that time. This delay is indispensable to enable me to put my
affairs in order. You may communicate with me by sending a
boat to the eastern point of the pass, where I will be found. You
have inspired me with more confidence than the admiral, your
superior officer, could have done himself; with you alone, I
wish to deal, and from you also I will claim, in due time the re-
ward of the services, which I may render to you. Yours, &c.

J. LAFITTE.

His object in writing that letter was, by appearing disposed to accede to their proposals, to give time to communicate the affair to the officers of the state government, and to receive from them instructions how to act, under circumstances so critical and important to the country. He accordingly wrote on the 4th September to Mr. Blanque, one of the representatives of the state, sending him all the papers delivered to him by the British officers with a letter addressed to his excellency, Gov. Claiborne of the state of Louisiana.

To Gov. CLAIBORNE.

Barrataria, Sept. 4th, 1814.
Sir—In the firm persuasion that the choice made of you to fill the office of first magistrate of this state, was dictated by the esteem of your fellow citizens, and was conferred on merit, I confidently address you on an affair on which may depend the safety of this country. I offer to you to restore to this state several citizens, who perhaps in your eyes have lost that sacred title. I offer you them, however, such as you could wish to find them, ready to exert their utmost efforts in defence of the country. This point of Louisiana, which I occupy, is of great importance in the present crisis. I tender my services to defend it; and the only reward I ask is that a stop be put to the proscription against me and my adherents, by an act of oblivion, for all that has been done hitherto. I am the stray sheep wishing to return to the fold. If you are thoroughly acquainted with the nature of my offences, I should appear to you much less guilty, and still worthy to discharge the duties of a good citizen. I have never sailed under any flag but that of the republic of Carthagena, and my vessels are perfectly regular in that respect. If I could have brought my lawful prizes into the ports of this state, I should not have employed the illicit means that have caused me to be proscribed. I decline saying more on the subject, until I have the honor of your excellency's answer, which I am persuaded can be dictated only by wisdom. Should your answer not be favorable to my ardent desires, I declare to you that I will instantly leave

the country, to avoid the imputation of having cooperated to-
wards an invasion on this point, which cannot fail to take
place, and to rest secure in the acquittal of my conscience.

I have the honor to be
your excellency's, &c.
J. LAFITTE.

The contents of these letters do honor to Lafitte's judgment, and evince his sincere attachment to the American cause. On the receipt of this packet from Lafitte, Mr. Blanque immediately laid its contents before the governor, who convened the committee of defence lately formed of which he was president; and Mr. Rancher the bearer of Lafitte's packet, was sent back with a verbal answer to desire Lafitte to take no steps until it should be determined what was expedient to be done; the message also contained an assurance that, in the meantime no steps should be taken against him for his past offences against the laws of the United States.

At the expiration of the time agreed on with Captain Lockyer, his ship appeared again on the coast with two others, and continued standing off and on before the pass for several days. But he pretended not to perceive the return of the sloop of war, who tired of waiting to no purpose put out to sea and disappeared.

Lafitte having received a guarantee from General Jackson for his safe passage from Barrataria to New Orleans and back, he proceeded forthwith to the city where he had an interview with Gov. Claiborne and the General. After the usual formalities and courtesies had taken place between these gentlemen, Lafitte addressed the Governor of Louisiana nearly as follows: "I have offered to defend for you that part of Louisiana I now hold. But not as an outlaw, would I be its defender. In that confidence, with which you have inspired me, I offer to restore to the state many citizens, now under my command. As I have re-marked before, the point I occupy is of great importance in the present crisis. I tender not only my own services to defend it, but those of all I command; and the only reward I ask, is, that a stop be put to the proscription against me and my adherents, by an act of oblivion for all that has been done hitherto."

"My dear sir," said the Governor, who together with General Jackson, was impressed with admiration of his sentiments, "your praiseworthy wishes shall be laid before the council of the state, and I will confer with my August friend here present, upon this important affair, and send you an answer to-morrow." At Lafitte withdrew, the General said, "Farewell; when we meet again, I trust it will be in the ranks of the American army." The result of the conference was the issuing the following order.

"The Governor of Louisiana, informed that many individuals implicated in the offences heretofore committed against the United States at Barrataria, express a willingness at the present crisis to enroll themselves and march against the enemy.

He does hereby invite them to join the standard of the United States and is authorised to say, should their conduct in the field meet the approbation of the Major General, that that officer will unite with the governor in a request to the president of the United States, to extend to each and every individual, so marching and acting, a free and full pardon."

These general orders were placed in the hands of Lafitte, who circulated them among his dispersed followers, most of whom readily embraced the conditions of pardon they held out. In a few days many brave men and skillful artillerists, whose services contributed greatly to the safety of the invaded state, flocked to the standard of the United States, and by their conduct, received the highest approbation of General Jackson.

BY THE PRESIDENT OF THE UNITED STATES OF AMERICA.
A PROCLAMATION.

Among the many evils produced by the wars, which, with little intermission, have afflicted Europe, and extended their ravages into other quarters of the globe, for a period exceeding twenty years, the dispersion of a considerable portion of the inhabitants of different countries, in sorrow and in want, has not been the least injurious to human happiness, nor the least severe in the trial of human virtue.

"It had been long ascertained that many foreigners, flying from the dangers of their own home, and that some citizens, forgetful of their duty, had co-operated in forming an estab-lishment on the island of Barrataria, near the mouth of the river Mississippi, for the purpose of a clandestine and lawless trade. The government of the United States caused the estab-lishment to be broken up and destroyed; and, having obtained the means of designating the offenders of every description, it only remained to answer the demands of justice by inflicting an exemplary punishment.

"But it has since been represented that the offenders have manifested a sincere penitence; that they have abandoned the prosecution of the worst cause for the support of the best, and, particularly, that they have exhibited, in the defence of New Orleans, unequivocal traits of courage and fidelity. Offenders, who have refused to become the associates of the enemy in the war, upon the most seducing terms of invitation; and who have aided to repel his hostile invasion of the territory of the United States, can no longer be considered as objects of pun-ishment, but as objects of a generous forgiveness.

"It has therefore been seen, with great satisfaction, that the General Assembly of the State of Louisiana earnestly rec-ommend those offenders to the benefit of a full pardon; And in compliance with that recommendation, as well as in consid-eration of all the other extraordinary circumstances in the case, I, James Madison, President of the United States of America, do issue this proclamation, hereby granting, pub-lishing and declaring, a free and full pardon of all offences committed in violation of any act or acts of the Congress of the said United States, touching the revenue, trade and navi-gation thereof, or touching the intercourse and commerce of the United States with foreign nations, at any time before the eighth day of January, in the present year one thousand eight

*hundred and fifteen, by any person or persons whatsoever,
being inhabitants of New Orleans and the adjacent country,
or being inhabitants of the said island of Barrataria, and the
places adjacent; Provided, that every person, claiming the
benefit of this full pardon, in order to entitle himself thereto,
shall produce a certificate in writing from the governor of the
State of Louisiana, stating that such person has aided in the
defence of New Orleans and the adjacent country, during the
invasion thereof as aforesaid.*

*And I do hereby further authorize and direct all suits, in-
dictments, and prosecutions, for fines, penalties, and for-
feitures, against any person or persons, who shall be entitled
to the benefit of this full pardon, forthwith to be stayed, dis-
continued and released: All civil officers are hereby required,
according to the duties of their respective stations, to carry
this proclamation into immediate and faithful execution.*

*Done at the City of Washington, the sixth day of February,
in the year one thousand eight hundred and fifteen, and of the
independence of the United States the thirty-ninth.*

By the President,
JAMES MADISON

JAMES MONROE,
Acting Secretary of State.

The morning of the eighth of January, was ushered in with the discharge of rockets, the sound of cannon, and the cheers of the British
soldiers advancing to the attack. The Americans, behind the breastwork, awaited in calm intrepidity their approach. The enemy advanced in close column of sixty men in front, shouldering their
muskets and carrying fascines and ladders. A storm of rockets preceded them, and an incessant fire opened from the battery, which
commanded the advanced column. The musketry and rifles from the
Kentuckians and Tennesseans, joined the fire of the artillery, and in a
few moments was heard along the line a ceaseless, rolling fire, whose

tremendous noise resembled the continued reverberation of thunder. One of these guns, a twenty-four pounder, placed upon the breastwork in the third embrasure from the river, drew, from the fatal skill and activity with which it was managed, even in the heat of battle, the admiration of both Americans and British; and became one of the points most dreaded by the advancing foe.

Here was stationed Lafitte and his lieutenant Dominique and a large band of his men, who during the continuance of the battle, fought with unparalleled bravery. The British already had been twice driven back in the utmost confusion, with the loss of their commander-in-chief, and two general officers.

Two other batteries were manned by the Barratarians, who served their pieces with the steadiness and precision of veteran gunners. In the first attack of the enemy, a column pushed forward between the levee and river; and so precipitate was their charge that the outposts were forced to retire, closely pressed by the enemy. Before the batteries could meet the charge, clearing the ditch, they gained the redoubt through the embrasures, leaping over the parapet, and overwhelming by their superior force the small party stationed there.

Lafitte, who was commanding in conjunction with his officers, at one of the guns, no sooner saw the bold movement of the enemy, than calling a few of his best men by his side, he sprung forward to the point of danger, and clearing the breastwork of the entrenchments, leaped, cutlass in hand, into the midst of the enemy, followed by a score of his men, who in many a hard fought battle upon his own deck, had been well tried.

Astonished at the intrepidity which could lead men to leave their entrenchments and meet them hand to hand, and pressed by the suddenness of the charge, which was made with the recklessness, skill and rapidity of practised boarders bounding upon the deck of an enemy's vessel, they began to give way, while one after another, two British officers fell before the cutlass of the pirate, as they were bravely encouraging their men. All the energies of the British were now concentrated to scale the breastwork, which one daring officer had already mounted. While Lafitte and his followers, seconding a gallant band of volunteer riflemen, formed a phalanx which they in vain assayed to penetrate.

The British, finding it impossible to take the city and the havoc in their ranks being dreadful, made a precipitate retreat, leaving the field covered with their dead and wounded.

General Jackson, in his correspondence with the secretary of war did not fail to notice the conduct of the "Corsairs of Barrataria," who were, as we have already seen, employed in the artillery service. In the course of the campaign they proved, in an unequivocal manner, that they had been misjudged by the enemy, who a short time previous to the invasion of Louisiana, had hoped to enlist them in his cause. Many of them were killed or wounded in the defence of the country. Their zeal, their courage, and their skill, were remarked by the whole army, who could no longer consider such brave men as criminals. In a few days peace was declared between Great Britain and the United States.

The piratical establishment of Barrataria having been broken up and Lafitte not being content with leading an honest, peaceful life, procured some fast sailing vessels, and with a great number of his followers, proceeded to Galvezton Bay, in Texas, during the year 1819; where he received a commission from General Long; and had five vessels generally cruising and about 300 men. Two open boats bearing commissions from General Humbert, of Galvezton, having robbed a plantation on the Marmento river, of negroes, money, &c., were captured in the Sabine river, by the boats of the United States schooner *Lynx*. One of the men was hung by Lafitte, who dreaded the vengeance of the American government. The *Lynx* also captured one of his schooners, and her prize that had been for a length of time smuggling in the Carmento. One of his cruisers, named the Jupiter, returned safe to Galvezton after a short cruise with a valuable cargo, principally specie; she was the first vessel that sailed under the authority of Texas. The American government well knowing that where Lafitte was, piracy and smuggling would be the order of the day, sent a vessel of war to cruise in the Gulf of Mexico, and scour the coasts of Texas. Lafitte having been appointed governor of Galvezton and one of the cruisers being stationed off the port to watch his motions, it so annoyed him that he wrote the following letter to her commander, Lieutenant Madison.

*To the commandant of the American cruiser, off the port of
Galvezton.*

*Sir—I am convinced that you are a cruiser of the navy, or-
dered by your government. I have therefore deemed it proper
to inquire into the cause of your living before this port without
communicating your intention. I shall by this message inform
you, that the port of Galvezton belongs to and is in the possession of the republic of Texas, and was made a port of entry
the 9th October last. And whereas the supreme congress of
said republic have thought proper to appoint me as governor
of this place, in consequence of which, if you have any demands on said government, or persons belonging to or resid-
ing in the same, you will please to send an officer with such
demands, whom you may be assured will be treated with the
greatest politeness, and receive every satisfaction required.
But if you are ordered, or should attempt to enter this port in
a hostile manner, my oath and duty to the government com-
pels me to rebut your intentions at the expense of my life.*

*To prove to you my intentions towards the welfare and
harmony of your government I send enclosed the declaration
of several prisoners, who were taken in custody yesterday,
and by a court of inquiry appointed for that purpose, were
found guilty of robbing the inhabitants of the United States of
a number of slaves and specie. The gentlemen bearing this
message will give you any reasonable information relating to
this place, that may be required.*

Yours, &c.
J. LAFITTE.

About this time one Mitchell, who had formerly belonged to
Lafitte's gang, collected upwards of one hundred and fifty desperadoes
and fortified himself on an island near Barrataria, with several pieces
of cannon; and swore that he and all his comrades would perish within
their trenches before they would surrender to any man. Four of this

gang having gone to New Orleans on a frolic, information was given to the city watch, and the house surrounded, when the whole four with cocked pistols in both hands sallied out and marched through the crowd which made way for them and no person dared to make an attempt to arrest them.

The United States cutter, *Alabama*, on her way to the station off the mouth of the Mississippi, captured a piratical schooner belonging to Lafitte; she carried two guns and twenty-five men, and was fitted out at New Orleans, and commanded by one of Lafitte's lieutenants, named Le Fage; the schooner had a prize in company and being hailed by the cutter, poured into her a volley of musketry; the cutter then opened upon the privateer and a smart action ensued which terminated in favor of the cutter, which had four men wounded and two of them dangerously; but the pirate had six men killed; both vessels were captured and brought into the bayou St. John. An expedition was now sent to dislodge Mitchell and his comrades from the island he had taken possession of; after coming to anchor, a summons was sent for him to surrender, which was answered by a brisk cannonade from his breastwork. The vessels were warped close in shore; and the boats manned and sent on shore whilst the vessels opened upon the pirates; the boat's crews landed under a galling fire of grape shot and formed in the most undaunted manner; and although a severe loss was sustained they entered the breastwork at the point of the bayonet; after a desperate fight the pirates gave way, many were taken prisoners but Mitchell and the greatest part escaped to the cypress swamps where it was impossible to arrest them. A large quantity of dry goods and specie together with other booty was taken. Twenty of the pirates were taken and brought to New Orleans, and tried before Judge Hall, of the Circuit Court of the United States, sixteen were brought in guilty; and after the Judge had finished pronouncing sentence of death upon the hardened wretches, several of them cried out in open court, "Murder—by God."

Accounts of these transactions having reached Lafitte, he plainly perceived there was a determination to sweep all his cruisers from the sea; and a war of extermination appeared to be waged against him.

In a fit of desperation he procured a large and fast sailing brigantine mounting sixteen guns and having selected a crew of one hundred and sixty men he started without any commission as a regular pirate determined to rob all nations and neither to give or receive quarter. A British sloop of war which was cruising in the Gulf of Mexico, having heard that Lafitte himself was at sea, kept a sharp look out from the mast head; when one morning as an officer was sweeping the horizon with his glass he discovered a long dark looking vessel, low in the water, but having very tall masts, with sails white as the driven snow. As the sloop of war had the weather gage of the pirate and could outsail her before the wind, she set her studding sails and crowded every inch of canvass in chase; as soon as Lafitte ascertained the character of his opponent, he ordered the awnings to be furled and set his big square-sail and shot rapidly through the water; but as the breeze freshened the sloop of war came up rapidly with the pirate, who, finding no chance of escaping, determined to sell his life as dearly as possible; the guns were cast loose and the shot handed up; and a fire opened upon the ship which killed a number of men and carried away her foretopmast, but she reserved her fire until within cable's distance of the pirate; when she fired a general discharge from her broadside, and a volley of small arms; the broadside was too much elevated to hit the low hull of the brigantine, but was not without effect; the foretopmast fell, the jaws of the main gaff were severed and a large proportion of the rigging came rattling down on deck; ten of the pirates were killed, but Lafitte remained unhurt. The sloop of war entered her men over the starboard bow and a terrific contest with pistols and cutlasses ensued; Lafitte received two wounds at this time which disabled him, a grape shot broke the bone of his right leg and he received a cut in the abdomen, but his crew fought like tigers and the deck was ankle deep with blood and gore; the captain of the boarders received such a tremendous blow on the head from the butt end of a musket, as stretched him senseless on the deck near Lafitte, who raised his dagger to stab him to the heart. But the tide of his existence was ebbing like a torrent, his brain was giddy, his aim faltered and the point descended in the Captain's right thigh; dragging away the blade with the last convulsive energy of a death struggle, he lacerated the wound. Again the reeking steel was upheld, and Lafitte placed his left hand near the Captain's heart, to make his aim more sure; again the dizziness of dissolution spread over his sight, down came the dagger into the captain's left thigh and Lafitte was a corpse.

The upper deck was cleared, and the boarders rushed below on the main deck to complete their conquest. Here the slaughter was dreadful, till the pirates called out for quarter, and the carnage ceased; all the pirates that surrendered were taken to Jamaica and tried before the Admiralty court where sixteen were condemned to die, six were subsequently pardoned and ten executed.

Thus perished Lafitte, a man superior in talent, in knowledge of his profession, in courage, and moreover in physical strength; but unfortunately his reckless career was marked with crimes of the darkest dye.

BLACKBEARD AND THE LADY

Benjamin Barker

CHAPTER ELEVEN

After having ordered his ship close alongside the *East Indiaman*, Blackbeard immediately descended to the place where sweet Ellen Armstrong was confined as a prisoner, and addressed its occupant, in the following manner,

'So Miss Armstrong, you acted the heroine to perfection, this afternoon.'

A look of utter loathing and contempt, being the only answer which the fair Ellen deigned to bestow on the pirate's words, he continued:

'You must certainly be mad, my lovely lily of the valley, to look so scornfully upon me, who at present holds in his hand the power of thy life or death.'

'As I am well assured that you will use the awful power you speak, to put a speedy end to my wretched existence,' replied Ellen, 'I must beg of you, instantly to retire, and thus rid me of your hateful presence.'

'Stop, stop, my pretty Miss,' exclaimed Blackbeard, 'not quite so fast, if you please. In the first place you must learn, that I have at present no intention of taking your life, but on the contrary, I intend to make you my wife, as soon as circumstances will permit.'

'Pirate, fiend, villain,' exclaimed Ellen, starting up from her seat and confronting Blackbeard, with all the majesty of injured innocence, 'learn, that rather than become the wife of a desperate robber like thyself, Ellen Armstrong will die, die by her own hand, and—'

'Ha, ha ha, there you go into heroics again,' interrupted the pirate, in a tone of scornful irony, 'but I will soon find a way to bring you back to your senses. Now, listen,' he continued, after a moment's pause, and in a tone of voice changed to stern severity, 'listen I say, to my words, and mark them well. From the curious scenes which transpired awile ago on the deck of this vessel, in which you chose to act a prominent part, I could draw but one inference, and that was, that you was deeply in love with Arthur Huntington, and now I would ask of you, if this inference is correct.'

'Had you any right to put such a question to me, I should not hesitate to answer it,' replied Ellen, who by this time had attained a sort of desperate courage which enabled her to bear up under the unaccountable horrors of her situation.

'If I have not a right, you will now perceive that I have the might to compel you to answer,' exclaimed Blackbeard, who having become by this time, thoroughly infuriated, drew a poniard from his belt, and advancing, towards Ellen, who sunk pale and terrified upon her knee, at his approach, he continued:

'It is far from my wish, Miss Armstrong, to harm even a hair of your head; but you must, (and mark me, I speak not unmeaningly,) you must, I repeat, answer my question, fairly, and without equivocation. Do you love Arthur Huntington?'

Ellen shuddered, and averted her head, but answered not. Finding his fair prisoner was not disposed to reply, Blackbeard, exclaimed with a horrid oath,

'I tell you, girl, that the pirate of the Roanoke, is not to be tampered with. Again, and for the last time, I command you to answer my question. Will you do so?'

'No,' replied Ellen firmly, 'I will not.'

'Then your blood be upon your head!' exclaimed the pirate, as springing suddenly forward, he inflicted a severe wound upon the person of sweet Ellen Armstrong, with his poniard, which caused her to fall fainting and bleeding upon the floor of the cabin.

'My God, what have I done,' muttered Blackbeard, as he gazed upon his prisoner's prostrate form.

'Murdered your sister!' exclaimed a shrill female voice, which emanated from a person who had entered the cabin unperceived, just after Ellen was wounded.

'Ha, who is that, that speaks of murder!' exclaimed the Pirate involuntarily.

'It is your mother, Elvira, who accuses you of having murdered that beautiful girl, who now lays gasping at your feet,' replied the strange female, who although she was far advanced in years, beyond the prime of life, still possessed a tall and commanding form, together with features, which, though they were somewhat wrinkled and withered, had once been pre-eminently fair and beautiful.

'Avaunt! hag,' exclaimed Blackbeard, as Elvira ceased speaking, 'begone I say, and if ever thou darest to call thyself, my mother, in my hearing, I will stab you to the very heart.'

'Am I not thy father's wife, Herbert?' replied the female.

'You say so, and it may be so,' rejoined Blackbeard, 'but at any rate you are only a social one.'

'If even that is allowed,' answered Elvira, 'you must own that it legally puts me in your mother's place.'

'By the bones of Captain Kid, it sounds well and appropriate for you, to talk about legality,' replied Blackbeard, ironically, 'you, who hast been born and bred amongst those, who acknowledge no laws, except those of their own making. Go to, you're an idiot.'

'But I am not a murderess,' replied Elvira.

'That is more than I could swear for,' said Blackbeard.

'At least I never killed my sister,' rejoined Elvira.

'What do you mean to insinuate by that?' asked the Pirate as his muscular frame trembled with a sort of indefinable emotion.

'I mean,' replied Elvira earnestly, 'not only to insinuate, but to solemnly assert, that, that unfortunate girl, who now lies bleeding before your eyes, is your only sister.'

'What!' exclaimed Blackbeard, driven by these singular words almost to frenzy, 'Witch of Bedlam, thou liest.'

A low, faint moan, here escaped from the lips of the wounded girl, which caused Elvira, thus to address the pirate:

'Say no more at present, Herbert, I entreat you, but leave the cabin, whilst I endeavor to restore this young creature to consciousness.'

'You asserted just now, that this girl was my only sister,' replied Blackbeard, 'and before I depart I must have an explanation of your words.'

'For the love of Heaven, Herbert,' said Elvira, 'leave me alone with this maiden for the present, and to-morrow I will explain everything.'

'Upon that consideration, I will go,' avowed the pirate, 'and after which you will carefully examine her wound, and if it is likely to prove fatal, beware how you lose any time in making me aware of the fact.'

So saying, and without awaiting Elvira's reply, Blackbeard immediately left the cabin.

'Lower away the boat there,' thundered forth the pirate, as he gained the brig's quarter deck. A score or two men promptly executed this order, the boat was soon manned; Blackbeard assumed his station in the stern sheets, and was soon pulled along side of the *Gladiator*, whose deck he quickly reached, where he earnestly inquired of the officer in charge, for Captain Rowland.

'He went ashore, sir,' replied the man to whom he had applied, 'about one hour ago, and left orders for you to follow him at your earliest convenience.'

Upon hearing this, Blackbeard without stopping to reply, hastily re-entered his boat, and ordered his coxswain to steer directly for the shore, which he soon reached, and having landed, made the best of his way to the palace, where we will for the present leave him, whilst we look further after the fortunes of our heroine.

No sooner had the pirate, taken his departure from the cabin, than the strange female hastened to the assistance of the wounded girl, whom she supported in her arms, and then conducted her into a small but neatly furnished state-room, which was Elvira's own apartment, where she had partly overheard the altercation which took place, as before related, between Blackbeard and Ellen, and from which she had noiselessly and unperceived entered the main cabin just after our unfortunate heroine had fallen to the floor. Here Elvira gently laid her fair charge upon her own soft couch, and proceeded immediately to examine her wound, which, although it had bled copiously, was but slight, then, after carefully dressing it, this strange woman, by the aid of appropriate restoratives soon succeeded in restoring 'sweet' Ellen Armstrong once more to consciousness.

As a confused sense of her situation began to dawn upon her mind, our heroine, after casting a wild glance around the state-room, addressed Elvira as follows:

'Good woman, for the love of Heaven, tell me where I am, and into whose hands I have fallen?'

'You are at present on board of a piratical vessel called the *Fury*, and in the hands of a merciless and cruel set of black-hearted villains.'

'And you,' exclaimed Ellen, hardly knowing what she said, 'how came you, a woman, to be in this horrid place?'

'That is a question,' replied Elvira 'much easier for you to ask, than it will be for me to answer, but, as some of the events connected with the sad history of my presence here, may be found to be somewhat connected with your present mysterious situation, I will lose no time in making you acquainted with the story of my past life, that is, if you think you possess strength enough to listen to the recital, which as it is to me a painful theme, I shall make as brief as possible.'

A strange and unaccountable interest in the words of the dejected being who stood before her, having taken possession of the sympathizing mind of our heroine, she signified to Elvira, that she felt strong enough to listen to any thing which might serve to explain the horrible mystery connected with her sudden captivity, and the subsequent events attendant upon it.

As Ellen finished speaking, Elvira, commenced her narration as follows:

'I was born in Lincoln, near fifty years ago. My parents were poor, but respectable trades-people, who, had they been permitted to live, until I, their only child, had reached the age of womanhood, might have, by religious counsel and strict government checked, if not wholly obliterated the reckless propensities of my passionate temper and wild, wayward disposition. But before my years had numbered ten, my parents both died within a few weeks of each other, leaving me to the care of a tyrannical old aunt, who I soon afterwards found, managed to hide, under an artful affection of religion and prudery, a base malignant and sensual character. I was immediately sent by my aunt to the parish-school, where, being naturally tractable and apt to learn I soon acquired the rudiments of a good education, and besides, I learnt also to become an expert needle-woman. No sooner did my aunt find that I was mistress of this latter accomplishment, than she took me at once from school, and compelled me to toil day and night at my needle, refusing me at the same time all necessary rest and recreation.

'Young and high-spirited as I then was, I found it impossible to bear such brutal treatment, and one day when I was about fourteen years of age, in a fit of anger and despair, I left the home of my cruel aunt, and found myself a wretched wanderer in the streets of London, without money, home, or friends. Still I wandered on, not realizing the horror of my situation, till the shades of evening began to cover the city, and the harsh knawings of cruel hunger, began inexorably to crave their natural satisfaction. Then it was that I felt myself compelled to look around for some place of shelter, but could find none, and would have returned again to my cruel aunt, but alas, all my efforts to find her habitation proved utterly fruitless, and having by this time reached the banks of the Thames, I plunged without a moment's hesitation, into its dark waters, resolving to end at once a life which promised nothing to its possessor, but wretchedness and wo. But my fatal resolution was frustrated by a man, who, unperceived had for some time previous watched my wild and desperate course, and who jumped into the water as I a second time rose to its surface, caught me by the arm, and held me tightly with one hand, whilst with the other he swam toward a small vessel, which, being but a short distance off, he managed to reach in safety.

'Having received on board this vessel every attention which the greatest delicacy and kindness could dictate, I soon became impressed with a strong desire to become acquainted, with the character and designs of the person who had so disinterestedly preserved my life. It so happened that during a short illness which was occasioned by the cold bath I had taken in the Thames, I was assiduously attended by a female, who, as I afterwards learnt, was the wife of one of the officers of the vessel. To this woman who was very kind and attentive to my wants, I applied for the gratification of my curiosity concerning my preserver, upon which she informed me that he was a young Spaniard of good family, who commanded the vessel in which we were then situated.

'This was all I could gather from her, but a day or two afterwards I had perfectly recovered so that I could verbally thank the generous man who had saved my life, to his face. After having listened with modest though marked attention to my warm protestations of gratitude, Don Almanzor, (for such was his name,) begged me to relate to him the untoward events which had driven me to desperation and almost death.

'In accordance with his request, I gave him a brief history of my previous life, after which in view as he said, of my helpless and desolate condition, he offered to take me to his home in Cuba, where he informed me I should become an inmate of his father's family, he taking upon himself to act towards me, in every respect, the part of a friend and generous brother.

'With redoubled expressions of sincere gratitude and respect, I eagerly consented to abide by Almanzor's generous offer, and a few days afterward, the vessel in which I had so strangely become a passenger, sailed for Havana, where she arrived after a pleasant passage of three weeks.

'During the voyage, Almanzor treated me with the most delicate attention and respect, and as he was young, handsome, and unmarried, you will not be surprised when I inform you, that long before its termination, I became deeply and fervently attached to him. However, I resolved to keep my passion a secret within my own bosom, until I should know whether my affection would be reciprocated by its object, and in the mean time, I became regularly domesticated in the family of Don Almanzor, which consisted of his father, who was a rich old Spanish slave-dealer, his mother, and himself. The old people treated me in all respects, as though I had been their only daughter, and for two years I lived with them in the enjoyment of a pure and tranquil happiness, which, at the expiration of that time, was enhanced beyond measure, by an honorable offer on the part of Almanzor, of his hand and heart. As might naturally be supposed, I readily accepted an offer which agreed so well with my own inclinations, and shortly afterwards we were married, and after two more years of increased felicity had passed, I became the mother of a lovely daughter.

'My husband was at this time absent on a trading voyage, and the vessel that he was in having encountered a severe hurricane, was stranded, and every soul on board of her found a watery grave.

'This dreadful news was brought to me by Captain Rowland, who visited the island at that time, in the capacity of master of an English brig, and need I say that the horrid tidings almost drove me frantic.

'Then the insiduous tempter came, and offered me his hand, which I accepted, and thus I became what you see me now, Rowland's wife.'

'And who is this Captain Rowland?' asked Ellen, eagerly.

'He is a noted pirate,' replied Elvira.

'Did you know that when you married him?'

'I did not, if I had, sooner would I have yielded my life than united my fortune, desperate as it was, with his. When I discovered his true character, I was his wife, on board of his vessel, and in his power, with no avenue through which I could escape, and for the sake of my child, I was forced to humble myself, and submit to his caprices.'

'Your situation must have been terrible beyond expression,' ejaculated Ellen, who had become deeply interested in the story of the unfortunate woman.

'God knows that it was so,' answered Elvira. 'The discovery of his deception came upon me suddenly, like a thunderbolt from the clouds of heaven, and I upbraided him for it in the bitterness of my heart, and he answered my reproaches at first with scornful laughter, and afterwards with a relation of the history of his past life, during which, to my utter astonishment and surprise, I learnt that he had been once before married, but that his wife had recently died, leaving two children, a son who was at that time in the vessel with his father, and an infant daughter, concerning whom, I could only then learn from Rowland, that she had been left in London, in the hands of such persons as would take good care of her.

'It was in vain after this, that I begged my cruel husband to return me and my child to Havana, he was utterly deaf to all my entreaties, although about two months after our embarcation he landed me on this desolate, but beautiful island, where, in his hours of leisure, he had with the assistance of his companions, erected and furnished with his rich but ill gotten spoils, that building which has been signified by the name of the Pirate's Palace.'

'That must be the horrid place,' exclaimed Ellen, 'which I saw this morning, and in which I fear Mary Hamilton is—is—'

'Now confined,' interrupted Elvira.

'Is it not worse than that,' exclaimed Ellen, eagerly, 'has she not met with a cruel death?'

'Oh no, that is no part of the purpose of those who have detained her,' answered Elvira.

'Do you know their true purpose, then,' asked Ellen, 'relative to her, myself, and the rest of the prisoners?'

'With regard to Miss Hamilton,' replied Elvira, 'Rowland's purpose is to force her into a union with his son.'

'And who may his son be?' again inquired Ellen.

'No other,' answered Elvira, impressively, 'but Herbert Rowland otherwise called Blackbeard, the famous pirate of the Roanoke, who is besides your only brother.'

'And Captain Rowland?'

'Is your father.'

'God of Heaven! Can it be possible?' exclaimed the fair Ellen.

'It is no less possible than true,' replied Elvira.

'Then, in Heaven's name, let us free Arthur from his fetters,' exclaimed Ellen, 'and all of us escape through the cabin window into the boat, that has, I perceive, been left astern.'

Upon hearing this, Elvira immediately left the cabin, but, to Ellen's greater joy, she shortly after returned, followed by Arthur Huntington, who assisted the females into the boat, after which he entered it himself and succeeded in getting, unperceived, out of sight of the brig, upon the bosom of the wide ocean.

THE EXPLOITS OF CAPTAIN CHARLES VANE

Charles Ellms

CHAPTER TWELVE

Charles Vane was one of those who stole away the silver which the Spaniards had fished up from the wrecks of the galleons in the Gulf of Florida, and was at Providence when governor Rogers arrived there with two men-of-war.

All the pirates who were then found at this colony of rogues, submitted and received certificates of their pardon, except Captain Vane and his crew; who, as soon as they saw the men-of-war enter, slipped their cable, set fire to a prize they had in the harbor, sailed out with their piratical colors flying, and fired at one of the men-of-war, as they went off from the coast.

Two days after, they met with a sloop belonging to Barbadoes, which they took, and kept the vessel for their own use, putting aboard five and twenty hands, with one Yeates the commander. In a day or two they fell in with a small interloping trader, with a quantity of Spanish pieces of eight aboard, bound for Providence, which they also took along with them. With these two sloops, Vane went to a small island and cleaned; where he shared the booty, and spent some time in a riotous manner.

About the latter end of May 1718, Vane and his crew sailed, and being in want of provisions, they beat up for the Windward Islands. In the way they met with a Spanish sloop, bound from Porto Rico to the Havana, which they burnt, stowed the Spaniards into a boat, and left them to get to the island by the blaze of their vessel. Steering between

St. Christopher's and Anguilla, they fell in with a brigantine and a sloop, freighted with such cargo as they wanted; from whom they got provisions for sea-store.

Sometime after this, standing to the northward, in the track the old English ships take in their voyage to the American colonies, they took several ships and vessels, which they plundered of what they thought fit, and then let them pass.

About the latter end of August, with his consort Yeates, came off South Carolina, and took a ship belonging to Ipswich, laden with logwood. This was thought convenient enough for their own business, and therefore they ordered their prisoners to work, and threw all the lading overboard; but when they had more than half cleared the ship, the whim changed, and they would not have her; so Coggershall, the captain of the captured vessel, had his ship again, and he was suffered to pursue his voyage home. In this voyage the pirates took several ships and vessels, particularly a sloop from Barbadoes, a small ship from Antigua, a sloop belonging to Curaçoa, and a large brigantine from Guinea, with upwards of ninety negroes aboard. The pirates plundered them all and let them go, putting the negroes out of the brigantine aboard Yeates' vessel.

Captain Vane always treated his consort with very little respect, and assumed a superiority over him and his crew, regarding the vessel but as a tender to his own: this gave them disgust; for they thought themselves as good pirates, and as great rogues as the best of them; so they caballed together, and resolved, the first opportunity, to leave the company, and accept of his majesty's pardon, or set up for themselves; either of which they thought more honorable than to be the servants to Vane: the putting aboard so many negroes, where there were so few hands to take care of them, aggravated the matter, though they thought fit to conceal or stifle their resentment at that time.

In a day or two, the pirates lying off at anchor, Yeates in the evening slipped his cable, and put his vessel under sail, standing into the shore; which when Vane saw, he was highly provoked, and got his sloop under sail to chase his consort. Vane's brigantine sailing best, he gained ground of Yeates, and would certainly have come up with them, had he had a little longer run; but just as he got over the bar, when

Vane came within gun-shot of him, he fired a broadside at his old friend, and so took his leave.

Yeates came into North Eddisto river, about ten leagues to the southward of Charleston, and sent an express to the governor, to know if he and his comrades might have the benefit of his majesty's pardon; promising that, if they might, they would surrender themselves to his mercy, with the sloops and negroes. Their request being granted, they all came up, and received certificates; and Captain Thompson, from whom the negroes were taken, had them all restored to him, for the use of his owners.

Vane cruised some time off the bar, in hopes to catch Yeates at his coming out again, but therein he was disappointed; however, he there took two ships from Charleston, which were bound home to England. It happened just at this time, that two sloops well manned and armed, were equipped to go after a pirate, which the governor of South Carolina was informed lay then in Cape Fear river cleaning: but Colonel Rhet, who commanded the sloops, meeting with one of the ships that Vane had plundered, going back over the bar for such necessaries as had been taken from her, and she giving the Colonel an account of being taken by the pirate Vane, and also, that some of her men, while they were prisoners on board of him, had heard the pirates say they should clean in one of the rivers to the southward, he altered his first design, and instead of standing to the northward, in pursuit of the pirate in Cape Fear river, turned to the southward after Vane, who had ordered such reports to be given out, on purpose to put any force that should come after him upon a wrong scent; for he stood away to the northward, so that the pursuit proved to be of no effect. Colonel Rhet's speaking with this ship was the most unlucky thing that could have happened, because it turned him out of the road which, in all probability, would have brought him into the company of Vane, as well as of the pirate he went after, and so they might have been both destroyed; whereas, by the Colonel's going a different way, he not only lost the opportunity of meeting with one, but if the other had not been infatuated, and lain six weeks together at Cape Fear, he would have missed him likewise; however, the Colonel having searched the rivers and inlets, as directed, for several days without success, at length sailed in prosecution of his first design, and met with the pirate accordingly, whom he fought and took.

Captain Vane went into an inlet to the northward, where he met with Captain Teach, otherwise Black Beard, whom he saluted (when he found who he was) with his great guns loaded with shot: it being the custom among pirates when they meet, to do so, though they are wide of one another: Black Beard answered the salute in the same manner, and mutual civilities passed between them some days, when, about the beginning of October, Vane took leave, and sailed farther to the northward.

On the 23d of October, off Long Island, he took a small brigantine bound from Jamaica to Salem in New England, besides a little sloop: they rifled the brigantine, and sent her away. From thence they resolved on a cruise between Cape Meise and Cape Nicholas, where they spent some time without seeing or speaking with any vessel, till the latter end of November; they then fell in with a ship, which it was expected would have struck as soon as their black colors were hoisted; but instead of this she discharged a broadside upon the pirate, and hoisted French colors, which showed her to be a French man-of-war. Vane desired to have nothing more to say to her, but trimmed his sails, and stood away from the Frenchman; however, Monsieur having a mind to be better informed who he was, set all his sails and crowded after him. During this chase the pirates were divided in their resolution what to do. Vane, the captain, was for making off as fast as he could, alleging that the man-of-war was too strong for them to cope with; but one John Rackam, their quarter-master, and who was a kind of check upon the captain, rose up in defence of a contrary opinion, saying, "that though she had more guns, and a greater weight of metal, they might board her, and then the best boys would carry the day." Rackam was well seconded, and the majority was for boarding; but Vane urged, "that it was too rash and desperate an enterprise, the man-of-war appearing to be twice their force, and that their brigantine might be sunk by her before they could reach to board her." The mate, one Robert Deal, was of Vane's opinion, as were about fifteen more, and all the rest joined with Rackam the quarter-master. At length the captain made use of his power to determine this dispute, which in these cases is absolute and uncontrollable, by their own laws, viz., the captain's absolute right of determining in all questions concerning fighting, chasing, or being chased; in all other matters whatsoever the captain being governed by a majority; so the brigantine having the heels, as they term it, of the Frenchman, she came clear off.

But the next day, the captain's conduct was obliged to stand the test of a vote, and a resolution passed against his honor and dignity, which branded him with the name of coward, deposed him from the command, and turned him out of the company with marks of infamy; and with him went all those who did not vote for boarding the French man-of-war. They had with them a small sloop that had been taken by them some time before, which they gave to Vane and the discarded members; and that they might be in a condition to provide for themselves by their own honest endeavors, they let them have a sufficient quantity of provisions and ammunition.

John Rackam was voted captain of the brigantine in Vane's room, and he proceeded towards the Carribbee Islands, where we must leave him, till we have finished our history of Charles Vane.

The sloop sailed for the bay of Honduras, and Vane and his crew put her in as good a condition as they could by the way, that they might follow their old trade. They cruised two or three days off the northwest part of Jamaica, and took a sloop and two perriaguas, all the men of which entered with them: the sloop they kept, and Robert Deal was appointed captain.

On the 16th of December, the two sloops came into the bay, where they found only one vessel at anchor. She was called the *Pearl of Jamaica*, and got under sail at the sight of them; but the pirate sloops coming near Rowland, and showing no colors, he gave them a gun or two, whereupon they hoisted the black flag, and fired three guns each at the *Pearl*. She struck, and the pirates took possession, and carried her away to a small island called Barnacho, where they cleaned. By the way they met with a sloop from Jamaica, as she was going down to the bay, which they also took.

In February, Vane sailed from Barnacho, for a cruise; but, some days after he was out, a violent tornado overtook him, which separated him from his consort, and, after two days' distress, threw his sloop upon a small uninhabited island, near the bay of Honduras, where she staved to pieces, and most of her men were drowned: Vane himself was saved, but reduced to great straits for want of necessaries, having no opportunity to get any thing from the wreck. He lived here some weeks, and was supported chiefly by fishermen, who frequented the island with small crafts from the main, to catch turtles and other fish.

While Vane was upon this island, a ship put in there from Jamaica for water, the captain of which, one Holford, an old buccaneer, happened to be Vane's acquaintance. He thought this a good opportunity to get off, and accordingly applied to his old friend: but Holford absolutely refused him, saying to him, "Charles, I shan't trust you aboard my ship, unless I carry you as a prisoner, for I shall have you caballing with my men, knocking me on the head, and running away with my ship pirating." Vane made all the protestations of honor in the world to him; but, it seems, Captain Holford was too intimately acquainted with him, to repose any confidence at all in his words or oaths. He told him, "He might easily find a way to get off, if he had a mind to it:—I am going down the bay," said he, "and shall return hither in about a month, and if I find you upon the island when I come back, I'll carry you to Jamaica, and there hang you." "How can I get away?" answered Vane. "Are there not fishermen's dories upon the beach? Can't you take one of them?" replied Holford. "What!" said Vane, "would you have me steal a dory then?" "Do you make it a matter of conscience," replied Holford, "to steal a dory, when you have been a common robber and pirate, stealing ships and cargoes, and plundering all mankind that fell in your way! Stay here if you are so squeamish!" and he left him to consider of the matter.

After Captain Holford's departure, another ship put into the same island, in her way home, for water; none of the company knowing Vane, he easily passed for another man, and so was shipped for the voyage. One would be apt to think that Vane was now pretty safe, and likely to escape the fate which his crimes had merited; but here a cross accident happened that ruined all. Holford returning from the bay, was met by this ship, and the captains being very well acquainted with each other, Holford was invited to dine aboard, which he did. As he passed along to the cabin, he chanced to cast his eye down into the hold, and there saw Charles Vane at work: he immediately spoke to the captain, saying, "Do you know whom you have got aboard there?" "Why," said he, "I have shipped a man at such an island, who was cast away in a trading sloop, and he seems to be a brisk hand." "I tell you," replied Captain Holford, "it is Vane the notorious pirate." "If it be he," cried the other, "I won't keep him." "Why then," said Holford, "I'll send and take him aboard, and surrender him at Jamaica." This being agreed upon, Captain Holford, as soon as he returned to his ship, sent his boat with his mate, armed, who coming to Vane, showed him a pistol, and told him he was his prisoner. No man daring to make opposition, he was brought aboard and put into irons; and when Captain Holford arrived at Jamaica, he delivered up his old acquaintance to justice, at which place he was tried, convicted, and executed, as was some time before, Vane's consort, Robert Deal, who was brought thither by one of the men-of-war. It is clear from this how little ancient friendship will avail a great villain, when he is deprived of the power that had before supported and rendered him formidable.

THE TREASURE HUNT

Robert Louis Stevenson

Partly from the damping influence of this alarm, partly to rest Silver and the sick folk, the whole party sat down as soon as they had gained the brow of the ascent.

The plateau being somewhat tilted towards the west, this spot on which we had paused commanded a wide prospect on either hand. Before us, over the tree-tops, we beheld the Cape of the Woods fringed with surf; behind, we not only looked down upon the anchorage and Skeleton Island, but saw—clear across the spit and the eastern lowlands—a great field of open sea upon the east. Sheer above us rose the Spy-glass, here dotted with single pines, there black with precipices. There was no sound but that of the distant breakers, mounting from all round, and the chirp of countless insects in the brush. Not a man, not a sail, upon the sea; the very largeness of the view increased the sense of solitude.

Silver, as he sat, took certain bearings with his compass.

"There are three 'tall trees'" said he, "about in the right line from Skeleton Island. 'Spy-glass shoulder,' I take it, means that lower p'int there. It's child's play to find the stuff now. I've half a mind to dine first."

"I don't feel sharp," growled Morgan. "Thinkin' o' Flint—I think it were—as done me."

"Ah, well, my son, you praise your stars he's dead," said Silver.

"He were an ugly devil," cried a third pirate with a shudder, "that blue in the face too!"

"That was how the rum took him," added Merry. "Blue! Well, I reckon he was blue. That's a true word."

Ever since they had found the skeleton and got upon this train of thought, they had spoken lower and lower, and they had almost got to whispering by now, so that the sound of their talk hardly interrupted the silence of the wood. All of a sudden, out of the middle of the trees in front of us, a thin, high, trembling voice struck up the well-known air and words:

"Fifteen men on the dead man's chest—

Yo-ho-ho, and a bottle of rum!"

I never have seen men more dreadfully affected than the pirates. The colour went from their six faces like enchantment; some leaped to their feet; some clawed hold of others; Morgan grovelled on the ground.

"It's Flint, by—!" cried Merry.

The song had stopped as suddenly as it began—broken off, you would have said, in the middle of a note, as though someone had laid his hand upon the singer's mouth. Coming through the clear, sunny atmosphere among the green tree-tops, I thought it had sounded airily and sweetly; and the effect on my companions was the stranger.

"Come," said Silver, struggling with his ashen lips to get the word out, "this won't do. Stand by to go about. This is a rum start, and I can't name the voice, but it's someone skylarking—someone that's flesh and blood, and you may lay to that."

His courage had come back as he spoke, and some of the colour to his face along with it. Already the others had begun to lend an ear to this encouragement and were coming a little to themselves, when the same voice broke out again—not this time singing, but in a faint distant hail that echoed yet fainter among the clefts of the Spy-glass.

"Darby M'Graw," it wailed—for that is the word that best describes the sound—"Darby M'Graw! Darby M'Graw!" again and again and again; and then rising a little higher, and with an oath that I leave out: "Fetch aft the rum, Darby!"

The buccaneers remained rooted to the ground, their eyes starting from their heads. Long after the voice had died away they still stared in silence, dreadfully, before them.

"That fixes it!" gasped one. "Let's go."

"They was his last words," moaned Morgan, "his last words above board."

Dick had his Bible out and was praying volubly. He had been well brought up, had Dick, before he came to sea and fell among bad companions.

Still Silver was unconquered. I could hear his teeth rattle in his head, but he had not yet surrendered.

"Nobody in this here island ever heard of Darby," he muttered; "not one but us that's here." And then, making a great effort: "Shipmates," he cried, "I'm here to get that stuff, and I'll not be beat by man or devil. I never was feared of Flint in his life, and, by the powers, I'll face him dead. There's seven hundred thousand pound not a quarter of a mile from here. When did ever a gentleman o' fortune show his stern to that much dollars for a boozy old seaman with a blue mug— and him dead too?"

But there was no sign of reawakening courage in his followers, rather, indeed, of growing terror at the irreverence of his words.

"Belay there, John!" said Merry. "Don't you cross a sperrit."

And the rest were all too terrified to reply. They would have run away severally had they dared; but fear kept them together, and kept them close by John, as if his daring helped them. He, on his part, had pretty well fought his weakness down.

"Sperrit? Well, maybe," he said. "But there's one thing not clear to me. There was an echo. Now, no man ever seen a sperrit with a shadow; well then, what's he doing with an echo to him, I should like to know? That ain't in natur', surely?"

This argument seemed weak enough to me. But you can never tell what will affect the superstitious, and to my wonder, George Merry was greatly relieved.

"Well, that's so," he said. "You've a head upon your shoulders, John, and no mistake. 'Bout ship, mates! This here crew is on a wrong tack, I do believe. And come to think on it, it was like Flint's voice, I grant you, but not just so clear-away like it, after all. It was liker somebody else's voice now—it was liker—"

"By the powers, Ben Gunn!" roared Silver.

"Aye, and so it were," cried Morgan, springing on his knees. "Ben Gunn it were!"

"It don't make much odds, do it, now?" asked Dick. "Ben Gunn's not here in the body any more'n Flint."

But the older hands greeted this remark with scorn.

"Why, nobody minds Ben Gunn," cried Merry, "dead or alive, nobody minds him."

It was extraordinary how their spirits had returned and how the natural colour had revived in their faces. Soon they were chatting together, with intervals of listening; and not long after, hearing no further sound, they shouldered the tools and set forth again, Merry walking first with Silver's compass to keep them on the right line with Skeleton Island. He had said the truth: dead or alive, nobody minded Ben Gunn.

Dick alone still held his Bible, and looked around him as he went, with fearful glances; but he found no sympathy, and Silver even joked him on his precautions.

"I told you," said he—"I told you you had sp'iled your Bible. If it ain't no good to swear by, what do you suppose a sperrit would give for it? Not that!" And he snapped his big fingers, halting a moment on his crutch.

But Dick was not to be comforted; indeed, it was soon plain to me that the lad was falling sick; hastened by heat, exhaustion, and the shock of his alarm, the fever, predicted by Dr. Livesey, was evidently growing swiftly higher.

It was fine open walking here, upon the summit; our way lay a little downhill, for, as I have said, the plateau tilted towards the west. The pines, great and small, grew wide apart; and even between the clumps of nutmeg and azalea, wide open spaces baked in the hot sunshine. Striking, as we did, pretty near north-west across the island, we drew, on the one hand, ever nearer under the shoulders of the Spy-glass, and on the other, looked ever wider over that western bay where I had once tossed and trembled in the oracle.

The first of the tall trees was reached, and by the bearings proved the wrong one. So with the second. The third rose nearly two hundred feet into the air above a clump of underwood—a giant of a vegetable, with a red column as big as a cottage, and a wide shadow around in which a company could have manoeuvred. It was conspicuous far to sea both on the east and west and might have been entered as a sailing mark upon the chart.

But it was not its size that now impressed my companions; it was the knowledge that seven hundred thousand pounds in gold lay somewhere buried below its spreading shadow. The thought of the money, as they drew nearer, swallowed up their previous terrors. Their eyes burned in their heads; their feet grew speedier and lighter; their whole soul was found up in that fortune, that whole lifetime of extravagance and pleasure, that lay waiting there for each of them.

Silver hobbled, grunting, on his crutch; his nostrils stood out and quivered; he cursed like a madman when the flies settled on his hot and shiny countenance; he plucked furiously at the line that held me to him and from time to time turned his eyes upon me with a deadly look. Certainly he took no pains to hide his thoughts, and certainly I read them like print. In the immediate nearness of the gold, all else had been forgotten: his promise and the doctor's warning were both things of the past, and I could not doubt that he hoped to seize upon the treasure, find and board the *Hispaniola* under cover of night, cut every honest throat about that island, and sail away as he had at first intended, laden with crimes and riches.

Shaken as I was with these alarms, it was hard for me to keep up with the rapid pace of the treasure-hunters. Now and again I stumbled, and it was then that Silver plucked so roughly at the rope and launched at me his murderous glances. Dick, who had dropped behind us and now brought up the rear, was babbling to himself both prayers and curses as his fever kept rising. This also added to my wretchedness, and to crown all, I was haunted by the thought of the tragedy that had once been acted on that plateau, when that ungodly buccaneer with the blue face—he who died at Savannah, singing and shouting for drink—had there, with his own hand, cut down his six accomplices. This grove that was now so peaceful must then have rung with cries, I thought; and even with the thought I could believe I heard it ringing still.

We were now at the margin of the thicket. "Huzza, mates, all to-gether!" shouted Merry; and the foremost broke into a run.

And suddenly, not ten yards further, we beheld them stop. A low cry arose. Silver doubled his pace, digging away with the foot of his crutch like one possessed; and next moment he and I had come also to a dead halt.

Before us was a great excavation, not very recent, for the sides had fallen in and grass had sprouted on the bottom. In this were the shaft of a pick broken in two and the boards of several packing-cases strewn around. On one of these boards I saw, branded with a hot iron, the name *Walrus*—the name of Flint's ship.

All was clear to probation. The cache had been found and rifled; the seven hundred thousand pounds were gone!

There never was such an overturn in this world. Each of these six men was as though he had been struck. But with Silver the blow passed almost instantly. Every thought of his soul had been set full-stretch, like a racer, on that money; well, he was brought up, in a single second, dead; and he kept his head, found his temper, and changed his plan before the others had had time to realize the disappointment.

"Jim," he whispered, "take that, and stand by for trouble."

And he passed me a double-barrelled pistol.

At the same time, he began quietly moving northward, and in a few steps had put the hollow between us two and the other five. Then he looked at me and nodded, as much as to say, "Here is a narrow corner," as, indeed, I thought it was. His looks were not quite friendly, and I was so revolted at these constant changes that I could not forbear whispering, "So you've changed sides again."

There was no time left for him to answer in. The buccaneers, with oaths and cries, began to leap, one after another, into the pit and to dig with their fingers, throwing the boards aside as they did so. Morgan found a piece of gold. He held it up with a perfect spout of oaths. It was a two-guinea piece, and it went from hand to hand among them for a quarter of a minute.

"Two guineas!" roared Merry, shaking it at Silver. "That's your seven hundred thousand pounds, is it? You're the man for bargains, ain't you? You're him that never bungled nothing, you wooden-headed lubber!"

"Dig away, boys," said Silver with the coolest insolence, "you'll find some pig-nuts and I shouldn't wonder."

"Pig-nuts!" repeated Merry, in a scream. "Mates, do you hear that? I tell you now, that man there knew it all along. Look in the face of him and you'll see it wrote there."

"Ah, Merry," remarked Silver, "standing for cap'n again? You're a pushing lad, to be sure."

But this time everyone was entirely in Merry's favour. They began to scramble out of the excavation, darting furious glances behind them. One thing I observed, which looked well for us: they all got out upon the opposite side from Silver.

Well, there we stood, two on one side, five on the other, the pit between us, and nobody screwed up high enough to offer the first blow. Silver never moved; he watched them, very upright on his crutch, and looked as cool as ever I saw him. He was brave, and no mistake.

At last Merry seemed to think a speech might help matters.

"Mates," says he, "there's two of them alone there; one's the old cripple that brought us all here and blundered us down to this; the other's that cub that I mean to have the heart of. Now, mates—"

He was raising his arm and his voice, and plainly meant to lead a charge. But just then—crack! crack! crack!—three musket-shots flashed out of the thicket. Merry tumbled head foremost into the excavation; the man with the bandage spun round like a teetotum and fell all his length upon his side, where he lay dead, but still twitching; and the other three turned and ran for it with all their might.

Before you could wink, Long John had fired two barrels of a pistol into the struggling Merry, and as the man rolled up his eyes at him in the last agony, "George," said he, "I reckon I settled you."

At the same moment, the doctor, Gray, and Ben Gunn joined us, with smoking muskets, from among the nutmeg trees.

"Forward!" cried the doctor. "Double quick, my lads. We must head 'em off the boats."

And we set off at a great pace, sometimes plunging through the bushes to the chest.

I tell you, but Silver was anxious to keep up with us. The work that man went through, leaping on his crutch till the muscles of his chest were fit to burst, was work no sound man ever equalled; and so thinks the doctor. As it was, he was already thirty yards behind us and on the verge of strangling when we reached the brow of the slope.

"Doctor," he hailed, "see there! No hurry!"

Sure enough there was no hurry. In a more open part of the plateau, we could see the three survivors still running in the same direction as they had started, right for Mizzenmast Hill. We were already between them and the boats; and so we four sat down to breathe, while Long John, mopping his face, came slowly up with us.

"Thank ye kindly, doctor," says he. "You came in about the nick, I guess, for me and Hawkins. And so it's you, Ben Gunn!" he added. "Well, you're a nice one, to be sure."

"I'm Ben Gunn, I am," replied the maroon, wriggling like an eel in his embarrassment. "And," he added, after a long pause, "how do, Mr. Silver? Pretty well, I thank ye, says you."

"Ben, Ben," murmured Silver, "to think as you've done me!"

The doctor sent back Gray for one of the pick-axes deserted, in their flight, by the mutineers, and then as we proceeded leisurely downhill to where the boats were lying, related in a few words what had taken place. It was a story that profoundly interested Silver; and Ben Gunn, the half-idiot maroon, was the hero from beginning to end.

Ben, in his long, lonely wanderings about the island, had found the skeleton—it was he that had rifled it; he had found the treasure; he had dug it up (it was the haft of his pick-axe that lay broken in the excavation); he had carried it on his back, in many weary journeys, from the foot of the tall pine to a cave he had on the two-pointed hill at the north-east angle of the island, and there it had lain stored in safety since two months before the arrival of the *Hispaniola*.

When the doctor had wormed this secret from him on the afternoon of the attack, and when next morning he saw the anchorage deserted, he had gone to Silver, given him the chart, which was now useless—given him the stores, for Ben Gunn's cave was well supplied with goats' meat salted by himself—given anything and everything to get a chance of moving in safety from the stockade to the two-pointed hill, there to be clear of malaria and keep a guard upon the money.

"As for you, Jim," he said, "it went against my heart, but I did what I thought best for those who had stood by their duty; and if you were not one of these, whose fault was it?"

That morning, finding that I was to be involved in the horrid disappointment he had prepared for the mutineers, he had run all the way to the cave, and leaving the squire to guard the captain, had taken Gray and the maroon and started, making the diagonal across the island to be at hand beside the pine. Soon, however, he saw that our party had the start of him; and Ben Gunn, being fleet of foot, had been dispatched in front to do his best alone. Then it had occurred to him to work upon the superstitions of his former shipmates, and he was so far successful that Gray and the doctor had come up and were already ambushed before the arrival of the treasure-hunters.

"Ah," said Silver, "it were fortunate for me that I had Hawkins here. You would have let old John be cut to bits, and never given it a thought, doctor."

"Not a thought," replied Dr. Livesey cheerily.

And by this time we had reached the gigs. The doctor, with the pick-axe, demolished one of them, and then we all got aboard the other and set out to go round by sea for North Inlet.

This was a run of eight or nine miles. Silver, though he was almost killed already with fatigue, was set to an oar, like the rest of us, and we were soon skimming swiftly over a smooth sea. Soon we passed out of the straits and doubled the south-east corner of the island, round which, four days ago, we had towed the *Hispaniola*.

As we passed the two-pointed hill, we could see the black mouth of Ben Gunn's cave and a figure standing by it, leaning on a musket. It was the squire, and we waved a handkerchief and gave him three cheers, in which the voice of Silver joined as heartily as any.

Three miles farther, just inside the mouth of North Inlet, what should we meet but the *Hispaniola*, cruising by herself? The last flood had lifted her, and had there been much wind or a strong tide current, as in the southern anchorage, we should never have found her more, or found her stranded beyond help. As it was, there was little amiss beyond the wreck of the main-sail. Another anchor was got ready and dropped in a fathom and a half of water. We all pulled round again to Rum Cove, the nearest point for Ben Gunn's treasure-house; and then Gray, single-handed, returned with the gig to the *Hispaniola*, where he was to pass the night on guard.

A gentle slope ran up from the beach to the entrance of the cave. At the top, the squire met us. To me he was cordial and kind, saying nothing of my escapade either in the way of blame or praise. At Silver's polite salute he somewhat flushed.

"John Silver," he said, "you're a prodigious villain and imposter—a monstrous imposter, sir. I am told I am not to prosecute you. Well, then, I will not. But the dead men, sir, hang about your neck like mill-stones."

"Thank you kindly, sir," replied Long John, again saluting.

"I dare you to thank me!" cried the squire. "It is a gross dereliction of my duty. Stand back."

And thereupon we all entered the cave. It was a large, airy place, with a little spring and a pool of clear water, overhung with ferns. The floor was sand. Before a big fire lay Captain Smollett; and in a far corner, only duskily flickered over by the blaze, I beheld great heaps of coin and quadrilaterals built of bars of gold. That was Flint's treasure that we had come so far to seek and that had cost already the lives of seventeen men from the *Hispaniola*. How many it had cost in the amassing, what blood and sorrow, what good ships scuttled on the deep, what brave men walking the plank blindfold, what shot of cannon, what shame and lies and cruelty, perhaps no man alive could tell. Yet there were still three upon that island—Silver, and old Morgan, and Ben Gunn—who had each taken his share in these crimes, as each had hoped in vain to share in the reward.

"Come in, Jim," said the captain. "You're a good boy in your line, Jim, but I don't think you and me'll go to sea again. You're too much of the born favourite for me. Is that you, John Silver? What brings you here, man?"

"Come back to my dooty, sir," returned Silver.

"Ah!" said the captain, and that was all he said.

What a supper I had of it that night, with all my friends around me; and what a meal it was, with Ben Gunn's salted goat and some delicacies and a bottle of old wine from the *Hispaniola*. Never, I am sure, were people gayer or happier. And there was Silver, sitting back almost out of the firelight, but eating heartily, prompt to spring forward when anything was wanted, even joining quietly in our laughter—the same bland, polite, obsequious seaman of the voyage out.

The next morning we fell early to work, for the transportation of this great mass of gold near a mile by land to the beach, and thence three miles by boat to the *Hispaniola*, was a considerable task for so small a number of workmen. The three fellows still abroad upon the island did not greatly trouble us; a single sentry on the shoulder of the hill was sufficient to ensure us against any sudden onslaught, and we thought, besides, they had had more than enough of fighting.

Therefore the work was pushed on briskly. Gray and Ben Gunn came and went with the boat, while the rest during their absences piled treasure on the beach. Two of the bars, slung in a rope's end, made a good load for a grown man—one that he was glad to walk slowly with. For my part, as I was not much use at carrying, I was kept busy all day in the cave packing the minted money into bread-bags.

It was a strange collection, like Billy Bones's hoard for the diversity of coinage, but so much larger and so much more varied that I think I never had more pleasure than in sorting them. English, French, Spanish, Portuguese, Georges, and Louises, doubloons and double guineas and moidores and sequins, the pictures of all the kings of Europe for the last hundred years, strange Oriental pieces stamped with what looked like wisps of string or bits of spider's web, round pieces and square pieces, and pieces bored through the middle, as if to wear them round your neck—nearly every variety of money in the world must, I think, have found a place in that collection; and for number, I am sure they were like autumn leaves, so that my back ached with stooping and my fingers with sorting them out.

Day after day this work went on; by every evening a fortune had been stowed aboard, but there was another fortune waiting for the morrow; and all this time we heard nothing of the three surviving mutineers.

At last—I think it was on the third night—the doctor and I were strolling on the shoulder of the hill where it overlooks the lowlands of the isle, when, from out the thick darkness below, the wind brought us a noise between shrieking and singing. It was only a snatch that reached our ears, followed by the former silence.

"Heaven forgive them," said the doctor; "'tis the mutineers!"

"All drunk, sir," struck in the voice of Silver from behind us.

Silver, I should say, was allowed his entire liberty, and in spite of daily rebuffs, seemed to regard himself once more as quite a privileged and friendly dependent. Indeed, it was remarkable how well he bore these slights and with what unwearying politeness he kept on trying to ingratiate himself with all. Yet, I think, none treated him better than a dog, unless it was Ben Gunn, who was still terribly afraid of his old quartermaster, or myself, who had really something to thank him for; although for that matter, I suppose, I had reason to think even worse of him than anybody else, for I had seen him meditating a fresh treachery upon the plateau. Accordingly, it was pretty gruffly that the doctor answered him.

"Drunk or raving," said he.

"Right you were, sir," replied Silver; "and precious little odds which, to you and me."

"I suppose you would hardly ask me to call you a humane man," returned the doctor with a sneer, "and so my feelings may surprise you, Master Silver. But if I were sure they were raving—as I am morally certain one, at least, of them is down with fever—I should leave this camp, and at whatever risk to my own carcass, take them the assistance of my skill."

"Ask your pardon, sir, you would be very wrong," quoth Silver. "You would lose your precious life, and you may lay to that. I'm on your side now, hand and glove; and I shouldn't wish for to see the party weakened, let alone yourself, seeing as I know what I owes you. But these men down there, they couldn't keep their word—no, not supposing they wished to; and what's more, they couldn't believe as you could."

"No," said the doctor. "You're the man to keep your word, we know that."

Well, that was about the last news we had of the three pirates. Only once we heard a gunshot a great way off and supposed them to be hunting. A council was held, and it was decided that we must desert them on the island—to the huge glee, I must say, of Ben Gunn, and with the strong approval of Gray. We left a good stock of powder and shot, the bulk of the salt goat, a few medicines, and some other necessaries, tools, clothing, a spare sail, a fathom or two of rope, and by the particular desire of the doctor, a handsome present of tobacco.

That was about our last doing on the island. Before that, we had got the treasure stowed and had shipped enough water and the remainder of the goat meat in case of any distress; and at last, one fine morning, we weighed anchor, which was about all that we could manage, and stood out of North Inlet, the same colours flying that the captain had flown and fought under at the palisade.

The three fellows must have been watching us closer than we thought for, as we soon had proved. For coming through the narrows, we had to lie very near the southern point, and there we saw all three of them kneeling together on a spit of sand, with their arms raised in supplication. It went to all our hearts, I think, to leave them in that wretched state; but we could not risk another mutiny; and to take them home for the gibbet would have been a cruel sort of kindness. The doctor hailed them and told them of the stores we had left, and where they were to find them. But they continued to call us by name and appeal to us, for God's sake, to be merciful and not leave them to die in such a place.

At last, seeing the ship still bore on her course and was now swiftly drawing out of earshot, one of them—I know not which it was—leapt to his feet with a hoarse cry, whipped his musket to his shoulder, and sent a shot whistling over Silver's head and through the main-sail.

After that, we kept under cover of the bulwarks, and when next I looked out they had disappeared from the spit, and the spit itself had almost melted out of sight in the growing distance. That was, at least, the end of that; and before noon, to my inexpressible joy, the highest rock of Treasure Island had sunk into the blue round of sea.

We were so short of men that everyone on board had to bear a hand—only the captain lying on a mattress in the stern and giving his orders, for though greatly recovered he was still in want of quiet. We laid her head for the nearest port in Spanish America, for we could not risk the voyage home without fresh hands; and as it was, what with baffling winds and a couple of fresh gales, we were all worn out before we reached it.

It was just at sundown when we cast anchor in a most beautiful land-locked gulf, and were immediately surrounded by shore boats full of Negroes and Mexican Indians and half-bloods selling fruits and vegetables and offering to dive for bits of money. The sight of so many good-humoured faces (especially the blacks), the taste of the tropical fruits, and above all the lights that began to shine in the town made a most charming contrast to our dark and bloody sojourn on the island; and the doctor and the squire, taking me along with them, went ashore to pass the early part of the night. Here they met the captain of an English man-of-war, fell in talk with him, went on board his ship, and, in short, had so agreeable a time that day was breaking when we came alongside the *Hispaniola*.

Ben Gunn was on deck alone, and as soon as we came on board he began, with wonderful contortions, to make us a confession. Silver was gone. The maroon had connived at his escape in a shore boat some hours ago, and he now assured us he had only done so to preserve our lives, which would certainly have been forfeit if "that man with the one leg had stayed aboard." But this was not all. The sea-cook had not gone empty-handed. He had cut through a bulkhead unobserved and had removed one of the sacks of coin, worth perhaps three or four hundred guineas, to help him on his further wanderings.

I think we were all pleased to be so cheaply quit of him.

Well, to make a long story short, we got a few hands on board, made a good cruise home, and the *Hispaniola* reached Bristol just as Mr. Blandly was beginning to think of fitting out her consort. Five men only of those who had sailed returned with her. "Drink and the devil had done for the rest," with a vengeance, although, to be sure, we were not quite in so bad a case as that other ship they sang about:

With one man of her crew alive,
What put to sea with seventy-five.

All of us had an ample share of the treasure and used it wisely or foolishly, according to our natures. Captain Smollett is now retired from the sea. Gray not only saved his money, but being suddenly smit with the desire to rise, also studied his profession, and he is now mate and part owner of a fine full-rigged ship, married besides, and the father of a family. As for Ben Gunn, he got a thousand pounds, which he spent or lost in three weeks, or to be more exact, in nineteen days, for he was back begging on the twentieth. Then he was given a lodge to keep, exactly as he had feared upon the island; and he still lives, a great favourite, though something of a butt, with the country boys, and a notable singer in church on Sundays and saints' days.

Of Silver we have heard no more. That formidable seafaring man with one leg has at last gone clean out of my life; but I dare say he met his old Negress, and perhaps still lives in comfort with her and Captain Flint. It is to be hoped so, I suppose, for his chances of comfort in another world are very small.

The bar silver and the arms still lie, for all that I know, where Flint buried them; and certainly they shall lie there for me. Oxen and wain-ropes would not bring me back again to that accursed island; and the worst dreams that ever I have are when I hear the surf booming about its coasts or start upright in bed with the sharp voice of Captain Flint still ringing in my ears: "Pieces of eight! Pieces of eight!"

PETER THE GREAT

Frank R. Stockton

CHAPTER FOURTEEN

Very prominent among the early regular buccaneers was a Frenchman who came to be called Peter the Great. This man seems to have been one of those adventurers who were not buccaneers in the earlier sense of the word (by which I mean they were not traders who touched at Spanish settlements to procure cattle and hides, and who were prepared to fight any Spaniards who might interfere with them), but they were men who came from Europe on purpose to prey upon Spanish possessions, whether on land or sea. Some of them made a rough sort of settlement on the island of Tortuga, and then it was that Peter the Great seems to have come into prominence. He gathered about him a body of adherents, but although he had a great reputation as an individual pirate, it seems to have been a good while before he achieved any success as a leader.

The fortunes of Peter and his men must have been at a pretty low ebb when they found themselves cruising in a large, canoe-shaped boat not far from the island of Hispaniola. There were twenty-nine of them in all, and they were not able to procure a vessel suitable for their purpose. They had been a long time floating about in an aimless way, hoping to see some Spanish merchant-vessel which they might attack and possibly capture, but no such vessel appeared. Their provisions began to give out, the men were hungry, discontented, and grumbling. In fact, they were in almost as bad a condition as were the sailors of Columbus just before they discovered signs of land, after their long and weary voyage across the Atlantic.

When Peter and his men were almost on the point of despair, they perceived, far away upon the still waters, a large ship. With a great jump, hope sprang up in the breast of every man. They seized the oars and pulled in the direction of the distant craft. But when they were near enough, they saw that the vessel was not a merchantman, probably piled with gold and treasure, but a man-of-war belonging to the Spanish fleet. In fact, it was the vessel of the vice-admiral. This was an astonishing and disheartening state of things. It was very much as if a lion, hearing the approach of probable prey, had sprung from the thicket where he had been concealed, and had beheld before him, not a fine, fat deer, but an immense and scrawny elephant.

But the twenty-nine buccaneers in the crew were very hungry. They had not come out upon those waters to attack men-of-war, but, more than that, they had not come out to perish by hunger and thirst. There could be no doubt that there was plenty to eat and to drink on that tall Spanish vessel, and if they could not get food and water they could not live more than a day or two longer.

Under the circumstances it was not long before Peter the Great made up his mind that if his men would stand by him, he would endeavor to capture that Spanish war-vessel; when he put the question to his crew they all swore that they would follow him and obey his orders as long as life was left in their bodies. To attack a vessel armed with cannon, and manned by a crew very much larger than their little party, seemed almost like throwing themselves upon certain death. But still, there was a chance that in some way they might get the better of the Spaniards; whereas, if they rowed away again into the solitudes of the ocean, they would give up all chance of saving themselves from death by starvation. Steadily, therefore, they pulled toward the Spanish vessel, and slowly—for there was but little wind—she approached them.

The people in the man-of-war did not fail to perceive the little boat far out on the ocean, and some of them sent to the captain and reported the fact. The news, however, did not interest him, for he was engaged in playing cards in his cabin, and it was not until an hour afterward that he consented to come on deck and look out toward the boat which had been sighted, and which was now much nearer.

Taking a good look at the boat, and perceiving that it was nothing more than a canoe, the captain laughed at the advice of some of his officers, who thought it would be well to fire a few cannon-shot and sink the little craft. The captain thought it would be a useless proceeding. He did not know anything about the people in the boat, and he did not very much care, but he remarked that if they should come near enough, it might be a good thing to put out some tackle and haul them and their boat on deck, after which they might be examined and questioned whenever it should suit his convenience. Then he went down to his cards. If Peter the Great and his men could have been sure that if they were to row alongside the Spanish vessel they would have been quietly hauled on deck and examined, they would have been delighted at the opportunity. With cutlasses, pistols, and knives, they were more than ready to demonstrate to the Spaniards what sort of fellows they were, and the captain would have found hungry pirates uncomfortable persons to question.

But it seemed to Peter and his crew a very difficult thing indeed to get themselves on board the man-of-war, so they curbed their ardor and enthusiasm, and waited until nightfall before approaching nearer. As soon as it became dark enough they slowly and quietly paddled toward the great ship, which was now almost becalmed. There were no lights in the boat, and the people on the deck of the vessel saw and heard nothing on the dark waters around them.

When they were very near the man-of-war, the captain of the buccaneers—according to the ancient accounts of this adventure—ordered his chirurgeon, or surgeon, to bore a large hole in the bottom of their canoe. It is probable that this officer, with his saws and other surgical instruments, was expected to do carpenter work when there were no duties for him to perform in the regular line of his profession. At any rate, he went to work, and noiselessly bored the hole.

This remarkable proceeding showed the desperate character of these pirates. A great, almost impossible task was before them, and nothing but absolute recklessness could enable them to succeed. If his men should meet with strong opposition from the Spaniards in the proposed attack, and if any of them should become frightened and try to retreat to the boat, Peter knew that all would be lost, and consequently he determined to make it impossible for any man to get away in that boat. If they could not conquer the Spanish vessel they must die on her decks.

When the half-sunken canoe touched the sides of the vessel, the pirates, seizing every rope or projection on which they could lay their hands, climbed up the sides of the man-of-war, as if they had been twenty-nine cats, and springing over the rail, dashed upon the sailors who were on deck. These men were utterly stupefied and astounded. They had seen nothing, they had heard nothing, and all of a sudden they were confronted with savage fellows with cutlasses and pistols.

Some of the crew looked over the sides to see where these strange visitors had come from, but they saw nothing, for the canoe had gone to the bottom. Then they were filled with a superstitious horror, believing that the wild visitors were devils who had dropped from the sky, for there seemed no other place from which they could come. Making no attempt to defend themselves, the sailors, wild with terror, tumbled below and hid themselves, without even giving an alarm.

The Spanish captain was still playing cards, and whether he was winning or losing, the old historians do not tell us, but very suddenly a newcomer took a hand in the game. This was Peter the Great, and he played the ace of trumps. With a great pistol in his hand, he called upon the Spanish captain to surrender. That noble commander glanced around. There was a savage pirate holding a pistol at the head of each of the officers at the table. He threw up his cards. The trick was won by Peter and his men.

The rest of the game was easy enough. When the pirates spread themselves over the vessel, the frightened crew got out of sight as well as they could. Some, who attempted to seize their arms in order to defend themselves, were ruthlessly cut down or shot, and when the hatches had been securely fastened upon the sailors who had fled below, Peter the Great was captain and owner of that tall Spanish man-of-war.

It is quite certain that the first thing these pirates did to celebrate their victory was to eat a rousing good supper, and then they took charge of the vessel, and sailed her triumphantly over the waters on which, not many hours before, they had feared that a little boat would soon be floating, filled with their emaciated bodies.

This most remarkable success of Peter the Great worked a great change, of course, in the circumstances of himself and his men. But it worked a greater change in the career, and possibly in the character of the captain. He was now a very rich man, and all his followers had plenty of money. The Spanish vessel was amply supplied with provisions, and there was also on board a great quantity of gold bullion, which was to be shipped to Spain. In fact, Peter and his men had booty enough to satisfy any sensible pirate. Now we all know that sensible pirates, and people in any sphere of life who are satisfied when they have enough, are very rare indeed, and therefore it is not a little surprising that the bold buccaneer, whose story we are now telling, should have proved that he merited, in a certain way, the title his companions had given him.

Sailing his prize to the shores of Hispaniola, Peter put on shore all the Spaniards whose services he did not desire. The rest of his prisoners he compelled to help his men work the ship, and then, without delay, he sailed away to France, and there he retired entirely from the business of piracy, and set himself up as a gentleman of wealth and leisure.

A HARROWING ESCAPE

Daniel Collins

CHAPTER FIFTEEN

DISTRICT OF MAINE, ss.

L. S.

BE IT REMEMBERED, THAT on this twenty-sixth day of April, in the year of our Lord one thousand eight hundred and twenty-five, and the forty-ninth year of the Independence of the United States of America, Mr. JOHN DORR, of the District of Maine, has deposited in this Office, the title of a Book, the right whereof he claims as Proprietor, in the words following, viz:

"Narrative of the Shipwreck of the Brig Betsey, of Wiscasset, and murder of five of her crew, by Pirates, on the coast of Cuba, Dec. 1824. By Daniel Collins, one of the only two survivors.

> *"——quæque ipse miserrima vidi,*
> *Et quorum pars magna fui."*
> *Wiscasset: Printed by John Dorr. 1825."*

In conformity to the Act of the Congress of the United States, entitled, "An Act for the encouragement of learning, by securing the copies of maps, charts, and books, to the authors and proprietors of such copies, during the times therein mentioned;" and also, to an act, entitled, "An Act supplementary

to an act, entitled, an act for the encouragement of learning,
by securing the copies of maps, charts, and books, to the au-
thors and proprietors of such copies, during the times therein
mentioned, and extending the benefits thereof to the arts of de-
signing, engraving, and etching historical and other prints."

J. MUSSEY, Clerk of the District Court of Maine.
A true copy as of record.—Attest,
J. MUSSEY, Clerk D. C. Maine.

On the 28th of November, 1824, I sailed from Wiscasset (ME), for Matanzas, in the Island of Cuba, on board the brig Betsey, laden with lumber; our officers and crew consisting of seven, viz. ELLIS HILTON, of Wiscasset, master; JOSHUA MERRY, of Edgecomb, 1st mate; DANIEL COLLINS, of Wiscasset, 2d mate; CHARLES MANUEL, (a Portuguese), SETH RUSSELL, and BENJ. BRIDGE, seamen; and DE-TREY JEOME, cook. On the 18th of December we passed the Berry Islands, and early next morning came to anchor within a league of Orange Key, on the Bahama Banks. It was the morning of the Sabbath, so calm and clear that even the lengthened billows of the Gulf Stream seemed sleeping around us, and the most untutored son of Neptune could not but remember that it was a holy day, consecrated to devotion and rest. Here we continued until noon, when a fresh breeze from the North invited us to weigh anchor and unfurl our sails, which, swelling with a fair wind, were as buoyant as our own spirits, at the increasing prospect of reaching our port of destination.

About sunset, a dark and stormy night approaching, I suggested to our Captain the propriety of shortening sail, to which he would not assent, presuming we might get into Matanzas the next day. The night was so dark that we could not discover objects distinctly beyond the length of the vessel, and the wind blew more than an usual wholesale breeze, which drove her, heavy-laden as she was, at the rate of 9 knots, calculating ourselves more than 6 leagues to the windward of the Double Headed Shot Keys. At half past 2 o'clock I was relieved at the helm, and after casting a glance over the lee side and discovering no alteration in the appearance of the water, I observed to my shipmate at the helm, "there is no fear of you"—went below and turned in with my clothes on. No one was below at this time except the Captain, who stood at the foot of the companion way viewing the appearance of the weather.

I had been in my berth about half an hour when I felt a tremendous shock, which covered me with the muskets that were over head, boxes, barrels and other cabin articles; the water pouring into my berth through the quarter. I cleared myself by a violent effort, ran for the companion way—it was gone—turned—leaped through the sky light, and was on deck in an instant. We were in the hollow of a sea, and I could just discern over our main peak the dark top of the rock, which we had struck, stem on, then going at the rate of nine knots. This rock, which some of our crew supposed to be a wreck, was concealed from the helmsman by the mainsail. Two of the crew were at the pumps—the deck load, which consisted of boards, scantlings and oars, piled on each side as high as their heads—the other two people were probably on the quarter deck. It was a careless watch for a dark night, even at our supposed distance from the Keys; but we were now in no situation to complain. A part of our stern and the yawl at the davits, had gone together. I ran forward to clear the anchors in order to prevent her from ranging ahead on another rock which I could perceive among the surf; but a greater part of the bows were gone, and with them the anchors.—The water was already groaning under the deck—she arose for the last time on the crest of another sea nearly to the top of the rock, quivering like a bird under its death-wound. Our Captain and crew were around the long-boat endeavoring to cut the leashings and right her, while I secured a compass, an axe, a bucket and several oars. The next sea we descended she struck; opened fore and aft, the masts and spars, with all sails standing, thundering against the rock, and the lumber from below deck cracking and crashing in every direction. We were all launched overboard on the lumber that adhered together, clinging hold of the long-boat as the seaman's last ark of refuge, and endeavoring to right her, which we did in a few moments; but not without the misfortune of splitting a plank in her bottom. We all sprang in, bearing with us nothing but the sea clothes we had on, the few articles before named, and some fragments of the boat's leashings. The Captain's dog, which a few moments before had been leaping from plank to plank after the cat, with as determined an enmity as though the pursuit had been through a farmyard, followed us; a companion by no means unwelcome to those, who, without provision or water, might have been compelled to depend on this faithful animal for the preservation of their lives.

A new difficulty now presented itself: Our boat leaked so fast that three hands, two with hats and one with the bucket, were unable to free her; but with the aid of the only knife we had saved, and the fragments of the leashings, I filled some of the seams, which helped to free her; but not so effectually as to relieve a single hand from bailing.

About a league from the rock we hung on our oars, watching the sea that ran mountains high, until day-light, when we pulled up under its lee, but could discover neither fresh water nor a particle of provisions, except a few pieces of floating bread that we dared not eat. Fragments of boards and spars were floating here and there, but the only article either of convenience or comfort we could preserve was a large blanket, which was converted into a sail and set; and being compelled by the violence of the sea, we put her away before the wind, steering S. half E.—a course that must have carried us far East of our intended track, had it not been for the strong Westerly current in St. Nicholas' Channel.

The rock on which we were wrecked, and from which we took our departure in the boat, proved to be one of the N. E. range of the Double Headed Shot Keys.

We steered the above course all that day, bailing and rowing without a moment's cessation, and approaching, as was then supposed, the Island of Cuba, the coast of which, except the entrance of Matanzas and Havana, was unknown to us. We knew, however, that the whole coast was lined with dangerous shoals and keys, though totally ignorant of the situation of those East of Point Yeacos. A hundred times during the day, were our eyes directed to every point of the compass, in search of a sail, but in vain—we were too far to the eastward of the usual track to Matanzas.

In a state of mind bordering on that insanity which is sometimes caused by hunger, thirst and despair united, we passed a most perilous night. At the very first dawn of light every eye was again in search of a sail. A small dark speck on the ocean was descried ahead, about 5 leagues distant! The joyful sound of land ran through our nerves like an electric shock, and gave new life to the oars. The wind being fair, the aid of our sail, which was equal to two additional oars, gave us such head way, that as the rays of the rising sun sported over the tops of the waves and fell on the small spot of land ahead, we found ourselves nearing one of the Cuba Keys.

The land we first discovered was a little Island of about three acres, that arose above the surrounding key, as high as the tops of the mangroves. The name of this key—the largest of its group—was of so sacred an import, that one would have supposed it had been a refuge no less from the storms of persecution, than those of the element around it.

The distance across was about three miles, two of which we had already passed, directly for the beach, a few rods from which as we had previously discovered, were two huts, inhabited by fishermen, whom we could now see passing in and out. When at the above distance from the reef, our attention was suddenly arrested by the appearance of two wrecks of vessels, of too large a size, one would have supposed, to have beaten over the reef. As the water grew shoaler I could see an even pipe clay bottom, on which our boat grounded an hundred yards from the shore. One of the inhabitants came off in a flat bottom'd log canoe about 25 feet long and 2-½ wide, hailed us in Spanish, demanding who we were, and was answered by Manuel our Portuguese.

As this Spaniard, who was the head fisherman, came along side, he was recognized by Capt. Hilton as the same of whom he had purchased some sugars the voyage before at Matanzas.

Early in the morning we turned out and we went down to the Cove before described, in order to bathe. While we were clothing ourselves on the shore at the head of the Cove, we discovered, at high-water mark, a number of human skeletons—(except the skulls)—bleached and partly decayed. The bones of the fingers, hands and ribs were entire. To me this was no very pleasant discovery, and I observed to Mr. Merry that "we might all be murdered in such a place without the possibility of its being known"; but the bones were, at the time, supposed to have belonged to seamen that might have been shipwrecked on the reef near this part of the key.

On our return to the hut we found breakfast awaiting us. This day we spent in rambling about the Island, and were generally followed by two of the fishermen, who manifested more than usual vigilance. During this as well as the preceding day they suspended their usual occupation, and passed their time in loitering about. My suspicions were increased by a number of circumstances to such a degree, that I urged Capt. Hilton to depart in our own boat bad as she was; but he expressed great confidence in the head fisherman, from his previous acquaintance with him at Matanzas.

As we had made arrangements to depart the next morning, all hands were preparing to turn in at an early hour when the master fisherman observed, it was too *hot* to sleep in the house, drew his blanket over his shoulders and went out.

It is a little singular that such a circumstance should not have produced on the minds of my shipmates the same effect it did on mine, as the weather was then uncomfortably cool to me within the hut. But in justice to them I ought to add, that a singular dream the night before our shipwreck, had produced on my mind a kind of sailor's superstition, which banished sleep from my eyes, even now while they were enjoying its refreshing influence.

After I had paced the room several times, one of the fishermen arose and extinguished the light, and when all was still, I went to the door that had been fastened after the master fisherman, drew the bolt without disturbing any one, and went out. At the threshold of the door I found an axe which I took in my hand, walked around the hut several times, but could not discover the object of my search. I at length found his blanket tucked up among the thatch under the eaves of the hut, and immediately re-entered the room to tell my companions I was apprehensive that this strange departure of the Spaniard was influenced by another motive than that expressed.

He could not go far without wading in the water, which was two or three feet deep all over this extensive key, except the spot around the huts, on which he was not to be found; and it is well known to mariners, that these keys are dissected by numerous creeks like the one already described, which in some instances extend miles among the mangrove bushes, where a sea robber might conceal himself for months without the fear of detection.

Without disturbing the Spaniards, I shook Mr. Merry and whispered to him my suspicions, on which we both went to the door and sat down to await the fisherman's return. When I first awaked him he trembled with fear that some unnatural fate awaited us. But the night passed without any further disturbance, and at day-light we all, by previous arrangement, commenced loading the two canoes, (which were of the same dimensions of that already described) by wading off to them with the fish in our arms. It was about sunrise when we had completed loading, and while we were all in the huts, the master fisherman suddenly entered—saluted Capt. Hilton in Spanish, and requested all our people and three of his own to accompany him to the schooner before named, in order to haul her out of the creek and moor her off, preparatory to our departure: this we did with no little labor, wading into the mud and water breast high. After we had anchored her about half a mile abreast of the huts, and discharged the fish from the canoes into her, we returned to the huts to breakfast.

When the master fisherman returned in the morning, I observed that his trowsers were wet up to his hips, and he appeared as though he had been wading several miles.

After breakfast we finished loading the little schooner, and returned to the huts to bring down some small stores. As we were all standing before the huts, the master fisherman was seen pointing to the Eastward and laughing with his companions. On looking in the direction he was pointing, I discovered the object of his amusement to be a small vessel just doubling an Easterly point of the key, about seven miles distant *within the Reef*, and bearing away for us. I had too often seen the grin of a Spaniard accompanied with the stab of his stiletto, to pass the circumstance unnoticed. By my request Manuel inquired of the Spaniards what vessel it was, and received for answer, that "it was the King's Cutter in search of Pirates." This answer satisfied us, and in a short time we were all hands, the master fisherman and three of his crew, on board our vessel. As soon as we were ready to weigh anchor, observing the Spaniard intent on watching the "Cutter," and delaying unnecessarily to get under way, I began to hoist the foresail, on which, he, for the first time, sang out to me in broken English, "no foresail, no foresail." By this time the sail was within three quarters of a mile of us. As I stood on the forecastle watching her, I saw one of her people forward, pointing at us what I supposed a spy glass; but in an instant the report of a musket and whistle of a bullet by my ears, convinced me of my mistake. This was followed by the discharge of, at least, twenty blunderbusses and muskets, from which the balls flew like hail-stones, lodging in various parts of our schooner; one of which pierced my trowsers and another Mr. Merry's jacket, without any essential injury.

At the commencement of the firing the four fishermen concealed themselves below deck, out of danger, and our Portuguese attempting to follow their example was forced back. I remained on the forecastle watching the vessel until the whistleing of six or seven bullets by my ears, warned me of my danger. At first I settled down on my knees, still anxious to ascertain the cause of this unprovoked outrage, until they approached within two or three hundred feet of us, when I prostrated myself on the deck, soon after which, the master fisherman arose, waved his hat at them, and the firing ceased. About forty or fifty feet abreast of us, she dropped anchor and gave orders for the canoe at our stern to come along side, which one of our fishermen obeyed, and brought on board of us their Captain and three men. The supposed Cutter was an open boat of about thirty-five feet keel, painted red inside and black without, except a streak of white about two inches wide; calculated for rowing or sailing—prepared with long sweeps, and carrying a jib, foresail, mainsail, and squaresail. She was manned by ten Spaniards, each armed with a blunderbuss, or musket, a *machete*, long knife, and pair of pistols. They were all dressed with neat jackets and trowsers, and wore palm-leaf hats. Their beards were very long, and appeared as though they had not been shaved for eight or nine months.

One of them had an extremely savage appearance, having received a blow, probably from a cutlass, across his face, that had knocked in all his front teeth and cut off a part of his upper lip, the scar extending some distance beyond the angles of the mouth—three of the fingers of his left hand, with a part of the little finger, were cut off, and the thumb was badly scarred. He was tall, well proportioned, and appeared to have some authority over the others. The Captain was stout, and so corpulent that I should not underrate his weight at 260 pounds. He reminded me strongly of a Guinea Captain I had formerly seen. He was shaved after the manner of the Turks; the beard of his upper lip being very long—was richly dressed—armed with a machete and knife on one side, and a pair of pistols on the other; besides which, he wore a dirk within his vest. After examining our papers, which had been accidentally saved by Capt. Hilton, he took out of a net purse, two doubloons, and presented them to the master fisherman in presence of all hands. This, we at first supposed to be intended as some compensation for the injury done, by firing at us. The account of our shipwreck, sufferings, and providential escape to the Island, was now related to him, by Manuel, which he noticed, by a slight shrug of the shoulders, without changing a single muscle of his face. He had a savage jeer in his look during the recital of our misfortunes, that would have robbed misery of her ordinary claims to compassion, and denied the unhappy sufferer even a solitary expression of sympathy.

After he had ascertained who we were, he returned to his own boat with three of his men, leaving one on board of us as a kind of prize master. Our master fisherman, who also accompanied him, was greeted by all on board the armed vessel in a manner that denoted him to have been an old acquaintance. We could see them passing to each other a long white jug, which, after they had all drank, they shook at us, saying in broken English, "Anglois, vill you have some *Aquedente*?" to which we made no reply. When they had apparently consulted among themselves about half an hour, they sent two men, with the jug, on board of us, from which we all drank sparingly, in order to avoid offence, and they returned to their own vessel, took in two more men and proceeded to the huts, which they entered and went around several times, then came down to our long boat and examined her carefully. After this they came off to our vessel with the two canoes, one of which, went to the armed boat and brought on board of us, all but the Captain and two of his men. Our little crew had thus far been the anxious spectators of these mysterious manoeuvres.

There were circumstances which at one time encouraged the belief that we were in the hands of friends, and at another, that these pretended friends were calmly preparing for a "foul and most unnatural
murder." Capt. Hilton was unwilling yet to yield his confidence in the
treacherous Spaniard, who, I did not doubt, had already received the
price of our blood. In this state of painful suspense, vibrating between
hope and fear, we remained, until the master fisherman threw on the
deck a ball of cord, made of tough, strong bark, about the size of a
man's thumb, from which they cut seven pieces of about nine feet
each—went to Capt. Hilton and attempted to take off his over-coat,
but were prevented by a signal from their Captain. They now commenced binding his arms behind him just above the elbows with one
of the pieces of cord, which they passed several times round, and drew
so tight, that he groaned out in all the bitterness of his anguish.

My fears that they were pirates were now confirmed; and when I
saw them, without temptation or provocation, cruelly torturing one
whom shipwreck had thrown among them, a penniless sailor, reduced
by sickness to an almost helpless condition, and entreating with all the
tenderness of a penitent that they would not cut him off in the blos-
som of his sins, and before he had reached the meridian of life—re-
minding them of the wife and parents he left behind, I burst into tears
and arose involuntarily as if to sell my life at the dearest rate, but was
shoved back by one of the pirates who gave me a severe blow on the
breast with the muzzle of his cocked blunderbuss. A scene of wo ensued which would have tried the stoutest heart, and it appeared to me
that even they endeavored to divert their minds from it, by a constant
singing and laughing, so loud as to drown the sound of our lamenta-
tions. After they had told Manuel they should carry us to Matanzas as
prisoners of war, they proceeded to pinion our arms as they had Capt.
Hilton's, so tight as to produce excruciating pain.

We were now completely in their power, and they rolled us about
with as much indifference as though we had been incapable of feeling,
tumbling us into the canoes without mercy. They threw me with such
force that I struck the back of my neck against the seat of the canoe
and broke it. Capt. Hilton, Mr. Merry, Bridge, and the Cook were in one
canoe; Russell, Manuel, and myself in the other. For the first time they

now informed us that they were about to cut our throats, which information they accompanied with the most appalling signs, by drawing their knives across their throats, imitating stabbing and various other tortures. Four pirates accompanied the other canoe and three ours, besides the four fishermen, two to manage each canoe. We were thus carried along side the piratical schooner, when all their fire arms were passed on board of her; the arm chest, which was in the stern sheets and covered with a tarpaulin, opened, several long knives and machetes taken out, their keen edges examined with the greatest scrutiny and passed on board the canoes for the expressed purpose of murdering us all.

The seven pirates and four fishermen, as before, now proceeded with us toward the beach until the water was about three feet deep, when they all got out; the two fishermen to each canoe, hauling us along, and the pirates walking by the side of us, one to each of our crew, torturing us all the way by drawing their knives across our throats, grasping the same, and pushing us back under the water which had been taken in by rocking the canoes. While some of us were in the most humiliating manner beseeching of them to spare our lives, and others with uplifted eyes were again supplicating that Divine mercy which had preserved them from the fury of the elements, they were singing and laughing, and occasionally telling us in broken English, that "Americans were very good beef for their knives." Thus they proceeded with us nearly a mile from the vessel, which we were now losing sight of by doubling a point at the entrance of the cove before described; and when within a few rods of its head, *where we had before seen the human bones*, the canoes were hauled abreast of each other, from twelve to twenty feet apart, preparatory to our execution.

The stillness of death was now around us—for the very flood-gates of feeling had been burst asunder and exhausted grief at its fountain. It was a beautiful morning—not a cloud to obscure the rays of the sun—and the clear blue sky presented a scene too pure for deeds of darkness. But the lonely sheet of water, on which, side by side, we lay, presented that hopeless prospect which is more ably described by another.

We had scarcely passed the last parting look at each other, when the work of death commenced.

They seized Captain Hilton by the hair—bent his head and shoulders over the gun-wale, and I could distinctly hear them chopping the bone of the neck. They then wrung his neck, separated the head from the body by a slight draw of the sword, and let it drop into the water;—there was a dying shriek—a convulsive struggle—and all I could discern was the arms dangling over the side of the canoe, and the ragged stump pouring out the blood like a torrent.

There was an imploring look in the innocent and youthful face of Mr. Merry that would have appealed to the heart of any one but a pirate. As he arose on his knees, in the posture of a penitent, supplicating for mercy even on the verge of eternity, he was prostrated with a blow of the cutlass, his bowels gushing out of the wound. They then pierced him through the breast in several places with a long pointed knife, and cut his throat from ear to ear.

The Captain's dog, repulsed in his repeated attempts to rescue his master, sat whining beside his lifeless body, looking up to these blood hounds in human shape, as if to tell them, that even brutal cruelty would be glutted with the blood of two innocent, unoffending victims.

Bridge and the Cook, they pierced through the breast, as they had Merry, in several places with their knives, and then split their heads open with their cutlasses.—Their dying groans had scarcely ceased, and I was improving the moment of life that yet remained, when I heard the blow behind me—the blood and brains that flew all over my head and shoulders, warned me that poor old Russel had shared the fate of the others; and as I turned my head to catch the eye of my executioner, I saw the head of Russel severed in two nearly its whole length, with a single blow of the cutlass, and even without the decency of removing his cap. At the sound of the blow, Manuel, who sat before me, leaped over board, and four of the pirates were in full chase after him. In what manner he loosed his hands, I am unable to say—his escape, I shall hereafter explain. My eyes were fixed on my supposed executioner, watching the signal of my death—he was on my right and partly behind me—my head, which was covered with a firm tarpaulin hat, was turned in a direction that brought my shoulders fore and aft the canoe—the blow came—it divided the top of my hat, struck my head so severely as to stun me, and glanced off my left shoulder, taking the skin and some flesh in its way, and divided my pinion cord on the arm. I was so severely stunned that I did not leap from the canoe, but pitched over the left side, and was just arising from the water, not yet my length from her, as a pirate threw his knife which struck me, but did not retard my flight an instant; and I leaped forward through the water, expecting a blow from behind at every step.

The shrieks of the dying had ceased—the scene of horrid butchery in the canoes was now over—Manuel and I were in the water about knee deep—two of the Pirates after me, and all the rest, with the fishermen, except one pirate, after Manuel. We ran in different directions; I, towards the mouth of the Cove, making nearly a semicircle in my track, to keep them over my shoulder, which brought me back again towards the canoes; and as the remaining pirate came out in order to cut me off, I was obliged to run between the canoes, so near the last pirate, that he made a pass at me and fell, which gave me the start. At the first of our race, I was after Manuel, with pirates before and behind. My object was to gain the bushes as soon as possible, supposing their cutlasses would be an obstacle, which I had the good fortune to prove. I lost sight of Manuel just as I entered the bushes; he was up to his breast in water, and the pirates near him. When I entered the bushes one of the pirates was within ten feet of me, and continued striking, hoping to reach me; and all of them yelling in the most savage manner, during the whole distance. The most of the way, the water and mud was nearly up to my hips—the mangroves were very thick, covered, as I before observed, with oyster shells up to high water mark. It was about noon when I entered these bushes, my course Westerly, the pirates after me, repeatedly in view, one of them frequently within three rods of me. Had it been on cleared land, I should soon have been overtaken by them; but the bushes were so large and thick as frequently to entangle their swords. I was barefoot; and had I worn shoes, they would soon have been lost in the mud. My feet and legs were so badly cut with the oyster shells, that the blood flowed freely; add to this, my head was very painful and swollen, and my shoulder smarted severely. In this manner and direction I ran till the sun about an hour high, when I lost sight of the pirates and paused for a moment, pulled off my jacket (the cord being yet on my right arm, which I slipped off) in which I rolled my hat, and taking it under my arm, I settled down on my knees, which brought the water up to my chin, in order to secrete myself. In this way I crept till nearly sunset, when, to my astonishment, I discovered the ocean, and just as the sun was setting, I crawled out to the border of the Island. I looked round and saw a very large bush of mangroves, the highest near, among the roots of which, I concealed myself. When the sun was setting, I could distinctly hear the splashing of water and cracking of bushes, and the pirates hallooing to each other, which increased my apprehensions, supposing they might discover my track through the muddy water. I was almost exhausted from a severe pain in my side, caused by running so long, though I had determined not to yield to them until I fell under the blow of their cutlass. Soon after the sun was down their noise ceased, and I crept up to the top of the tall mangrove, put on my hat and jacket, where I set all night, until the sun rose the next morning, that I might discover if they had come round the Island to intercept my passage.

As I ran through the bushes, I disturbed numberless birds, among which was the Flamingo, who was extremely bold, flying around me with such a noise, that I feared it would betray me, by serving as a guide to my pursuers.

When the sun had arisen, without a cloud, I could discover nothing to increase my apprehension. I descended the mangrove and proceeded to the border of the Key—looked across the water before me, where lay another Key, which I judged 2½ or 3 miles distant. Here I stripped myself to my shirt, the sleeves of which I tore off, and with my trowsers, threw them into the sea. I then tied my jacket, which was of broad cloth, by means of the cord that was on my arm, slung it over my neck, and put my hat on, to protect my wounded head from the sun. In this plight I committed myself to the sea, first supplicating, on my knees, a Divine blessing on my undertaking; but doubting whether I should ever reach the opposite Key. Being, however, an excellent swimmer, having before swum nearly 2 miles on a wager, I reached the opposite Key without any other injury than the galling of my neck with the cord; and with much less fatigue than I could have supposed. This Key was much of the description of the last, but smaller. I made but little pause, continuing my course South Westerly across it, which was, I should suppose, about three miles; and as I had not hurried, owing to my fatigue, when I arrived at its border, it was about the middle of the afternoon. At about 2 miles distance, I descried another Key, to which I swam, slinging my jacket as before. When I arrived at this, which was the third Key, it was a little before sunset. I proceeded into the bushes about three-fourths of a mile, it being a small Key, and came out nearly to its margin, where I passed the night, leaning against a bunch of mangroves, with the water up to my hips. Such had been my fatigue and mental excitement, that even in this unpleasant situation, I slept soundly, until I was disturbed by a vision of the horrible scene in the canoes—the images of Capt. Hilton and Mr. Merry, mangled as when I last saw them, came before my eyes; and in my fancied attempt to rescue them, I awoke, but could not convince myself it was a dream, until I grasped my own flesh. Again I slept interruptedly until day-light. Being excessively hungry, for this was the third day since I had taken a single particle of food or drink, I plucked some of the greenest of the leaves; this relieved my hunger but increased my thirst. About sun-rise I departed from this Key, wading with the water, at times, up to my neck, for nearly a mile, when it grew deeper.

The next and fourth Key, being about another mile distant, I swam to. This day I kept on about the same course, South Westerly, and crossed three more small Keys, about a mile distant from each other. I had now arrived at the seventh and last Key; on this I passed the night, having prepared a kind of flake of old roots, on which I slept soundly, for the first time out of water, since I left Cruz del Padre. Between day-light and sun-rise, having eaten of the green leaves as before, and having been refreshed by sleep, I departed from the last Key; by this time so weak that I could scarcely walk. The water was not so deep but I could wade until within half a mile of what afterward proved to be Cuba; but of which I was ignorant at the time.

While I was crossing this last passage, I had to contend with a strong current probably from the mouth of the very river I afterward forded; and when but a few rods from the shore a shark approached within a rod; but to my great joy, he turned and left me.

I had now swam about nine miles beside the distance I had travelled through mud and water, and the hunger and thirst I had endured, having tasted neither food nor drink, except a few salt leaves of mangroves, during my flight. And to add to my sufferings, my almost naked body was covered with moschetoes, attracted by the blood and sores produced by my escape from Cruz del Padre.

Observing that this shore varied a little from those I had passed, I followed it in an Easterly direction, which was reversing my former course, for nearly two miles, when I came to a large yawl, with her foremast standing. As I set me down on her gun-wale, the thought struck my mind that this boat, like our own, might have preserved some unfortunate crew from the fury of the storm, in order to offer them up to the pitiless pirate, who, perhaps, had not suffered a solitary individual to escape and say, that the vengeance of man, on these encrimsoned shores, had sacrificed those whom the mercy of God had spared amid the dangers of his "mighty deep." While I was employed by these reflections, the gnawings of hunger were suddenly aroused by the appearance of two Craw-fish under the stern sheets; one of which, I caught and devoured with such greediness, that it was very soon rejected; and although I at first thought I could have eaten a dozen of them, the exhaustion, produced by my efforts to vomit, destroyed all relish for the other.

I again proceeded on my old course, South Westerly, until about the middle of the afternoon, when I approached dry land, and set me down on a wind-fall to contemplate my situation; to a description of which, I might well have adapted the language of JOB: "My flesh is clothed with worms and clods of dust; my skin is broken and become loathsome." Near the roots of this tree, as I sat viewing some holes formed by land crabs, I observed water issuing from one of them. A more grateful and unexpected sight the Israelites could not have witnessed at the smitten rock; for I soon found the water proceeded from a boiling spring: and without it, I am sure I could not have survived another day; for it will be recollected that this was the first fresh water I had tasted since the morning my shipmates were murdered. But pure as it was, my parched stomach would not retain it, until after repeated trials, I succeeded in quenching my thirst. I again proceeded South Westerly, the land gradually elevating, until there suddenly opened upon me an immense plain, where the eye could reach over thousands of acres without the obstruction of a tree, covered with cattle of every age and description; some of which came snuffing around, so near, that in my crippled condition, I feared they might board me. But a swing of my hat set them capering and snorting in every direction. The number and variety of wild cattle collected on these plains is immense. I should think I saw more than five hundred hogs, chiefly of a dark colour, and more than half that number of horses, principally white; bulls, and cows with calves by their sides, goats, mules, &c.

I travelled on my course with as much rapidity as my feeble and exhausted condition would allow, until dusk, when I arrived at the bank of a small River; here I reposed uninterruptedly until day-light next morning. When I first attempted to arise, my limbs refused their duty; and I was compelled to seize hold of a bush that was near, in order to raise myself upon my feet. This is not strange, when we consider the fatigue and hunger I had endured, the wounds all over my limbs, and the numbness produced by sleeping without a covering, exposed to the dampness that arises from a fresh water river, in a climate like that of Cuba.

I paused on the bank a few moments observing the current, in order to ascertain the direction of its source, towards which, I proceeded, travelling on the bank until noon, when I entered a beautiful lime grove, the fruit of which, completely strewed the ground. After I had devoured as many of these, rind and all, as satisfied the cravings of hunger, I filled my jacket pockets, fearing I might not again meet with such a timely supply.

By this time I had discovered a winding foot path, formed by droves of wild cattle; but in vain did I search for the impression of a human foot step. This path I followed until it lead to a fording place in the river, where I paused, dreading the effect of fresh water on my sores, some of which had begun to scab over. But my situation would not admit delay; I therefore forded the river, which had been so swollen by recent rains, that I was compelled to wade up to my arm-pits. This produced the apprehended effect; for I had no sooner reached the opposite shore, than my sores began to bleed afresh, and smart severely. My supply of limes recruited my strength sufficiently to pursue my path until sunset, when I again halted and set me down on a log.

The only article of clothing I had to cover my nakedness, was my jacket; for the body of my shirt, I had left on one of the Keys, fearing that the blood stains upon it, might bring on me some unjust suspicion. My numerous sores, owing to the alternate influence of heat and fresh water, had now become so offensive as to occasion a violent retching, that nearly overcame the feeble powers of my stomach; and had it not been for my providential supply of limes, that afterward, in some degree corrected their fœtor, I must have laid me down by this log, a mass of corruption, and given my body up a prey to the birds and wild beasts of the forest. The reader will not think this an exaggeration; for while I was sitting here, the numerous Turkey-buzzards that were roosting over my head, attracted by my offensive smell, alighted within a few feet of me, and began to attack each other with as much ferocity as if they were already contending for their prey. I arose, as if to convince them that I yet possessed the power of motion; though I doubted within myself whether they would not have possession of me before the setting of another sun. But onward I travelled as far and as fast as my feeble condition would permit, until it was too dark to follow the path, when I laid down and passed a restless night, annoyed, as usual, with moschetoes. In the morning I arose feeble and dejected; and in my prayers, which I had daily addressed to HIM whose mercy-seat had so often covered me from the tempest, and whose "pillar of cloud by day and pillar of fire by night" had not yet forsaken me in the wilderness, I desired that I might meet this day, (the sixth of my miraculous escape,) some being to whom I could relate my sufferings, and the murder of my companions, as an appeal to my country, (bound as she is, to protect the humblest of her citizens,) to arise in the majesty of her naval power, and stay the hands of those who are colouring these barbarous shores with the blood of her enterprising seamen.

My life glass appeared to be nearly up, and I now began to yield all hopes of being relieved. My feet and limbs began to swell, from the inflammation of the sores, and my limes, the only sustenance I had, although they preserved life, began to create gnawing pains in my stomach and bowels. I however wandered on, following the intricate windings of the path, until the middle of the forenoon, when I discovered, directly in the way, several husks of corn, and soon after, some small sticks like bean poles, that had evidently been sharpened at one end by some human hand. This discovery, trifling as it may appear, renewed my spirits and strength to such a degree, that I made very little pause until about sun-set, when I espied in the path, not a great distance ahead, a man on horse back, surrounded by nearly twenty dogs! Fearing he might not observe me, I raised my hat upon my walking stick, as a signal for him to approach. The quick-scented dogs were soon on the start, and when I saw that they resembled blood hounds, I had serious apprehensions for my safety; but a call from their master, which they obeyed with prompt discipline, put my fears to rest. The man was a negro, mounted on a kind of mat, made of the palm leaf, and generally used for saddles by the plantation slaves on this Island.—When within a few rods of me he dismounted, approached with his drawn sword (machete) and paused in apparent astonishment; I pointing to the sores on me, fearing from his attitude he might mistake me for some highway robber. He now began to address me in Spanish, of which I knew only enough to make him understand I had been shipwrecked; on which he made signs for me to mount the horse. This I attempted, but was unable to do, until he assisted me. He then pointed in the direction of the path for me to go on, he following the horse, with his sword in his hand.

After travelling nearly three miles, I discovered a number of lights, about half a mile distant; and when we came up with them we halted near a large bamboo grove, where, with his aid, I dismounted, and by a signal from him, set down until he went to a hut and returned with a shirt and pair of trowsers, with which he covered my nakedness. He now took me by the hand and led me into a large house, occupied by his master, the owner of the plantation. A bench was brought me, on which I seated myself, and the master of the house, a grey headed Spaniard, probably turned of seventy, came toward me with an air of kindness, understanding from the black I had been shipwrecked. As the old man was examining my sores, he discovered on my arm a handsome impression of the crucifix that had been pricked in with indelible ink, in the East Indies some years before, which he kissed with apparent rapture, saying to me, "Anglois very much of the christian," supposing me to be a Roman Catholic.—This drew around me all the members of the family, who kneeled in succession, kissing the image and manifesting their sensibility by tears, at the sufferings which they perceived by my sores and emaciated appearance, I must have endured. I was then conducted by an old lady, whom I took to be his wife, into another apartment, in the corner of which, was a kind of grate where a fire was kindled on the ground. Here a table was spread that groaned under all the luxuries which abound on the plantations of this Island; but it was perhaps fortunate for me, that my throat was so raw and inflamed I could swallow nothing but some soft-boiled rice and coffee. After this refreshment, the kind old Spaniard stripped me, dipped a clean linen cloth into pure virgin honey and rubbed it over my sores. He then pointed to the bed, which had been prepared for me in the same room. I gave him to understand, by signs, that I should besmear his clean sheets; but this was negatived by a shake of the head; so without further ceremony I turned in—it was the softest pillow I ever did, or expect to, lay my head on;—yet it was rest, not sleep.

The old man had ordered a servant to attend me during the night, fearing the little food I had taken, after so long an abstinence, might produce some serious illness. Every time I groaned or turned, this servant would run to me with a bowl of strong hot coffee, which I could not refuse without disobeying his master's orders. Early in the morning, before I arose, the old planter came to my bed side, examined my pulse and tongue, and brought me a quart bowl of fresh tamarinds, more than half of which, he compelled me to eat, in order to prepare my stomach for the after reception of food, and prevent those symptoms of inflammation, which his intimate knowledge of the healing art had enabled him to discover.

I arose, put on my clothes and walked out to survey the possessions of this wealthy old planter, to whose hospitality I had been indebted for my life.

HENRY MORGAN'S PRECIOUS TEN MINUTES

Cyrus Townsend Brady

CHAPTER SIXTEEN

Gracious Majesty, King Charles II of England, in sportive—and acquisitive—mood, had made him a knight; but, as that merry monarch himself had said of another unworthy subject whom he had ennobled—his son, by the left hand—"God Almighty could not make him a gentleman!"

Yet, to the casual inspection, little or nothing appeared to be lacking to entitle him to all the consideration attendant upon that ancient degree. His attire, for instance, might be a year or two behind the fashion of England and still further away from that of France, then, as now, the standard maker in dress, yet it represented the extreme of the mode in His Majesty's fair island of Jamaica. That it was a trifle too vivid in its colors, and too striking in its contrasts for the best taste at home, possibly might be condoned by the richness of the material used and the prodigality of trimming which decorated it. Silk and satin from the Orient, lace from Flanders, leather from Spain, with jewels from everywhere, marked him as a person entitled to some consideration, at least. Even more compulsory of attention, if not of respect, were his haughty, overbearing, satisfied manner, his look of command, the expression of authority in action he bore.

Quite in keeping with his gorgeous appearance was the richly furnished room in which he sat in autocratic isolation, plumed hat on head, quaffing, as became a former brother-of-the-coast and sometime buccaneer, amazing draughts of the fiery spirits of the island of which he happened to be, *ad interim*, the Royal Authority.

But it was his face which attested the acuteness of the sneering observation of the unworthy giver of the royal accolade. No gentleman ever bore face like that. Framed in long, thin, gray curls which fell upon his shoulders after the fashion of the time, it was as cruel, as evil, as sensuous, as ruthless, as powerful an old face as had ever looked over a bulwark at a sinking ship, or viewed with indifference the ravaging of a devoted town. Courage there was, capacity in large measure, but not one trace of human kindness. Thin, lean, hawk-like, ruthless, cunning, weather-beaten, it was sadly out of place in its brave attire in that vaulted chamber. It was the face of a man who ruled by terror; who commanded by might. It was the face of an adventurer, too, one never sure of his position, but always ready to fight for it, and able to fight well. There was a watchful, alert, inquiring look in the fierce blue eyes, an intent, expectant expression in the craggy countenance, that told of the uncertainties of his assumptions; yet the lack of assurance was compensated for by the firm, resolute line of the mouth under the trifling upturned mustache, with its lips at the same time thin and sensual. To be fat and sensual is to appear to mitigate the latter evil with at least a pretence at good humor; to be thin and sensual is to be a devil. This man was evil, not with the grossness of a debauchee but with the thinness of the devotee. And he was an old man, too. Sixty odd years of vicious life, glossed over in the last two decades by an assumption of respectability, had swept over the gray hairs, which evoked no reverence.

There was a heavy frown on his face on that summer evening in the year of our Lord, 1685. The childless wife whom he had taken for his betterment and her worsening, some ten years since—in succession to Satan only knew how many nameless, unrecognized precursors—had died a few moments before, in the chamber above his head. Fairly bought from a needy father, she had been a cloak to lend him a certain respectability when he settled down, red with the blood of thousands whom he had slain and rich with the treasure of cities that he had wasted, to enjoy the evening of his life. Like all who are used for such purposes, she knew, after a little space, the man over whom the mantle of her reputation had been flung. She had rejoiced at the near approach of that death for which she had been longing almost since her wedding day. That she had shrunk from him in the very articles of dissolution when he stood by her bedside, indicated the character of the relationship.

To witness death and to cause it had been the habit of this man. He marked it in her case, as in others, with absolute indifference—he cared so little for her that he did not even feel relief at her going—yet because he was the Governor of Jamaica (really he was only the Vice-Governor, but between the departure of the Royal Governor and the arrival of another he held supreme power) he had been forced to keep himself close on the day his wife died, by that public opinion to which he was indifferent but which he could not entirely defy. Consequently he had not been on the strand at Port Royal when the *Mary Rose*, frigate, fresh from England, had dropped anchor in the harbor after her weary voyage across the great sea. He did not even yet know of her arrival, and therefore the incoming Governor had not been welcomed by the man who sat temporarily, as he had in several preceding interregnums, in the seats of the mighty.

However, everybody else on the island had welcomed him with joy, for of all men who had ever held office in Jamaica Sir Henry Morgan, sometime the chief devil of those nefarious bands who disguised their piracy under the specious title of buccaneering, was the most detested. But because of the fortunate demise of Lady Morgan, as it turned out, Sir Henry was not present to greet My Lord Carlingford, who was to supersede him—and more.

The deep potations the old buccaneer had indulged in to all outward intent passed harmlessly down his lean and craggy throat. He drank alone—the more solitary the drinker the more dangerous the man—yet the room had another occupant, a tall, brawny, brown-hued, grim-faced savage, whose gaudy livery ill accorded with his stern and ruthless visage. He stood by the Vice-Governor, watchful, attentive, and silent, imperturbably filling again and again the goblet from which he drank.

"More rum," said the master, at last breaking the silence while lifting his tall glass toward the man. "Scuttle me, Black Dog," he added, smiling sardonically at the silent maroon who poured again with steady hand, "you are the only soul on this island who doesn't fear me. That woman above yonder, curse her, shuddered away from me as I looked at her dying. But your hand is steady. You and old Ben Hornigold are the only ones who don't shrink back, hey, Carib? Is it love or hate?" he mused, as the man made no answer. "More," he cried, again lifting the glass which he had instantly drained.

But the maroon, instead of pouring, bent his head toward the window, listened a moment, and then turned and lifted a warning hand. The soft breeze of the evening, laden with the fragrance of the tropics, swept up from the river and wafted to the Vice-Governor's ears the sound of hoof beats on the hard, dry road. With senses keenly alert, he, also, listened. There were a number of them, a troop possibly. They were drawing nearer; they were coming toward his house, the slimmer house near Spanish Town, far up on the mountain side, where he sought relief from the enervating heats of the lower land.

"Horsemen!" he cried. "Coming to the house! Many of them! Ah, they dismount. Go to the door, Carib."

But before the maroon could obey they heard steps on the porch. Some one entered the hall. The door of the drawing-room was abruptly thrown open, and two men in the uniform of the English army, with the distinguishing marks of the Governor's Guard at Jamaica, unceremoniously entered the room. They were fully armed. One of them, the second, had drawn his sword and held a cocked pistol in the other hand. The first, whose weapons were still in their sheaths, carried a long official paper with a portentous seal dangling from it. Both were booted and spurred and dusty from riding, and both, contrary to the custom and etiquette of the island, kept their plumed hats on their heads.

"Sir Henry Morgan——" began the bearer of the paper.

"By your leave, gentlemen," interrupted Morgan, with an imperious wave of his hand, "Lieutenant Hawxherst and Ensign Bradley of my guard, I believe. You will uncover at once and apologize for having entered so unceremoniously."

As he spoke, the Governor rose to his feet and stood by the table, his right hand unconsciously resting upon the heavy glass flagon of rum. He towered above the other two men as he stood there transfixing them with his resentful glance, his brow heavy with threat and anger. But the two soldiers made no movement toward complying with the admonition of their sometime superior.

"D'ye hear me?" he cried, stepping forward, reddening with rage at their apparent contumacy. "And bethink ye, sirs, had best address me, who stand in the place of the King's Majesty, as 'Your Excellency,' or I'll have you broke, knaves."

"We need no lessons in manners from you, Sir Henry Morgan," cried Hawxherst, angry in turn to be so browbeaten, though yesterday he would have taken it mildly enough. "And know by this, sir," lifting the paper, "that you are no longer Governor of this island, and can claim respect from no one."

"What do you mean?"

"The *Mary Rose* frigate arrived this morning, bringing Lord Carlingford as His Majesty's new Governor, and this order of arrest."

"Arrest? For whom?"

"For one Sir Henry Morgan."

"For what, pray?"

"Well, sir, for murder, theft, treason—the catalogue fills the paper. You are to be despatched to England to await the King's pleasure. I am sent by Lord Carlingford to fetch you to the jail at Port Royal."

"You seem to find it a pleasant task."

"By heaven, I do, sir!" cried the soldier fiercely. "I am a gentleman born, of the proudest family in the Old Dominion, and have been forced to bow and scrape and endure your insults and commands, you bloody villain, but now——"

"'Tis no part of a soldier's duty, sir, to insult a prisoner," interrupted Morgan, not without a certain dignity. He was striving to gain time to digest this surprising piece of news and thinking deeply what was to be done in this entirely unexpected crisis.

"Curse it all, Hawxherst!" Ensign Bradley burst out, pulling at the sleeve of his superior. "You go too far, man; this is unseemly."

Hawxherst passed his hand across his brow and by an effort somewhat regained his self-control.

"Natheless 'tis in this paper writ that you are to go to England a prisoner on the *Mary Rose*, to await the King's pleasure," he added, savagely.

"His Gracious Majesty hath laid his sword upon my shoulder. I am a knight of his English court, one who has served him well upon the seas. His coffers have I enriched by—but let that pass. I do not believe that King Charles, God bless him——"

"Stop! The *Mary Rose* brings the news that King Charles II is dead, and there reigns in his stead His Gracious Majesty King James."

"God rest the soul of the King!" cried Morgan, lifting his hat from his head. "He was a merry and a gallant gentleman. I know not this James. How if I do not go with you?"

"You have ten minutes in which to decide, sir," answered Hawxherst.

"And then?"

"Then if I don't bring you forth, the men of yonder troop will come in without further order. Eh, Bradley?"

"Quite so, Sir Henry," answered the younger man. "And every avenue of escape is guarded. Yield you, sir; believe me, there's naught else."

"I have ten minutes then," said the old man reflectively, "ten minutes! Hum!"

"You may have," answered the captain curtly, "if you choose to take so long. And I warn you," he added, "that you'd best make use of that time to bid farewell to Lady Morgan or give other order for the charge of your affairs, for 'twill be a long time, I take it, before you are back here again."

"Lady Morgan is dead, gentlemen, in the room above."

At this young Bradley removed his hat, an example which Hawxherst followed a moment after. They had always felt sorry for the unfortunate wife of the buccaneer.

"As for my affairs, they can wait," continued Morgan slowly. "The game is not played out yet, and perchance I shall have another opportunity to arrange them. Meanwhile, fetch glasses, Carib, from yonder buffet."

He nodded toward a huge sideboard which stood against the wall immediately in the rear of Ensign Bradley, and at the same time shot a swift, meaning glance at the maroon, which was not lost upon him as he moved rapidly and noiselessly in obedience.

"Gentlemen, will you drink with me to our next merry meeting?" he continued, turning to them.

"We're honest soldiers, honorable gentlemen, and we'll drink with no murderer, no traitor!" cried Hawxherst promptly.

"So?" answered Morgan, his eye sparkling with baleful light, although he remained otherwise entirely unmoved.

"And let me remind you," continued the soldier, "that your time is passing."

"Well, keep fast the glasses, Carib, the gentlemen have no fancy for drinking. I suppose, sirs, that I must fain yield me, but first let me look at your order ere I surrender myself peaceably to you," said the deposed Governor, with surprising meekness.

"Indeed, sir——"

"'Tis my right."

"Well, perchance it may be. There can be no harm in it, I think; eh, Bradley?" queried the captain, catching for the moment his subaltern's eye.

Then, as the latter nodded his head, the former extended the paper to Morgan. At that instant the old buccaneer shot one desperate glance at the maroon, who stood back of the shoulder of the officer with the drawn sword and pistol. As Hawxherst extended the paper, Morgan, with the quickness of an albatross, grasped his wrist with his left hand, jerked him violently forward, and struck him a vicious blow on the temple with the heavy glass decanter, which shivered in his hand. Hawxherst pitched down at the Governor's feet, covered with blood and rum. So powerful had been Morgan's blow that the brains of the man had almost been beaten out. He lay shuddering and quivering on the floor. Quickly as Morgan struck, however, Carib had been quicker. As the glass crashed against the temple of the senior, the maroon had wrenched the pistol from the junior soldier's hand, and before he realized what had happened a cold muzzle was pressed against his forehead.

"Drop that sword!" cried Morgan instantly, and as the weapon fell upon the floor, he continued, smiling: "That was well done, Black Dog. Quite like old times, eh?"

"Shall I fire?" asked Carib, curling his lips over his teeth in what passed with him for a smile.

"Not yet."

"Your Excellency," gasped poor Bradley, "I didn't want to come. I remonstrated with him a moment since. For God's sake——"

"Silence, sirrah! And how much time have I now, I wonder?" He looked at his watch as he asked the question. "Three minutes! Three minutes between you and instant death, Ensign Bradley, for should one of your men enter the room now you see what you would have to expect, sir."

"Oh, sir, have mercy——"

"Unless you do exactly what I say you will be lying there with that carrion," cried Morgan, kicking the prostrate body savagely with his jewelled shoes.

"What do you want me to do? For God's sake be quick, Your Excellency. Time is almost up. I hear the men move."

"You are afraid, sir. There still want two minutes——"

"Yes, yes, but——"

"Go to the window yonder," cried the old man contemptuously—whatever he was he was not afraid—"and speak to them. Do you, Carib, stand behind, by the window, well concealed. If he hesitate, if he falter, kill him instantly."

"Pistol or knife?"

"The knife, it makes less noise," cried the buccaneer, chuckling with devilish glee. "Only one minute and a half now, eh, Mr. Bradley?"

"They're coming, they're coming!" whispered Bradley, gasping for breath. "Oh, sir——"

"We still have a minute," answered Morgan coolly. "Now, stop them."

"But how?"

"Tell them that you have captured me; that my wife is dead; that you and Lieutenant Hawxherst will spend the night here and fetch me down to Port Royal in the morning; that I have yielded myself a prisoner. Bid them stay where they are and drink to your health in bottles of rum, which shall be sent out to them, and then to go back to Port Royal and tell the new Governor. And see that your voice does not tremble, sir!"

There was a sudden movement outside.

"If they get in here," added Morgan quickly, "you are a dead man."

Bradley, with the servant clutching his arm, ran to the window. With the point of his own sword pressed against the back of his neck he repeated the message which Morgan had given him, which was received by the little squadron with shouts of approbation. He turned from the window, pale and trembling. Moistening his lips he whispered:

"I stopped them just in time."

"Well for you that you did," said Morgan grimly. "Come hither! Face that wall! Now stand there! Move but a hair's-breadth, turn your head the thousandth part of a degree, and I run you through," he added, baring his sword. "Rum for the men without, Carib," he added, "and then tell me when they are gone."

While the two were left alone in the room, Morgan amused himself by pricking the unfortunate officer with the point of the weapon, at the same time enforcing immobility and silence by the most ferocious threats of a speedy and cruel death. The men outside drank noisily and presently departed.

"Bind this fool," Morgan commanded briefly. "Then bid the slaves keep close in their cabins on pain of my displeasure—they know what it is. Then fetch the fastest horse in the stable to the front door. Get my riding-boots and cloak, and before you go hand me that little desk yonder. Be quick about it, too, for time presses, although I have more of it than these gentlemen would have allowed me."

As the maroon, after carefully lashing the officer with a seaman's expertness, rushed out to busy himself in carrying out these commands, Morgan opened the desk which he had handed to him and took from it several rouleaux of gold and a little bag filled with the rarest of precious stones; then he made a careful examination of the body on the floor.

"Not quite dead yet," he murmured, "but there is no use wasting shot or thrust upon him, he won't survive that blow. As for you, sir," looking at the paralyzed ensign, lying bound upon the floor, "you thought you could outwit the old buccaneer, eh? You shall see. I dealt with men when you were a babe in arms, and a babe in arms you are still. Ho! Ho!"

He laughed long and loudly, though there was neither mirth nor merriment in his sinister tones. The blood of the poor listener froze in his veins at the sound of it.

The brief preparations which Morgan had indicated as necessary for the journey were soon made.

He was always promptly obeyed by his own people; the slaves fled his presence when they could as if he had been a pestilence. At a sign from his taciturn body-servant at the open door that the horse was ready, he rose to his feet.

"Shall I kill this one now?" asked the maroon.

Morgan looked at the young man reflectively. The tongue of the ensign clave to the roof of his mouth; the sweat stood out on his forehead; he could not utter a word from fright. He was bound and trussed so tightly that he could not make a move, either. His eyes, however, spoke volumes.

"Well," said Sir Henry deliberately, "it would be a pity to kill him—" he paused; "in a hurry," he added.

"Dead men tell no tales."

"Eh, well, we can take care of that. Just lay him near his friend, lock the doors when I am gone and set the place on fire. The people are all out of the house. See they remain away. 'Twill make a hot, glorious blaze. You know the landing opposite Port Royal?"

The half-breed nodded.

"Meet me there as quick as you can. Lose no time."

"Aye, aye, sah," answered the Carib. "And Lady Morgan, sah?"

"Let her burn with the other two. She is so saintly she may like the fire, for I am afraid there will be none where she has gone. Good-by, Master Bradley. You allowed me ten minutes. I take it that this house will burn slowly at first, so perhaps you may count upon—let us say— half an hour. I'm generous, you see. Harry Morgan's way! 'Tis a pity you can't live to take my message to Lord Carlingford. The next time he sends any one for me let him send men, not fools and—cowards."

"You villain! You cursed, murdering villain!" gasped Bradley at last.

"To our next meeting, Mr. Bradley, and may it be in a cooler place than you will be in half an hour!"

THE AUDACIOUS BARBAROSSA

Stanley Lane-Poole

CHAPTER SEVENTEEN

The island of Lesbos has given many gifts to the world—Lesbian wine and Lesbian verse, the seven-stringed lyre, and the poems of Sappho; but of all its products the latest was assuredly the most questionable, for the last great Lesbians were the brothers Barbarossa, who struck terror in the early 16th century.

When Sultan Mohammed II conquered the island in 1462, he left there a certain Sipāhi soldier, named Ya'kūb—so say the Turkish annalists, but the Spanish writers claim him as a native Christian—who became the father of Urūj Barbarossa and his brother Kheyr-ed-dīn. Various stories are told of their early career, and the causes which led to their taking to the sea; but as Lesbos had long been famous for its buccaneers, whether indigenous or importations from Catalonia and Aragon, there was nothing unusual in the brothers adopting a profession which was alike congenial to bold hearts and sanctioned by time-honoured precedent.

Urūj Barbarossa, according to the testimony of those who remember him, was, when he died, about forty-four years of age. He was not very tall of stature, but extremely well set and robust. His hair and beard perfectly red; his eyes quick, sparkling and lively; his nose aquiline or Roman; and his complexion between brown and fair. He was a man excessively bold, resolute, daring, magnanimous, enterprizing, profusely liberal, and in nowise bloodthirsty, except in the heat of battle, nor rigorously cruel but when disobeyed he was highly beloved, feared, and respected, by his soldiers and domestics, and when dead was by them all in general most bitterly regretted and lamented. He left neither son nor daughter. He resided in Barbary fourteen years, during which the harms he did to the Christians are inexpressible.

Urūj, the elder, soon became the reïs, or captain, of a galleon, and finding his operations hampered in the Archipelago by the predominance of the Sultan's fleet, he determined to seek a wider and less interrupted field for his depredations. Rumours had reached the Levant of the successes of the Moorish pirates; prodigious tales were abroad as to great argosies, laden with the treasures of the New World, passing and repassing the narrow seas between Europe and Africa, and seeming to invite capture; and it was not long (1504) before Captain Urūj found himself cruising with two galleons off the Barbary coast, and spying out the land in search of a good harbour and a safe refuge from pursuit.

The port of Tunis offered all that a Corsair could wish. The Goletta in those days was but slightly fortified, and the principal building, besides the castle, was the custom-house, where the wealth of many nations was taxed by the Sultan of the House of Hafs. The very sight of such an institution was stimulating to a pirate. Urūj paid his court to the King of Tunis, and speedily came to an understanding with him on the subject of royalties on stolen goods. The ports of Tunis were made free to the Corsair, and the king would protect him from pursuit, for the consideration of a fixed share—a fifth—of the booty. The policy of the enlightened rulers of Tunis evidently no longer suited their latest representative.

The base of operations thus secured, Urūj did not keep his new ally long waiting for a proof of his prowess. One day he lay off the island of Elba, when two galleys-royal, belonging to his Holiness Pope Julius II, richly laden with goods from Genoa, and bound for Cività Vecchia, hove in sight. They were rowing in an easy, leisurely manner, little dreaming of Turkish Corsairs, for none such had ever been seen in those waters, nor anything bigger than a Moorish brigantine, of which the Papal marines were prepared to give a good account. So the two galleys paddled on, some ten leagues asunder, and Urūj Reïs marked his prey down. It was no light adventure for a galleon of eighteen banks of oars to board a royal galley of perhaps twice her size, and with no one could tell how many armed men inside her. The Turkish crew remonstrated at such foolhardiness, and begged their captain to look for a foe of their own size: but for reply Urūj only cast most of the oars overboard, and thus made escape impossible. Then he lay to and awaited the foremost galley She came on, proudly, unconscious of danger. Suddenly her look-out spied Turkish turbans—a strange sight on the Italian coast—and in a panic of confusion her company beat to arms. The vessels were now alongside, and a smart volley of shot and bolts completed the consternation of the Christians. Urūj and his men were quickly on the poop, and his Holiness's servants were soon safe under hatches.

Never before had a galley-royal struck her colours to a mere galleon. But worse was to follow. Urūj declared he must and would have her consort. In vain his officers showed him how temerarious was the venture, and how much more prudent it would be to make off with one rich prize than to court capture by overgreediness. The Corsair's will was of iron, and his crew, inflated with triumph, caught his audacious spirit. They clothed themselves in the dresses of the Christian prisoners, and manned the subdued galley as though they were her own seamen. On came the consort, utterly ignorant of what had happened, till a shower of arrows and small shot aroused her, just in time to be carried by assault, before her men had collected their senses.

Urūj brought his prizes into the Goletta. Never was such a sight seen there before. "The wonder and astonishment," says Haedo, "that this noble exploit caused in Tunis, and even in Christendom, is not to be expressed, nor how celebrated the name of Urūj Reïs was become from that very moment; he being held and accounted by all the world as a most valiant and enterprizing commander. And by reason his beard was extremely red, or carroty, from thenceforwards he was generally called Barba-rossa, which in Italian signifies Red-Beard."

The capture of the Papal galleys gave Urūj what he wanted—rowers. He kept his Turks for fighting, and made the Christian prisoners work the oars; such was the custom of every Corsair down to the present century, and the Christian navies were similarly propelled by Mohammedan slaves. The practice must have lent a strange excitement to the battle; for then, assuredly, a man's foes were of his own household. A Venetian admiral knew well that his two or three hundred galley slaves were panting to break their irons and join the enemy; and the Turkish Corsair had also his unwilling subjects, who would take the first chance to mutiny in favour of the Christian adversary. Thus it often happened that a victory was secured by the strong arms of the enemy's chained partizans, who would have given half their lives to promote a defeat. But the sharp lash of the boatswain, who walked the bridge between the banks of rowers, was a present and acute argument which few backs could withstand.

Urūj had made his first *coup*, and he did not hesitate to follow it up. Next year he captured a Spanish ship with five hundred soldiers on board, who were all so sea-sick, or spent with pumping out the leaky vessel, that they fell an easy prey to his galleons. Before five years were out, what with cruising, and building with the timber of his many prizes, he had eight good vessels at his back, with two of his brothers to help. The port of Tunis now hardly sufficed his wants, so he established himself temporarily on the fertile island of Jerba, and from its ample anchorage his ships issued forth to harry the coasts of Italy.

To be king of Jerba was all too small a title for his ambition. He aimed at sovereignty on a large scale, and, Corsair as he was by nature, he wished for settled power almost as much as he delighted in adventure. In 1512 the opportunity he sought arrived. Three years before, the Mohammedan King of Bujēya had been driven out of his city by the Spaniards, and the exiled potentate appealed to the Corsair to come and restore him, coupling the petition with promises of the free use of Bujēya port, whence the command of the Spanish sea was easily to be held. Urūj was pleased with the prospect, and as he had now twelve galleons with cannon, and one thousand Turkish men-at-arms, to say nothing of renegades and Moors, he felt strong enough for the attempt. The renown of his exploits had spread far and wide, and there was no lack of a following from all parts of the Levant when it was known that Urūj Reïs was on the war-path. His extraordinary energy and impetuosity called forth a corresponding zeal in his men, and, like other dashing commanders, he was very popular.

Well supported, and provided with such a siege-train as the times permitted, he landed before Bujēya in August, 1512, and found the dethroned king expecting him at the head of three thousand mountain

Berbers. The Spanish garrison was collected in the strong bastion, which the Count Don Pedro Navarro had fortified when he took the city, and for eight days the fortress withstood the battering of the Corsair's ordnance. Just when a breach began to be opened, Urūj was disabled; a shot took his left arm away above the elbow. In the absence of their leader's heroic example, the Turks felt little confidence in their superiority to Spanish steel; they preferred carrying their wounded captain to the surgeons at Tunis. Bujēya for the moment escaped, but the Corsairs enjoyed some little consolation in the capture of a rich Genoese galleon which they met on its voyage to the Lomellini's mart at Tabarka. With this spoil Urūj returned to recover from his wound, while his brother, Kheyr-ed-dīn, kept guard over the castle of the Goletta, and began to bring the galleons and prizes through the canal into the Lake of Tunis, where they would be safe from pursuit.

He was too late, however. The Senate of Genoa was highly incensed at the loss of the galleon, and Andrea Doria, soon to be known as the greatest Christian admiral of his time, was despatched with twelve galleys to exact reparation. He landed before the Goletta, and drove Kheyr-ed-dīn before him into Tunis. The fortress was sacked, and half Barbarossa's ships were brought in triumph to Genoa. Thus ended the first meeting between Doria and Kheyr-ed-dīn: the next was less happy for the noble Genoese.

Kheyr-ed-dīn, well aware of his brother's fierce humour, did not dare to face him after this humiliation, but left him to fume impotently in his sickroom, while he stole away to Jerba, there to work night and day at shipbuilding. Urūj joined him in the following spring—the King of Tunis had probably had enough of him—and they soon had the means of wiping out their disgrace. The attempt was at first a failure; a second assault on the ominous forts of Bujēya (1514) was on the point of success, when reinforcements arrived from Spain. The Berber allies evinced more interest in getting in their crops after the rain than in forcing the bastion; and Barbarossa, compelled to raise the siege, in a frantic rage, tearing his red beard like a madman, set fire to his ships that they might not fall into the hands of the Spaniards.

He would not show himself now in Tunis or Jerba. Some new spot must shelter him after this fresh reverse. On his way to and from Bujēya he had noticed the very place for his purpose—a spot easy to defend, perched on inaccessible rocks, yet furnished with a good harbour, where the losses of recent years might be repaired. This was Jījil, some sixty miles to the east of Bujēya; whose sturdy inhabitants owed allegiance to no Sultan, but were proud to welcome so renowned, although now so unfortunate, a warrior as Barbarossa. So at Jījil Urūj dwelt, and cultivated the good-will of the people with spoils of corn and goods from his cruisers, till those "indomitable African mountaineers," who had never owned a superior, chose him by acclamation their king.

The new Sultan of Jījil was now called to a much more serious enterprize than heading his truculent highlanders against a neighbouring tribe—though it must be admitted that he was always in his element when fisticuffs were in request. An appeal had come from Algiers. The Moors there had endured for seven years the embargo of the Spaniards; they had seen their *fregatas* rotting before their eyes, and never dared to mend them; they had viewed many a rich prize sail by, and never so much as ventured a mile out to sea to look her over: for there were keen eyes and straight shots in the Peñon which commanded the bay, and King Ferdinand the Catholic held a firm hand over the tribute which his banished subjects had to pay him for his condescension in ruining them. Their occupation was gone; they had not dragged a prize ashore for years; they must rebel or starve.

At this juncture Ferdinand opportunely died (1516), and the Algerine Moors seized their chance. They stopped the tribute, and called in the aid of Salim, the neighbouring Arab sheykh, whose clansmen would make the city safe on the land side. "But what are they to do with the two hundred petulant and vexatious Spaniards in the fort, who incessantly pepper the town with their cannon, and make the houses too hot to hold them; especially when they are hungry? Little would the gallant Arab cavalry, with their fine Libyan mares and horses, rich coats-of-mail, tough targets, well-tempered sabres, and long supple lances, avail them against the Spanish volleys. And who so proper to redress this grievance as the invincible Barbarossa, who was master of a naval force, and wanted not artillery? Had he not been twice to reinstate the unfortunate King of Bujēya, and lost a limb in his service?

"Without the least deliberation Prince Salim despatched a solemn embassy to Jījil, intreating Barbarossa, in whom he and his people reposed their entire confidence, to hasten to their assistance. No message whatever could have been more welcome to the ambitious Barbarossa than one of this nature. His new-acquired realm brought him in but a very scanty revenue; nor was he absolute. . . . He had been wretchedly baffled at Bujēya, but hoped for better success at Algiers, which, likewise, is a place of much greater consequence, and much more convenient for his purpose, which, as has been said, was to erect a great monarchy of his own in Barbary."

With some six thousand men and sixteen galleons Urūj set forth by sea and land to the rescue of Algiers. First he surprised Shershēl, a strong position fifteen leagues to the west of Algiers, which had been occupied by Moors from Granada, and was now commanded by a bold Turkish Corsair, Kara Hasan, who, emulating his old comrade's success with the people of Jījil, had induced the Shershēl rovers to accept him as their leader. Urūj had no liking for two Kings of Brentford, and took off Black Hasan's head as a friendly precaution, before exposing himself to the perils of another contest with the Spaniards.

Soon he was at Algiers, hospitably lodged and entertained, he and all his men, Turks and Jījilis alike, by Sheykh Salim and the people of the town. There, at the distance of a crossbow-shot, stood the fortress he had come to reduce, and thither he sent a message offering a safe conduct to the garrison if they would surrender. The Spanish captain made reply that "neither threats nor proffered courtesies availed aught with men of his kidney," and told him to remember Bujēya. Upon which Urūj, more to please his unsuspicious hosts than with much prospect of success, battered the Peñon for twenty days with his light field-pieces, without making any sensible breach in the defences.

Meanwhile, the Arabs and Moors who had called him to their aid were becoming aware of their mistake. Instead of getting rid of their old enemy the Spaniard, they had imported a second, worse than the first, and Urūj soon showed them who was to be master. He and his Turks treated the ancient Moorish families, who had welcomed them within their gates, with an insolence that was hard to be borne by descendants of the Abencerrages and other noble houses of Granada.

Salim, the Arab Sheykh, was the first to feel the despot's power: he was murdered in his bath—it was said by the Corsair himself. In their alarm, the Algerines secretly made common cause with the soldiers of the Peñon, and a general rising was planned; but one day at Friday prayers Barbarossa let the crowded congregation know that their designs were not unsuspected. Shutting the gates, the Turks bound their entertainers with the turbans off their heads, and the immediate decapitation of the ringleaders at the mosque door quelled the spirit of revolt. Nor was a great Armada, sent by Cardinal Ximenes, and commanded by Don Diego de Vera, more successful than the Algerine rebellion. Seven thousand Spaniards were utterly routed by the Turks and Arabs; and to complete the discomfiture of the Christians a violent tempest drove their ships ashore, insomuch that this mighty expedition was all but annihilated.

An adventurer who, with a motley following of untrained bandits and nomads, could overthrow a Spanish army was a phenomenon which the Christian States now began to eye with considerable anxiety. From the possessor of a strong place or two on the coast, he had become nothing less than the Sultan of Middle Barbary (*Maghrib el-Awsat*). When the Prince of Tinnis raised the whole country side against him, and a mighty host was rolling down upon Algiers, Urūj marched out with one thousand Turks and five hundred Moors, and never a cannon amongst them, and smote the enemy hip and thigh, and pursued them into their own city. The prince of Tinnis took to the mountains, and Urūj Barbarossa reigned in his stead (1517). Then Tilimsān fell into his possession, and save that the Spaniards held Oran and two or three fortresses, such as the Peñon de Alger and Bujēya, his dominions coincided with modern Algeria, and marched with the kingdoms of Tunis and Fez. He was in a position to form alliances with Fez and Morocco. His galleons were punctilious, moreover, in returning the call of Don Diego de Vera, and many an expectant merchant in Genoa, or Naples, or Venice, strained his eyes in vain for the argosy that, thanks to the Corsair's vigilance, would never again sail proudly into the harbour.

When all this came to the ears of the new King of Spain, afterwards the Emperor Charles V, he yielded to the prayer of the Marquis de Comares, Governor of Oran, and despatched ten thousand veterans to make an end of the Corsairs once and for ever. Urūj Barbarossa was then stationed at Tilimsān with only 1,500 men, and when the hosts of the enemy drew near he made a bolt by night for Algiers, taking his Turks and his treasure with him. The news soon reached the enemy's scouts, and the Marquis gave hot pursuit. A river with steep banks lay in the fugitives' path: could they pass it, they would have the chances in their favour. Urūj scattered his jewels and gold behind him, vainly hoping to delay the greedy Spaniards; but Comares trampled over everything, and came up with the Turkish rear when but half their force had crossed the river. Their leader was already safe on the other side, but the cries of his rear-guard brought him back. The Corsair was not the man to desert his followers, and without an instant's hesitation he recrossed the fatal stream and threw himself into the fray. Hardly a Turk or a Moor escaped from that bloody field. Facing round, they fought till they dropped; and among them the vigorous figure of Barbarossa was ever to be seen, laying about him with his one arm like a lion to the last.

THE LAST OF THE NORTH ATLANTIC PIRATES

Arthur Hunt Chute

CHAPTER EIGHTEEN

In the farther end of the Bay of Fundy, about a mile off from the Nova Scotian coast, is the Isle of Haut. It is a strange rocky island that rises several hundred feet sheer out of the sea, without any bay or inlets. A landing can only be effected there in the calmest weather; and on account of the tremendous ebb of the Fundy tides, which rise and fall sixty feet every twelve hours, the venturesome explorer cannot long keep his boat moored against the precipitous cliffs.

Because of this inaccessibility little is known of the solitary island. Within its rampart walls of rock they say there is a green valley, and in its center is a fathomless lake, where the Micmac Indians used to bury their dead, and hence its dread appellation of the "Island of the Dead." Beyond these bare facts nothing more is certain about the secret valley and the haunted lake. Many wild and fabulous descriptions are current, but they are merely the weavings of fancy.

Sometimes on a stormy night the unhappy navigators of the North Channel miss the coast lights in the fog, and out from the Isle of Haut a gentle undertow flirts with their bewildered craft. Then little by little they are gathered into a mighty current against which all striving is in vain, and in the white foam among the iron cliffs their ship is pounded into splinters. The quarry which she gathers in so softly at first and so fiercely at last, however, is soon snatched away from the siren shore. The ebb-tide bears every sign of wreckage far out into the deeps of the Atlantic, and not a trace remains of the ill-starred vessel or her crew. But one of the boats in the fishing fleet never comes home, and from lonely huts on the coast reproachful eyes are cast upon the "Island of the Dead."

On the long winter nights, when the "boys" gather about the fire in Old Steele's General Stores at Hall's Harbor, their hard gray life becomes bright for a spell. When a keg of hard cider is flowing freely the grim fishermen forget their taciturnity, the ice is melted from their speech, and the floodgates of their souls pour forth. But ever in the background of their talk, unforgotten, like a haunting shadow, is the "Island of the Dead." Of their weirdest and most blood-curdling yarns it is always the center; and when at last, with uncertain steps, they leave the empty keg and the dying fire to turn homeward through the drifting snow, fearful and furtive glances are cast to where the island looms up like a ghostly sentinel from the sea. Across its high promontory the Northern Lights scintillate and blaze, and out of its moving brightness the terrified fishermen behold the war-canoes of dead Indians freighted with their redskin braves; the forms of *cœur de bois* and desperate Frenchmen swinging down the sky-line in a ghastly snake-dance; the shapes and spars of ships long since forgotten from the "Missing List"; and always, most dread-inspiring of them all, the distress signals from the sinking ship of Mogul Mackenzie and his pirate crew.

Captain Mogul Mackenzie was the last of the pirates to scourge the North Atlantic seaboard. He came from that school of freebooters that was let loose by the American Civil War. With a letter of marque from the Confederate States, he sailed the seas to prey on Yankee shipping. He and his fellow-privateers were so thorough in their work of destruction, that the Mercantile Marine of the United States was ruined for a generation to come. When the war was over the defeated South called off her few remaining bloodhounds on the sea. But Mackenzie, who was still at large, had drunk too deeply of the wine of a wild, free life. He did not return to lay down his arms, but began on a course of shameless piracy. He lived only a few months under the black flag, until he went down on the Isle of Haut. The events of that brief and thrilling period are unfortunately obscure, with only a ray of light here and there. But the story of his passing is the most weird of all the strange yarns that are spun about the "Island of the Dead."

In May, 1865, a gruesome discovery was made off the coast of Maine, which sent a chill of fear through all the seaport towns of New England. A whaler bound for New Bedford was coming up Cape Cod one night long after dark. There was no fog, and the lights of approaching vessels could easily be discerned. The man on the lookout felt no uneasiness at his post, when, without any warning of bells or lights, the sharp bow of a brigantine suddenly loomed up, hardly a ship's length in front.

"What the blazes are you trying to do?" roared the mate from the bridge, enraged at this unheard-of violation of the right of way. But no voice answered his challenge, and the brigantine went swinging by, with all her sails set to a spanking breeze. She bore directly across the bow of the whaler, which just grazed her stern in passing.

"There's something rotten on board there," said the mate.

"Ay," said the captain, who had come on the bridge, "there's something rotten there right enough. Swing your helm to port, and get after the devils," he ordered.

"Ay, ay, sir!" came the ready response, and nothing loth the helmsman changed his course to follow the eccentric craft. She was evidently bound on some secret mission, for not otherwise would she thus tear through the darkness before the wind without the flicker of a light.

The whaler was the swifter of the two ships, and she could soon have overhauled the other; but fearing some treachery, the captain refrained from running her down until daylight. All night long she seemed to be veering her course, attempting to escape from her pursuer. In the morning, off the coast of Maine, she turned her nose directly out to sea. Then a boat was lowered from the whaler, and rowed out to intercept the oncoming vessel. When they were directly in her course, they lay on their oars and waited. The brigantine did not veer again, but came steadily on, and soon the whalemen were alongside, and made themselves fast to a dinghy which she had in tow. A few minutes of apprehensive waiting followed, and as nothing happened, one of the boldest swung himself up over the tow-rope on to the deck. He was followed by the others, and they advanced cautiously with drawn knives and pistols.

Not a soul was to be seen, and the men, who were brave enough before a charging whale, trembled with fear. The wheel and the lookout were alike deserted, and no sign of life could be discovered anywhere below. In the galley were the embers of a dead fire, and the table in the captain's cabin was spread out ready for a meal which had never been eaten. On deck everything was spick and span, and not the slightest evidence of a storm or any other disturbance could be found. The theory of a derelict was impossible. Apparently all had been well on board, and they had been sailing with good weather, when, without any warning, her crew had been suddenly snatched away by some dread power.

The sailors with one accord agreed that it was the work of a sea-serpent. But the mate had no place for the ordinary superstitions of the sea, and he still scoured the hold, expecting at any minute to encounter a dead body or some other evil evidence of foul play. Nothing more, however, was found, and the mate at length had to end his search with the unsatisfactory conclusion that the St. Clare, a brigantine registered from Hartpool, with cargo of lime, had been abandoned on the high seas for no apparent reason. Her skipper had taken with him the ship's papers, and had not left a single clue behind.

A crew was told off to stand by the *St. Clare* to bring her into port, and the others climbed into the long-boat to row back to the whaler.

"Just see if there is a name on that there dinghy, before we go," said the mate.

An exclamation of horror broke from one of the men as he read on the bow of the dinghy the name, *Kanawha*.

The faces of all went white with a dire alarm as the facts of the mystery suddenly flashed before them. The *Kanawha* was the ship in which Captain Mogul Mackenzie had made himself notorious as a privateersman. Every one had heard her awe-inspiring name, and every Yankee seafaring man prayed that he might never meet her on the seas. After the *Alabama* was sunk, and the *Tallahassee* was withdrawn, the *Kanawha* still remained to threaten the shipping of the North. For a long time her whereabouts had been unknown, and then she was discovered by a Federal gunboat, which gave chase and fired upon her. Without returning fire, she raced in for shelter amongst the dangerous islands off Cape Sable, and was lost in the fog. Rumor had it that she ran on the rocks off that perilous coast, and sank with all on board. As time went by, and there was no more sign of the corsair, the rumor was accepted as proven. Men began to spin yarns in the forecastle about Mogul Mackenzie, with an interest that was tinged with its former fear. Skippers were beginning to feel at ease again on the grim waters, when suddenly, like a bolt from the blue, came the awful news of the discovery of the *St. Clare.*

Gunboats put off to scour the coast-line; and again with fear and trembling the look-out began to eye suspiciously every new sail coming up on the horizon.

One afternoon, toward the end of May, a schooner came tearing into Portland harbor, with all her canvas, crowded on, and flying distress signals. Her skipper said that off the island of Campabello he had seen a long gray sailing-ship with auxiliary power sweeping down upon him. As the wind was blowing strong inshore, he had taken to his heels and made for Portland. He was chased all the way, and his pursuer did not drop him until he was just off the harbor bar.

Many doubted his story, however, saying that no one would dare to chase a peaceful craft so near to a great port in broad daylight. And, again, it was urged that an auxiliary vessel could easily have overhauled the schooner between Campabello and Portland. The fact that the captain of the schooner was as often drunk as sober, and that when he was under the influence of drink he was given to seeing visions, was pointed to as conclusive proof that his yarn was a lie. After the New Bedford whaler came into port with the abandoned *St. Clare*, it was known beyond doubt that the *Kanawha* was still a real menace. But nobody cared to admit that Mogul Mackenzie was as bold as the schooner's report would imply, and hence countless arguments were put forward to allay such fears.

But a few days later the fact that the pirates were still haunting their coast was absolutely corroborated. A coastal packet from Boston arrived at Yarmouth with the news that she had not only sighted *Kanawha* in the distance, but they had crossed each other's paths so near that the name could be discerned beyond question with a spyglass. She was heading up the Bay of Fundy, and did not pause or pay any heed to the other ship.

This news brought with it consternation, and every town and village along the Fundy was a-hum with stories and theories about the pirate ship. The interest, instead of being abated, was augmented as the days went by with no further report. In the public-houses and along the quays it was almost the only topic of conversation. The excitement became almost feverish when it was known that several captains, outward bound, had taken with them a supply of rifles and ammunition. The prospect of a fight seemed imminent.

About a week after the adventure of the Boston packet Her Majesty's ship *Buzzard* appeared off Yarmouth harbor. The news of the *Kanawha* had come to the Admiral at Halifax, and he had dispatched the warship to cruise about the troubled coast.

"That'll be the end of old Mogul Mackenzie, now that he's got an English ship on his trail," averred a Canadian as he sat drinking in the "Yarmouth Light" with a group of seafaring men of various nationalities. "It takes the British jack-tar to put the kibosh on this pirate game. One of them is worth a shipload of Yankees at the business."

"Well, don't you crow too loud now," replied a Boston skipper. "I reckon that that Nova Scotian booze-artist, who ran into Portland the other day scared of his shadow, would not do you fellows much credit."

"Yes; but what about your gunboats that have had the job of fixing the *Kanawha* for the last three years, and haven't done it yet?" The feelings between Canada and the United States were none too good just after the Civil War, and the Canadian was bound not to lose this opportunity for horse-play. "You're a fine crowd of sea-dogs, you are, you fellows from the Boston Tea-Party. Three years after one little half-drowned rat, and haven't got him yet. Wouldn't Sir Francis Drake or Lord Nelson be proud of the record that you long-legged, slab-sided Yankees have made on the sea!"

"Shut your mouth! you blue-nosed, down-East herring-choker!" roared the Yankee skipper. "I reckon we've given you traitors that tried to stab us in the back a good enough licking; and if any more of your dirty dogs ever come nosing about down south of Mason and Dixon's Line, I bet they'll soon find out what our record is."

"Well, you fools can waste your tongue and wind," said a third man, raising his glass, "but for me here's good luck to the *Buzzard*."

"So say we all of us," chimed in the others, and the Yankee and the Canadian drank together to the success of the British ship, forgetting their petty jealousies before a common foe.

Everywhere the news of the arrival of the British warship was hailed with delight. All seemed to agree that her presence assured the speedy extermination of the pirate crew. But after several days of futile cruising about the coast, her commander, to escape from a coming storm, had to put into St. Mary's Bay, with the object of his search still eluding his vigilance. He only arrived in time to hear the last chapter of the *Kanawha*'s tale of horrors.

The night before, Dominic Lefountain, a farmer living alone at Meteighan, a little village on the French shore, had been awakened from his sleep by the moaning and wailing of a human voice. For days the imminent peril of an assault from the pirates had filled the people of the French coast with forebodings. And now, awakened thus in the dead of night, the lonely Frenchman was well nigh paralyzed with terror. With his flesh creeping, and his eyes wide, he groped for his rifle, and waited in the darkness, while ever and anon came those unearthly cries from the beach. Nearly an hour passed before he could gather himself together sufficiently to investigate the cause of the alarm. At last, when the piteous wailing had grown weak and intermittent, the instinct of humanity mastered his fears, and he went forth to give a possible succor to the one in need.

On the beach, lying prostrate, with the water lapping about his feet, he found a man in the last stage of exhaustion. The blood was flowing from his mouth, and as Dominic turned him over to stanch its flow, he found that his tongue had been cut out, and hence the unearthly wailing which had roused him from his sleep. The beach was deserted by this time, and it was too dark to see far out into the bay.

Dominic carried the unfortunate man to his house, and nursed him there for many weeks. He survived his frightful experiences, and lived on for twenty years, a pathetic and helpless figure, supported by the big-hearted farmers and fishermen of the French shore. Evidently he had known too much for his enemies, and they had sealed his mouth forever. He became known as the "Mysterious Man of Meteighan," and his deplorable condition was always pointed to as a mute witness of the last villainy of Mogul Mackenzie.

On the night following the episode of the "Mysterious Man of Meteighan," a wild and untoward storm swept down the North Atlantic and over the seaboard far and near. In the Bay of Fundy that night the elements met in their grandest extremes. Tide-rips and mountain waves opposed each other with titanic force. All along the bleak and rock-ribbed coast the boiling waters lay churned into foam. Over the breakwaters the giant combers crashed and soared far up into the troubled sky; while out under the black clouds of the night the whirlpools and the tempests met. Was ever a night like this before? Those on shore thanked God; and those with fathers on the sea gazed out upon a darkness where no star of hope could shine.

Now and again through the Stygian gloom a torrent of sheet-lightning rolled down across the heavens, bringing in its wake a moment of terrible light. It was in one of these brief moments of illumination that the wan watchers at Hall's Harbor discerned a long gray ship being swept like a specter before the winds towards the Isle of Haut. Until the flash of lightning the doomed seamen appeared to have been unconscious of their fast approaching fate; and then, as if suddenly awakened, they sent a long thin trail of light, to wind itself far up into the darkness. Again and again the rockets shot upward from her bow, while above the noises of the tempest came the roar of a gun.

The people on the shore looked at each other with blanched faces, speechless, helpless. A lifetime by that shore had taught them the utter puniness of the sons of men. Others would have tried to do something with what they thought was their strong arm. But the fishermen knew too well that the Fundy's arm was stronger. In silence they waited with bated breath while the awful moments passed. Imperturbable they stood there, with their feet in the white foam and their faces in the salt spray, and gazed at the curtain of the night, behind which a tragedy was passing, as dark and dire as any in the annals of the sea.

Another flash of lightning, and there, dashing upon the iron rocks, was a great ship, with all her sails set, and a cloud of lurid smoke trailing from her funnel. She was gray-colored, with auxiliary power, and as her lines dawned upon those who saw her in the moment of light, they burst out with one accord, "It's the *Kanawha*! It's the *Kanawha*!" As if an answer to their sudden cry another gun roared, and another shower of rockets shot up into the sky; and then all was lost again in the darkness and the voices of the tempest.

Next morning the winds had gone out with the tide, and when in the afternoon the calm waters had risen, a boat put off from Hall's Harbor and rowed to the Isle of Haut. For several hours the rocky shores were searched for some traces of the wreck, but not a spar or splinter could be found. All about the bright waters laughed, with naught but the sunbeams on their bosom, and not a shadow remained from last night's sorrow on the sea.

So Mogul Mackenzie, who had lived a life of stress, passed out on the wings of storm. In his end, as always, he baffled pursuit, and was sought but could not be found. His sailings on the sea were in secret, and his last port in death was a mystery. But, as has been already related, when the Northern Lights come down across the haunted island, the distress signals of his pirate crew are still seen shooting up into the night.

THE HOARD OF TRINIDAD

Ralph D. Paine

CHAPTER NINETEEN

O f all the freebooters' treasure for which search is still made by means
of curious information having to do with charts and other plausible
records, the most famous are those buried on Cocos Islands in the Pacific
and on the rocky islet of Trinidad in the South Atlantic. These places are
thousands of miles apart, the former off the coast of Costa Rica, the latter several hundred miles from the nearest land of Brazil and not to be
confused with the better known British colony of Trinidad in the Leeward
Islands group of the West Indies.

Each of these treasures is of immense value, to be reckoned in millions of dollars, and their stories are closely interwoven because the
plunder came from the same source at about the same time. Both nar-
ratives are colored by piracy, bloodshed and mystery, that of Cocos Island perhaps the more luridly romantic of the two by reason of an
earlier association with the English buccaneers of Dampier's crew.
Each island has been dug over and ransacked at frequent intervals
during the last century, and it is safe to predict that expeditions will
be fitting out for Cocos or Trinidad for many years to come.

The history of these notable treasures is a knotty skein to disen-
tangle. Athwart its picturesque pages marches a numerous company of
bold and imaginative liars, every man of them ready to swear on a
stack of Bibles that his is the only true, unvarnished version of the
events which caused the gold and jewels and plate to be hidden. However, when all the fable and fancy are winnowed out, the facts remain-

ing are enough to make any red-blooded adventurer yearn to charter a rakish schooner and muster a crew of kindred spirits.

During the last days of Spanish rule on the west coast of South America, the wealthiest city left of that vast domain won by the Conquistadores and held by the Viceroys, was Lima, the capital of Peru. Founded in 1535 by Francisco Pizarro, it was the seat of the government of South America for centuries. The Viceregal court was maintained in magnificent state, and the Archbishop of Lima was the most powerful prelate of the continent. Here the religious orders and the Inquisition had their centers. Of the almost incredible amount of gold and silver taken from the mines of the country, much remained in Lima to pile up fortunes for the grandees and officials, or to be fashioned into massy ornaments for the palaces, residences, churches, and for the great cathedral which still stands to proclaim the grandeur that was Spain's in the olden days.

When Bolivar, the Liberator, succeeded in driving the Spanish out of Venezuela, and in 1819 set up the free republic of Colombia, the ruling class of Peru took alarm which increased to panic as soon as it was known that the revolutionary forces were organizing to march south and assault Lima itself. There was a great running to and fro among the wealthy Spanish merchants, the holders of fat positions under the Viceroy, and the gilded idlers who swaggered and ruffled it on riches won by the swords of their two-fisted ancestors. It was feared that the rebels of Bolivar and San Martin would loot the city, and confiscate the treasure, both public and private, which consisted of bullion, plate, jewels, and coined gold.

Precious property to the value of six million sterling was hurried into the fortress of Lima for safe keeping and after the capture of the city by the army of liberation, Lord Dundonald, the English Admiral in command of the Chilian fleet assisting the revolutionists, offered to let the Spanish governor depart with two-thirds of this treasure if he would surrender the remainder and give up the fortifications without a fight. The Peruvian liberator, San Martin, set these terms aside, however, and allowed the Spanish garrison to evacuate the place, carrying away the six million sterling. This immense treasure was soon scattered far and wide, by sea and land. It was only part of the riches dispersed by the conquest of San Martin and his patriots. The people of

Lima, hoping to send their fortunes safe home to Spain before the plundering invaders should make a clean sweep, put their valuables on board all manner of sailing vessels which happened to be in harbor, and a fugitive fleet of merchantmen steered out from the hostile coast of Peru, the holds piled with gold and silver, the cabins crammed with officials of the state and church and other residents of rank and station. At the same time there was sent to sea the treasure of the great cathedral of Lima, all its jeweled chalices, monstrances, and vestments, the solid gold candle-sticks and shrines, the vast store of precious furniture and ornaments, which had made this one of the richest religious edifices of the world.

There had not been so much dazzling booty afloat at one time since the galleon plate fleets were in their heyday during the sixteenth and seventeenth centuries. In 1820 there were no more of those great buccaneers and gentlemen adventurers who had singed the beard of the King of Spain in the wake of Francis Drake. They had sailed and fought and plundered for glory as well as gain, or for revenge as much as for doubloons. Their successors as sea rovers were pirates of low degree, base wretches of a sordid commercialism who preyed on honest merchant skippers of all flags, and had little taste for fighting at close quarters. The older race of sea rogues had been wolves; the pirates of the early nineteenth century were jackals.

Many a one of these gentry got wind of the fabulous treasure that had been sent afloat from Lima, and there is no doubt that much of it failed to reach Spain. While in some instances, these fleeing ships were boarded and scuttled by pirate craft, in others the lust of gold was too strong for the seamen to whom the rare cargoes had been entrusted, and they rose and took the riches away from their hapless passengers. It has been believed by one treasure seeking expedition after another, even to this day, that Captain Thompson of the British trading brig, *Mary Dear* received on board in the harbor of Lima as much as twelve million dollars' worth of gold and silver, and that he and his crew, after killing the Spanish owners, sailed north in the Pacific and buried the booty on Cocos Island.

Captain Thompson somehow escaped and joined a famous pirate of that time, Benito Bonito, who accumulated a large treasure which he also buried on Cocos Island. The British Admiralty records show that Bonito was overhauled in his turn by the frigate *Espiegle* and that rather than be hanged in chains, he very handsomely blew out his brains on his own deck.

This same treasure of Lima, or part of it, furnished the foundation of the story belonging to the volcanic islet of Trinidad in the South Atlantic. One version of this is that the pirates who chose this hiding-place had been the crew of a fast English schooner in the slave trade. While at sea they disposed of their captain by the unpleasant method of pinning him to the mainmast with a boarding pike through his vitals. Then the black flag was hoisted and with a new skipper they stood to the southward, finding a great amount of plunder in a Portuguese ship which had on board a "diamond dealer" among other valuable items. After taking an East Indiaman, and other tempting craft, they buried the total proceeds on the desolate, uninhabited island of Trinidad, intending to return for it before the end of the cruise.

Unfortunately, for the successful pirates, they ran afoul of a heavily armed and manned merchant vessel which shot away their rudder, tumbled their spars about their rascally ears, boarded them with great spirit and determination, and clapped the shackles on the twenty gentlemen of fortune who had survived the engagement. These were carried into Havana and turned over to the Spanish authorities who gleefully hanged nineteen, not twenty, mark you, for one had to make a marvelous escape in order to hand down the secret of the treasure to posterity. This survivor died in bed in England at a very great age, so the story runs, and of course he had a chart to set the next generation to digging.

The earlier statements of this narrative may be cast aside as worthless. The real, true pirate of Trinidad was not in the slave schooner which captured the "diamond dealer" of the Portuguese ship. An odd confusion of facts caused the mistake. While Benito Bonito was harrying the Spanish shipping of the Pacific and burying his treasure on Cocos Island, there was on the Atlantic a bloodthirsty pirate by the name of Benito de Soto. He was a Spaniard who sailed out of Buenos Aires in the year 1827, bound to Africa to smuggle a cargo of slaves. The crew was composed of French, Spanish, and Portuguese desperadoes, and led by the mate and De Soto they marooned the captain and ran away with the ship on a pirate voyage. They plundered and burned and slaughtered without mercy, their most nefarious exploit being the capture of the British merchant ship *Morning Star*, bound from Ceylon to England in 1828, and carrying as passengers several army officers and their wives and twenty-five invalided soldiers. After the most fiendish conduct, De Soto and his crew, drove the survivors into the hold of the *Morning Star*, and fastened the hatches, leaving the vessel to founder, for they had taken care to bore numerous auger holes in her bottom. By a miracle of good fortune, the prisoners forced the hatches and were taken off next day by a passing vessel.

Benito de Soto met his end as the result of being wrecked in his own ship off the Spanish coast. He was caught in Gibraltar and hanged by the English Governor. An army officer who saw him turned off related that he was a very proper figure of a pirate, "there was no driveling fears upon him,—he walked firmly at the tail of the fatal cart, gazing sometimes at his coffin, sometimes at the crucifix which he held in his hand. This he frequently pressed to his lips, repeated the prayers spoken in his ear by the attendant clergyman, and seemed regardless of everything but the world to come. The gallows was erected beside the water, and fronting neutral ground. He mounted the cart as firmly as he had walked behind it, and held up his face to Heaven and the beating rain, calm, resigned, but unshaken; and finding the halter too high for his neck, he boldly stepped upon his coffin, and placed his head in the noose. Then watching the first turn of the wheels, he murmured, 'farewell, all,' and leaned forward to facilitate his fall."

This Benito, who died so much better than he had lived, was not hanged at Havana, it will be perceived, and the version of the Trinidad treasure story already outlined is apparently a hodgepodge of the careers of Benito de Soto, and of Benito of Cocos Island, with a flavor of fact in so far as it refers to the twenty pirates who were carried to Cuba to be strung up, or garroted. The Spanish archives of that island record that this gang was executed and that they had been found guilty of plundering ships sailing from Lima shortly after the city had been entered by the revolutionists. Their association with the island of Trinidad is explained herewith as it was told to E. F. Knight, an Englishman, who organized and commanded an expedition which sailed in search of the treasure in 1889.

There was at that time near Newcastle, England, a retired sea captain who had been in command of an East Indiaman engaged in the opium trade in the years 1848 to 1850. "The China seas were then infested by pirates," said Mr. Knight's informant, "so that his vessel carried a few guns and a larger crew than is usual in these days. He had four quarter-masters, one of whom was a foreigner. The captain was not sure of his nationality but thought he was a Finn. On board the vessel the man went under the name of 'The Pirate' because of a deep scar across his cheek which gave him a somewhat sinister appearance. He was a reserved man, better educated than the ordinary sailor, and possessing a good knowledge of navigation.

"The captain took a liking to him, and showed him kindness on various occasions. This man was attacked by dysentery on the voyage from China to Bombay, and by the time the vessel reached port he was so ill, in spite of the captain's nursing, that he had to be taken to the hospital. He gradually sank, and when he found that he was dying he told the captain, who frequently visited him, that he felt very grateful for the kind treatment given him, and that he would prove his gratitude by revealing a secret which might make his captain one of the richest men in England. He then asked the skipper to go to his chest and take out from it a parcel. This contained a piece of old tarpaulin with a plan of an island of Trinidad upon it.

"The dying soldier told him that at the spot indicated, that is at the base of the mountain known as Sugar Loaf, there was an immense treasure buried, consisting principally of gold and silver plate and ornaments, the plunder of Peruvian churches which certain pirates had concealed there in the year 1821. Much of this plate, he said, came from the cathedral of Lima, having been carried away from there during the war of independence, when the Spaniards were escaping the country and that among other riches were several massive gold candle-sticks.

"He further stated that he was the only survivor of the pirates, as all the others had been captured by the Spaniards and executed in Cuba some years before, and consequently it was probable that no one but himself knew the secret. He then gave the captain instructions as to the exact position of the treasure in the bay under the Sugar Loaf, and enjoined him to go there and search for it, as it was almost certain that it had not been removed."

Mr. Knight, who was a young barrister of London, investigated this story with much diligence, and discovered that the captain aforesaid had sent his son to Trinidad in 1880 to try to identify the marks shown on the old pirate's tarpaulin chart. He landed from a sailing ship, did no digging for lack of equipment, but reported that the place tallied exactly with the description, although a great landslide of reddish earth had covered the place where the treasure was hid. This evidence was so convincing that in 1885 an expedition was organized among several adventurous gentlemen of South Shields who chartered a bark of six hundred tons, the *Aurea*, and fitted her at a large outlay with surf boats, picks, shovels, timber, blasting powder, and other stores. This party found the island almost inaccessible because of the wild, rock-bound coast, the huge breakers which beat about it from all sides, and the lack of harbors and safe anchorage. After immense difficulty, eight men were landed, with a slender store of provisions and a few of the tools. The dismal aspect of the island, the armies of huge land crabs which tried to devour them, the burning heat, and the hard labor without enough food or water, soon disheartened this band of treasure seekers, and they dug no more than a small trench before courage and strength forsook them. Signaling to their ships, they were taken off, worn out and ill, and thus ended the efforts of the expedition.

In the same year, an American skipper chartered a French sailing vessel in Rio Janeiro, and sailed for Trinidad with four Portuguese sailors to do his digging for him. They were ashore several days, but found no treasure, and vanished from the story after this brief fling with the dice of fortune. Now, Knight was of different stuff from these other explorers. He was a first-class amateur seaman who had sailed his yacht *Falcon* to South America in 1880, and was both experienced and capable afloat and ashore. While bound from Montevideo to Bahia he had touched at Trinidad, curious to see this remote islet so seldom visited. This was before he heard the buried treasure story. Therefore when he became acquainted, several years later, with the chart and information left by the old pirate, he was able to verify the details of his own knowledge, and he roundly affirmed:

"In the first place, his carefully prepared plan of the island, the minute directions he gave as to the best landing, and his description of the features of the bay on whose shores the treasure was concealed, prove beyond doubt to myself and others who know Trinidad, that he, or if not himself some informant of his, had landed on this so rarely visited islet; and not only landed but passed some time on it, and carefully surveyed the approaches to the bay, so as to be able to point out the dangers and show the safest passage through the reefs. This information could not have been obtained from any pilot-book. The landing recommended by previous visitors is at the other side of the island. This bay is described by them as inaccessible, and the indications on the Admiralty chart are completely erroneous.

"And beyond this, the quartermaster must have been acquainted with what was taking place in two other distant portions of the world during the year of his professed landing on the desert island. He knew of the escape of pirates with the cathedral plate of Lima. He was also aware that, shortly afterwards, there were hanged in Cuba the crew of a vessel that had committed acts of piracy on the Peruvian coast.

"It is scarcely credible that an ordinary seaman,—even allowing that he was superior in education to the average of his fellows,—could have pieced these facts together so ingeniously into this plausible story."

This argument has merit and it was persuasive enough to cause Knight to buy the staunch cutter *Alerte*, muster a company of gentlemen volunteers, ship a crew, and up anchor from Southampton for Trinidad.

There was never a better found treasure expedition than this in the *Alerte*. The nine partners, each of whom put up one hundred pounds toward the expenses, were chosen from one hundred and fifty eager applicants. Articles of agreement provided that one-twentieth of the treasure recovered was to be received by each adventurer and he in turn bound himself to work hard and obey orders. In the equipment was a drilling apparatus for boring through earth and rock, an hydraulic jack for lifting huge bowlders, portable forge and anvil, iron wheel-barrows, crow-bars, shovels and picks galore, a water distilling plant, a rapid fire gun, and a full complement of repeating rifles and revolvers.

A few days before the *Alerte* was ready to sail from Southampton an elderly naval officer boarded the cutter and was kind enough to inform Mr. Knight of another buried treasure which he might look for on his route to Trinidad. The story had been hidden for many years among the documents of the Admiralty, and as a matter of government record, it is, of course, perfectly authentic. In 1813, the Secretary of the Admiralty instructed Sir Richard Bickerton, commanding at Portsmouth, to send in the first King's ship touching at Madeira a seaman who had given information concerning a hidden treasure, in order that the truth of his story might be tested.

The Admiralty order was entrusted to Captain Hercules Robinson of the *Prometheus* and in his report he states that "after being introduced to the foreign seaman referred to in the above letter, and reading the notes which had been taken of his information, he charged him to tell no person what he knew or what was his business, that he was to mess with the captain's coxswain, and that no duty would be required of him. To this the man replied that that was all he desired, that he was willing to give his time, and would ask no remuneration for his intelligence."

While the *Prometheus* was anchored at Funchal, Madeira, Captain Robinson closely questioned the mysterious seaman whose name was Christian Cruse. He declared that he had been in a hospital ill of yellow fever, several years before, and with him was a shipmate, a Spaniard, who died of the same malady. Before his death he told Cruse that in 1804 he had been in a Spanish ship, from South America to Cadiz, with two millions of silver in chests. When nearing the coast of Spain, they were signaled by a neutral vessel that England had declared war and that Cadiz was blockaded. Rather than risk capture by the British fleet, and unwilling to run all the way back to South America, the captain resolved to try to gain the nearest of the West Indies and save his treasure.

Passing to the southward of Madeira, a cluster of small, uninhabited islands, called the Salvages, was sighted. Thereupon the crew decided that it was foolishness to continue the voyage. The captain was accordingly stabbed to death with a dirk, and the ship steered to an anchorage. The chests of Spanish dollars were landed in a small bay, a deep trench dug in the sand above highwater mark, and the treasure snugly buried, the body of the captain deposited in a box on top of it. The mutineers then sought the Spanish Main where they intended to burn their ship, buy a small vessel under British colors, and return to carry off the two million dollars.

Near Tobago they suffered shipwreck because of poor navigation and only two were saved. One died ashore, and the other was the Spanish seaman who made the dying declaration to Christian Cruse in the hospital at Vera Cruz.

Captain Hercules Robinson was a seasoned officer of His Majesty's navy, used to taking sailors' yarns with a grain of salt, but that he was convinced of the good faith of Christian Cruse and of the truth of the narrative is shown by his interesting comments, as he wrote them down a century ago:

"May Cruse not have had some interested object in fabricating this story? Why did he not tell it before? Is not the cold-blooded murder inconceivable barbarity, and the burying the body over the treasure too dramatic and buccaneer-like? Or might not the Spaniard have lied from love of lying and mystifying his simple shipmate, or might he not have been raving?

"As to the first difficulty, I have the strongest conviction of the honesty of Christian Cruse, and I think I could hardly be grossly deceived as to his character, and his disclaiming any reward unless the discovery was made, went to confirm my belief that he was an honest man. And then as to his withholding the information for four or five years, be it remembered that the war with Denmark might have truly shut him out from any intercourse with England. Next as to the wantonness and indifference with which the murder was perpetrated, I am afraid there is no great improbability in this. I have witnessed a disregard of human life in matters of promotion in our service, etc., which makes the conduct of these Spaniards under vehement temptation, and when they could do as they pleased, sufficiently intelligible.

"But certainly the coffin over the treasure looked somewhat theatrical and gave it the air of Sadler's Wells, or a novel, rather than matter of fact. I enquired, therefore, from Christian Cruse why the body of the captain was thus buried, and he replied that he understood the object was, that in case any person should find the marks of their proceedings and dig to discover what they had been about, they might come to the body and go no further."

After further reflection, Captain Robinson convinced himself that the Spanish seaman had been clear-headed when he made his confession to Cruse, and that it would have been beyond him deliberately to invent the statement as fiction. The *Prometheus* was headed for the Salvages, and arriving off the largest of these islands, a bay was found and a level white patch of beach above high water mark situated as had been described to Christian Cruse. Fifty sailors were sent ashore to dig with shovels and boarding pikes, making the sand fly in the hope of winning the reward of a hundred dollars offered to the man who found the murdered captain's coffin.

The search lasted only one day because the anchorage was unsafe and Captain Robinson was under orders to return to Madeira. Arriving there, other orders recalled his ship to England for emergency duty and the treasure hunt was abandoned. So far as known, no other attempt had been made to find the chests of dollars until Mr. Knight decided to act on the information and explore the Salvages in passing.

Of this little group of islands it was decided by the company of the *Alerte* that the one called the Great Piton most closely answered the description given Christian Cruse by the Spanish pirate. A bay was found with a strip of white sand above high-water mark, and Mr. Knight and his shipmates pitched a camp nearby and had the most sanguine expectations of bringing to light the rude coffin of the murdered captain.

A series of trenches was opened up after a systematic plan, and some crumbling bones discovered, but the ship's surgeon refused to swear that they had belonged to a human being. The trouble was that the surface of the place had been considerably changed by the action of waves and weather, which made the Admiralty charts of a century before very misleading. The destination of the *Alerte* was Trinidad, after all, and the visit to the Salvages was only an incident, so the search was abandoned after four days. In all probability, the treasure of the Salvages is still in its hiding-place, and any adventurous young gentlemen seeking a field of operations will do well to consult for themselves the documentary evidence of Captain Hercules Robinson and Christian Cruse, as filed among the records of the British Admiralty Office.

Trinidad is a much more difficult island to explore than any of the Salvages group. In fact, this forbidding mass of volcanic rock is a little bit of inferno. It is sometimes impossible to make a landing through the surf for weeks at a time, and when a boat makes the attempt in the most favorable circumstances, the venture is a hazard of life and death. As a vivid summary of the aspect of this lonely treasure island, I quote from Mr. Knight, because he is the only man who has ever described Trinidad at first hand:

"As we neared it, the features of this extraordinary place could gradually be distinguished. The north side, that which faced us, is the most barren and desolate portion of the island, and appears to be utterly inaccessible. Here the mountains rise sheer from the boiling surf,—fantastically shaped of volcanic rock; cloven by frightful ravines; lowering in perpendicular precipices; in places overhanging threateningly, and, where the mountains have been shaken to pieces by the fires and earthquakes of volcanic action, huge landslips slope steeply in the yawning ravines,—landslips of black and red volcanic debris, and loose rocks large as houses, ready on the slightest disturbance to roll down, crashing, into the abysses below. On the summit of the island there floats almost constantly, even on the clearest day, a wreath of dense vapor, never still, but rolling and twisting into strange shapes as the wind eddies among the crags. And above this cloud-wreath rise mighty pinnacles of coal-black rock, like the spires of some gigantic Gothic cathedral piercing the blue southern sky. It would be impossible to convey in words a just idea of the mystery of Trinidad. The very coloring seemed unearthly, in places dismal black, and in others the fire-consumed crags are of strange metallic hues, vermilion red and copper yellow. When one lands on its shores, this uncanny impression is enhanced. It bears all the appearances of being an accursed spot, whereupon no creatures can live, save the hideous land-crabs and foul and cruel sea birds."

An ideal place, this, for pirates to bury treasure, you will agree, and good for nothing else under Heaven. The South Atlantic Directory, the shipmaster's guide, states that "the surf is often incredibly great, and has been seen to break over a bluff which is two hundred feet high." Trinidad was first visited by Halley, the astronomer, after whom the famous comet was named, who called there in 1700 when he was a captain in the Royal Navy. Captain Amos Delano, the Yankee pioneer in the Far Eastern trade, made a call in 1803, prompted by curiosity, but as a rule mariners have given the island a wide berth, now and then touching there when in need of water or fresh meat in the shape of turtles.

At one time the Portuguese attempted to found a settlement on Trinidad, probably before the forests had been killed by some kind of volcanic upheaval. The ruins of their stone huts are still to be seen as humble memorials of a great race of explorers and colonists in the golden age of that nation.

With tremendous exertion, the party from the *Alerte* was landed with its tools and stores, and headquarters established close to the ravine which was believed to be the hiding-place of the treasure as indicated by the chart and information of the Finn quartermaster with the scar across his cheek. It was found that there had been no actual landslide, but the ravine was choked with large bowlders which at various times had fallen from the cliffs above. These were packed together by the red earth silting and washing during the rainy season when the ravines were flooded.

Along the whole of the windward coast were found innumerable fragments of wreckage, spars, timbers, barrels. From the position of the island, in the belt of the southeast trade winds, many derelict vessels must have been driven ashore. Some of this immense accumulation of stuff may have lain there for centuries, or ever since vessels first doubled the Cape of Good Hope. Here and there were the gaunt rows of ribs to show where a ship had been stranded bodily, and doubtless much valuable property in silver and gold, in bars, ingots, and doubloons, lies buried in the shattered hulks of these old Dutch East Indiamen, and galleons from Peru.

As particular landmarks near the ravine, the pirate had mentioned three cairns which he and his comrades had heaped up. Sure enough, the previous treasure seekers of the *Aurea* expedition from England had found the three cairns, but foolishly demolished them on the chance that gold might be buried underneath. Mr. Knight could find traces of only one of them, and he discovered also a water-jar, a broken wheelbarrow and other tools to show where the others had been digging. The crew of the *Alerte* were confident that they were at the right place, and they set to work with the most admirable zeal and fortitude, enduring hardships cheerfully, and during the three months of their labors on Trinidad, removing earth and rock literally by the thousands of tons, until the ravine was scooped out to a depth of from eight to twenty feet.

Their vessel had to anchor far off shore, and once forsook them for a fourteen hundred mile voyage to Bahia to get provisions. These London lawyers and other gentlemen unused to toil with the hands became as tough and rough and disreputable to see as the pirates who had been there aforetime. In costume of shirt, trousers, and belt, they became ragged and stained from head to foot with the soil, and presented a uniform, dirty, brownish, yellow appearance like so many Brazilian convicts. Their surf boat was wrecked or upset at almost every attempt to land or to go off to the *Alerte*, and when they were not fishing one another out of the surf, they were diving to recover their submerged and scattered stores. Their leader, Mr. Knight, paid them a tribute of which they must have been proud:

"They had toiled hard and had kept up their spirits all the while and what is really wonderful under circumstances so calculated to try the temper and wear out the patience, they had got on exceedingly well with each other, and there had been no quarreling or ill feeling of any sort."

At length the melancholy verdict was agreed upon in council. All the bright dreams of carrying home a fortune for every adventurer were reluctantly dismissed. The men were worn to the bone, and it was becoming more and more difficult to maintain communication with the *Alerte*. The prodigious excavation was abandoned, and Mr. Knight indulged himself in a soliloquy as he surveyed the "great trenches, the piled-up mounds of earth, the uprooted rocks, with broken wheelbarrows and blocks, worn-out tools, and other relics of our three months strewn over the ground; and it was sad to think that all the energy of these men had been spent in vain. They well deserved to succeed, and all the more so because they bore their disappointment with so much pluck and cheerfulness."

But, in truth, the expedition had not been in vain. The toilers had been paid in richer stuff than gold. They had lived the true romance, nor could a man of spirit and imagination wish for anything more to his taste than to be encamped on a desert island, with the surf shouting in his ears, the sea birds crying, all hands up with daybreak to dig for buried treasure whose bearings were found on a tarpaulin chart that had belonged to a pirate with a deep scar across his cheek. How it would have delighted the heart of Robert Louis Stevenson to be one of this company of the *Alerte* at Trinidad! The gallant little vessel, only sixty-four feet long she was, filled away for the West Indies, homeward bound, while the men aboard amused themselves by wondering how many nations might have laid claim to the treasure, had it been found;—England which hoisted its flag on Trinidad in 1770; Portugal because Portuguese from Brazil made a settlement there in 1750; Brazil, because the island lay off her coast; Spain, to whom the treasure had belonged, and Peru from whose cathedral it was taken, and lastly the Roman Church.

In conclusion, Mr. Knight, to whose fascinating narrative, "The Cruise of the *Alerte*," I am indebted for the foregoing information, sums it up like a true soldier of fortune:

"Well, indeed, it was for us that we had not found the pirates' gold; for we seemed happy enough as we were, and if possessed of this hoard, our lives would of a certainty have become a burden to us. We should be too precious to be comfortable. We should degenerate into miserable, fearsome hypochondriacs, careful of our means of transit, dreadfully anxious about what we ate or drank, miserably cautious about everything. 'Better far, no doubt,' exclaimed these cheerful philosophers, 'to remain the careless, happy paupers that we are.'

"'Do you still believe in the existence of the treasure?' is a question that has been often put to me since my return. Knowing all I do, I have very little doubt that the story of the Finn quartermaster is substantially true,—that the treasures of Lima were hidden on Trinidad; but whether they have been taken away, or whether they are still there and we failed to find them because we were not in possession of one link of the directions, I am unable to say."

In later years, E. F. Knight became a war correspondent, and lost an arm in the Boer campaign. I met him at Key West during the Spanish war in which he represented *The London Times* and found him to be a solid, well-ballasted man who knew what he was about and not at all one to have gone treasure seeking without excellent reasons. That he was adventurous in his unassuming way he proved by landing on the Cuban coast near Havana in order to interview the Spanish Captain-General. A newspaper dispatch boat ran close in shore, the skipper risking being blown out of water by the batteries of Morro Castle, and Knight was transferred to a tiny flat-bottomed skiff of the tonnage of a bath-tub. Equipped with a note-book, revolver, water bottle, and a small package of sandwiches, he said good-by in his very placid manner, and was seen to be standing on his head in the surf a few minutes later. He scrambled ashore, probably recalling to mind a similar style of landing on the coast of Trinidad, and vanished in the jungle. That he ran grave danger of being potted for an *Americano* by the first Spanish patrol he encountered appeared to give him no concern whatever. It was easy to perceive that he must have been the right kind of man to lead a treasure-hunting expedition.

Since the *Alerte* sailed on her dashing quest in 1889, the pirates' gold of Trinidad has figured in an adventure even more fantastic. Many readers will doubtless remember the career of the late Baron James Harden-Hickey who attempted to establish a kingdom of his own on the islet of Trinidad. He belonged in another age than this and he was laughed at rather more than he deserved. Duelist, editor, *boulevardier*, fond of the tinsel and trappings of life, he married the daughter of John H. Flagler of the Standard Oil Company and with funds from this excessively commercial source created a throne, a court, and a kingdom. He had seen the island of Trinidad from a British merchant ship in which he went round the Horn in 1888, and the fact that this was a derelict bit of real estate, to which no nation thought it worth while to lay formal claim, appealed to his active imagination.

A would-be king has difficulty in finding a stray kingdom nowadays, and Harden-Hickey bothered his head not in the least over the problem of populating this god-forsaken jumble of volcanic rock and ashes. Ere long he blossomed forth most gorgeously in Paris and New York as King James I of the Principality of Trinidad. There was a royal cabinet, a Minister of Foreign Affairs, a Chancellerie, and uniforms, court costumes, and regalia designed by the king himself. Most dazzling of all the equipment was the Order of the Insignia of the Cross of Trinidad, a patent and decoration of nobility to be bestowed on those deemed worthy of the signal honor.

The newspapers bombarded King James I with gibes and jeers, but he took himself with immense, even tragic seriousness, and issued a prospectus of the settlement of his kingdom, inviting an aristocracy of intellect and good breeding to comprise the ruling class, while the hard work was to be done by hired menials. He mustered on paper some kind of a list of resources of Trinidad, although he was hard put to name anything very tangible, and laid special stress on the buried treasure. It was to be dug up by the subjects and, if found, to be divided among the patriots who had bought the securities issued by the royal treasury. Surely a pirates' treasure was never before gravely offered among the assets of a kingdom, but King James had no sense of humor, and the lost treasure was as real to him as any other of his marvelous dreams.

Some work was actually done at Trinidad, building material landed, a vessel chartered to run from Brazil, and a few misguided colonists recruited, when in 1895 the British Government ruthlessly knocked the Principality of Trinidad into a cocked hat and toppled over the throne of King James I. The island was wanted as a cable landing or relay station, and a naval officer raised the red ensign to proclaim annexation by reason of Halley's discovery in 1700. At this Brazil set up a protest on the ground that her Portuguese had been the original settlers. While the diplomats of these two powers were politely locking horns over the question of ownership, that unfortunate monarch, King James I of the Principality of Trinidad, Baron Harden-Hickey of the Holy Roman Empire, perceived that his realm had been pulled out from under him, so to speak. Whichever nation won the dispute it meant no comfort for him. Trinidad was no longer a derelict island and he was a king without a kingdom.

He surrendered not one jot or tittle of his rights, and to his Minister of Foreign Affairs he solemnly bequeathed the succession and the claim to proprietorship. And among these rights and privileges was the royal interest in the buried treasure. Harden-Hickey, when he could no longer live a king, died as he thought befitting a gentleman, by his own hand. It seems a pity that he could not have been left alone to play at being king, and to find the pirates' gold.